Do You Believe In Always

◆ A FICTIONAL MEMOIR ◆

NICI DAMON

DO YOU BELIEVE IN ALWAYS Copyright © 2014 by Nici Damon

For information contact:

Nici Damon
nici.damon@hotmail.com
www.nicidamon.com

The lines from "you said is". Copyright © 1973, 1983, 1991 by the Trustees for the E. E. Cummings Trust. Copyright © 1973, 1983 by George James Firmage, from COMPLETE POEMS: 1904-1962 by E. E. Cummings, edited by George J. Firmage. Used by permission of Liveright Publishing Corporation.

Web design by: Leilani Doornbosch
www.customcoverpro.com

Cover design by: Daria Brennan
www.beegraphica.com

ISBN 978-0-9909757-0-0
First Edition: February 2015

10 9 8 7 6 5 4 3 2 1

Do You Believe In Always

TO MORGAN

When I remember us together, I always rewind to my favorite scenes.
Which, for me, was everything from the opening credits to the stinger.

CAST OF CHARACTERS

Anna Maison – the heroine. A chronicle of the absurd

Lee – Anna's first husband. She married him in high school, father of Morgan

Jason – the first hero. A two year life-altering relationship after Lee and before Ben, with a do-over attempt 30 years later

Andy – Anna's second husband. He adopted Morgan and remains her father, which makes him a hero for real

Benjamin Stevenson (Ben) – the second hero. A twenty-five year relationship that continued far too long with the inevitable personal conflict

Marcus – Ben's oldest son

Paul – Anna's third husband

Mr. Lucky – "lucky" enough to be a 15-year live-in relationship. Never a hero but one who ended with a heroic effort

Gabriel – the last of the heroes. Or not

Shane / Son – Gabriel's married son and only child

JB and the Brothers Grimm – the brothers of Gabriel … along with a host of other Fairy Tale characters

Bastardo Romantico™ – a Match.com Valentine's Day blind date. A hero only in his own mind

Morgan – Anna's daughter, an actress/model

Jarred – Morgan's husband, a London-born New York based actor

Travis – Anna's grandson

Kayla – Anna's granddaughter

Maggie – Anna's stepmother

Bobbi – Anna's lifelong best friend, now living in Florida

Golden Knight – a long-time personal friend of Anna

JournalLand – an online diary/journal site, where all the original unedited entries appeared. A locked journal can only be seen by the writer

— *"Do You Believe in Always"* (a public journal, later locked)

— *"LuvACowboy"* (a locked private journal)

— *"cUnHell"* (a locked private journal documenting an illness)

OnTheRadio, Poppy, Randi, etc. – other *JournalLand* writers

And a supporting cast of thousands

> Do you believe in always, the wind
> said to the rain
> I am too busy with
> my flowers to believe, the rain answered …
>
> ~~e.e.cummings "you said Is (XIII)"

PROLOGUE

He was right about a lot of things. About the fact that having been told I am attractive almost all of my adult life I have attracted a lot of attention. More than a lot. A LOT.

Some of it was what I wanted – what I went after. And some of it just came to me unbidden, like a virus that attacks without warning.

Being attractive had its pitfalls. When I was out with another woman, she tended to get all the play. I finally had an opportunity to ask "Why her and not me?" Just curious you know. And his answer? "Because I was more likely to be shot down by the pretty one."

I've been fortunate. I've been in love. I've been loved. I've even been someone's greatest love three times. Which is assuredly something if you think about it.

But I've never expected it. Or taken it for granted.

And my heart has been just as broken as any girl who hasn't been as lucky. Or as pretty.

Finally, one day, I just stopped believing.

I'm not sure you should read this. It is little more than an annotation of life-altering emotional events and because there was no place else to put it, I vomited everything I was feeling onto these pages. So you will not learn about courage. Or resiliency. Or kindness. Or strength. Or loyalty – which has caused me the greatest heartache of all.

And those are the things I would rather you learn about me.

Like life, the story starts halfway through and ends before it is finished.

FIRST DANCE

I was born in the 50's, did high school in the 60's, and partied in the 70's – ok, and the 80's. Deviant sex, hard drugs, and rock 'n roll. I watched Oswald die on live TV, saw man's first step on the moon, protested for Civil Rights and against the war in Vietnam.

What my generation didn't start, stop, or overturn, we went out of our way to put In Their Face.

Take it from an old hand who's actually been there. Looking through Rose's tinted glasses at that shaken, not stirred, is a sure guarantee he'll get laid and you'll get fucked.

BEN

02-14-1977 — **Two Lovers Tangle**

I started this journal to tell the epic tale of Ben and Anna, two lovers separated by time, distance, and space. And ended it … well, what is an end, anyway?

Ben and Anna met in the spring of 1977, across a swing dance floor. "Don't even bother," whispered her friend. "Many have tried, none have succeeded."

She asked him to dance and they danced, and they lunched, they played darts, and sat in the park, and they talked. They rode in his VW convertible to feel the sun on their face. But she was married, couldn't leave, and feared the fall. ("Did you leave for me?" "No my love, I left for me.")

He dared take her to *Oh Calcutta* and they went home and made love for the first time. And she fell in love with him, as he had fallen in love with her the moment he saw her on that dance floor all those months before.

Five years later, he walked out of her life. She kept everything – the cards, the letters, the pictures, even the sticky notes – hidden far back in the darkest part of the deepest closet. Not thinking too hard about him because it hurt too much. But never genuinely forgetting.

03-16-1989 — **A Letter**
A Letter to Anna from Benjamin

I question myself – why I called you again, whether I am now able to make a life-long commitment to someone, whether we could be happy together. Maybe it's the 1000 miles between us that makes it easier. But there is one thing I know – you care about me, care what happens to me, think about me, want to be with me even as I want to be with you. It feels right to admit I still love you.

I don't understand why I've always been attracted to you. You are a strange and deeply complex mixture. An inquisitive, challenging, involved, vulnerable, and passionate woman I was afraid to live with then, but haven't been able to live without since.

I'm finding myself slowly but surely aching to be with you. I want to hold you, kiss you, be inside of you – in the best way. I feel connected to you, bound to you.

09-30-1989 — **Again**

And here we are. But a few months after all the "Iloveyouandcan'tspendan-othermomentwithoutyou's" and barely a word for weeks. How I treasure the letters and cards he has written this last year. All the plans and hints and promises, which unlocked those feelings I hid away so long ago. We were together five years and then, the moment I was free to be his … silence.

I remember the night, weeks later, when I walked into our dance club and found him there with someone else. It was only then I understood that he could not do forever with someone ready to do forever with him.

Why does he speak to me of love when he cannot commit to anything? And so I remain in the same space, waiting until he can honestly say, "Come to Me."

10-01-2000 — **Déjà Vu**

When you are a "been there, done everything" kind of person you can expect a bit of déjà vu now and again. The slightest sight, smell, sound, or taste can bring a long hidden memory to the surface. Or not – as sometimes you know it is intimately familiar, just not from where.

In my teen years, I dated a young man several years older than myself. Don't "tut tut." In those days, your parents decided the appropriateness of a relationship, not the government. My parents met him, and his parents, and everyone decided it was fine with them (with stringently enforced curfews, of course, and the typical parental exhortations regarding behavior).

My two best friends met his two best friends and it became a Saturday night sextet most weekends. (minds out of the gutter – sextet means SIX). The boys would get the beer, and drive their '57 Chevys out to a nice country road where we would sit on the cars, share the beer (drinking right from the bottle), and smoke our cigarettes.

But at the end of the evening, there was always an hour or so left for another visit to the country road. Where, despite my parent's belief in the appropriateness, we were (eventually) getting busy with something that would not likely be deemed at ALL appropriate.

As to that déjà vu – I'm coming to it.

Earlier this week, I had the good fortune to spend a lovely couple of hours with a delightful man I met some time ago. And by a couple of hours I meant we chose to get together and get busy with something that would not likely be deemed at ALL appropriate. Again – no tut-tutting. I'm a big girl, I've never been all that "P.C.," and in that area of my life I have no issues with choosing to be properly ravished by a delectable, unpredictable man without him having bought me dinner and drinks first.

At one point, during a particularly passionate kiss, that sense of déjà vu was overwhelming and I knew it instantly. You see, I rarely kiss someone who smokes. He does (but was so polite about it I hardly noticed) and was enjoying a beer as he enjoyed me. And his mouth brought back a warm, comforting remembrance of those carefree teenage years when life was simple, hearts hadn't been broken, and my soul still believed in Always.

10-15-2000 — **Your Letter**
A Letter to Anna from Benjamin

Received your letter and sorry I missed your call the other night. May I call you? Write you? Are you willing to see me again?

Are you with someone else? Fill me in. I am living alone again, but have been seeing someone for about a year.

10-31-2000 — **I'd Like to See You Too**
Personal email to Benjamin from Anna

I've thought of you every day since we talked.

Wonder what that means?

But have decided Yes – I do want to see you – if you have the time.

12-18-2000 — **Welcome Home Dear Anna**
An email to Anna from Benjamin

Welcome back from India. I hope the culture shock wasn't too traumatic. I remember how it was when I flew back to the states after 2 weeks in Central America. Third World to First in only three hours.

It would be nice to have you stay an extra day. I will pick you up from the airport.

01-07-2001 — **Smiling**
Personal email to Benjamin from Anna

It's been a long time since I was with someone as caring and loving as you.

What an exquisite brief feeling that there was someone there that truly cared about me, had always cared about me, and wanted the best for me. I think now about how much I'm missing by choosing to "settle."

I am an extremely strong, capable, independent individual and the power to change whatever I want to change lies in my own hands.

Someday, someone will publish our letters and notes in a little book – like Emily Dickenson's love poems. I love to read and hold your letters. And this time, no matter what, you're never getting them back.

01-08-2001 — **Smiling too**
Personal email to Anna from Benjamin

I've been smiling a lot lately, thinking about last week and our three days together. It didn't take long for us to "re-acquaint" did it? Your memory lingers. And your scent.

I still want to dance with you.

01-11-2001 — **Shake, Rattle and Roll**

He shakes me up. He always wants me to share my innermost insecurities – the ones I hide even from myself. It frightens me to trust, to wish for a future that may never be, to feel the strength and depth of emotion that flowed between us after so long a time. It was so easy to be wrapped in his arms and I want so much to stay there; yet fear the fall.

01 22 2001   **I'm Alive and Well**
Personal email to Anna from Benjamin

Current rumors notwithstanding, I have been sighted from time to time within the last several days. I've remained relatively quiet and isolated since returning from my son's house. He's 30 and a grown man, but still seems so young and unsure. I blame myself – if only I hadn't moved 300 miles away when he was 4 and so vulnerable and impressionable. My journeys to see him invariably kick in bouts of guilt over the past.

01-23-2001 — **Pay the Nurse!**
Personal email to Benjamin from Anna

Even when a child has grown, we never see the man or woman; only the child they once were. Marcus may be your son, but ... HE's AN ADULT! I know, it's the toughest part of being a parent. Letting go. At some point, you have to stop parenting him and start just being his friend.

Allow him to take responsibility for his own actions and let HIM be guilty for the ones that don't work. Remember when you became an adult (I think I was 6 or so) and realized the choice was yours to become the person you wanted to become. (Pay the nurse!)

Wish I knew the ending. The whole ending. When I know where I'm going it's much easier. If life was like writing a book, I could lay out the chapters, the characters, and the scenes. Put together a project plan and timeline. Then start taking one step at a time until it's all completed.

Life isn't quite like that. There's never an ending. Never knowing WHERE you're going until somehow you get there.

PS: Enjoy the visuals.

01-24-2001 — **Lost it!**
Personal email to Anna from Benjamin

Pant, pant, pant! Heart pounding, pulse increasing, sweat beads forming on my forehead, shallow breathing, faint stirrings "below the belt!" Wow, what a picture! Do you have any idea what kind of effect a photo like that has on me? When I saw that picture, I wanted to bend down, lightly kiss your belly, raise your butt off the bed, and begin to pull down your jeans. It's hard trying to figure out what to do with you a thousand miles away.

By the way, when are you coming back?

I danced with you again yesterday. I got up, walked over to you, took your hand, put my arm around your waist, and moved to the rhythm of our song. I won't soon forget that memory. It was the first physical contact we had in 12 years you know. The next significant contact wasn't too shabby either! Love you Hon.

01-24-2001 — **Oh My, Oh My, Oh Goodness**!
Personal email to Benjamin from Anna

Does your last email mean you want to see me again?

Or was it a slip of the tongue after seeing the photo. I've tried to respect your wishes and not call – or email – too much. It's unquestionably HARD!

02-04-2001 — **Checklist to Myself**

Since 1991, I have lived with my boyfriend/business partner, which makes life complicated.

He was an intelligent, funny, gregarious person who enjoyed life, who allowed me freedom and independence in my outside hobbies, who appeared to love and respect me, and was sexually liberated.

Three years later, he had an affair with a married doctor. He pleaded with her to marry him so "we could all live together as a family." His lifelong dream of a threesome. She said no. He begged me for forgiveness. I stayed. And it is no consolation prize to drive a paid-for car, be allowed to enjoy my hobbies, and after years of struggling, finally be debt free.

I cannot fault him his dream. I've been in love with one man most of my adult life. I mostly kept it safely locked away, inside a small box deep inside my heart, the key in a secret place I rarely visited. Now I want to open the box and see if it is real, or just a memory of something long gone.

I have always believed, with all my soul, that someday before I die, this man and I need to explore the possibility of our being together, to see if it is all I think it could be. If, at long last, we find it's there for us – I'll walk away from that nice house, take that debt free existence, and drive that paid-for car halfway around the world without a single regret, without a single backward glance, and come into his arms.

02-13-2001 — **It Occurs To Me**

Think that I am suffering from a case of *How to Lose a Man in 10 Days*. Six months ago I suddenly called Ben, declared I was still crazy about him after all these years, and fell into his bed. Then started with how we're going to spend our 85th birthdays together.

I'm thinking it's romantic, while he's trying to figure out if he's at all interested in pursuing a possibility of maybe at some point getting to know me again. As always, I was reading the last chapter, while he was still perusing the table of contents.

02-14-2001 — **Happy Valentine's Day**
Personal email to Anna from Benjamin

You are special, no doubt about it – one of a kind, so unique. You intrigue me, challenge me. I could spend a lifetime trying to understand what makes you tick.

02-17-2001 — **Fire and Ice**

There is 20 inches on the ground, and it's still snowing and sleeting.

Reminds me of when I moved to the East Coast. I'm in Las Vegas for a swing dance competition – 90 degree plus temperatures – warmest January they've had in years. I had already packed up my apartment, left my excess luggage in a St. Louis airport storage locker, and had a friend meeting me at the terminal with my two cats so I could land, pick up the extra luggage, and get right on another plane.

Unfortunately, the East Coast was snowbound, so the cats and I sit for HOURS until I can get a flight.

At the other end, I can't get a car. They've had 25 inches of snow – nothing's open! And no hotels who will take pets! A limo driver finally agrees to take the chance. We get stuck twice and I walk the last half-mile, dragging my suitcases through the snowdrifts to my temporary housing.

It snowed four more times before the end of the month. The city had to haul it away in dump trucks. Meanwhile I'm driving around in a rental car with no map, going to work every day, and trying to find an apartment before the movers, my car, and my dog show up!! What a month!! January 1987.

And that's the way it was.

2-19-2001 — **Patience**
Personal email to Anna from Benjamin

It is probably a good thing you're so far away. If you were here, well … I'm somewhat vulnerable. Always was a sucker for your soft, slender, sexy body – the way it feels, moves, responds, tastes. I would ravage it if I could. The distance between us is like a cold shower – makes me think before I act.

This may be just as well. If you were here it would be a lot more difficult to maintain discipline.

Please be patient as I try to sort things out using both head and heart.

2-21-2001 — **Discipline**
Personal email to Benjamin from Anna

Discipline is for monks, priests, nuns, and dominatrix. Which are you?

I'm not looking for your decision to climb the mountain. I'm just hoping, at some point, that you will agree to pick up the travel brochure. We can't decide our futures, we can't look into a crystal ball, and we can't bridge a 12-year gap in a month, or six months, or even a year.

02-25-2001 — **Do What You Have To**
Personal email to Anna from Benjamin

I loved you then and in a certain way I still do (probably always will, no matter if we're together or apart). Even if we do not end up as a couple, my hope is that we remain the best of friends, caring for one another, supporting, and encouraging each other, being there for one another.

It wouldn't surprise me in the least if, before we both kick over, we end up together.

I've heard it said that God has a great sense of humor – this would certainly prove it. And wouldn't our friends and families chuckle and shake their heads!

02-26-2001 — **Do What You Have To?**

Ah-the problems of complete indecision. When what you want in your heart, and what you need in your head, are completely diverse. Or are the same thing, but there's too much "stuff" in the way" to accomplish the task and do what you want to do, in the way you want to do it.

He is afraid of spending the rest of his life struggling to make ends meet – although it is the result of changing professions again and again. I would love him rich or poor. He should love himself the same way. I spent most of my life trying to figure out how to have enough to go around, so I'll admit I'm more content in many ways when the outgo and income match. But it leaves me very unsatisfied in others. I'm honestly not sure which is worse.

As to his everything else, there are a finite number of years left in our lives. The years left to me will go by so quickly it often frightens me to the point of panic. I don't know how I will be able to face the world, at the end, when it asks me "were you happy, were you loved, and what did you accomplish in your life?" If the question were to be put to me now – the answer would be "not for a long time, maybe once, and nothing of any consequence."

If the answers are going to be any different – my life needs to change. That's the goal – it's the timeline that's more difficult. So you see – I understand. My wish for him is that when the world asks him the same questions he can answer, "yes, yes, and everything I had hoped."

03-28-2001 — **Get Well Soon**
Personal email from Anna to Benjamin

I'm so sorry to hear that you: (fill in appropriate blank)

____Are so sick in bed that you can't get up

____Became so hoarse from a cold/flu that you can't talk

____Were hit by a car and broke your arm, making keyboarding impossible

____Smashed your fingers with a hammer, making writing improbable

____Have been so depressed that you are on medication, which is keeping you in a semi-comatose state

____Are saving your money by shutting down your internet connection, turning off your cell phone, and generally leading a local, celibate lifestyle

____Got accepted into the seminary school and decided you'd better, once again, give up the idea of a remarkable woman who is determined to turn your world topsy-turvy. In which case, if we're both still alive – see you in another 10 years.

Here's hoping you feel better soon. Please keep me informed of your progress.

04-02-2001 — **Gone But Not Forgotten**

At last, a call that sounded less like a Christmas card annual insert and more like one that comes from the heart. I sometimes feel (and not the "feel" word as prescribed by the hourly visit once a week) as if he is afraid of communicating with me, of sharing that which is "him." I seek his passion, the thoughts that come from within, that have meaning and substance. Not blowing the dam, but negotiating a controlled release drop by drop.

Thinking of him sometimes brings a smile and sometimes brings almost unbearable grief. I'm so torn between wanting to pack a suitcase and show up on his doorstep to see what he would do with me and continuing to live my everyday life – knowing that 25% of another year is gone, never to be recovered.

04-07-2001 — **Isn't it Strange**

I feel as if I'm going through each day waiting for something to happen. Waiting for the catalyst that will allow him to know he wants me, needs me, desires for me to make a move. Changing scares me, staying in one place scares me. I don't trust anyone else, and I don't trust myself. I feel like any decision I make is going to be the wrong one.

Will there ever be anyone in my life that stays? Will there ever be anyone who doesn't just mouth the words, but truly wants the real me?

There are a dozen books about it – but they all say the same thing. You can't change another person and don't get into a relationship thinking that you can. I'm the first to know that it is true – three times true as a matter of fact.

I want happilyforeverafter, not a quickie that lasts until the sex becomes too comfortable.

Life's rules repeat – don't get too close, don't make too many plans, don't have too many wishes – because they don't ever come true.

06-13-2001 — **Changes**

After 11 years of helping Mr. Lucky build the business up, then watching him tear it down over and over while I came in behind and built it up again (all without acknowledgement of course) – I am now in the line of fire.

Mr. Lucky needs to be king of the hill, the cream of the crop, the A number One. But the economy is killing us and he is now sullen, angry, mean, and depressed, blaming the decline on anyone and everyone else. The rest of us stepped up to the plate but as long as "it's MY company and I'll do WHAT I want to do, HOW I want to do it, and WHEN I want to do it" while making inappropriate choices, there's little we can do. So I said I was quitting.

Whatever happens, happens, and now that it's done, I'm not scared anymore. It just took doing I think. So – one step at a time.

06-21-2001 — **Losses**

My beautiful Kaz kitty is gone. She died in my arms just weeks after Azazel. After 18 years, it's almost too much too much to bear that they are both gone. It is times like this when I ache to hear his voice in my ear telling me it will be all right.

07-08-2001 — **Visit**
Personal email from Anna to Benjamin

I haven't heard from you in a while, but I wanted to let you know I'm coming home to see an old girlfriend, attend my class reunion, and visit my stepmom of course. Would you like to get together while I'm there? Maybe Friday evening for dinner?

07-31-2001 — **Place Your Order – Weekend II**
Personal email to Anna from Benjamin

I fell in love with you the first time I laid eyes on you – couldn't help it. Still love you – can't help it. Probably always will. Can we risk being friends with one another? Will you be willing to start there? Or is it all or nothing?

So I'll again offer to sleep on the sofa and give you the bedroom. However, if you desire to either invite me in to join you or to come out and join me I would be ecstatic! You ARE the best lover I've ever had. I take thorough delight in your body – just love looking at it and touching it.

08-06-2001 — **At Your Computer**
Personal email to Benjamin from Anna

You left for work a couple hours ago. I already miss you as I sit here at your computer, sending you a message before the airport taxi arrives. I have genuinely enjoyed our visit together and look forward to the next one.

My fondest hopes and dearest dreams would be that we could spend this kind of time together each time we both need it. It rejuvenates me, renews me, and reminds me – above all – that I love, and am loved by, a very special person.

09-10-2001 — **I Came … I Saw … I …**

I thought to see before I saw
I thought to do before I lived
I thought to be before I was
I thought to love before I died.

09-15-2001 — **Tara's Theme**

Mankind raised himself to walk on two legs and got himself a Scarlett O'Hara attitude.

I'll think about it tomorrow.

So simple really. Why didn't I think of it before?

09-18-2001 — **Dorothy, your ride is here**

If this just don't beat the band. 40 Days and 40 Nights of rain give way to a somewhat decent interlude that will now conclude with a HURRICANE.

But of course – what else?

09-26-2001 — **Wheels Go Round & Round**

I'm off today to Abingdon, Virginia for a bike ride, and other weird stuff. Group of 20 going to go down (or up, as some are coming from Atlanta), see a play with a strange name called *Liquid Moon: A Porn Play,* then bike 38 miles tomorrow down a mountain.

Yes – I said down. Apparently, the group is ferried UP the mountain, and then it's our job to get back down. A total ride of 38 miles.

Used to do the River Ramble in St. Louis – 26 miles to and from Grafton State Park along the River Road. Hundreds of riders of all ages participated every year. The ground was so flat Morgan did it two years in a row as an adventurous little girl on a small-wheeled motocross bike.

09-22-2001 — **A Nod is as Good as a Wink**

Why do we believe that we can't find love because we haven't met the right man, or the right woman?

It has nothing to do with meeting anyone. It has to do with the capability of loving. Until we answer the basic question *can I actually love another person*, it won't matter who we meet. If we don't know how to do it, we wouldn't know love if it slapped us across the face.

10-02-2001 — **Sideways in Time**

> *We assume that the future is a line instead of a coordinate, a path instead of a direction. We assume that if we travel to futureward, there is but one possible destination. And that is as absurd as it would be to ignore the possibility of traveling to eastward in any other line than due east …*
> ~~Murray Leinster, "Sidewise in Time"

I've taken it on faith that somewhere, in one of the worlds slightly parallel to my own, the other me lives in love. And I think I will be happy for me.

10-08-2001 — **A Bird in the Hand**

> *When you want water, a rock is useless. But it's the best thing in the world when you want to keep something important from flying away.*
> ~~*Numb3rs*, Dr. Larry Fleinhardt (paraphrase)

Ah, Dr. Fleinhardt, I too have always had exactly, precisely, automatically at hand what I wanted and needed yesterday.

10-24-2001 — **Hello Again**
Personal email to Anna from Benjamin

I haven't forgotten about you. You are, after all, absolutely unforgettable.

When are you going to take me to one of those bondage/dominant-submissive/
s&m/fetish/3-somes/swingers type of gatherings we talked about that you used
to be into?

There are certain "fantasies" I want to experience before I grow up and fall in
love and get married again. You certainly know more of these matters than I do.
Think about it and so will I.

10-26-2001 — **Now and Then**

I haven't answered. I don't know what to say. Has he moved beyond me when I
wasn't watching, or was he already there? If this is where he is, I cannot join
him.

I spent years in that time – but that time was then, and now is not then, now is
now. If I go back to then, just for a now and again, will I return to now, or be
stuck once more in when.

10-13-2001 — **Sometimes I Dream**

> If you dream of less
> sometimes you end up
> with more.

11-10-2001 — **Let's Make Plans**
Personal email from Anna to Benjamin

I am so looking forward to our weekend together and dancing with you at the
dance club's anniversary dance. What shall be the schedule? Shall I come in
Thursday or Friday? Do you want the extra day (night!)?

I need your arms around me again.

11-22-2001 — **Memory's a Funny Thing**

Well, I'm off to the dance. With or without him, two nights in a hotel by myself with candles, bubble bath, and a good book.

Or perhaps throw caution to the winds, go to a bar, pretend like it's a Saturday night in the 70's, and pick up a stranger for a night of mad passionate lovemaking. Whatever I do, it won't be a total loss …

Had an epiphany late last night after his email changing all the plans. He forgot. He just plain forgot his friend's wedding and the dance were on the same weekend and he already has a date for the wedding. It's why he tried to put me off instead of asking me to go with him, and was too embarrassed to tell me.

I think I won't be very understanding, should he actually decide to show up Sunday night. Or then again … melt into his arms. I don't remember when I didn't love him.

11-25-2001 — **Thus Spake The Email**
Personal email to Benjamin from Anna

As always, making love to you, being made love to by you, makes everything so much more confusing. I cannot leave you. I know because I've tried through twenty years and through five marriages between us. Thought it would be best. Thought I should release both of us because maybe it was only my stubborn, damn the torpedoes, chin up, jaw clenched never let go heart that was keeping the someday we will be together belief alive.

And finally I knew, I just knew, it's simply more powerful than both of us. So all I ask of you right now – please be my friend, watch over me, and love me *Same Time Next Year*. With you, there is no other world.

11-30-2001 — **Bad Boys**

Anna has always gone for bad boys. Hot rodders in high school, rockers with earrings in her 20's, dopers in her 30's, and motorcycle leathers in her 40's. It wasn't until she went for the straight guys that her life turned to shit.

Rock on little girl.

12-17-2001 — **What I Know**

We talked tonight. I think I've not called him sometimes when I wanted to for fear I would learn things I'd rather not know. After all – I don't know what I don't know until I know what I don't know and I don't want to know what I don't know.

Sleep tight my dearest one. I will think of you just before I slip off to sleep so that if perchance I do not arise at dawn, you might someday read this and know you were my last thought in this life.

12-31-2001 — **Resolutions**
Personal email from Anna to Benjamin

We're at the end of Twenty Oh One. I'll raise my glass to you at midnight and click the rim you hold aloft 1000 miles away from me. Last year at this time we were in each other's arms and I cannot help but wonder ... how have we managed to do less, when we had a year to plan?

I resolve that this year's resolutions shall not be promises ... they shall be the blueprint for my actions.

I resolve to do as much for me as I do for others.

I resolve to see more of the glad than the sad.

I resolve to look forward in hope, not backward in regret.

I resolve to start what I dream, and finish what I start.

I resolve to love you a little more, and a little better, and a little more often this year than last.

02-02-2002 — **Life, Interrupted**

> *You made me suffer a lot, but you will bring me back from this deep pit, and give me new life ... and take my sorrow away.*
> ~~Psalm 71, vs. 20-21. The Holy Bible, KJV (Paraphrased)

A dear friend I've never met sent me a note that his wife of 47 years passed away last January. He's done my taxes, long distance, for as long as I can remember. He says he will continue to work indefinitely, as he now has no reason to retire.

Love is the power that keeps you on the road life puts before you.

Life, interrupted, and the road forks.

If I were smarter – then – the valium would have done its job. I wasn't – and it didn't. And yet, all the roads I could have taken still remain just out of reach.

So tell me ... exactly when will You bring me back from the pit?

01-09-2002 — **Depression and Religion**

There are those that believe their Creator is kind and wonderful, and we are not born with original sin – but are simply "heaven sent" with the ability to make our own decisions, either good or bad. And, therefore, we make our own hell both here, and in the hereafter.

There are those that adhere to a belief system that says good works don't assure you a ticket into their heaven, so no matter how evil you are, just believe in the right prophet, at the last minute, and the ticket will be waiting.

Bull.

I've said before that Christians are a cheeky lot. Nothing I've heard over all these years changes my mind. Christianity is not the only religion, and Jesus is not the only prophet. And I refuse to believe that good works don't get you somewhere, both here and in whatever the hereafter is gonna be – whether you accept or don't accept that Jesus is the real deal.

However, enough about me and my half-baked theories. Since no one knows, I simply pose the following to all those Believers: exactly why didn't that great "Creator" just do it right the first time?

Lies, murder, old age, death, the punishment of good and the rewards of evil, the platypus, the appendix, the common cold, the Old Testament (which had to be completely rewritten, thereby leaving everyone confused).

And let's not forget Noah's Ark, the original reboot 2.0.

Time to get on with a life teetering on the edge while that same time pushes persistently from behind. One more day. One more time.

03-22-2002 — **The voodoo that you do**
Personal email from Anna to Benjamin

i just wanted to say hello. well, that's not entirely true. i also wanted to ask you to do me a big favor. could you stop practicing witchcraft/black magic/voodoo or whatever it is you are doing? you keep popping up in my mind and every time i try to block you out, i feel this sharp pain in the center of my chest.

i've tried everything to protect myself. garlic, crosses, horseshoes, rowan, vodka (that one was my idea) but to no avail. i suspect you're using some lost, ancient, mid western form of the dark arts that i can't protect myself against. something involving bratwurst, toasted ravioli, and a pagan mask with a "go rams" logo on it.

so if you could sacrifice one less chicken, chant one fewer incantation, summon up one less demon against me, i'd appreciate it. and for god's sake, cut out the tickleme objects in my nether regions!

07-30-2002 — **Still trying and getting nowhere**

There comes a time in life when you just have to admit that age catches up to you – wrinkles here, sags there. When you walk down the street and people just don't notice you anymore. I think I understand why movie stars in their declining careers so often commit suicide.

Anna doesn't know what's happened to him, of course. As always, summer arrives, Ben disappears, and this time she may leave it alone. Perhaps after all these years it's the right thing to do.

Or perhaps, sometime this fall, she'll give him a call and suggest (once again) a time for same time next year.

Her life has been the novel she will never write. With all the clichés. She felt his presence ... they were meant for one another ... someday they will ... what teen-age drivel from someone approaching the end of her days.

Perhaps, like Merlin, she lives forward and ages backward.

09-11-2002 — **On 9/11**

I flew shortly after 9/11 – in fact, almost as soon as the planes were back in the air. I wasn't at all afraid – as if my very presence made us both invincible.

I feel pretty smug about it, seeing as how I live less than half a mile from the Pentagon, where tanks and anti-aircraft guns still line the road.

On the other hand, the sound of a low-flying plane forces my eyes upward to follow its path and that's way too often, seeing as how I also live on the flight path to Washington International.

11-06-2002 — **Same Time, Next Year**

And so it goes. Fall it is. And the usual call. Should I, would I, could I. And I agreed, because it was an odd day. On odd days, I still love him. And on even days, I don't. The day we meet will be an odd day. But midnight comes.

12-01-2002 — **Morgan's Message**

Morgan knew we had been together again – and chastised me for it via email, providing suggestions on what I should do with my life.

Stay with Mr. Lucky, but find things that are positive about him. And have my affair with Ben since it seems that is the only way we work together and we just can't seem to stay away from each other.

Move out and start a new life wherever I wish, but keep my old acquaintances (meaning Ben I suppose) a part of it.

Lastly, move out but spend at least a year dating NEW people, and not seeing the old ones. See what life would be like to be single again.

How did my daughter get into Ben's relationship 12-step group? And funny - she's right. I don't seem to want to stay away from him, do I?

12-04-2002 — **Minority Report and the usual cluttered mind**

There are two rules that determine the course of the universe: Choice [...] And Chance. For instance, you choose to throw a cupful of dice, taking the chance that you may lose. See how it works? A choice is made without knowing the outcome, because chance always chooses the outcome. Choice and Chance determine your existence and, inevitably, chooses your destiny.
~~Q (Jarman 72)

There was a good message in *Minority Report* wasn't there? Destiny ... I thought about that a lot after it was all over. The Pre-Crime program was based on the fundamental belief that each person's life was only a destiny fulfilled. You are destined to be someone ... you are destined to do something ... you are destined to turn right, or turn left, at each fork in the road.

Do you remember what Agatha said to John, when it was almost time for him to kill Crow? "You still have a choice."

Think about it. No matter what you do, or when you do it or how you do it ... it is done by your choice. Peer pressure made you do it? No ... you chose to go along with them. You made a bad mistake by accident? No ... it was a bad choice. Stay, leave, love, hate, trust, believe, turn right, turn left, U-turn.

I am reconciled that it has been my choices every step of the way which led me-then to be me-now.

Everyone is headed somewhere, one way or another. A series of right choices will get you to your dream; a series of wrong choices will get you to your nightmare. You and I make extraordinary choices every day because we can.

His scent stayed with me. His breath was in my lungs and I didn't want to exhale for fear of losing it. I wanted to stay with him, to squeeze out all the space between our bodies and allow our hearts to beat with one sound. It always takes a long time for the intensity that is "us" to fade back to reality.

12-11-2002 — **Gaslight Square and meanderings of a cluttered mind**

I used to go to a pub in the Central West End called O'Connell's. Other than Balabans, it was my favorite place.

I started going with a group of friends, much older than me. They bought me wine, let me play darts with them without complaining about my less than spectacular skills, made sure I had eaten (as in those days I may not have that day), didn't mind how young and (no doubt) silly I could be, and one particular one almost always took me home with him. I was 22 and he was 46 but the difference seemed inconsequential in the delicate way he made love to me.

I bring this up because the O'Connell's of those early years had been there since the 60's Gaslight Square days and had some of the most spectacular poetry/haiku I have ever read ... written on the bathroom walls. Each writer trying to outdo the other in a cornucopia of reading pleasure, its very essence preventing the obscenities more commonly found in such places.

Some of the haiku came from a little book that was popular at the time. I wish I could remember the name instead of just the phrase "everyone should love one drab brown thing."

O'Connell's moved to the new location and took those walls with them. Tradition moved, we moved with it, and my dart game steadily improved. Eventually my friend fell in love, and moved to Mexico to write, but not before he had helped me learn a little more about being a grown-up. I have often wondered if he ever published and what ever happened to that interesting group of people.

I recently ran across a poem from a book of old Japanese literature called *Hyaku-nin Isshu* (100 Verses from 100 Poets). I knew the poem ... and I could only have known it from those bathroom walls.

> *How desolate my former life,*
> *Those dismal years, ere yet*
> *I chanced to see thee face to face;*
> *'Twere better to forget*
> *Those days before we met.*
> ~~(Atsutada 42-43)

12-17-2002 — Sing me Goodnight

Ben called to wish me a goodnight. "I can't promise you anything" he says, then proceeds to picture how we would talk about our day before we sleep. He would want me across his chest, he says, our day moving from one mouth to the next, sharing the same breath.

"And will we still hold hands when we walk together at 90?" he asks. "Will you still want me?"

But he can't promise. Or ask. And feels he must warn me of the commitment phobia and that it may never be what I want because relationships are not always the TV movie that ends with the big kiss.

After so many, many years, perhaps he is just a bad habit I should learn to break.

12-20-2002 — Sometimes you need to hear it

This festive season I took time to pick out some truly wonderful cards for a few people I have known an especially long time. Special people who always take the time to listen, who never judge me, and who always accept me for just who I am. I still call these wonderful people my friends, even if I have not seen some of them in years.

As for the story – shortly after I moved to the East Coast I was lucky enough to meet three great guys: Paul, Mr. Lucky, and Golden Knight. I dated them all for over a year, finally giving up two of them in heart wrenching, tearful final dates to concentrate on Paul who became my third husband – lasting an embarrassingly short amount of time before separation and divorce.

I picked back up where we'd left off with Mr. Lucky and Golden Knight but, once again, chose Mr. Lucky over Golden Knight. Despite two disappointments, he remained a loving friend, a confidant, and has always just been there. He remembers my birthday and Valentine's Day, and never fails to change any of his own plans to have lunch or dinner upon request every two or three months. He has remained in that role over all these years.

I never thought of him as anything more than … well, what do you call that kind of person? Friend, certainly, but what else? In a conversation a few months ago, the occasion arose to put a "name" on our relationship and I was hard-pressed to come up with one. He's just always been there.

He phoned to say thank you for his card and to let me know he hadn't called recently because he has a new roommate – after 35 years alone. A woman he'd known for a while and they were going to see how spending time together felt. I was happy for him, but sad too, and I joked, "Couldn't wait any longer for me huh?"

After a brief silence, he took a deep breath and proceeded to tell me that he has always cared very much for me, always thought of me even when we would not see each other for extended periods, and if he had to put words to it – he loves me.

My silence was perhaps a bit longer than intended, but I decided to take the sentiment for what it was worth. After all, he is trying a new kind of relationship out and I have never wanted anything more than we've had. But it got me to wondering.

What if he had said that years ago? What if he'd been brave enough to voice his emotions rather than keeping that distance – letting me always lead the way through the friendship? What if he had taken a giant leap of faith off the emotional cliff?

We'll never know now, but I'm having lunch with him next week just to get that hug he's always ready to give me, wonderfully happy and contented to know that I've had a much better friend than I ever knew.

It occurs to me that I should probably say the same thing to more people along the way. Remind them that even though they are out of sight, they are never out of mind. We shouldn't be afraid to tell others we love them, just as we shouldn't be afraid to hear it.

12-24-2002 — **Santa is coming to town**

Full moon, stars, cold, but beautiful. The fat man should have no problem finding us tonight! Opening presents in the morning, and a big Christmas dinner planned. Kids put up the tree last night AND will cook!

We were at the grocery today, at the breakfast bar section. There was Morgan in all her glory – her photo on the Quaker breakfast bars box. As we stood admiring her, a guy walks up and I ask him if he wants to buy a box – as the star is standing right there. He not only insists on having his picture taken with her, but also has her autograph the box! Her head was so swelled!

Hope your Christmas Eve is lovely … Kisses, hugs, and all that good stuff to each and every one of you, and may the Fat Man bring you at least one of the things you wish for.

12-26-2002 — **OH dear!**

This morning I told Mr. Lucky I was leaving him.

It's not the first time we've had the conversation over the years, but it may well be the last. He has been the worst ever on any holiday, I think, and it was a natural segue. It's been embarrassing for me and uncomfortable for the kids, although they've been troopers and just enjoyed my company.

I can't stand it any longer and see why I need to move sooner, not later. Funny – the only thing he could think of is to make sure my name is off the business checkbook. Thus I see my real importance.

12-30-2002 — **Cure needed, contribute to your local charity drive!**

I wonder what taking care of Anna would truly feel like. Would the he-doesn'tunderstandme, wenevermakeloveanymore, allwedoisfight, whyamialwayswrong syndromes still be there?

After all, every relationship starts with a promise. Some start with love, honor, and obey, some with love and cherish, some with romance, friendship, and sex. Each of them starts with the same convictions that we will grow old and die together.

Maybe *Grey's Anatomy* is right. Relationship killers are genetic and all relationships inherit them automatically. With no vaccination, no pill, and no cure, these diabolical killer genes just lay in wait to sicken and kill any relationship standing in their way.

And, if that's true, can anything ever really change, or will I always just trade one face for another.

12-31-2002 — The Substance of Things Hoped For, the Evidence of Things Not Seen

> *What is faith then but persistent hope in the face of relentless doubt.*
> Brother Carmen Jane, *A Case For Consciousness* CY 10087
> ~~"Decay of the Angel"

faith: *noun.*
1. Confident belief in the truth, value, or trustworthiness of a person, idea, or thing.
2. Belief that does not rest on logical proof or material evidence. See Synonyms at belief. See Synonyms at trust.
3. Loyalty to a person or thing; allegiance: keeping faith with one's supporters.
4. A set of principles or beliefs.

01-04-2003 — I thought to, or not, then again …

I thought to send you a little message today. Or not. Then again … it is almost tomorrow and I am back to thinking.

I've often missed the messages you used to send. The sweet nothings, the wisdom, the review of your day-to-day life. Those transient bits and bytes flying through the unknown cloud drew me to a place of joy while reading about your comings and goings.

Sometimes you wrote of fear, sometimes of courage, but always of, and from, your heart. I miss your soul, though I've found I can live without it for periods of time still unknown.

01-11-2003 — Time and Time Again

> *time, if you could hear me, i would vainly scream a deafening yell directly into*
> *your left ear just hoping, somehow, that i could inflict upon you, in some*
> *small degree, the pain that you have inflicted upon me all these years.*
> ~~Beagle47, December 2002

when does time become the enemy?

when new year's eve seems to come every three months. when you can actually see the new lines in the mirror. when a birthday looms that reminds you that there is much less of your life ahead than you've already left behind.

so i ask the important question. if a visit to your favorite internist left you with the news that there is much less time than you'd counted on – what changes would you make?

would you jump off the proverbial relationship cliff hand in hand to spend it with love. would you ask for what you want because now is all the future you have. would you take the chances you've been setting aside for later, since there's little later left. would you charge into battle with time, and know you can win. or wouldn't you?

01-12-2003 — **Did I tell ya thanks?**

A very dear friend of mine was living in Phuket, Thailand when the tsunami hit and although I knew he was ok, I couldn't help but worry. He was never an emotional guy, but has managed to form lasting friendships with dozens of people across the world – which is surely the sign of a big heart.

He called tonight to say, "You've sent more emails than my mom – so I figured you needed to hear my voice." He was so right.

To: SaltyDawg
Subject: Did I tell ya thanks?

In case I didn't – thanks. Thanks for the call. Thanks for thinking of me. Thanks for not giving me TOO much grief for my inevitable personal investment in the things that happen to, and around, the people I care about.

I have come to regret that I didn't spend more time with you when you lived so much closer. Funny isn't it. Age has a way of catching up with your "gee, I wish I woulda's."

Am surely glad you are well, happy, and apparently very contented with your life. While I suspect you already know it, it bears repeating. If there's ever anything you need from me, just only have to ask.

Anna

To: Anna
Subject: re: Did I tell ya thanks

You have now. And thank you for being a good friend. They're hard to find.

SaltyDawg

1-13-2003 — **Serendipity**

ser·en·dip·i·ty: *noun.*
1. The faculty of making fortunate discoveries by accident.
2. The fact or occurrence of such discoveries.
3. An instance of making such a discovery.

It's midnight and I should have been asleep hours ago – but my dearest Ben called at 10 and we just hung up. He didn't get the email I was out of town and hoped he might call. He just "felt like talking to you tonight."

If life were like a book, we would wake each morning with the next chapter under our pillow. A complete manual for the day including the right answers to all the questions.

And, perhaps, for a lucky few – we'd find an early script of the entire last chapter. Just so we'd know we were taking the right steps to get there.

01-14-2003 — **When you're right** ...

I do so wish I were more perfect. I have always believed the people in my world would like me better and trust me more if they didn't think me broken.

02-08-2003 — **Buy Now or Cancel**

On the website to make a reservation to go see him I sat there, finger poised above the *Buy Now – Cancel* buttons.

What causes the desire to go to him when his random messages are without depth, and bereft of emotion. What force of nature propels me unerringly towards the great sadness that is leaving?

Since I couldn't answer the questions, I allowed my finger to descend and pressed the key gently.

Men often wonder why women use the word "trust." I suspect they believe it is an overused word whether it is a noun or verb.

But, being a woman, I understand it completely. Trust me.

02-14-2003 — A Valentine Card

You gave me the greatest gift – the time we spent together this weekend. So this is your Valentine's card. Something to tuck away in that box you've labeled "Anna." To re-read on the occasion you want to remember.

Here is my heart. You are the only person I've ever trusted to keep it safe.

03-14-2003 — Today is Your Birthday
Personal email to Anna from Benjamin

Happy Birthday! I hope you did something nice for yourself today, even if someone else didn't. I don't think Easter is going to work out for us this year. Perhaps later this spring or early summer?

03-15-2003 — Easter
Personal email from Anna to Benjamin

As Simon Cowell says on *American Idol*, "can I be honest with you?"

It makes me feel very disappointed that you don't want to see me on Easter. I realize "intellectually" that the reasons are yours personally, and they are not ones you have chosen to share and that they are actually none of my business. But "emotionally" my heart hurts.

So let's leave it as this. The last few times I've asked to see you. This time, when you want to get together again – let me know. I'm going to leave it to you.

03-17-2003 — **The Box**

Do you have a box? A cigar box, a little book box, maybe a heart shaped box that once held Valentine chocolate. It's probably hidden away somewhere on a shelf, or in the lingerie drawer, or in the bottom drawer of your desk. Perhaps you wrote a name on it, maybe you didn't, because you will always, always, know who is in it.

Inside that box are the mementos from the most special relationship you ever had. The menu from your first dinner, the movie tickets when you first held hands, the ribbon from the first rose, the sentimental birthday card, and the four-leaf clover you found in the park that day when you discovered you were loved. And, for some of us, the letter that said goodbye.

Each of us yearns to believe that there is a box, somewhere, with our name on it. We want to believe that when we made love it transcended everything that came before, and every one that came after. The existence of that box reassures us that the sum of our relationship together meant the same to them as it did to us. We want to believe our box is unique and cherished beyond measure.

So what do you do when you find out you are not special. What does it mean when there is more than one box?

There she had been, in the middle of the best visit they had enjoyed in a long time. A visit to celebrate a holiday, to spend it together for the first time in years. She was writing the Valentine card. Putting everything that filled her heart into making it something that would go into her box with a kiss, to be read, and re-read, each time he sought reassurance of her feelings.

She went to his office desk to find a red pen. Happy coincidence, a red pen right there in the cup on top.

She went back out the door and as she turned to shut it, her eyes were drawn up to the shelves on the far side of the room. And there was a box. Another box. And the name on the box was not hers.

It was hard to breathe for a moment. Oddly enough, her head said it is possible we all have more than one box. We start each relationship not knowing where it will lead and the contents of each box are little pats on the back that we achieved lovability, even if we are no longer a couple.

It wasn't what she had hoped for on this day. But life hardly ever gives you what you hope for.

03-19-2003 — **Let's talk about The One**

> *When we are together*
> *Life is a sweet surrender*
> *Where I could stay forever*
> *Where every moment with you*
> *Is a moment to treasure*

Most people want to believe there is someone out there that is their other half. Whether you believe in a heart broken in heaven and sent to earth in two pieces destined to seek and find, a chemistry that will only match one other, or a Hallmark card true love, we are all looking for "The One." So what do you do when you've found The One, but you are not your One's One?

Anna pondered this enigma just days past her fifty f(throat clearing) birthday. Nine men have said I love you, resulting in three marriages come and gone, and a current participant in a sad dissatisfying long term living arrangement. None of them has been "The One."

She had known who The One was for twenty-eight years. Half her life. He's gone in and out. Between two of his marriages and two of hers. They went ten years once without speaking, but when one of them can't stand to be away from the other one any longer they get together in every woman's passionate dream and every man's fantasy. The middle of the romantic novel you can't put down until you read the last page.

Anna is ready. As ready as she's ever been to spend her life with him. No reservations, no regrets. He's not. Still doubting. Still looking for something else, something she can't give him. The issues are endless. Trust, childhood trauma, lovability, everything every self-help book and 12-step program tells you should be wrong with you. Sometimes Anna believes pop psychologists have done nothing more than give us excuses for not growing up, for not making decisions, for not taking responsibility for our lives, our decisions, and our futures. We can always blame it on something or someone because blaming it on anything but ourselves is so much simpler.

Lately she's beginning to ask herself. Is the reason she can't find another "One" because she can't give up this one. Is there only enough room in a heart for one "One"?

And if that's true, how do you let it go?

03-20-2003 — **To Imagine is Everything**

To know is nothing at all; to imagine is everything.
~~Anatole France (*The Crime of Sylvestre Bonnard*, 113)

I don't know why I feel the need to be perfect. Or maybe I do. If I were perfect, then how could someone not love me? There's nothing to dislike, nothing to resent, nothing to worry about with a perfect person.

When I see that I'm not so perfect it scares me some, and when I allow myself to show my less than perfect self to someone like him, it scares me more. I feel like he adds another checkmark to his "why not to" list.

03-27-2003 — **Decide What You Really Want**

Anna went to dinner with Golden Knight last night. A belated birthday dinner with all the trimmings at a restaurant he knew she loved. And Anna was more than curious about his new relationship.

"Are you happy?" Anna inquired.

"Yes, I suppose I must be" he replied. "Neither of us are the kinds of people who will stick around and suffer through a mediocre relationship. It is either giving us everything we expect, or the potential for everything, or we walk away without regret. So yes, I suppose I must be since she's still there after six months."

Anna lowered her eyes, took a breath, and leaned forward slightly to look up at him. "But are you Hallmark card happy? Have you found IT?"

"I don't think there is such a thing, Anna. Consider this. You and I could have been born in a hut in Haiti, in the Harlem ghetto, or in a village in India. We weren't. We were born in the most prosperous and free country in the world. We both have beautiful homes, cars, and enough money to be greater than just comfortable. These things came to us because we were born in the right place at the right time. Happiness, on the other hand, is not a birthright. It's a choice."

"But I want more" Anna cried. "I know I'm not mistreated in the classic sense. But my heart needs more, my soul needs more. I ask myself every day why can't I be satisfied with the things I have. Why am I always looking for love to go along with it?"

"I can't answer that Anna," he said. "But you can't always have everything. Maybe you should consider that being happy doesn't mean everything's perfect. It means you've decided to see beyond the imperfections."

Anna's eyes filled with tears as she stared at him and said, "Many years ago, when I had only been out on my own for a short time, I had run out of money. I rarely asked my dad for anything, but this time I did. He sent me a check, and wrapped around it was a letter. He wrote:

> *There's not much advice I can give you except this. You have an intellect of remarkable quality, but it's worth only what you use of it. You can't have everything. Decide what you really want, then work to achieve it.*
> ~~Daddy"

Anna reached into her purse for a tissue as she said, "I've never forgotten the advice, but I don't think I ever learned how to use it."

04-01-2003 — When The Missing is Real

Today is Friday. Anna hasn't heard from Ben since his call of Monday midnight. So perhaps the "shesnotreallyrightforme" new girl has become more right after all.

It's not that she couldn't find it, somehow, in her to write him off. It's that she can't admit her uselessness to him. She can't allow herself to be written out of HIS life.

04-02-2003 — **View from the Peanut Gallery**

The greatest love stories in literature revolve around couples who are kept apart by seemingly insurmountable odds. Sometimes they are separated by distance, sometimes by space, sometimes by positions in life, and occasionally even by time itself. Sometimes one, or even both, is already involved in a relationship of dubious quality. Whatever the situation, they are inextricably attracted to one another and the entire book, film, or play is about the driving need to overcome the obstacles standing in their way of being together forever.

Hundreds and thousands of such stories have convinced even the most jaundiced of us that there is, indeed, merit – even reward – in doing whatever is necessary because Love Is All There Is. So I guess this begs the question – is never ending true love just a compulsion? And where is the line between love and obsession?

Some years ago I observed that Anna had always gone for bad boys. It wasn't until she went for the straight guys that her life turned to shit.

The actual truth was that once she got them, she didn't actually believe she could keep them. Maybe because she knew going in that the bad boys were only good for a hot toss and the reasons for good boys were needs that quickly passed. Win some, lose some, she consoled herself with the lie that she didn't want them anyway, there's always another one around the corner.

Then one walked away from her. Three times. And the lies didn't work. Is that love, or is it a desperate last-ditch compulsion to hang on because, for once, she just can't have the one she wants.

I wonder ... is loving Ben just an obsession that could be cured by a good therapist?

04-02-2003 — **The Floor is Now Open for Questions**

Last Tuesday night, 11:00 p.m.

Mr. Lucky: "Can you take me in the morning for my colonoscopy?"
Anna: "Sure, what time is the appointment?"
Mr. Lucky: "I don't know."

Anna: "Ok, what time are you supposed to be there?"
Mr. Lucky: "I don't know."
Anna: "Which hospital is it?"
Mr. Lucky: "I don't know."
Anna:

Note to self: Life is apparently NOT about the answers. It's about the questions.

04-04-2003 — How Do I Get There

I got to thinking why you are still the first thing I think about in the morning, laying there under soft covers, drowsy with sleep. And why you are the last thing I think about at night, snuggled down into the pillows, considering what dreams should be made of.

Because after all these years, it's still where I want to be.

When we first met, you charmed me with your patience. You came to my office, took me to lunch, walked with me in the park, and beat me at darts. When I pulled away from your kisses, you held my hand instead, and gave me the time I needed to let you into my heart.

People often talk about how the changes they experience over the years move them too far apart. I believe that our experiences built a solid bridge where we can meet in the middle.

So forgive me if it makes you uncomfortable when I sometimes need to say I still believe in you. That I still want to walk in the park with you holding my hand, and will never pull away from you again when you try to kiss me.

And forgive me that I am sometimes the little voice that whispers in your ear, reminding you that you are loved. Because I think to believe it's truly real, we sometimes need to hear it out loud.

I can be the patient one this time.

04-06-2003 — **Note to Friends**

Welcome to the 2003 edition of getting to know your friends. The theory is that you will learn many little things about your friends, if you did not know them already. Try it yourself. Pass it along and then back to me. I'll wait.

1. **What time did you get up this morning**? Forced awake at 8 a.m. by a knock on the door

2. **Diamonds or pearls**? Pearls – I've been to India

3. **What is your favorite TV show**? I'm an addict because I have a TiVo (or do I have a TiVo because I'm an addict?). This year, maybe *Alias*.

4. **What did you have for breakfast**? Slimfast – and a chocolate/peppermint mint patty (well, they were there, weren't they)

5. **What is your middle name**? Margaret, named after my maternal grandmother. Someone thought it was cute.

6. **What is your favorite food**? I eat to live, I don't live to eat. St. Louis Pizza (the Provel cheese gets me every time), bacon, rib-eye steak – rare, baked sweet potatoes with brown sugar and cinnamon, home-made baking powder biscuits with sweet butter and honey, and of course, anything that contains chocolate. And if it's made by anyone other than me – it's an automatic favorite.

7. **What foods do you dislike**? Hot dogs, mushrooms, any food so spicy you can't taste the flavor underneath, and cumin (the spice).

8. **What is your favorite CD at the moment**? If I were on a deserted island, I'd have to have the Sarahs – Brightman and McLachlan – and Norah Jones. I'm also a sucker for Doo-Wop, and 60's R&B.

9. **What car do you drive**? Electric blue 1994 Mitsubishi Eclipse with a sunroof

10. **Favorite sandwich**? Bacon, Lettuce, Tomato on toast with LOTS of sweet pickles, mayonnaise, and mustard

11. **What characteristic do you despise**? Liars, drivers who can't get going from a stop and don't use turn signals, loud eaters, men who don't put the seat down, and store clerks who put your coins on TOP of the bills when they hand you change.

12. **Favorite item of clothing**? Levi 501 jeans. Had to order them over the internet to get a 35" inseam – worn them since their invention I think.

13. **If you could go anywhere in the world on vacation, where would you go**? Right now, Italy, but Greece and Egypt are close seconds. China and Australia are on that same list.

14. **Where would you retire**? Anywhere near my daughter, but it had better be warm year round. (are you listening dear?) The ideal would be a little beach

house for winter, and a little cabin in the woods for summer. The best of both my worlds.

15. **What was your most memorable birthday?** When I was 22. I was the center of attention in at my favorite local bar, surrounding by a room full of friends, and the bartender knew my name. The worst? 21 and 33. Alone after big break-ups.

16. **Favorite sport to watch?** Football, although I also like baseball

17. **Which fabric detergent do you use?** Cheer, because I grew up with it.

18. **Coke or Pepsi?** Coke – cause I grew up with it (oh, you mean the pop drink!).

19. **Are you a morning person or a night owl?** Like Snoopy, I don't do mornings!

20. **Do you have any pets?** Yes, Mango, a female Jenday Conure who used to be a kind, loving bird when she went to work with me every day. Then she stayed at home all the time and became a sullen creature that bites any stranger who comes near her.

21. **What did you want to be when you were little?** An actress. Be careful what you wish for.

04-09-2003 — **Through the Looking Glass**

> *The door opens.*
> *The edges meet.*
> *Step through and you find yourself lost.*
> *Stay where you are and you go nowhere.*
> Wayfinder Hasturi, A.K.A. The Mad Perseid, AFC 217
> ~~"Totaled Recall"

It has been said we never truly think about our last breath until we are about to take it. But Anna was thinking about it.

Perhaps it was the everyday way in which the technician provided the services for the annual mammogram. Tug, push, pull, place, squeeze, hit the button and you're done, thank you just go out that door we'll call you in two weeks.

Perhaps it was the birthday that reminded her once again that she was older by far than her mother had been when she died of the cancer a mammogram was supposed to find. Any opportunity to heal the relationship buried with her.

Perhaps it was the letter from her dear cousin, telling her of his mother's passing last fall. She had planned to finally visit her aunt in the spring, to ask of her father, to ask for tales of his childhood, to hear the stories that had never had a chance to be told in life. The last of his siblings dead and gone, and another opportunity lost forever.

Perhaps it was wondering why she hadn't responded to the email from the apartment complex telling her the apartment she looked at all those months ago when she visited Ben would be available in June. But responding meant making a decision now. It meant starting the real process of leaving. Hiring the attorneys, deciding who gets what, how, and when, then the anger and recriminations, the fear and doubts that always followed.

She had made those lists before. The deciding, the dividing, the things to be left behind that you didn't want to give back, the things you don't honestly want but can't bear to throw away because it's all you have left.

It's not as if Mr. Lucky is a wildly inappropriate person. What if, when it's all finished, there's no "whew, I'm glad that's over." What if (like the last time) when she's finally available, Ben can't, or won't, be there. In a life of infinite choices, how do you know when you've made the right one? How do you know when it's time to step through the door?

Hindsight is 20/20. It's always easier to look back and see things clearly that we couldn't see at all then. It's easier to be wiser about the mistakes we made yesterday than the ones we are in the process of making today.

Learning from the past is supposed to give meaning, and purpose, to the pain and heartache experienced along the way. Maybe what she should have learned is that there isn't anything any better. All relationships change over time. Maybe what she has right now is just as good as it's ever going to get with any of them.

So, if she chooses to stay where she is, to stop looking for a truly great relationship and settle for a just ok one, what answer will she give as she takes that last breath. What will she say when faced with the question, "What did you do with the gift of your life?"

Life is not lost by dying;
life is lost minute by minute,
day by dragging day,
in all the thousand small uncaring ways.
  ~~Stephen Vincent Benet, "A Child is Born: A Drama of the Nativity"

04-17-2003 — **Love-forsaken**

In my heart part
love you comegoes
there odd days
even not –
one three five yours
two four six love-forsaken
core trembles
sputters
out

04-18-2003 — **If I Could Sing Like the Birds**

Oh, how beautiful, the Tadpole whispered to himself.
What? asked the Lizard.
That singing, cried the Tadpole.
Oh, if I could only sing like those Birds.
      ~~M'Louise Jones, "More Ways Than One"

You know how when there's something important you should have done, but you've forgotten, and when you remember, your stomach turns? Or that feeling that comes into your throat, when you see the person you loved with another person, even if you're no longer together?

The only way to remember Ben during all those years without him had been to block out certain feelings. Now every feeling she ever had is bubbling up all over the place with nowhere to go but out her eyeballs. He is who he is; he's never going to change. His ability to love is limited and she needs to accept that.

But she is left to wonder, just how dangerous is a broken heart?

04-23-2003 — **Searching for Love in All the Right Places**

According to a recent article from Match.com, love is a basic human instinct. We need to love and be loved, and we spend most of our life searching for it.

If love is such a natural instinct within each of us, why do we so often fight the state of it?

Pop-shrinks have decided that we aren't smart enough to trust our own feelings. Love is just too confusing for us poor human beings, and we need help understanding and interpreting it. Thus we have become so afraid of loving we use everything around us to tell us how. Novels, movies, web sites, 12-step programs, commercials, TV shows, group therapy, and hundreds of books by suddenly well-known authors have become our blueprints for a successful relationship. In other words – don't follow your heart, follow their plans.

Ben has always known where to find Anna. Instead, like most men, he peers over the fence wondering if that pasture next door might just be a little greener. He still reads the books, listens to the TV shows, and goes to the meetings.

Wouldn't it be funny if, after all his searching, he found that what he has been looking for all his life has been right there in front of him the whole time …

04-23-2003 — **Chains of Bondage**

Ben: Hi, I thought I'd give you a call. Hope it's not too late. I'm just on my way to Borders before it closes. How are you?

Anna: Hi, this is unexpected. How am I? Why I'm …

how am I? I am terminally ill with a broken heart. An unknown author once wrote, "Love comes to those who still hope even though they've been disappointed, those who still believe, even though they have been betrayed, and those who still love even though they've been hurt before." I hope not, I believe not. That leaves only pain to bind me inextricably to you. If I miss you in this lifetime, I will find you in the next, if just to say, "I waited a lifetime to hear you say I want you … "

Why I'm just fine, really fine. And how about you?

04-24-2003 — Six Degrees of Separation

Six degrees of separation is the theory that anyone on the planet can be connected to any other person on the planet through a chain of acquaintances that has no more than five intermediaries. In 1967, American sociologist Stanley Milgram devised a way to test the theory by mailing a package (Barabási). In 2001, Duncan Watts, a professor at Columbia University recreated Milgram's experiment on the Internet finding that the average number of intermediaries was, indeed, six (827-829).

A user at my journal site recently left me a note that said, in part:

> *I was just thinking about how things tend to come full circle. An obvious example is a note from catz-eyes, who you added as a favourite, which I thought was interesting. He's a favourite of yours, which is a favourite of mine, which is a favourite of the-cad, which is a favourite of (BAM!) catz-eyes*
> ~~candoor, April 2003

Is it possible *JournalLand* is just a giant "six degrees" ring?

Sitting here now with a glass of wine in hand, getting more than a little tipsy, I remember the original internet search that brought me to *JournalLand*. "What the ... " was my first thought for, despite the fact that the words "computer" and "consultant" appear on my business card, this was my first look at an on-line diary/journal. Ok, so I'd heard the word Blog but it sounded like a Rorschach inkblots test.

The reason for starting this thing in the first place was to have a safe backup for Ben and Anna's thoughts and correspondence. Sharing was not part of the plan.

I didn't start with a fancy template. But the words ... it was a new adventure every day. By now, I've enjoyed bits of diaries from all over the world, from Goth to God, warlocks to wankers, middle-schoolers to the overthe50s diary ring.

So, *JournalLand*ers, I come at long last to the point. I raise my wineglass to you.

Cheers, Prosit, Saœde, Kan bei, Skal, Proost, Kippis, A votre sant, Auf ihr wohl, Eis Igian, Okole maluna, L'Chaim, Kedves egeszsegere, Cin cin, Slante, Kampai, Salud, Kia ora, Sto Lot, Na zdorovia!!

If you don't mind, I really like being here in your company.

04-26-2003 — SWF looking for %M%... Fill in the Blanks

> *You men have no idea what we're dealing with down there. Teeth placement, and jaw stress, and suction, and gag reflex, and all the while bobbing up and down, moaning and trying to breathe through our noses. Easy? Honey, they don't call it a job for nothin'.*
> ~~Samantha Jones, "Easy Come, Easy Go"

When Anna was 20, she enjoyed the oh-so experienced pleasures of a man of 40. A gorgeous writer with expensive tastes, wealthy friends, a huge cock, and an experienced tongue he loved to use regularly.

When she was 40, she spent an inordinate amount of time with a man of 20. A poor actor with eccentric tastes, show business friends, a huge cock, and an experienced tongue he loved to use regularly.

Believe me, the only noticeable difference was what she had been served for dinner and the choice of music accompanying the evening's main event.

The young actor helped get Ben off her mind. She was starting to obsess which led to nothing but trouble. The sleepless nights, the gray days, the restraining orders … (just kidding on that last one).

Why is it in the movies and TV, whenever the plucky young heroine has to clamber through the sewers from one relationship to another she never gets dirty? In real life, that sewer is dirty, dark, and smells. And the things living in it don't run away; they get confused, turn around, and come back *at* you.

Right now, the thought of another body next to hers seems like something out of a dream. But when real people fall down, they get right back up. Anybody out there got any hot 25-year-old friends looking for good company and truly fantastic sex?

Men! You can't live with them, and you can't get them to dress up in a skimpy little leather G-string, handcuff you to the bed, and turn on the closest vibrator ...

~~Emo Philips

04-27-2003 — **One ringy dingy ... two ringy dingies**

Mr. Lucky had been gone for three days. "He won't be home till midnight Tuesday; we have the whole weekend to play." Tuesday, at midnight, he finally called.

Anna: Mr. Lucky just walked in the door, sorry but I can't talk now.
Ben: Can I call you tomorrow morning?
Anna: Of course, as long as you don't mind spending your minutes.

He did call. Ninety minutes in peak time. A veritable indulgence for him. A potpourri of catching up, giggling, and news. News of his current class and tales of an old professor he had known years ago. And when they spoke of forgiveness, she told him she had recently found the strength to forgive her mother, which led to a conversation about the molds we come from. And so on.

He asked how her move was progressing. "Slowly" she answered. "I can't seem to get the momentum." She didn't want to say it was because the move had a lot to do with him and she wasn't so sure there was anything there for her anymore.

And so on. He asked about his rival, the one waiting in the wings, the one who said I love you every day and wanted her to leave Mr. Lucky and live with him foreverafter. "You know I've told him we aren't a good match."

And she asked about hers. "She's doing fine." Which didn't answer the question at all of course, but she left it alone.

When the last goodbyes were said, and the last agreements to call soon, and the last promises that her birthday present honestly WAS in the mail, she replaced the phone and thought a kiss. Then the day, a little lighter and a little brighter, continued.

04-28-2003 — **can hearts break**

> is it really true you can smell success
> is the taste of fear sour or sweet
> if you lose yourself, where were you left
> on the desk or a subway seat
> which direction does your stomach turn
> and how does it work upside down
> are tongues really tied, do brains turn to mush
> will all ears burn, can sorrows drown
> and do you suppose a heart can break
> and if it can, what does it take
> to put it back together again
> all the king's horses, or all the king's men?

05-03-2003 — **Find a Little Tenderness**

Let's face it, thrills are not cheap. Those little rubber items are downright expensive and don't even get me started on the spiraling cost of batteries. But with a bit of ingenuity, there are plenty of playthings around the house.

Zucchinis are a turn on. And you can cut them to size. Vacuum cleaners are quite erotic depending on the attachments. Closets are crammed with usable objects: belts, suspenders, ties, and scarves – and there's always a little something there for dress-up.

Into leather? Kissing toes encased in Manolo Blahniks is a definite turn-on (you might as well be classy about it). And as long as you're down there lip-caressing expensive cowhide, describe to me how you feel about that nice long spiky heel.

There are an amazing number of dishwasher safe kitchen implements available for double duty and have you looked at some of the interesting tools just lying around on the workbench doing nothing?

If you're into something kinky, it doesn't take a lot of money. It just takes a little imagination. After all, look what Albert Finney and Joyce Redman did with a dinner roll and a bowl of fruit.

I'll bring the Mazola!

05-05-2003 — **The End of the Road**

Our love won't die because I won't give up on it! It's epic, it's massive. It's Romeo and Juliet, Anthony and Cleopatra, Ben and Jennifer [...] All tragedies, I might add.

~~"The Seven Year Witch"

At one point, after months of not hearing from Ben, Anna's first ever love contacted her. She hadn't heard from Jason in over 30 years. An instant connection formed, and after several months of exciting correspondence, phone calls, IMs, and emails, she was ready to see him face-to-face.

As usual, fate had other ideas.

Jason and Ben both live in her old hometown, 1000 miles away. Just as she had agreed to visit Jason, Ben called "I need to see you again; I've missed you so much." Conflicted, she made airline and hotel reservations that allowed her to spend the first day with Ben "just to have lunch" before meeting Jason the next afternoon. As anyone who reads these pages regularly could guess, lunch turned into dinner, the hotel room was cancelled, and they danced the same dance that has kept them together all these years. And Ben is still The One.

I pause only to mention that the visit with Jason went on as planned. Disappointing anyone, especially a man, is not Anna's strong suit.

And that fickle finger?

By the end of last year, and after a particularly horrific period with Mr. Lucky, Anna made up her mind she was moving out. With two men in the same town anything could happen, so she put her name on the reservation list of a local apartment complex, and began planning her escape.

Jason was ecstatic, having begged her to move since the first visit, expressing undying love, and planning their future together in every "we/us" detail. Ben was enthusiastically non-committal, never having asked her to share anything, except time, since their first years together. The "L" word is an email signature, and commitment is a phobia. He can't say "I want you" but he can't let her go.

Moving meant giving up a home she loved, friends she cared about, a job she was good at, and the security of a good salary to move back to a city she barely remembered. When the apartment complex called to say an apartment had become available – she got cold feet.

It was right then she realized that, while she would give up everything to be with Ben, she was not willing to give up anything to be with Jason.

> *When you come to the place where there's no more road,*
> *is that the end, or the beginning?*

05-15-2003 — Riddle of Desperation

> *A building without walls is where we live, hope without dreams is all we*
> *have. To run is to embrace despair.*
> ~~Telemachus Rhade – Nietzschean Riddle of Desperation

Some days are no more than a commonplace miracle where I live from one tentative conclusion to the next, thinking each one is final.

The closer I get to you, the more I realize I'm just one wrong step away from where I used to be.

One foot in front of the next, I cannot turn away, I cannot move on.

In the quiet moments without you, I still feel you next to me. Lovers, friends joined, my heart does not stop.

05-16-2003 — A Fine Line Between Love and Hate

> *I don't know if you can die from a broken heart.*
> *I do know you can't live with one.*
> ~~catz-eyes, May 2003

I hate you
Because you didn't walk away. Because you pursued me and persistently insisted on courting me until I fell in love with you.

I hate you
Because when you make love to me we fit perfectly, and rose to the kinds of

passion only found in fairy tales and poetry, and I know I will never have this passion with anyone else.

I hate you
Because you stayed with me for years, sending me letters, and notes, and pretending to love me more than anyone has ever loved me, and made me believe in you.

I hate you
Because you couldn't understand how afraid I was of making another bad choice by leaving my other life, and after five years together you wouldn't love me enough to wait just six more months.

I hate you
Because when you left, the pain of that broken heart was greater than any person should have had to bear and you didn't care.

I hate you
Because you always left me when the grass seemed greener on the other side of the fence, then returned time and again forcing me to watch you leave once more for those same empty pastures.

I hate you
Because I've wasted twenty-five years of my life loving you and believing that someday you would love me again the same way too.

I hate you
Because you won't say go away I will never want you, and instead keep my hopes alive by giving me hints and glimpses of a perfectly possible future together.

I hate you
Because every time you leave you take more of my heart with you and this time there's nothing left at all.

I hate you
Because after all these years of searching for you in everyone else I've ever met, I feel destined to live out the rest of this pitiful life knowing you are out there somewhere without me.

I hate you
Because when everything we gave to each other slowly fades away, when you are only here as a dream, and when the words "I love you" are scripts of the past, I will always have the memories that were once moments, and I will always know that I once had a chance to be loved by you.

> *One of the hardest things ... is realizing that the person who dumped you probably isn't suffering as badly as you are ... That's what hurts the most: the prospect that they were right to move on, when for you, they felt like the one.*
> ~~Karley Sciortino

05-20-2003 — School Days

> *Conformity is the jailer of freedom and the enemy of growth.*
> ~~John F. Kennedy

TheChemister is a beautiful, articulate *JournalLand* teen I love to read and she is having some doubts about high school in particular, and life in general.

Having been a mom to a beautiful, articulate teen, reading her is like peeking into the diary I never found.

I was a goose in school. More worried about boyfriends, what round I'd be picked in the "choosing up sides" games, and my popularity rating based on votes for Student Council, or Homecoming Court. Well, that's another entry too.

But boy, if I could do it over again ... the changes I would make now that I know what is unquestionably important about school.

I was also a completely rebellious, totally outspoken, too bright for my own good, wacko kid with one "oh so typical I could throw up every time I hear someone blame all their problems on" abusive, and one normal, parent.

I grew up in a conservative, all white, Germanic settled small Midwestern town (5000 souls) near St. Louis, and attended the only high school (graduating class: 105).

I was 10 in the summer of 1960; the same year John F. Kennedy ran for President and civil rights was in its infancy. Kennedy was a CATHOLIC (oh my gawd) and he supported the civil rights movement (double OMG). And I supported him – altho I suspect it was because my parents did.

In honor of the presidential debates (it was a famous one with Richard M. Nixon) our teacher decided to have a debate. Two of us would take opposite sides, as if we were the candidates, and discuss the issues. Then the class would vote. I was selected to speak, and guess which one I chose.

I lost that debate, as you might imagine, but the prodigious research required taught me so much more than I lost.

My point, I suppose, is that you don't always have to take the popular side in order to win. In fact, the popular side isn't always the right side.

The message today is one I wish I could have more effectively passed to my own daughter.

We are in school, living at home and supported by our parents, only 15% of our lives. The other 85% we are on our own as adults – saddled with thousands of responsibilities, decisions, disappointments, and heartbreaks – and using every single day what we learned during that first 15%.

In school, we get to study the past, explore science and math, take apart literature, and create new works. We don't learn *how* to think – we learn *to* think. And it's FREE.

I wish I had put as much effort into the rest of my school years as I did into that grade school debate. Can you imagine how much better I could have been?

An education isn't how much you have committed to memory, or even how much you know. It's being able to differentiate between what you know and what you don't.

~~Anatole France (attrib.)

05-25-2003 — **The Pledge**

> I never pledged
> until death do us part
> as the last line
> of a sentence mouthed
> falteringly
> in a flower-strewn
> sanctuary.
>
> I pledged my troth
> in simple language
> given continuity and meaning
> by all the every days
> I have lived and loved you. (Bosche)

06-03-2003 — **June 3 – National Love Conquers All Day**

If you live to be a hundred, I want to live to be a hundred minus one day so I never have to live without you.
~~A. A. Milne

"Amor Vincit Omnia" translates as "love conquers all," a motto engraved on the brooch worn by the Prioress in Chaucer's Canterbury Tales (8). The full quote from the Roman poet Virgil's Ecologues X, 69 dated to 38 BC is "omnia vincit Amor: et nos cedamus Amori" or, "Love conquers everything, let us yield ourselves to Love!" (120)

Anna and Ben have watched the first dawn and last dusk of the world together. Names and faces change, but the connection is as close as the waves are bound to the sea.

If this life has been lived, their time truly passed, then in the next life they will find one another. Anna asks only this; let her dust be mingled with his forever, and forever, and forever.

06-13-2003 — **An Unexpected Trip**

Anna's entire trip to Florida was plagued with 100% humidity, hours of afternoon thunderstorms, and temperatures that barely topped 78 degrees. She managed to avoid the hurricane, and arrived home to lower humidity and a daily high of 95 degrees predicted for the week. Ahh … this home is like … well, home!

When you grow up without air conditioning in a particularly hot and humid location your relationship with summer is complex and contradictory. You were told to go outside and play amid stories that sunlight is dangerous and burns the skin.

Not that summers in a small Midwestern town weren't fun. She had a great time and has a long list of mosquito bite and poison ivy stories to prove it. There were hours spent lounging under the shade of the neighbor's carport, or the boughs of the backyard willow tree. Too hot to ride bikes, play tennis, or form a sandlot baseball game, the dog days of summer mostly included sitting around and talking.

She has no idea what a big group of kids from 8   12 found to talk about, but talk they did for hours at a time. She still wonders if some of those conversations contained the answer to everything, long forgotten upon entering the world of adulthood.

There are plenty of climatically wonderful places to be in the United States this time of year – places that make you feel good to be alive without having to seek out a shade tree around 3 p.m. Unfortunately, she doesn't live in any of them and vacation's over for another few weeks.

Of course sitting on her desk, taunting her, is that free roundtrip ticket. To take the trip she fantasizes about. Where she races to the airport, and goes to Ben, invited or not. She knocks on his door and, at that moment, it forces him to admit the truth, whatever the truth might be.

In her fantasies, he takes her in his arms. In reality, it could be the final good-bye. Thirty years gone to the past. Thirty years of the future to be without him. Where shall she go … where *shall* she go.

> *When all falls apart and sinks below the surface, the only dream that matters to me is that in this life you love me.*
> ─Fabienne Gassmann, *Hope, Joy, Peace, Love*

06-18-2003 — **press Enter to send**

> *I wanted a perfect ending […] Now I've learned, the hard way, that some*
> *poems don't rhyme, and some stories don't have a clear beginning, middle,*
> *and end. […] [Life] is about not knowing, having to change, taking the*
> *moment and making the best of it, without knowing what's going to happen*
> *next. Delicious ambiguity […]*
> ~~Gilda Radner (237)

She thought about it. Every time she woke up and found herself thinking of him before her eyes had opened. And every time she went to sleep and found him in her dreams. And every time she called and he never picked up even when she knew he could have, or should have, or would have.

She went back through her entries and found the right one. The one she had written and never actually sent. The one she wrote in anger and despair and desperation. **A Fine Line Between Love and Hate.**

And she opened an email. And copied it in. And addressed it. And pressed **Send**.

> *Being deeply loved by someone gives you strength; while loving someone deeply*
> *gives you courage.*
> ~~Lao Tzu

08-24-2003 — **A Fine Line Between Hate and Love**

> *Where you used to be,*
> *there is a hole in the world,*
> *which I find myself constantly walking around in the daytime,*
> *and falling in at night.*
> ~~Edna St. Vincent Millay (102)

Anna writes. She writes what she can no longer send to someone who can no longer hear and bears the singular knowledge that creating her own ending is oh so very, very easy.

I loved you
Because you persistently insisted on pursuing me when I didn't want pursuing,

courting me in the old-fashioned way with cheap red wine in mismatched glasses, a view of the stars, and tickets to *Oh Calcutta.*

I loved you
Because you never failed to ask, 'and how are you' and you wanted to listen.

I loved you
Because for ever so long you gave me ever so long to find the right time to come to you when you could have left the first day, or the first week, or even the first hour of that perfectly perfect first night.

I loved you
Because, even driving with one hand, you could reach over with a lover's unerring accuracy and no one has ever found that spot again.

I loved you
Because when you held me in your arms no one existed but we two in every instant of every hour of every day I was made to love you and, having been there, I never wanted to be anywhere else.

I loved you
Because falling in love with you gave me the only until death do us part moments I will ever have, no matter how many white veils I may put on.

I loved you
Because when you led, I knew where to follow and for one brief instant in time, I was someone's One.

I loved you
Because every time I hear our song I will feel your body outside inside mine.

I loved you
Because with you I glimpsed Paradise, and the memories assure me of the sweet dreams only lovers can dream in all of the midnights of the rest of my days.

I loved you
Because you have my heart for safekeeping, my soul in the palm of your hands, and my belief that we will find one another again in our next life.

I loved you
Because I meant it when I said I would love you
Always and forever

09-05-2003 — **Just as simple as that**

Anna returned home from the wedding celebrations of her only child to find an email from Ben.

> *"Dearest Anna,*
> *Sorry I've been out of touch lately— nothing personal, nothing against you.*
> *Caught snippets of some of your emails – sorry you're in such distress over*
> *us. Thanks for your poetry and sentiments.*
> *A&F, Benjamin"*

An email. As if nothing she had sent had been read, or understood. Perhaps her subtlety had been TOO subtle, too poetic, too naïve. What about her messages could have been unclear? Anna fought the need to pick up the phone, but lost to a hand that moved with a life of its own.

"Hello Ben."

"Hello Anna. You caught me at a good time; I've at least an hour until I need to get some sleep."

How could he sound so nonchalant?

"Ben, snippets? You read snippets? Did you not read the last message I sent, or understand it? You email me as if I've said nothing at all important." Anna forced herself to calm down.

"I'm sorry Anna. You mean the last message with the kiss off?" Ben sounded almost puzzled, as if she couldn't possibly have meant it.

And so the conversation went. Questions, answers, reminisces, always the same conversations in the same directions. Questions about the girlfriend (no, he hadn't gone back with her yet) questions about Jason (yes, she had broken it off and yes, even without Ben in her life, it would have happened anyway.)

"Ben, can you not accept that I don't know how not to love you?" It was a summation of everything Anna had asked before.

"I know Anna, and I've known from the beginning. We fit; when we touch we become a single person. We feel what the other feels, think what the other thinks. Even without words we've remained linked through the years, like matched halves." This from Ben, always the romantic.

"Yes Ben. Only you can find that place in me. And it is you I have looked for in everyone else. Jason tried, but the chemistry – it just wasn't there. Perhaps I should be satisfied in having experienced it so deeply once." Anna heard the resignation in her voice and felt the tears welling in her eyes.

"What are we Anna, friends, lovers ... what do we call it after all this time?" His voice became wistful. "Anna, I've been thinking. Perhaps we should make a pact. If you still want me in four years – four years from my birthday – and we have somehow not come together before then – let's agree to try it."

Anna held her breath for the space of a single heartbeat. "Yes my love, I will agree. But until then, can we find a name for this and a way to stay in each other's life without pain?"

Ben was silent for only a moment. When he spoke, she could hear the catch in his voice. "Yes dear Anna, perhaps it is just as simple as that."

> *And ever has it been that love knows not its own depth until the hour of separation.*
> ~~Kahlil Gibran (7)

09-10-2003 — **if you should die (before me)**

if you should die before me
(and surely Fate cannot be so unkind)
i would ask those I love come
plead my case when i be gone.
allow my heart be joined with yours
in our eternal rest.
would that they give in death
what you denied me in life

The heavens burned,
the stars cried out
And under the ashes of infinity,
Hope, scarred and bleeding, breathed its last.
  ~~Ulatempa Poetess "*Elegy for the Commonwealth*" CY 9823
          "Angel Dark, Demon Bright"

LAST DANCE PART FIRST

Sometimes I think I'm terminally ill with a broken heart. And heaven will mean finally seeing this black and white world in Technicolor.

I have been madly, passionately, happilyforeverafter like you see on made for TV movies in love three times. But I never married any of them. Yet, I wasn't afraid to fall in love again.

For all the pain love has caused me, it left me with the knowledge it exists in the world. And I must truly believe it will come for me again – probably when I am least expecting it. I must keep my heart ready, just in case, and try every day to improve myself as a person, and learn from life around me.

When Ben and I met, way back then, he was my Clark Gable. My William Powell. My Spencer Tracey. I fell in love with him almost overnight. If I didn't show it enough, or didn't know how to tell him enough to make him believe it, I'm sorry.

When we split, it was the hardest thing I've ever done. And I hope he never believes he has never been loved. He was loved more than life itself – at least once.

With him, I glimpsed paradise, Paris for lovers, and went on a honeymoon each time we came together. I loved him passionately, blindly, brutally. I had exquisite tastes of love's cup and will cherish the joys forever. Nothing can take away the sweet, sweet memories, and no heartache can destroy my gratitude and wonder at the gifts that he gave me.

I still long to talk endlessly, greeting sunrises with idle chatter and profound discoveries. My heart races for new horizons, a warm smile, whispers in my ear. I yearn for long sensual massages, quiet naps, wine in front of a fire, bubble baths, long walks in busy cities and primitive forests. I want to wake up to the smell of his body. I want my heart to pound at the sound of his voice or the look in his eye. I want to cry on his naked shoulder. I want to seduce and be seduced.

I still grieve my losses, my mistakes, all my bad choices. I believe life's coin has only two sides, love and fear, and that all emotions originate there. And if those are the choices, I will not be afraid to live my dreams for I'll wither and die if I don't.

I believe a relationship is an opportunity to know and be your highest self. I believe in an open, honest expression of needs and wants, and I believe in the integrity of boundaries. I believe in soul mates, unconditional love, and Tantric sex. And I still believe in always with all my heart and soul.

May your New Year be everything you need, and want, it to be.

GABRIEL

05-11-2005 — Cherub

The Angel calls me cherub in his inscrutable way
it gives me the warm fuzzy feel goods
even though I know it may
be repeated the same in everyone's comments and could
quite simply be his way of making us all
Feel quite extra special today.

Thank you Gabriel, I do so wish I could return the favor!

05-12-2005 — ME, ME, ME

1. Tell me about your childhood pets? A turtle, a parakeet named Blue Boy, a Siamese cat named Boo, and a cocker spaniel named Corky – an occasional visitor who would run away from his own home several miles across town to come see us. The first time he was lost, but no one could ever explain the next four times.

2. Tell me about your adult pets? Mostly cats. Kaz (18) and Azazel (16) passed away recently. Before them was Patches, wagged home as a stray by Morgan and destined to terrorize her hamsters. A gorgeous German shepherd named Peter, and Ernst Stavro Blofeld – a five pound Oscar who lived in a 45 gallon tank and ate goldfish. Currently – Mango, a Jenday conure.

3. Tell me about your husbands? Three. The first was my daughter's father. We married as seniors in high school and stayed together 2 years. The second was five years later and lasted 8 years but remains a Great Dad to Morgan. The third was six years later and lasted two years. I haven't married the fourth – but we've been living together 13 years.

4. Tell me about your lovers? Ha Ha Ha – they are in the triple digits – maybe higher. Seriously. I understand the concept of casual sex.

5. Tell me about one wild place you've had sex? In a DJ booth at a disco while 700 people danced on the floor. With the DJ. Fortunately, it was during the days of extended play LP's.

6. Tell me about the great loves of your life? Two. The first was Jason, shortly after my first husband. It lasted two years and I was devastated. The last was Ben, lasting (in and out) for twenty-five years.

7. Tell me something funny about a first date?

We made the date and he's picking me up. My watchful German shepherd Peter begins to bark when he hears the knock. I point to the other side of the room and speak in loud tones "Lay down Peter, go lay down. Now." I open the door to a very shocked, wide-eyed date – named "Peter."

8. What would you change about the men in your life? I wouldn't change them. I'd change me. I'd learn why I pick ones that are so bad for me and why I don't pick up on their addictions and co-dependencies.

9. Tell me one of your most embarrassing moments? I'm at a vaudeville dinner theater where the acts are hilarious. I have one too many drinks and get the guffaws. A lone guitarist hits the stage, begins a sad love song and I was drowning him out. The waiter came over and asked that I please be quiet. Was my face red. The time I danced on the tables is another story.

10. What is your most disappointing childhood memory? When I was eight, our Brownie troop embroidered tea towels for Mother's Day. It was difficult work for little hands, and a very small towel, so I embroidered "Mom" and was so proud of my hard work. Mother put it in the drawer with a tight smile, and it never came out again.

I won't discuss the times Mother would twist my arm, push me to the floor, kick me, and scream, "Cry, dammit."

05-13-2005 — **Have It Your Way**

> *Hold the pickles hold the lettuce, special orders don't upset us,*
> *all we ask is that you let us serve it your way.*
> *Have it your way, have it your way at Burger King*
> ~~Burger King Commercial 1980's

I bring this up only because I went to the "Have It Your Way" fast food franchise yesterday to reward myself with a Chicken Club (made like a Whopper please) meal.

> Chicken Whopper Sandwich, Med Fries, and Coke:
> 1130 calories (Recommended daily: 1500)
> 75 mg cholesterol (Recommended daily: 300)
> 2050 mg sodium (Recommended daily: 500)

Oops.

I grabbed the death-in-a-bag and smugly left the premises through a glass door clearly marked, in big letters: **PUSH**. As I went through, I noticed a very small sign just at chest level.

You can have it your way and pull if you want, but this door can be pretty stubborn.

That door and I have so much in common!

05-14-2005 — **ME ME ME TOO**

1. What is your lucky number? It has always been 7, and multiples of 7 like 14, 21, 28. I was born on the 14th (Pisces), and so was Morgan (Sagittarius)!

2. What are your hobbies? Swing dancing, sailing (Hobie 16), stamp collecting, dragons. My parents believed we should know how to do a little of everything so I shoot a mean bow and arrow, can hold my own on a trampoline, and know how to roller skate and square dance.

3. What is your favorite Holiday? I'm a sap for Christmas although being an agnostic means it's definitely the lights, the tree, and the prezzies. Moreover, I always dressed up for Halloween to embarrass my daughter.

4. What is your favorite wine? An Italian red – Sangiovese. I stopped drinking Boone's Farm years ago.

5. What is your favorite beer? Black and Tan. LOVED Ireland.

6. What kind of car do you want? A 1957 Chevy with four on the floor. It happens to be the same model in which I lost my virginity.

7. What do you look like? I'm a small-busted 5'7" and weigh 106 pounds, naturally. That's one pound more than I weighed at 18. I have chin-length chestnut brown hair and very blue eyes. My hair was below my waist most of my life. Cher was my Halloween costume for years.

8. So, why didn't you get a boob job when everyone else was getting one? I adopted a "more than a mouthful" philosophy about the STILL perky little things. I don't think I've ever missed a chance to get laid because they were too small!

9. Were you called any names in grade school? King Kong. I was the tallest person in my class.

10. How many rooms does your house have? Twenty-three – if you count the bathrooms and master closet (hey, it's 13 x 21 … it's a room!)) – and I've painted and redecorated every single one of them.

Now for the BONUS QUESTIONS:

11. Have you ever been arrested? Labor Day Weekend, 1973, Los Angeles, possession of tear gas. After four days of intense questioning, the FBI let me go. They actually wanted the people we knew … well, that HE knew. Who then wanted me – because they weren't sure what I might know, or be willing to say. I lived under an assumed name for five years.

12. Have you ever done drugs? HELLO – I lived with two addicts! Hell yes I've tried drugs … PCP, Heroin, Cocaine, hash, pot, 'shrooms, LSD … but it stopped at "trying." It's been a long time since anything stronger than a 5mg Valium before a dental visit.

13. What do you see when you look straight ahead? A framed collage of pictures Morgan created. It is my father, Morgan, and I, shortly before he died of cancer.

On it, she wrote, "Love is the soil in which we bloom and grow."

05-30-2005 — **A Moment of Silence – Memorial Day**

Daddy
1923 – 1993
U.S. Army 1943 – 1946
78th Lightening Division
Forward Artillery Spotter
Fought at the Battle of the Bulge
Fought at the Remagen Bridgehead

In memory of those who have died serving our country.
In honor of those who have dedicated their lives to
Protecting everything we hold dear.
In appreciation of the men and women
Standing strong around the world.

06-02-2005 — **Designs of the Times**

My best friend loves me … I think. She often buys without trying on – then hands over the never worn garments when she doesn't like the color or fit because we are exactly the same size. This time, the tops, skirts, and capris were all cotton.

When I was young, we did not have steam irons. Or air conditioning in any but the wealthy homes and major stores. Or dryers with Permanent Press cycles. Or detergents that could wash in cold water.

My family washed clothes in an electric washing machine in hot water. In the summer, they went outside where there shortly appeared a parade of wooden people holding flapping sheets and underwear between their toes. In the winter, the masses of wet cotton were pinned securely to the lines that ran across the ceiling of the utility room like so many spider webs.

Air-dried pure cotton dries stiff and wrinkled. In the summer, ironing was a very, very hot process and often fell to me to accomplish.

That process came to mind as I ironed all my new sleeveless cotton summer tops, skirts and Capri slacks, clones of the tops and bottoms I ironed through-out my younger years. Dressed in a new outfit, I look exactly like a picture of myself in 1960.

And it occurred to me that designers haven't gone anywhere in 55 years. The last radically new idea for women was the mini-skirt and that was a natural outgrowth of constantly changing hemlines – the only place left to go was up. The last new idea for men was the long tie and even that was simply a narrow cravat.

In recent years, designers have simply gone back and forth through the previous decades to find fashion inspiration. Up and down with the hemlines, sleeves or no sleeves, full or princess seamed. Empire waists and full skirts are back again, for the second or third time in my lifetime.

Faced with an obvious lack of new ideas, there was only one thing fashion conscious designers could do. Match not just the color, but also the actual fabric itself to the decade. Welcome back 100% cotton, goodbye Permanent Press.

06-15-2005 — **One, Two, Three, Go**

I had dinner with Golden Knight on Wednesday. We did eat, but as I lay in his arms later, I looked up, caught his eye, and asked him, "Are you in love with her?"

He hesitated a moment, squinted a bit, curled his mouth in thought and said quite sincerely, "Yes, I think I am." Quite an admission for a man who has been single most of his life.

I posed the question I had been considering. "Then why are you here?"

Surprisingly, he didn't react as I had expected. He simply answered quietly and honestly. "Because we are so much more than friendship. Everything about you is so special to me and I don't want to ever lose you."

> *Between birth and death lies desire,*
> *Desire for life, for love,*
> *for everything good.*
> *And this is the source of all suffering*
> > Outcast Consensus 17, *Why Existence?*
> > ~~"The Sum of Its Parts"

06-17-2005 — **Ona huh**

> Beep bang clang and clap
> Rumble thump bump and slap
> Pop poof boom and chirp
> Crackle buzz squeak and burp
> Tweet snap click and hiss
> Ding dong creak and kiss
> Swoosh gush coo and cluck
> Pitter-patter fizz and fuck
> Onomatopoeia's fun
> Wham bam thanks I'm done.

06-19-2005 — **A *JournalLand* Note from Gabriel**

Good Evening Ms Anna:

Thank you for adding me to your favorites list. If it is not too terribly personal, may I ask if you are the pretty Woman kissing the Ben Affleck clone in the picture on your profile?

My name is Gabriel. I have just started reading your entries and I have enjoyed what I have read. You seem to be of a sensitive nature and I enjoyed the statement on your profile. I also believe in Always.

Ms Anna I should warn you, I'm a bit of a tease, a rather large flirt, and love nothing more than playing with my friends. Oh, and although I have a little touch of the Bad Boy in me (in a good way) I'm always a gentleman. I am looking forward to getting to know you. Good Night Ms Anna.

06-20-2005 — **He's Just Not That Into You**

Everyone knows I do NOT like self-help relationship books. I have no inclination to pay $21.95 to hear the same stupid bullshit spouted by some tinhorn pop psychologist clone. For me to admit I not only PAID $21.95 for a book (ok, I had a coupon for 20% off, but that's not the point) but read the whole thing … twice … then read it again, should get your attention.

Are you ready? Are you waiting for it? *fanfare, drums, trumpets, and naked chorus girls singing "The Impossible Dream"*

He's Just Not That Into You by Greg Behrendt and Liz Tuccillo

Don't take my word for it. Go to your local bookstore and read just the first few pages. Then plunk down your credit card immediately, take it home, and become a true believer.

Greg, a comedian and writer for *Sex and the City*, started it on the show and the introduction says simply:

> Men are not complicated … And sadly (and most embarrassingly), we would rather lose an arm out a city bus window than tell you simply, 'you're not the one'.
> I know the guy you're dating … He's that guy that's so tired from work, so stressed about the project he's working on. […]
> … As soon as it all calms down he'll leave his wife, girlfriend, crappy job. God, he's so complicated.
> He is a man made up entirely of **your** excuses. And the minute you stop making excuses for him, he will completely disappear from your life. (6-7)

At 165 small pages, it's a simple read – took me about thirty minutes. Run, don't walk. Go now. That's alright. I'll wait for you. Buy one for yourself, and another one for that best friend that's always whining about her new boyfriend, and read the *He's Just Not That Into You* signs.

Done? How damn simple it is.

> When a guy is into you, he lets you know it. He calls, he shows up, he wants to meet your friends, he can't keep his eyes or hands off you, and when it's time to have sex, he's more than overjoyed to oblige. I don't care if he's starting his new job as president of the United States the next morning at 4 a.m. He's coming up!! (5)

> *Profound love is uplifting, joyous, inspiring, and intoxicating and [you] should never settle for anything less. Shitty relationships make you feel shitty, and that's not what you were put on this earth for.*
> ~~Greg Behrendt (161-162)

06-25-2005 — State of the Union

> If everyone wants
> to be loved so badly
> why the hell
> does everyone fight
> the state of it?

06-30-2005 — A *JournalLand* Note from Gabriel

I have investigated your entries and, oddly, I seem strangely stimulated – actually, it's more of a need – to get to know you better. I hardly know you, yet here I am with a small crush. Odd isn't it? You seem to be one of those folks whose words dance about one's sensibilities; they fill cracks in one's heart, all the while tickling that very same heart. In one entry, it felt as though your words took hold of me and we were slow dancing cheek to cheek.

I think of Romance as one of the finer qualities of Life and hope we can speak via email sometime soon.

07-03-2005 — **It is indeed a small world**
Personal email to Anna from *Gabriel*

It's evening here in Dominica and I've just finished today's scenes. How nice to find your email waiting for me.

Since we are going to get to know one another quite well – I wanted to talk about privacy. It is very important to me. Most actors in the early part of their careers do everything to be noticed by anyone, but once we realize it is becoming a career, privacy becomes important or the letters from the inmates start to arrive!

Would you like to exchange photos? I have been described as handsome and the bad boy charmer type. Tell me of you. Would you be willing to brush my long hair and tell me I'm pretty?

07-04-2005 — **So Many Questions, So Little Time**
Personal email to *Gabriel* from Anna

I often find it odd that folk who have "made it," especially in the entertainment and sports industries, have to spend an inordinate amount of time guarding their minds, bodies, and especially their hearts, against all the people attracted to them because they have worked hard, studied hard, and become good at their chosen profession.

It's not that I don't understand. For those existing in lives of quiet desperation, living vicariously through (or with) a successful person is a yearning passion hard controlled. The media doesn't make it any easier as we get a chance to peer into all the corners and around the edges and under the covers until we think we know them inside out and backwards. We become their lovers, their confidants, their best friends – and will never meet them face-to-face.

I'm too old to be star-struck and too confident to need the security blanket of another's success. Should we become pen pals, you will find that everything you read in my journal is the absolute truth. Even the stories I weave are true in every detail, although they may have happened on a date other than when they are captured on paper.

Lest you think I am not real, I can be *Googled*. As a joke, I tried my name, and I was there 698 times – and not in any stories about the Butcher of Seville. How bizarre to know my entire life is on the internet.

I have taken some time to start reading your journal entries from the beginning. You seem to be a "what you see is what you get" charming bad boy. My cynical side remembers that every bad boy I've ever met has broken my heart – there is usually nothing much more there than an overwhelming desire for casual sex and a young boy's need to have their ego stroked – but I so very much LOVE bad boys.

I will leave you with the following. You only need to know two things about me and you will know me. First, there has never been a situation, an environment, a conversation, or a surrounding, with which I have not been comfortable – whether the diamonds were around my neck at the governor's ball, or in the star-studded sky when I climbed the hill to bay at the moon. Second, in the deepest most secret corner, hidden even from myself most of the time and despite everything I say – I believe in love.

07-05-2005 — **Understanding, Broken Hearts and Bad Boys**
Personal email to Anna from *Gabriel*

I certainly do believe you are real and from what I know of you, and what others at *JournalLand* say, you are indeed a wonderful person. Your words show me you are intelligent, kind, and a romantic. I was a bit smitten by your words for, as they say, it takes one to know one. I can't imagine a world without Romance – not one I'd want to live in anyway.

I have had my heart broken a time or two. The worst was losing my wife. Before she passed on she left a letter to be given to me a year after her death. In it she asked that I remain the man she loved, never closing my heart but leaving it open to share with others.

Despite your having been through some rough times, you leave your heart open, choosing to live life and remain open to its possibilities. Like me, you see love as joy, not pain. You believe in Romance and this is why I am drawn to you.

If it is okay with you, I'd like to send you a photo or two of me. Remember, I play bad guys and the hair and makeup people do everything possible to make me look mean and ugly. I have two different colored eyes, long hair, and a scar on my left cheek.

My bad boy only comes out in in appropriate times and places but, as you say, all women love bad boys in certain situations. If so, think of me as your Huckleberry Finn.

07-05-2005 — **Understanding Redux**
Personal email to *Gabriel* from Anna

You are a bad boy indeed – I do so love to read words, especially those directed personally to me (I absolutely swoon for handwritten letters … and they are so seldom received nowadays).

Yes, I would enjoy a visual. So send away. I've been imagining you as a real Pirate (considering your current role) – probably with a peg leg, one eye, and six teeth. I'll do the same if I can find something where I am not squinting, sticking out my tongue, riding a roller coaster, or sitting on Santa's lap in a string bikini.

I actually think I'm a little older than you are – but blessed with good skin, clear eyes, and small bones so we may look the same age. Everything (and I mean everything) is natural. I just couldn't face giving up what nature gave me for sacks of gel – no matter how great they may make me look in clothes.

I like my job, I love my home, and I see no reason to leave the "stuff" I like to live by myself in a cramped apartment on the third floor of a smelly walkup going out to bars to be hit on by dingly dongly men without a clue.

Tell me more about you!

07-05-2005 — **Body Language**

> *Sixty percent of all human communication is non-verbal body language, and thirty percent is tone. That means 90% of what you are saying is not coming out of your mouth.*
> ~~Will Smith in *Hitch*

Pen to paper, keyboard to screen, arresting words skip and play between there and here. Answer question answer forms a linking chain across the miles of space and time. Thrust and parry word games of practical romantics. Online miscreants weaving the tales dreams are made of ... when we remember when

in that first moment a movement of muscle tendon, blood under supple skin, an arresting double take of broad shoulder, quick hand, slim hip

voice tones echo between your spaces, feathers of laughter float and carry on the wind; an eyebrow arches, pearls of white in two straight rows when tender lips turn corners up

the head lifts, they turn just so, light reflected eyes chance glance seek and soul travels to soul in an instant

fingers brush and that touch travels up bouncing swirling whirling round and round until desperate need to share the same breath overwhelms the mind

curve of cheek, brush of lash, sweep of hair, arch of neck, length of limb. desire to trace the circles planes and angles when skin-to-skin two bodies syncopate for one moment in time

Hearts are lost in the blink of an eye. So, in that first dawning moment, should you walk away from every perfectly possible future knowing heartache and hopelessness are almost always the final reward?

> *No woman wakes up saying, "God, I hope I don't get swept off my feet today."*
> ~~Will Smith in *Hitch*

07-05-2005 — **Photos, Bad Teeth, Age and Bad Boys**
Personal email to Anna from *Gabriel*

I am sending photos. The best is of me at age 1 showing off my two colored eyes. When I lived in Hawaii, the natives freaked out when I looked at them. The eyes of Pele the Volcano Goddess are dual colored, so it is called giving the "Stink Eye." But it did let me surf all the good spots.

I have a Bachelors of Science Degree (minoring in chemistry and math) and was an Airborne Infantry Officer in an Army Ranger Company. I have had outside interests in business and design and done Martial Arts for years and years. I paint, professionally at times. I write, and am the king of run on sentences. I have been around the world three times and would like to make it four.

I play the worst sort of people on the screen, but I'm a Pacifist to the point of surrender. We can argue like heck and I will never strike in anger. I love women, and have many women friends – I value their opinions, seek out their wisdom, and enjoy their friendship. And, of course, there is the lovely softer side of women. Your sensitivities, your sweetness, and the abundance of kindness that all men wished they possessed. Your creativity, intellect, and coy charm.

I was not the peg legged one-eyed Pirate in your favorite movie this year, but did I ever have bad teeth. Yikes! I am a hair under 5'11" usually I'm about 180 lbs.; I keep my body in good shape.

Post scripted: I'll be in Maryland in Late September visiting some *JournalLand* friends. Maybe you could join us for lunch or dinner.

07-06-2005 — **I Used to Like Me Better**

> *When you're young, your whole life is about the pursuit of fun. Then you grow up and learn to be cautious. You could break a bone or a heart. You look before you leap, and sometimes you don't leap at all because there is not always someone there to catch you. And in life, there is no safety net. When did it stop being fun and start being scary?*
> ~~Carrie Bradshaw, "Hop, Skip, and a Week"

I used to like so many things about myself.

I liked the thick dark hair that hung to my waist and twisted in loose S-shaped waves when it was wet.

I liked the color of my eyes that were so blue my photographer almost lost a competition when the judge insisted they had been retouched.

I liked my skin in the summer, tanned the color of sugared pecans.

I liked the crooked little fingers inherited from my father because they helped me remember him after he died.

I liked the fact that the *"this little piggy stayed home"* toe was longer than the first, oft pointing it out to those who had to make do with the plain tapering kind.

I liked the fact that there was, below an "inny" belly button, a perfect hollow by each hipbone creating a pair of natural handles for ardent lovers.

But I got older. I cut my hair, even though I have regretted it every day. There are permanent laugh lines by those blue eyes and sun is purported to be bad for the skin. Those little fingers are attached to hands that have too many bones. The hip hollows remain, but when I look down all I notice is knees who have attracted some never before seen wrinkles, even if the ardent lovers don't seem to mind the change.

I became the age that men my age replace women my age with trophy wives while ogling twenty-somethings at cafes and coffee bars. And wish I was still a twenty-something … even a thirty-something would be nice.

At least the little piggy is still at home, standing tall and proud. I should be grateful for small things.

> *You can't help getting older, but you don't have to get old.*
> ~~George Burns

07-06-2005 — **Pictures, Poems, Travel and Names (oh my)**
Personal email to *Gabriel* from Anna

Baby picture was adorable. Absolutely adorable. And fair's fair. I've attached one for you of ME at age one.

07-06-2005 — **Howling**
Personal email to Anna from *Gabriel*

The evening is off to a nice start, I got an email from you! But you still haven't guessed my age!

I loved your Baby photo; I believe those two kids make a great couple. I liked your last *JournalLand* entry, all but the ending. Isn't there a possibility that disappointment is shelved, Heartbreak takes a break, and love prevails?

One fact you may find interesting, I have remained friends with all my old girlfriends. I'm no Saint, but I don't say hateful things to friends and never ever to Lovers. I am always a Gentleman who is willing to sit down and talk. If I am wrong, I admit to it – sometimes slowly – but I do come around.

How was your day? I ask because I honestly want to know. Be it a friend or a lover I am interested in those around me. After all, what makes life so interesting is the interaction of those with whom we share this planet.

07-07-2005 — **Questions and Work and Answers and Such**
Personal email to *Gabriel* from Anna

In one of your emails, you said, "I do tease and I'm very playful and I do pay extra attention to some of the writers in *JournalLand* who believe no one hears them."

I wonder where Anna fits in that potpourri of correspondence.

I have stayed friends with almost all my lovers/husbands too. I figure that if you liked them enough to grant them premier status, their actions would have to be extreme to end the friendship.

I hate to fight – hate it. I like to TALK. I like to DEBATE issues about which I feel passionate. I like to solve a problem by sitting down and discussing it like adults. You listen and try to understand how I feel, and I listen and try to understand how you feel – and we find a solution that satisfies both our needs.

My day was extremely busy with work, home, feeding myself, and looking up some pictures for a certain actor gentleman (and I use one of those terms loosely) I'm getting to know. I would rather have been writing, or swimming, or painting, or sailing, or dancing.

PS: I hate to guess ages. But oh, ok – you've asked twice so I'll take a stab at it. it's hard to tell. 45-50? And if I'm way off it's your fault for asking.

07-07-2005 — **Cute Toes and Strange Eyes**
Personal email to Anna from *Gabriel*

A good guess on my age! I told you I was older than you were. Now that I have completely scared you away, and you have no interest in meeting a senior citizen I suppose it's okay to ask your age. I prefer older women, never dating anyone under 35 – and even at that age, I prefer them mature in heart and mind.

As far as the category you fit into – the fact is, you don't. You have your own category but I won't get into that until I hear from you again. I'd hate to make a fool of myself especially if you now look to me as the Grandfather type.

07-09-2005 — **AARP and Senior Citizen Discounts**
Personal email to *Gabriel* from Anna

Congratulations for making this far. You're right, you are older than I am, but only by two years, and you are indeed well preserved. Guess that's what good living and early alcohol pickling can do for you!

Attached is my favorite picture ever, which is saying a lot because I've never believed I took good pictures. My face in photos always has too many angles and shadows. I love this one because it showed the little girl inside that was mostly scared she wouldn't be able to do it right. I was 21. The first man I had ever loved had left me. I moved from St. Louis to Chicago just to escape the memories and was doing a little modeling on weekends.

An amateur photographer who didn't understand F-stops took this in the middle of a photo shoot. He said "Anna?" I turned, and he clicked.

07-09-2005 — **Too Old? Nonsense, You came at the perfect time**
Personal email to Anna from *Gabriel*

You and I both know age has very little to do with anything other than Wine, Cheese and hamburger left in the refrigerator a little too long. In order for me to properly woo you, you need to know I prefer women who have NOT out-grown Romance, enjoy Sex, and are in possession of a young Heart. They must be willing to wake in the morning ready to seize the day. Accept the fact there will be problems but problems that can be worked out. Choose to be Happy – after all, it is a choice we must all make every day.

There is no need to change who we are. Habits and quirks? There can be compromise, but the person you are, please stay the same. With that out of the way, may I please get to know you?

I'm going for broke here and in doing so may subject myself to ridicule, contemptuous scorn, belittling, and bitter mocking. You asked where someone like yourself might fit in with the Women I correspond with at *JournalLand*. I believe you have your own category, a lofty one, towards the top, near the apex or just above it.

I believe I'm smitten. You have a kind Heart; you're a sweet Person with a sharing Soul. You're a Romantic who believes in Love, you crave adventure of both body and mind. You still seek the man you can give your heart to without fear, the man you can step into, as well as he into you, the one with whom you can become one. The one who will allow you to stand alone when needed, who will support you unconditionally, the one who will love you in the worst of times.

I too am looking for that kind of Woman. I believe you came around at the perfect time – after all, it's all in the timing!

07-10-2005 — As Old As you Feel, and a Long Story
Personal email to *Gabriel* from Anna

Your emails are intriguing and a bit overwhelming – but don't stop. You are honest, you seem to have integrity, you are smart, and you enjoy life. I have a funny feeling we have an awful lot in common and I don't want you to be any other way. But let me tell you a story.

In 1970, I fell in love. For the very first time. Truly, passionately, completely. I lived an idyllic life for just under two years. Then he left. I was the first woman he had allowed himself to love completely and the fear of settling down, of finding a way to support a wife and child, and the possibility I might figure out that he wasn't perfect was too much for him. It took many, many years for me to understand and be able to fall in love again.

Three years ago, he found me through the internet. It started with a card. Then another card. Then an email. Then a flood of emails back and forth. I was surprised, then smitten, and at last overwhelmed by everything he wrote. His words created images. They romanced me, enveloped me in their loving kindness, said everything I felt and wanted someone to feel about me. And, maybe, everything I had wanted him to feel all those many years ago.

We spoke on the phone. The same rich, resonant voice. Saying the same things. A romantic who believes in love, looking for that special one to whom he can give his heart.

We agreed to fly cross-country to meet, and as much as I wanted it, had hoped for it, had dreamed of the possibilities of it, the chemistry wasn't there. It was the same words, the same voice. But when he looked in my eyes, took my hand, and kissed me, I didn't feel anything.

I don't know how to explain it. How can someone pour out everything that is inside them, tell you more than most couples ever learn about one another before they walk down the aisle for the "I do's," speak to you in a language every woman seeks her entire life, and upon meeting, it's not there.

What causes that electric spark that travels between two people – that runs up their arms and explodes in their hearts and brains in tiny little fireworks. When they know that they want to spend time with this person, and know them in all the ways you cannot know a person using words, and you want to melt into them and lose yourself.

That's almost the end of my story. I let it go on a little too long, thinking I would feel differently, that I would learn to love again this man I once couldn't spend life without. But even after visiting twice more, it didn't change. The chemistry, that unknown quantity, never happened.

Where is this going you ask? Well, maybe that's the problem with internet dating. There's a picture. Written words, maybe even a phone call. You can usually weed out the crazies, or the ones with whom you have nothing in common. But you will never, ever, know if they are worth pursuing until you look in that person's eyes the first time. Until you touch their hand, or their cheek, or brush their hair away from their neck.

I will be REALLY embarrassed if I have taken everything you've written completely the wrong way (and feel free to disabuse me of such crazy notions), but I THINK you are saying you may be interested in pursuing the possibility of something more than being pen-pals at some point in the future. And I guess I'm saying that is of interest to me too.

But once burned …

Everything you said in your last email is true – and you can find almost the same words written by me in my entries. I think of myself as a romantic pragmatist. That's someone who trusts completely, loves absolutely, and knows where the emergency exit is located.

That said – here is my cell number. Your mission, should you choose to accept, is to decide the next step.

07-10-2005 — **Genes, Chemistry and Falling in Love**
Personal email to Anna from *Gabriel*

First, I have to say, at 16, you were pretty, at 21, you were beautiful, and now you are … I couldn't possibly use a single word, it just doesn't work. Is there a need to proclaim that the Magnificent Rocky Mountains are beautiful? That the Pacific Ocean is vast and deep? In describing Michelangelo's *David*, or Van Gogh's *Starry Night* would one word do? I have found my Helen; I feel the urge to build a Thousand Ships.

Should my words frighten you, and I hope they don't, know that I speak from the Heart. I am a man of confidence and when something is heartfelt, I feel the need to express myself.

I tried years ago to overcome my emotions, to pack them up and hide them away. Funny thing about emotions – hide them away and they grow in the dark, gaining strength. I hide them no longer, I face them and if need be I hang out with them. If sad, be sad for a while, if angry, face it, and put it away. If joyous, for God's sake be joyous.

That said, I think you're near perfect! All that is missing is a longhaired two different color eyed, fun loving former bad boy gentleman with a huge heart.

07-12-2005 — **Spirits**

The smell is beginning to fade in his old shirt. The one he had thrown on and she had eventually taken off to caress the hollows and curves of him. To join with him, her heart so full to bursting it filled every part of her with the joy of him.

He put it back on, unbuttoned, almost casually, when they had finished, when he was still moist from their love. He wore it to sit outside under the stars, to sip their wine, and consider the yesterdays and tomorrows of their life together.

Much later, she crept from their bed to find it and it made its way into her luggage before she came back to tuck herself once again into and around all the places where she fit so well.

It smelled of him, of his body, and the scent of his cheek and hair. She could slip her arms into the sleeves, close her eyes, and be held by him or bury her nose in the essence of him.

The smell is beginning to fade in his old shirt and Ben is a silent shadow, moving just out of her sight. Sometimes, if she turns her head just right, she can almost see him there. Almost hear his voice calling her name. A ghost that belongs in the past and she rather likes that she has put him there.

07-12-2005 — **Back from the Capitol**
Personal email to Anna from *Gabriel*

I thought about you constantly today. It was a pretty day, with a warm breeze, there was a flowery scent in the air, and the Sun, although bright, wasn't scorching. I wandered off to the nearest beach, stuck my feet into the warm Caribbean Sea, and wondered aloud what could make this day better? Immediately your lovely face was in my mind's eye.

07-13-2005 — **Have Credit Card, Will Travel**

> *A woman is closest to being naked when she is well dressed.*
> ~~Coco Chanel

AAARGH! Summer sales are so difficult, especially when they occur in the middle of summer. When summer went on sale at the *end* of summer it was so much simpler to close my eyes and walk on by. Save the ogling and leftover budget for the warm rich colors of fall because summer was OVER.

Now, summer sales start before Memorial Day and 40% off looks so darn delicious in the heat of the moment. I suspect that, at the rate we are going, summer sales will eventually begin immediately upon the heels of the after Christmas sales of the year before.

I love clothes. I have a closet full of clothes. I have a dresser full of clothes. I have clothes with the tags still attached. I guarantee that whether the occasion is mud wrestling or tea with the Queen I have the perfect outfit. I even have saris. Yes – saris (what woman in her right mind can resist gold threaded silk?).

One would think when I travel I would take a mountain of suitcases. NOT. I packed for my last trip to India (everything from a multi-day camel trek in the Thar Desert to a formal Hindu wedding in a five-star hotel) in a 22" collapsible backpack that fit in the overhead luggage rack. Morgan also took one. Two women, two weeks. Two backpacks.

> *Oh, never mind the fashion. When one has a style of one's own, it is always twenty times better.*
> ~~Margaret Oliphant, *Miss Marjoribanks (449)*

07-13-2005 — **Love's Labour Lost**

Candoor, a wonderful diarist in *JournalLand*, left a comment on one of my older entries – and I just found it. It was an entry about loving a lost love forever. He said:

> and I ask myself for one more uncounted time, what to do … how to love again … who will ever understand that as perfectly wonderful as they are and as happy as I am with them, that they were still a second choice … who would ever put up with that fact and still love and stay with me? … nobody, I fear … but I do not want to be alone … so I dream …

Have you ever thought about what it would be like to love another person? To give yourself permission to let go of the old, and open yourself up to the possibilities of a different future. Would your feelings for the lost love compromise what you could be together, what you could share. What would they think, knowing about the one who came before? Would they believe? Would they be jealous? Would they feel second best? Interesting questions.

07-13-2005 — **A Brief History**
Personal email to Anna from *Gabriel*

Very busy with the shoot going into over drive because of the possibility of the Hurricane coming to visit us, plus pounding out fifty pages a day for our sitcom in development, and YOU constantly darting in and out of my little pea sized brain causing me to dream day and (as of late) night dreams twice now. Fortunately, they are still GP, and I don't need a lot of sleep.

My parents were dream makers, they planted seeds of adventure and showed us that life was something to enjoy – not just walk through it, but also truly live it, to be and do everything you wanted.

By the time I was three, I was reading and writing. I graduated High School at 16. In my college sophomore year, I completed Quantum Mechanics and Astrophysics. It looked as though I'd be in some sort of science career but there was a war going on so, like the fool I was, I wanted to see it, do my part and follow in my family's tradition. With two years of college, I was able to enter the Army's Officers Candidate School. Commissioned a 2nd LT at 19, I became an Airborne Infantry Officer in an Army Ranger company.

During 18 months in Vietnam, I was wounded three times. The third was a doozy … spent 15 months in the Army Hospital and still have a scar on the left cheek of my face, a small steel plate on the top rear of my skull, three pieces of metal in my brain, and bullet fragments in my left shoulder. After four years in the service, I came back to complete my degree.

You should know that I have fallen in pretty good like with you. I find you interesting, intelligent, a romantic, incredibly good looking, and you are close to my age, thank God. You are sweet, kind, and basically a good person and I want to get to know you better. I am interested in establishing a solid friendship with you in the hopes it may lead to something else in the future, but should that not happen I always have room for one more friend and hopefully you do too. I expect absolutely nothing from you other than you allowing me to get to know you.

One last thing you should know, I have had cancer twice. Acute Lymphocytic Leukemia (ALL) and beat it. It's been 10 years since my last episode. I have had trouble with my wounds over the years, mostly minor stuff. I am in great shape. I don't smoke or use drugs and only have an occasional drink.

I'm very active. I surf all the time, ski, snowboard, work out in the Martial Arts, run daily, and spend time with my weights 3 times a week. I am a great Cook! I am responsible, pay my bills, have great credit, I am able to do just about anything I want, I love to travel, own two homes and other business properties.

Should something wonderful happen between us, I have the wherewithal to conduct a long distance relationship. I have a wonderful attorney. When the time comes, he would make available to you all information concerning my financial situation.

I know it seems weird talking about such things so early, but it is my experience that once this stuff has been established, the relationship can move forward with less stress. I don't care about your financial situation unless you're going to prison soon for owing the IRS millions (but I'll come see you on weekends) and expect nothing from you except your letting me get to know you.

Think of the above the same as the government mandated Warning Label on the side of a package we are thinking of buying!

I figure if this doesn't scare you away nothing will. I promise not to bring this stuff up again. Bye for now.

07-14-2005 — **Background check**
Personal email to *Gabriel* from Anna

How odd that you would talk about the strangely taboo subjects that are not supposed to be the measure of a man or woman, and are so highly improper to bring up in polite company. The mundane things that don't usually find their way into a conversation until very late in a blossoming relationship, sometimes until it's too late to stop the commitment of the emotional self, or until you've said I will and found out you should have said I won't and run far, far, away.

What a difference life would have been if such things could have been discussed earlier. Or if we were, perhaps, less influenced by pretty words, and a melodious voice, and the feel of strong arms and a willing body.

How shall I address the practical in a few short paragraphs, leaving something for the future to explore? Perhaps the easiest is to say, just read what has already been written and ask the questions that haven't already been answered.

I'm healthy. Physically, mentally, and emotionally. I love to ride bicycles, sail catamarans, swim, and Swing Dance. I was a Midwestern girl, so I never learned to surf or snow ski, but I could do a back flip on a trampoline, swim for miles, and actually like to bowl.

I don't have the time to do the things I love. I'm a fair writer, an ok poet, and I take beautiful pictures. I am an artistic, passionate, and devoted Pisces and the arts are everything to me. I want to decorate, create, paint, color, and build. And someday I will be an old woman with a silver white braid trailing down her back discussing her latest avant-garde creation.

My family and friends keep asking why I stay here with my partner. I've thought about it over and over. I live a somewhat independent life, he is not cruel, and we are reasonably friendly. But mostly I keep the hope alive that there is someone out there looking for me. I want to be found.

07-15-2005 — **In search of a Creative/Artistic Old Woman with A Silver/white braid down her back**
Personal email to Anna from *Gabriel*

I was raised a Gentleman, which is not something one does on occasion, it is a way of life. I am a provider, not a taker. If you should, sometime in the future, feel the need to lavish upon me soft kisses and kind words, and offer me your sweet Heart and kind Soul, I'm inclined to believe I would graciously accept.

I have one Son named Shane who is 31. He is brilliant, and a good human being, and I am very proud of him. He is very good looking with blue eyes like his Mother and thick blondish brown hair. After a short career in pro ball, he works for one of the teams. Like his Dad, he still surfs, skis, snowboards, and likes dirt bikes.

He is married and deeply in love with a beautiful, smart woman, and has two highly intelligent, good-natured young children. I have a large family, most good looking, most intelligent, the majority successful, and we are very close.

I have to say I admire your strength in raising your daughter alone at such a young age. Raising a five year old, after losing my wife to cancer, was the toughest and most rewarding thing I have ever done. Shane and I are not only Father and Son, we are the best of friends.

I believe this is another thing we have in common. Our children, and the difficulties that arose from our losses, showed us we are capable of great strength and courage. The more I know of you, the more I like you.

07-15-2005 — **Love After Love (inspired by Peter David)**

He has not lost all who has still the future left him.
      ~~Christian Nestell Bovee (29)

Somewhere deep inside her a tiny half-formed thought broke free, rising and bubbling to the surface, expanding millimeter by millimeter to fill her mind with a great shining light.

Her full time occupation has been living a life mourning not only for those things that were lost, but for those she was going to lose (David, 63).

What would it be like to be at peace? She had lost that ability and had never been able to find it again. No matter what she was doing, or how well things were going, she always thought of it as transient and waited for it all to be snatched away (141).

What would happen if she started thinking dangerous thoughts such as, *Is true love still possible? Could there possibly be someone, somewhere, whose heart I could share, who would believe in always?* It would be an accomplishment to move forward with life, however much time it may take. To open her heart to the prospect of another.

Something, any something, is better than this nothing. And so she began.

Take down the love letters from the bookshelf,
the photographs, the desperate notes,
peel your image from the mirror.
Sit. Feast on your life.
      ~~Derek Walcott, *Love After Love* (328)

07-15-2005 — **A *JournalLand* Note from Gabriel**

So you do Like Me? ☺

07-15-2005 — **Perhaps a Bit OCD**
Personal email to *Gabriel* from Anna

yes, i think you're someone i'm getting to know. here lately there's so much rolling around in my head it's all i can do to get it onto paper fast enough.

sometimes i have to get up in the middle of the night because i can type faster than i can write (like FAST fast). in fact i once had a job where i typed as he extemporaneously dictated his reports – and HE was a structural engineer (so first i had to learn how to spell all the big new words!)

did i ever mention i have a bit of ocd? it's small and comes out at odd times – like not being able to leave the house overnight with dirty dishes in the sink or an unmade bed. my house is not shiny, but usually clean enough for company. and yet, strangely enough – i can get very very dirty without batting an eye … digging in the garden, hauling stuff around, painting walls, stripping antique furniture, camping, canoeing … go figure. Sogno di me

7-16-2005 — **Dreams**
Personal email to Anna from *Gabriel*

Sogno di Me? But of Course!

Sogno di lei di notle a volta nelli Italiano. AT OTHER TIMES, Ich traum von Ihnen auf Deutsche. THEN AGAIN, Sur quelques nuits et pendant le jour vous me,venez dans la Villa Paris de Lumieres je le reve de vois et moi a Paris. The point is – I dream of you. (It's been a while, so don't be surprised if the translation of the above is something like "I sometimes wear a toilet on my head.")

I am using the never-ending power of my little pea size brain, and my day off, to build a cell phone booster. I raided the Sound guy's equipment trailer and borrowed a few items to build my own power tower so I can get a call out to you soon. Well Darling, So Long from Mr. Wizard.

07-16-2005 — **Romance Languages**
Personal email to *Gabriel* from Anna

You set this poor girl's heart aflutter. Goodness gracious. I do want to talk with you. That said, the timing is somewhat important. I have tried to be completely honest about my current living arrangements and that I think a certain respect is due within it. My motto is … just because a guy at the bar buys you a drink doesn't mean you should go home and get a (figuratively speaking) divorce.

Does that make sense? (PS: I love your name)

7-16-2005 — **He Who Is Like God**
Personal email to Anna from *Gabriel*

Gabriel was one of God's angels, and means Strength of God … in my case that would be a lesser God!

I understand your situation and I'm sorry. It must be very hard for someone like yourself who places so much value on Romance and Love. I also understand the need for security and the desire to remain a kind person.

The Idea of You and I talking is to bring a bit of extra fun into your day. I won't lie to you and tell you I'm not interested in you because I am. I hope my words tickle your sweet Heart. I may, on occasion, bend the boundaries of Decorum, and move a toe or a foot across the line of prudence, but with words only. Although should we meet face to face I can't guarantee I won't attempt to steal a kiss.

07-16-2005 — **I think I'm all confused**
Personal email to *Gabriel* from Anna

I spent some time today reading up on some of our mutual *JournalLand* writer friends and kept running into your notes to them, and their notes to you. Whew, some of them were pretty … I think I'll stop here except to say that if I am imparting more meaning into this correspondence than you, I apologize in advance for getting carried away by a pretty Pirate.

As to boundaries, I will hold you to no line, and prudence is not required or expected. Should we ever meet, and the sparks fly, I will guarantee you the word "chaste" will not enter into our actions. There's always the chance that the chemistry won't be there – but let's not put the cart before the horse shall we? Just bring the Viagra, and the Mazola, and let the chips fall where they may.

7-17-2005 — **Confused?**
Personal email to Anna from *Gabriel*

Confused? Rest assured, one thing you don't have to be confused about is how I feel for you. I am past liking you and I'm falling into deep Like. I read your words before getting to know you and it built a small fire in the old stove that is my heart. That hasn't happened in a very long time.

I am not doing this with anyone else, there are no intimate emails, no exposing each other's Hearts to one another. Anna I believe it's your heart I'm seeking.

I have a bit of an odd feeling coursing through me at this moment. First it heads in one direction then the other. I feel sorry there is no love left in your relationship, because that is truly sad for two people who once loved each other BUTTTTTT I am truly elated there is a vacancy in your heart for me.

I do understand there is always the chance there will be no chemistry but, for now, let's park your cart and horse around the corner, keep an open mind, and see what happens. I have to warn you, I have a tendency to grow on people and you just might like me.

07-17-2005 — **Good Night Kiss**
Personal email to Anna from *Gabriel*

At last we speak, if only for one moment before the connection died. So Lovely Anna, may I call again tonight?

I had a dream of You and I kissing last night. I am a man of passion and believe a kiss can be powerful, you can feel its urgency, its intensity, as it runs from your lips to all those lovely destinations needed for a wondrous Union.

I believe it's the kiss that orchestrates the union between two lovers; it is the kiss that transfers the energy which throws the breaker switch that causes the implosion of atoms leading to glorious release. It is the kiss that ends the night as we fall into each other's arms for sleep … it is the kiss that starts the day anew. So how do YOU feel about kissing?

07-17-2005 — **When the Shoe Drops**

> *Men always want to be a woman's first love –*
> *women like to be a man's last romance.*
> ~~Oscar Wilde

Some time ago, after Ben had been long silent, Anna began an unexpected correspondence with her first true love. From a magnificent potential, it came to pass that he wanted more of her than she was able to give and he asked for an explanation.

... the little prick that sits on my shoulder keeps telling me this was your diabolical vendetta and now that you've completely seduced me all over again we're even, because you got to dump me this time.

Jason,

you have asked me for honesty, to tell you what happened, what changed. For years I have lived with the memory of the romantic starry-eyed bit of perfection that was our time together. You were the first person to whom I gave my heart. When it was over, I tried to erase everything, but I could never forget how extraordinary it felt to love and be loved. Or what it felt like when it wasn't there any longer.

When we began corresponding, your words overwhelmed me. You said everything I wanted to hear then, and everything I had needed and desired and hoped you would say if we ever met again. The romantic in me was intrigued, and spellbound.

When we met at last, I found you to be the wonderful, kind, intelligent, romantic man I expected. But the chemistry we once shared so long ago was no longer there and I realized, with sadness, I had been writing to the young man in my photo album. I should have stopped it then, and blame myself for letting it go on so long. And I am deeply sorry for causing you pain.

I haven't said this very well. I hope that you can understand ... and that you will someday find that I will always be your friend.

Love, Anna

Jason never wrote again, but Anna did not expect it.

Anna made a stern promise to herself after Jason. It is far too easy to get lost in the words. To imagine the person writing the passages, giving them the qualities she wants them to possess. She doesn't so much read the words as hear their voice, as if sitting across the table from them while sipping her wine.

She recently broke that promise by beginning, almost accidently, another on-line correspondence. This time with a stranger, another writer, another diarist. His words seduce, flatter, tease, convey a pleasing personality, and stir an attraction she wasn't expecting. And there is no past to haunt her dreams.

She finds it effortless ... this creation of tomorrows without dwelling on yesterdays. And wonders, like any practical romantic, when the other shoe will drop.

> *A man falls in love through his eyes, a woman through her ears.*
> ~~Woodrow Wyatt

07-18-2005 — **Kodachrome**

I was not a cheerleader. Or a prom queen. I wasn't the class president. In the "picking sides" popularity contest, I was not picked first, or second, or third.

My school years were a love-hate relationship. Every molecule of me loved the process of learning and hated the environment required to accomplish it. School was simple scholastically and brutally lonely.

It wasn't that I fell into any of the labels modern young scholars have created. I was just a tall, skinny kid with curly hair who wanted more than anything to be liked by the pretty girls with long blond ponytails.

This entry occurred to me after spending a delightful hour poring over old photo albums with my new son-in-law and distinctly remembering the day my daughter decided to quit first grade. "Everyone hates me, I don't have any friends."

Some of you may know the feeling. Having gained the wisdom that comes with graduation and meeting the real world head-on for the first time, I promised her with every ounce of newly gained confidence it would get better. And through the years I continued to teach the lessons I wished my parents had been able to teach me in my youth.

As she learned to be comfortable in her own skin, she learned to tolerate school (which is – honest to God, nothing more than a passing phase) and gained a wide and varied circle of friends and acquaintances. And like her mother before her, she managed to get through that gawky, awkward, "I'm ugly, nobody likes me I'm gonna go eat worms" tomboy stage of life and has had every success choosing her own friends and way of life.

Over our girl-talk lunches or long distance calls, we laugh hysterically to see where we have come from those oh-so-long ago and oh-so-unbelievably-unimportant days.

07-19-2005 — Night of the Howling Moon

This was the night when the temperature was so warm it lay upon her like a second skin.

This was the night the Moon Goddess rose high into a cloud-strewn sky, only two or three of the brightest stars peeking through the breaks to keep her company.

This was the night of a long, leisurely, teasing perfect call from the man who was becoming her friend, who was intent on finding all the secret passages into her mind and soul, ignoring all the roadblocks she tried to erect, passing all the seen and unseen tests.

This was the night she stepped out into the moonlight, leaving her clothes in a soft puddle at the door.

This was the night she raised her head and howled at the moon.

07-19-2005 — Look for a Sign
Personal email to Anna from *Gabriel*

Tonight I shall hover in the sky until I locate your sweet dreaming heart. I shall swoop down and I shall love you as you've never been loved before. Tonight I shall show you the places I speak of, naughty fun places. I will leave before you wake in the morning, look for a sign I was there.

07-20-2005 — Planes, Trains and Automobiles
Personal email to *Gabriel* from Anna

You asked if life has infected me with trust issues. I don't like to call them "issues" as that implies they need some sort of please lie back on the couch sessions to resolve them, but I suppose my nature has become wary of strangers bearing gifts of kindness and friendship.

We have been making our way past what's your sign to tell me about your exes. But I guess I'm suggesting that I'd hate for you to put a lot of your very limited personal time, and what seems like unlimited phone minutes, into someone you may not feel a connection with when you meet them.

So where I was going was — should you decide you would like to meet in person, I've decided I am ready, willing, and able. I know your schedule is packed for the foreseeable future but when the time is right you can buy me dinner and show me the sights of wherever we meet.

And I'm happy to take the couch.

07-20-2005 — **You Worry Me A Little**
Personal email to Anna from *Gabriel*

I feel we are getting to know each other and I think we are going at an appropriate speed. I guess we all take a chance when getting to know someone over the phone/computer and I suppose some folks get disappointed when they finally meet in person.

My profession exposes me to beautiful women all the time, but I have often found there is no chemistry once I get to know them.

I'm not going to lie to you and say looks aren't important, but I'd be willing to bet they don't add up to much more that 25% of a long relationship. My Grandparents, Aunts, and Uncles are as much in love now as when they were young and beautiful. I have come to appreciate the magic of how a kind heart and sweet soul can quickly spread to the outside of one's physical self.

You and I are headed towards old age but, although we will be decent looking, it is our hearts that will make us beautiful. You may have made an initial decision to speak with me based on my looks, but you owe it to yourself to take the time to get to know my heart.

I like you a lot. My mind is made up and I don't care about your past, your present, or your wrinkles. I would like to see you in person and I'll pay for the airfare. I have five bedrooms in the Malibu Home and four in the one further south. Although my couches may be comfy, you may have your own bedroom.

07-21-2005 — **Kodachrome II**
Personal email to *Gabriel* from Anna

I really (REALLY) like your new photo. It's a little different from the TV headshot ones you sent before – more approachable. You legitimately are a handsome devil of a guy! And bad boy enough to make the toes curl ... yummy.

I want to envision your environment. Tell me about when you are at home. White walls, mini-blinds, and three pieces of furniture like the typical bachelor (TV, chair, and bed)? In a subdivision with yard? Or a condo with no yard to care for? Are you far from the ocean?

07-21-2005 — **You Make Me Laugh**
Personal email to Anna from *Gabriel*

You make me laugh. I own and live in a 3-story house that sits on a private beach. I assure you it is completely furnished, each and every room! Let me add there is not a single beanbag chair or patio chair inside the house. It is decorated with furniture I have collected from around the world. I am particularly fond of my desk made of Brazilian Rosewood.

My house is rather big and tall, it has three decks – one for each floor – and all face the Ocean. At low tide, my back yard stretches for 200 yards, and at extreme high tide the Ocean comes right under half the house.

Well, Sweetheart it's time for bed, unfortunately not together. Sweet dreams.

07-22-2005 — **Good Lovers, Bad Boys**

> *Love is a matter of chemistry*
> *Sex is a matter of physics*
> *But kinkiness requires engineering.*
> ~~Anonymous, *AllGreatQuotes.com*

I can assume my father and mother made love, as I am the product of that marriage (and as I inherited some of his physical traits, I didn't belong to the milkman who delivered three times a week). Unlike Morgan and I who discuss everything, their generation did not <u>ever</u> discuss what happened behind closed doors. So I am left to wonder if they were each as happy with one another there, in that private sanctuary, as they were outside of it. He was a good man, and he and my mother certainly loved one another.

But over the years I've learned a strange thing. Good men do not always make good lovers and bad men bad ones. My second husband was as good as you could get, but physically and emotionally inept. And there were a couple of bad boys I can think of, really bad boys, who were glorious. And glorious sex has always been extremely high on my list of gotta haves.

I consider myself lucky. Although my teenaged boyfriends were little more than fumblers, I was fortunate that, by the age of 20, I had a much older friend with monumental skill who gave easily and received with joy.

I started this thought standing at a Metro stop musing about how far should you take a new relationship before giving in to the increasing desire to sample first hand. How sometimes the chemistry is there, but the aptitude isn't. And how, sometimes, even knowing doesn't always tell you how it's going to turn out.

Mr. Lucky, so called because he's lucky I've stuck around this long, is not a bad person. Selfish, emotionally detached, self-centered, but not what I call bad. For the first 18 months of our (now 14 year) relationship he was at least a 4 in the 0-10 scale. Didn't have any stamina, but had decent manual dexterity and knew his female anatomy. Of course, he tended to believe his own press – as his ex-wives and numerous girlfriends apparently never said, "Honey, we need to talk."

The years passed. Once or twice a month he'll still turn to me during a commercial pause and say "Wanna have some sex?"

I tried over the years to teach the old dog new tricks – or remind him of ones he used to know – but it has been in vain, and now it just doesn't matter.

I've been honest with Gabriel, my new Online Friend, who not only emails multiple messages but also speaks with me at least an hour a day. The other day he asked me if I still have a physical relationship with Mr. Lucky. All I could say was "Yes, occasionally." Sometimes there's no way to give an explanation without sounding all wrong.

07-24-2005 — **Life As I Know It**

Saturday, 7/23/05 1:30 p.m.

"Oh," says Mr. Lucky. "Did I tell you that I invited D over this weekend to work on some business stuff?"

"No," says I, already re-arranging my planned weekend work. But, I reason, I like D and the house is usually company ready and if it isn't – well, that's why they are called friends. "When is he coming?"

"Sunday."

"When on Sunday?" At least it wasn't today which means there's still time.

"Noon."

"Hmm ... " say I, thinking this doesn't sound complete. "By himself?"

"No, K is coming with him."

Clarity is coming to me. The oh-so-unsociable I can't be bothered with small talk Mr. Lucky has actually invited D and his wife K to our house.

At Noon.

Food preparation is needed and, while the cupboards are not bare, they are bereft of the ingredients required for a solid summer meal. Drop-ins have to make do with catch as catch can. Invitees deserve better.

"What were you thinking of having for lunch?" I mentioned offhandedly – not thinking he would get the hint.

"Hamburgers on the grill. And, you know, all the stuff you always make for a Bar-B-Que." Here he pauses dramatically, puffing up in manly pride. "And I'll go to the store."

I eye him suspiciously, but who am I (who now needs to at least clean out the bird cage, vacuum the kitchen rug, make sure there is paper and towels in the guest bathroom, hose down the deck, make some side dishes, and finish today the work I had planned to spread out over the two day weekend) to complain.

"That's lovely, wonderful in fact. Let me make you a list." And I pull out a paper and start naming the items – adding careful explanations because if I say "Fruit on the Bottom" yogurt he will call me from the store … and ask what flavor fruit and if I say "loaf of bread" I'll get a second call … what kind of bread. And so on down the entire list, one item at a time, up one aisle and down the other. At least two vital ingredients will be ignored ("I didn't see them") so I always pad with some secondary items to use as back-ups.

List complete, with verbal reinforced explanations for each item, I hand it over. He stares at it as if it were a poisonous snake, presses his lips together into a hard, straight line, wrinkles his nose, then raises his eyes to mine. "I was just going to get some hamburger."

5:30 p.m. Update

Fourteen grocery items on the list. He got nine of them. (Apparently, tomatoes, ice cream, hamburger buns, mustard, and fruit were not on sale).

sigh

07-25-2005 — **Down the Yellow Brick Road**
Personal email to *Gabriel* from Anna

I've found that relationships often end, not because of the big stuff, but because of the little stuff. Toilet seats, wall color, a new sofa, hanging up shower towels, dishes in the sink, and literally hundreds of others. Do "behaviors" become the reasons the relationships deteriorate, or are the behaviors just an excuse for giving up. Does one work on the behaviors, or work on the big stuff so the behaviors won't matter as much?

Some minds work part-time. Some minds work over-time. And some minds work all the time. I am blessed (read, cursed) with the latter … except when it short circuits. There are things I believe, things I believe in, things I want to believe and believe in. I believe in love at first sight because it once happened to me. I believe in communication, I believe in passion, I believe that sometimes you just have to trust one another.

Your calls and messages are … they uplift me, they make me giggle, they warm me, they excite me, they give me sweet dreams at night, and somehow (how can this be possible so soon) they make me want to know you so much more.

If I could change six things about myself (tried to do five, but it just didn't work … aha see #1):

1. I would listen more, and talk less.
2. I would work harder to trust earlier.
3. I would be less judgmental about things and people I don't know enough about.
4. I would live more spontaneously and with less fear.
5. I would seek and learn the secret to taming my ego and discard narcissism.
6. I would forget that my life is more than half over, and that I still have so much to do, so much to learn, and so much love to give. It is my greatest sorrow.

I don't know where we are headed, but may I hold your hand until we get there?

07-25-2005 — **More Stuff**
Personal email to Anna from *Gabriel*

Sweetie, my wish for you is that you're happy, and should you and I become a we, then we'll just take life as it is, hand and hand, enjoy it, learn a little, work on fine-tuning ourselves (because, after all, we are both already nearly perfect).

One of the most rewarding things in life is to face problems, deal with them, and overcome them. I look at what You have been through and how things ended up … you should be very proud of yourself.

07-25-2005 — **Extraordinary**
Personal email to *Gabriel* from Anna

I find myself, every day, wanting to know more and more. Even if it takes years and years to find out everything.

I suspect you have put a spell on me. Which, for some reason, seems perfectly acceptable.

As for the questions on today's call – yes Gabriel. I like you. A lot. I don't understand it. But I'm willing to accept it, and let it go wherever it's headed. I prefer men with a strong, confident lead. Just ask me to dance.

07-26-2005 — **I can't stand behind a line I can't see**
Personal email to *Gabriel* from Anna

A thought came to me today as you were speaking of "privacy." You talk of it often, and I'm not quite sure where your line is. Perhaps you can elaborate at some point so I don't cross over it accidently.

I'm an open book. I can keep secrets that need keeping, and maintain privacy, as long as I'm clear on the lines. Where your friends are concerned (*JournalLand* or otherwise) you can tell them whatever you want about me. If you've ever read much of my journal, you will see there is NOTHING private or sacred. I've laid out my very soul for strangers to mock.

07-28-2005 — **The Heart of the Heart**

Do you think it's ok if I find dozens of things in a day I want to share with him, as long as I limit the emails to one?

Do you think it's ok that I count the hours until he has a break from work and can find the time to call for the third (or fourth) time in a day.

Do you think it's ok that I sometimes sound like a little kid on the other end of the line, laughing and giggling for no reason at all but because he's there.

Do you think it's ok that I bound out of bed in the morning, hoping he sent a message. Even if it's just "Good night."

When is it too early to respond to a question of an intimate nature with an honest answer?

When is it too early to trust someone else, if only for a moment?

I know my motives. I want to fill all the empty spaces so full there's no room for anyone else. What if his aren't?

07-29-2005 — **More Than Lovers – Fall – 1972**

There are three great things in this world.
The first thing is for you to love someone.
The second thing is for someone to love you back
and the third greatest thing is for the first
and second thing to happen at the same time … .
~~Unknown, *RomanticLoveMessages.com*

More than lovers, we're friends …

"Come out tonight," she pleaded with Anna, but with a sweet smile. She was a mom, like Anna, celebrating her 17th birthday, and despite the five year age difference the friendship had formed easily.

"It's just a little neighborhood place. I know the doorman and there's a singer. You know you love musicians." So Anna went.

We built no walls, we left the doors wide open …

And they took their seats. And he took the stool, and lifted his 12-string, and opened his mouth, and his voice washed over her like cool rain.

You hold me tight, and I'm secure …

The sound of her heartbeat filled the room, the strings connecting them hummed with anticipation. She couldn't speak, she couldn't breathe.

Feelin' as free as the wind …

And when their eyes met, he invited her in and she accepted, lovers already.

The sky opens up, we're a part of it too …

He came to her, hand out, and she slipped hers within its warm protective space. "Tomorrow," he whispered and he had no need to hear the answer.

Our love will never end …

Tomorrow came and they laughed, and they sang, and they went to his house, and the four white walls welcomed the stranger in its midst. And she stayed for two years. Until staying became so very much more difficult than leaving.

We're more than lovers, much more than lovers …

They lived hard, loved hard, cried hard, and died hard.

*We're friends.**

Is it still ok to believe in love at first sight?

*Unpublished Words and music by Gari, A. Born 1944. Died: somewhere, somewhen

07-30-2005 — **Things That Go Bump In the Night**

> *A good marriage is at least 80 percent good luck in finding the right person at the right time. The rest is trust.*
> ~~Nanette Newman

For the many, many years I was involved with Ben, I always knew he was a man who had suffered a lousy childhood, a bad first marriage, and a worse second one. His past so colored his present and future that he had devoted his life to fixing everything about himself he thought was broken.

After we split the first time, he began reading all the books, working on all the "issues." Did therapy. Went to (and even taught) some 12-Step Courses. The buzzwords were part of normal conversation. He became extremely religious, almost fundamentalist in a very left wing sort of way, actually considering the ministry (and a decade ago, doing most of the schoolwork required before quitting). Eventually his need to fix himself spilled over into believing I needed fixing too.

Where is this going, you ask? Well, it goes to the basis of any good relationship … Trust.

The stumbling blocks to our relationship were difficult for him – religion, commitment, and fidelity. He needed me to believe in a God I did not accept. While seeking his own perfection, he could not make a commitment to a life together. And, as he was "the other man" in my heart during all the years I waited for that commitment, he could not believe in my fidelity.

Writing about it helped me to understand that a relationship with him would take more from me than I could ever get back, eventually draining me. So, after two and a half decades I put this beautiful, expressive, emotional man away. Once I did, I realized my rational self had put him away long ago. My emotional self was simply clinging, like a shipwrecked sailor, to the side of the last lifeboat.

And, as Gabriel reminded me recently, part of trust is two people choosing to love and accept each other exactly as they are. It should always be just that simple.

> *You may be deceived if you trust too much, but you will live in torment if you don't trust enough.*
>
> ~~Frank Crane (172)

07-31-2005 — **Travel Section**
Personal email to *Gabriel* from Anna

My favorite part of the Sunday paper is the Travel Section. There is always a front-page article on an exotic location describing the roads less travelled. Sometimes it's an overseas destination, sometimes right here in the good old USA. Kitschy places to buy tiddlydinks and out of the way places to stay.

With such extravagances beyond my budget, I wistfully I turn to page three. The What's the Deal page with the Bargain of the Week. Here are displayed the getaway deals. Fly non-stop to Bristol England for $402. Eight night Alaskan white-water rafting trips, a $999 fare from California to Australia or spend Thanksgiving in Italy for a package of $699.

sigh But the thing that caught my eye was the Travel Q&A. The writer asks if there is a Caribbean island that can match Kauai. The answer was Dominica. Orchid-filled rainforests, a 150-foot waterfall, Ti-Tou Gorge, Champagne Bay which fizzes like a large glass of warm bubbly, steel drums, calypso, and the Rainforest Aerial Tram.

How I envy you dear. Being paid to do what you love in paradise.

07-31-2005 — **They Didn't Say Anything About**
Personal email to Anna from *Gabriel*

Cutie, I was wondering, in that Dominica travel section ... did they mention Pirates who commandeer Production vehicles and build power boosters from spare parts in order to talk to their future Lover by cell phone?

Did they speak of a certain Southern Boy who is so smitten that the best part of his day is talking to his Yankee Country Girl? Any talk of a two different colored eyed Surfer driving around the Island talking on his cell phone for hours at a time?

No? Really? Hmm, how used to you I have already become, actually it would be better stated to say I have become wonderfully comfortable with you. I do know that by the time I wake up I'm thinking of you, and not much more ... actually the bottom line is I spend most of the day thinking about you.

08-01-2005 — **Captain Blood and Old Fashioned Girls**

There is a strangely old-fashioned girl living in my body. A girl typically kept pinned to the ground with my famous two-armed crank elbow lock-jaw wrestling move. A girl I ignore with hands over ears, eyes closed, humming loudly "la la la la." Because the very strong, confident, self-reliant, I can do anything and everything *all by myself* girl has been required on center stage for most of the past twenty years.

But no matter how often I refuse to acknowledge her presence, the Yankee country girl lives on, undeterred, inside me. Manifesting herself in the oddest ways, and at the strangest times. And clambering to get out.

In my ideal world, the captain of a pirate ship (a la Errol Flynn) would put into port to seek the woman he has seen only in an artist rendering stolen in the last raid. He would slash and burn his way into the villa to vanquish the evil tyrannical villain who holds me hostage, sweep me up into his arms, put me on his ship, and sail away – at which time I would fall madly in love with him and we would sail around the world happily forever after. Well, if life were like a romance novel anyway.

But real life isn't a romance novel, and pirates don't exist – at least the movie-perfect Errol Flynn kind of pirates we have grown to adore.

I sometimes suspect women's lib — for all the good it has done — has stolen men's ability to be heroes, and women's ability to believe they still exist. Men often fear doing what they were taught, or taking on any of the traditionally male roles in a relationship ... because "traditional" roles must be wrong in the modern live your life by the latest "how to fix everything wrong with you" book and what you see on *The Jerry Springer Show* kinda' world. So, let me set the record straight.

When you take my arm, open the door, or pull out my chair, I will not assume you think me incapable of doing it for myself. Nor will I assume you believe me incapable of defending myself when you make sure I get to my car safely.

When you help with the hard stuff, the heavy stuff, the ladder required stuff, or the tough to get at stuff, or the stuff that requires the use of power tools, without looking at me blankly and saying "ummm, guess you want me to do that, huh" I will not assume you are making a statement on my physical prowess, strength, or ability to use said power tools.

When you make plans for our date on Saturday evening, including which restaurant and at what time, I will not assume you think me unable to handle my daily schedule or make my own decisions.

When, without me even knowing, you make sure that I have some extra money in my wallet — just in case — and gas in my car, and check to see whether there's milk in the fridge when you're going to the store anyway, I will not assume you think me unable to take care of my day to day activities, and our needs as a family.

And when, expecting nothing in return, you reach out to hug away the tears that sometimes show up without me even knowing why, the old-fashioned girl in me will smile contentedly and know she has found exactly the hero she was looking for all along.

08-02-2005 — **It Takes One Look – Summer 1985**

Some years ago, I was able to prove, beyond a shadow of a doubt, that men spend too much time on the obvious.

Three of us, two girls and a guy friend, were sitting at a back table in a small neighborhood bar. It was an old wood floor beer and peanuts place, but it had a dance floor in front, and was blessed that night with a delightfully memorable musical act covering some of my favorite Burton Cummings, Harry Nilsson, and Little River Band classics.

We got to talking and HE complained about how hard it was to approach a seemingly unapproachable attractive member of the fair sex in this kind of small place, as there was always the embarrassing chance of getting shot down – which made approaching the second target almost impossible unless she had somehow failed to miss the original humiliating encounter.

WE said that, bottom line, he needed to understand that the ball was always in our court. When a girl was interested, the signals may be subtle, but always directed at the object of our desire – and he **would** cross the room. If he didn't want to be shot down (we asked with some rolling of the eyes) why didn't he just respond to the girls who were giving him the right signals?

HE said, "Signals, what signals?"

WE said (with a sigh, a shake of the head, and a pitying *tsk tsk* sound) "Exactly!"

HE said, "Prove it. No talking, no hand signals, no display of womanly assets, no obvious *I'll do you if you ask*. Your most subtle effort."

"I'll take that challenge," I said. "In fact, YOU pick out the guy. I'll have any unaccompanied guy in the place sitting at this table by the next band break."

"Fine," HE said, looking around, "the lead singer in the band." And, crossing his arms, sat back with a smug expression.

I arched my brow, swiveled round to take a look, and decided he was not only worth the effort, but if he decided to take me right there on the beer stained table amongst the peanut shells with the entire bar cheering us on, I would have been happy to oblige.

I did leave the table for the dance floor briefly, but I played by the rules.

The band broke ten minutes later, slightly ahead of schedule, and the lead singer was sitting beside me, at that back table, 60 seconds after that.

HE has never forgotten the lesson he learned that day and WE have giggled about it every time we've told the story. *giggle*

PS: that beautiful singer did take me, or perhaps I took him, not only that night but for many, many days and nights afterward.

08-02-2005 — **We May Be Sleeping ... but**
Personal email to Anna from *Gabriel*

Tonight I slip beneath the sheets and melt in behind you. Our bodies meet and press against each other, magically changing shape, ebbing and flowing, and no one can see where You end and I begin. Tonight we are one.

I softly kiss the side of your sweet neck and, with the tip of my tongue just barely touching, slowly and gently glide up to your ear. My tongue softly teases your earlobe then kisses it, as my hand traces the line of your thigh. It rests there on your hip and My heart beats together with Yours in the sweet music our Souls dance to till morning.

I leave energized for the day with a morning's kiss, knowing the night did you no harm. But as I leave, I wish the Sun would fall from the sky, causing the Moon to rise so I could once again Join with You as our souls dance through another night. Good Night Dream Lover

08-03-2005 — **You Should Have Told Me**
Personal email to Anna from *Gabriel*

Your neighborhood watch National Night Out party sounds like it was a rousing success: Pizza, Ice Cream, Heartburn, Cramps in the Pool, a drowning or two. Perfect. I wish I could have been there.

I'm about to get into bed and immediately fall asleep so I can once again hold you in my arms. I long for the night when I can actually feel you in my arms for real, feel your heart beat against me. I truly want to feel your breath against my chest as you sleep. I want you safe with me.

08-03-2005 — **Before We Sleep**
Personal email to Anna from Benjamin

Anna,

Every night I say goodnight to you. Whether you hear me or not. I wonder if you still think of me? If you still want to grow old with me?

What does life feel like to you? Have you forgotten? Does your attention/affection belong to someone else? Do you care if I care?

Do you read our emails? Do you ever read our letters? Did I wait too long?

Does anyone care about your day better than I? Are you working? Loving? Dancing? Singing? Reading? Will you still tell me?

My head has always ignored my heart. But in its own way, my heart has always been yours. Even if I've never had the courage to make you mine. I could release you if you chose and be forever grateful for the glimpse of heaven we have shared, for the precious gifts you gave me, and satisfied.

You may think you have written the last chapter. But you have not. We have many miles to go before we sleep. I wish you peace.

Always & Forever,

Ben

08-04-2005 — **Carrie, and Mr. Big, and Me**

I was not a *Sex and the City* fan when it was playing. I know, I can't figure it out either. I can only assume it was on a night when something that seemed better was on another station, or I was busy with work, sex, or some commitment. But thanks to the miracle of TiVo and the TNT station, I was able to watch every one recently. **sigh** now I know what everyone was talking about.

For any of you who have lived with your head in a hole, the show is about a quartet of single 30-something women living in New York and their day-to-day issues with life, work, love, and friendship. I cannot tell you the number of times I would shake my head and say, *"Yep – been there, done that, took home the booby prize."*

But there was one episode in particular … Mr. Big, Carrie's long-term lover, had moved to Paris for six months without making a commitment to Carrie, and she spent the time he was gone thinking she could get over him, while simultaneously waiting for him to get back. Because she didn't believe love could end so easily, or her trust in him be so easily broken. Because she didn't believe their story was done.

Some months after he left, Carrie and her friends attend a big party in The Hamptons. She looks up, and there is Mr. Big, not only back in the country without having called her, but with a date. A much younger, beautiful woman he brought home from Europe, and is apparently engaged to.

Carrie staggers out the French doors to the beach, looks out over the wide expanse of empty ocean, turns, and throws up from the sheer raw emotion of it. Because she had kept alive the hope she would be The One and everything she had been afraid of all along was right there in front of her. And being broken as it now was, believing in it again would no longer be second nature, or natural, or easy. It would forevermore be hard.

The ability to love, without reservation, was once simple. So I had complete trust in the man who seemed perfect until he started coming home drunk, then slapped me around and kidnapped my daughter, and I believed in the one that ended up stealing everything I owned to finance a coke habit I didn't know he had because the ones that knew didn't tell me before I married him, and had a great deal of love and even respect for the one that paraded his mistress in front of my friends and family and they didn't tell me either.

When they were gone, I just kept asking myself why I didn't know, why I didn't see what was in front of my face, why didn't someone tell me. I should have been smarter, I should have been more cynical, and I should have protected myself better. I questioned my own intelligence because only a genuinely stupid person could be so easily taken advantage of by someone she loved.

Then I put away my ability to trust anyone and questioned everything.

It's happened to you too hasn't it? It's the feeling you get when you go out with your girlfriend to tell her about the exciting new man in your life – and he's at the back table holding hands with another woman who is wearing an engagement ring. The feeling you get when you meet his friends on the street and he doesn't introduce you. The feeling you get when, quite by accident, you find the letters he's written, and then the credit card receipts, and then the pictures.

You know the feeling.

> **Carrie:** *There is no way that the love that I had with Big is the same thing that he has with Natasha.*
> **Miranda:** *"Natasha?" When did you stop calling her "the idiot stick figure with no soul?"*
> ~~Carrie Bradshaw and Miranda Hobbes, "Ex and the City"

08-04-2005 — I'm in the last Airport and almost home …
Personal email to Anna from *Gabriel*

and already see the time difference is going to take a mathematical genius to figure out when to call you a hundred times a day. Good thing that's me!

Choosing to trust is always a tough thing – jump in or jump out. If I choose to trust and play fair, and know I didn't do anything wrong, and it still doesn't work out, I have nothing to be ashamed of – even if my trust is violated. It may hurt for a while, but as the adage goes, I would rather have Loved and lost than to never Love at all.

By the way, I'm working on the schedule for my trip to Maryland in September. I was just wondering if, during the second week of my stay, you would like to go with me to Tampa? You would not be lying when you say you are visiting your girlfriend Bobbi, as we will also do that. But I think I'd like playing with you all over Western Florida.

08-06-2005 — ME ME ME THREE

In honor of **Blogathon 2005** I am forgoing a serious entry – and going back to interview Anna.

1. **How did you get your (real) first name?** It was a shortened form of my (first) married last name, and given to me by a boyfriend when I was 21.

2. **Where were you born?** E. St. Louis, IL. When the town slogan was "Garden Center of the Midwest"

3. **Where do you live now?** Outside Washington D.C.

4. **When is your birthday?** I'm a Pisces.

5. **Which was the happiest time of your life?** The disco years – 1976–1983. The music, the clothes, the dance floors, the mirror balls ...

6. **How old do you wish you were?** 35

7. **Who would play you in a movie about your life?** Living: Sharon Stone. Dead: Katherine Hepburn.

8. **Who would you cast to play a significant other?** Living: Someone Tall, Dark, and Hunky. Dead: Errol Flynn

9. **How would this movie end?** Ever see *Gone With the Wind*, or *The Thornbirds*? It's the way it's always ended.

10. **You're going to die a natural death. What is the cause?** Suddenly, while having the greatest sex of my life.

11. **You're going to die a sudden, tragic death. What is the cause?** Suddenly, shot by the ex-girlfriend of the man with whom I am having the greatest sex of my life.

12. **How long do you plan on living?** I'm going to live long enough for aliens to land and let us know GOD is actually a kid who created Earth as a high school science project – and hasn't thought about us since graduation!

13. **Introvert or extrovert?** Extrovert

14. **Creation or evolution?** Evolution. Period.

15. **Mounds or Almond Joy?** Mounds for the dark chocolate, then I stick almonds in it!

16. **Do YOU feel like a nut?** No, I like to feel a nut though

17. **Favorite word?** Epiphany.

18. **Favorite historical figure?** Michelangelo. To have such a mind ...

19. **Which historical figure could we have done without?** Pope Urban II – the pope who launched the first Crusade in 1096.

20. **Favorite pick-up line?** "Would you like to get naked and howl at the moon?"

21. **Favorite curse word?** Dren

22. **Favorite kids movie?** *Cinderella*

23. **What happened in the last dream you remember?** I had just retrieved a very important microchip and reader from a potential traitor and hidden it in my towel (don't ask). I went into the closet to read it. I heard a movement in my room, the light went on, and I forced my eyes to open ... and woke up. Darn, hope there was nothing important on that chip.

24. **What annoys you?** Stupidity

25. **How many licks does it take to get to the center of a tootsie pop?** Once I start licking, I get so excited I just want it all in.

26. **What would Jesus do?** Throw up his hands in disdain and horror over what has been done in his name.

27. **Who was the third gunman on the grassy knoll?** The FBI

28. **What did you like to make believe as a child?** I was adopted and my real parents were coming to get me.

29. **Did you have an imaginary friend?** Not until I started dating

30. **If you had the choice to live forever, would you?** Absolutely.

31. **Do you believe in Vampires?** Yes. You've never met anyone who sucked the life from you?

32. **What are your turn ons in the opposite sex?** A good brain, proportionate body parts, humor, romance.

33. **Do you follow your head, your heart, or your crotch?** There's a difference?

34. **What was the name of your first boyfriend?** Jack

35. **What is your weakness?** Love

36. **Do you feel like your physical self matches your personality?** Yes, except I should be shorter.

37. **Have you ever hallucinated?** Yes. Although the drugs may have had something to do with it!

38. **What do you like most about the opposite sex?** Duh!

39. **How did you find out that there was no Santa Claus?** Logic. He couldn't possibly get everywhere in one night when he was sitting in Macy's all day.

40. **End this survey with your favorite quote:** "How do you bounce back when reality batters your belief system and love does not, as promised, conquer all." – Carrie Bradshaw, "Unoriginal Sin"

08-06-2005 — **Hello Lover**
Personal email to *Gabriel* from Anna

Spending hours on the phone with you today while you did your errands was remarkable. Almost felt like we spent a whole Saturday together as you ran around doing regular things, instead of being on a set somewhere doing un-regular stuff. It occurs to me that if you have a big party tomorrow I may not speak with you until evening or so. Can't wait.

08-07-2005 — Where Are You??
Personal email to Anna from *Gabriel*

Woke up and, lo and behold, no morning email, ouch! Have I been dumped already? What a huge Bummer.

08-07-2005 — Fruit of the Knowledge Tree

> How can I bear the knowledge
> that all of this is
> instant replay of the
> night before
> and that tomorrow night
> will be a
> replay of
> me
> and forever down the long line.
>
> How can i
> and still lay with you upon your bed
> (seeing the leftovers from the night before)
> and knowing it is so.

08-08-2005 — You Asked Me How I Feel
Personal email to *Gabriel* from Anna

> *... don't say you're old. You are a little girl baby all the time. God made it so you spent yo' ole age first wid somebody else, and saved up yo' young girl days to spend wid me.*
> ~~ Tea Cake, *Their Eyes Were Watching God*

You asked me this morning how I felt and I remembered some months ago when someone else asked me that very same question.

Last night I sat outside for two hours, my feet propped up and my head tilted back, watching clouds move across a moonless expanse of sky. As the candles around me danced to the music of "Surrender," you used your voice to speak of stroking my hair, cupping my face to follow the curve of my brow across my cheek and down my neck, stopping at the pulse point, and waiting until our

111

hearts beat as one sound. Face and neck and lips. Because you knew it was the perfect moment for exactly that, and no more.

I said, "I've long dreaded having to figure out what I would have to give up when I leave here, and I wonder if it is what has frozen me into inaction. Just silly things – like Christmas. I ADORE Christmas and the tree covered with the boxes of ornaments I've been gathering all my life.

"Last year, as I began making the lists of my stuff that needed to be packed, I looked up at them on the shelves in the garage, and I looked at all my books that would have no place to go, and my beautiful dragons from all over the world, and the antique cabinet where my crystal is kept that is so awfully hard to move (even though it has moved with me four times), and I couldn't continue, because I would have to give up too much.

"I remind myself all the time I should be less attached to STUFF, but I had so little for so long and much of it is truly precious – like photos and scrapbooks. But limited funds only go so far – so it would be all lost at once."

And you said, "Getting rid of stuff, what? Are you crazy? That's why it's called My Stuff or Your Stuff, you're supposed to keep it, silly woman.

"To rid one's self of Christmas ornaments is a serious Sin. You get rid of Fleas, a bad Lover, garbage, not stuff and never ever Christmas stuff ... ever. Those that do are Skunks of the First Order. We can always alternate, mix and match my stuff with yours then store what's left over. You will never have to give up stuff that's important to you to be with me."

I realized, at that very moment, that this relationship would not be about having to give up anything to be in it. It's about learning how to merge all the "stuff" that makes up who, and what, we are.

Forty days until you are beside me for the first time.

> ... *love ain't somethin' lak uh grindstone dat's de same thing everywhere and do de same thing tuh everything it touch. Love is lak de sea. It's uh movin' thing, but still and all, it takes its shape from de shore it meets, and it's different with every shore*
> ~~Janie, *Their Eyes Were Watching God* (Hurston, 226)

08-08-2005 — Photos of Morgan, Jarred, the Tree and Scrooge
Personal email to Anna from *Gabriel*

I had a wonderful time talking with you last night, it seems as though we have tumbled a little further to my ultimate goal. I already have really really really really really really really really fallen in the deepest of like with you.

Ahhh last year's Christmas Tree looks wonderful, Morgan is nearly as beautiful as her Mom, Jarred is a fine looking Man, and Ebenezer is every bit the Scrooge I thought him to be.

Sweetheart, after you come to me I promise Christmas will always be the true celebration it is meant to be.

08-09-2005 — Home and Missing You
Personal email to Anna from *Gabriel*

Sweetheart, I'm home, I'm tired, and I miss you. God this is happening fast and normally I probably would be alarmed, but I am not … I love this feeling.

I'm extra Happy, I feel even more alive than normal, which – trust me on this – is saying a lot!

It's weird; I already know what you feel like. As a matter of fact I feel that I know you so much, both emotionally and physically that I truly miss you.

I shall dream of you once again darling, and in doing so, I shall have a wonderful night.

08-10-2005 — Michael Duggan – We Barely Knew Ye

One early spring in the mid-1960's I turned sixteen. I still walked back and forth to school every day, because my best friend wouldn't get a car until the fall, when she would pick me up every morning so we could act cool and smoke a cigarette on the way.

There was a country bar – no, rather a bar in the country – my soon to be steady boyfriend had taken me to a few times. It was miles away, age didn't matter much to order a beer, and the music was loud and live.

One night, a friend and I ran off in her beat up 1955 Chevy, up one road and down another until we found ourselves in that bar in the country and the fella' that hustled me drinks was a sweet faced man/boy named Michael. He was 18, and something about him tickled my fancy.

Michael got a sweet kiss or two that night, and he got my phone number. Neither of us had a car so he would schedule a time to call me long distance a couple times a week.

Sometimes I'd be late starting the walk home from school. The all-out sprint up and down the hills caused a stitch in my side, and my stomach would be all curled up and knotty with butterflies for fear that ringing phone would echo in an empty house, and he would be gone before I got there.

We talked for hours just flirting and playing, he mailed me little notes and letters, and over the summer we found a way to get together a few more times. He got as far as second base, but he wouldn't go any farther even when I made it clear he was the one I wanted to satisfy the primal urges stirring up in me.

In the fall, school started again, my future steady boyfriend became my steady boyfriend, and the conversations with Michael became fewer and fewer, and finally stopped.

One day, there was a letter in my mailbox. I recognized the handwriting immediately, such big curves of the M's and K's of my name. Inside was the news that he was going to Vietnam, and he wanted to let me know. And a picture of him in his uniform to remember him by.

I wrote back, but never received an answer. And I still don't know what happened to that sweet faced boy.

Twenty-four months later, as I was on the way to the hospital to deliver the baby, everyone in the car reminded me I hadn't chosen a boy's name yet. I don't know if Michael became my favorite boy's name because of those sweet long-gone childhood memories, or if it had been my favorite all along. But had she been a boy, Michael Lee it would have been.

As I wait here, with butterflies in my stomach, for the next phone call from another sweet faced man/boy who has caught my fancy, I was reminded of those hills, and those butterflies.

> *Some people are settling down, some people are settling, and some people re-*
> *fuse to settle for anything less than butterflies.*
> ~~Carrie Bradshaw, "I Love a Charade"

08-09-2005 — **Summer Moon**
Personal email to *Gabriel* from Anna

The summer moon spoke to me tonight with your voice as I sat admiring it and talking with you. I'm not sure *when* you got to know me so well, but am sure glad you took the time.

08-10-2005 — **Concentrating**
Personal email to Anna from *Gabriel*

I spent the evening smiling at the most inappropriate times. I was reading my script with a fellow actor when I actually laughed aloud. The actor looked at me and asked, "What?" I smiled and said I was thinking of a very special lady who seems to be on my mind an infinite amount lately.

He grinned and said, "Dude, Cupid's arrow has hit you dead center – everyone on set has noticed that goofy look on your face! And who are you always talking to on your cell?"

Well, ah, er actually that's the same person I've been thinking about.

Do I know her? I said if you did you wouldn't be asking these questions, you'd know immediately why I am the way I am lately.

Pretty huh? Nope, spectacular, lovely, gorgeous, magnificent absolutely beauti-ful, and those adjectives barely do her justice. She is Helen reborn. With her by my side, we will capture our Golden Fleece and so much more.

He said this sounds serious; I assured him that it is. Is this headed somewhere? I said I certainly hope so.

From that moment on, he has referred to me as Loverboy and I don't mind cause I miss you Sweetheart.

08-10-2005 — **Reading minds … NOT**
Personal email to *Gabriel* from Anna

One of the most delightful things I'm learning about you is that I don't have to try and read your mind. Hurrah! First, I've always been kinda good at that empathetic stuff when I try, and second, I don't usually like to try cause I'm usually disappointed at what I find.

You, on the other hand, have never disappointed me. You are very happy to just say, or ask, or sometimes insist. On anything you have something to say, or ask about, or insist on. Right out there, plain and simple.

Today you challenged me by asking what kind of work I would (or would not) like to do, should you convince me to join you on the West Coast. I find I like your idea of working at playing with you as often and for as long as you wish, helping with the details, and taking off at a moment's notice. That said, maybe I'll want to work, or consult, or write. But mostly I know I'll be happy that you truly want me to choose, and any choice I make will be all right with you.

What a wonderful and extraordinary part of my life you are becoming.

08-11-2005 — **ll io kv ee you**

Gabriel sent me an email this evening —

> I sat on my deck looking at the Quarter Moon and just to its left you could see Venus. I thought to myself – it's you and I jumping across the Moon. If it's true that Men are from Mars and Women are from Venus, our planetary system is in for a change. For when I bring my Mars to your Venus and we join as one, then there will be eight planets instead of nine.
>
> I've been mixing and blending certain words all day long. I can't figure it out. It seems as though the words are in some sort of transition, as if they are about to become something else. The crazy thing is, it seems to be subconscious.
>
> I want you to know I really ll io kv ee you.
>
> Good Night Darling

Can I learn how to love him? I think so.
Can he learn how to love me? I think so.
How do I know?

Because he knows the worst things about me and it's still ok. Because when you know each other's deepest darkest secrets, that's when you're free to love without fear. There's always a chance I'm at the wrong place, at the wrong time, with the wrong man once again. But I don't think so.

Love is trust, responsibility, taking the weight for your choices and feelings, and spending the rest of your life living up to them. It is when you have the grace, compassion, and fortitude to walk beside each other in this thing called life. And, most importantly, it's about not hurting the object of that love.

> *Take my hand and grow young with me; don't rush; be a beginner; [...]*
> *weave pearls in your hair; grow potatoes; [...] light the candles, keep the*
> *fire; dare to love someone; tell yourself the truth; stay inside the rapture.*
> ~~Marlena De Blasi, *A Thousand Days in Venice* (73)

08-12-2005 — **Sorry**
Personal email to Anna from *Gabriel*

I am writing this as you're sleeping. I'm a bit worried I may have scared you during our call. When I said "I love you" it was something I wanted to say and you are under no obligation whatsoever to respond in kind. It has been trying to jump from my lips for a number of days now. I have held it back, forced it back, choked it back, and it was becoming a bit of a problem.

Love is a strong and powerful emotion, one has to release its energy or suffer the consequences. Like most emotions, love can mutate and change if left alone in the dark. I am sorry but I had to release it, it needed to be set free. The love I feel doesn't need company at this time. It's how I feel about you, and it's a great feeling. If nothing else, just know there is someone who Loves You.

If this bothers you I will curb my enthusiasm, but it won't change the fact. If you can accept this is how I feel and know I'm not looking for any kind of declaration from You, we'll be fine and we can continue with our Wooing.

I didn't mean to frighten you, but I also thought you might like to know.

08-13-2005 — **If Wishes Were Horses**

> *Life has taught us that love does not consist in gazing at each other but in looking outward together in the same direction.*
> ~~Saint-Exupery (215)

Before I knew him, everything moved so fast. My mind would be stuck in Monday, while my body was in Friday. It rushed by me and before I knew it another week of life was gone. Now it moves slowly, from one phone call to the next, from one email to another, and there is a yearning inside of me that has taken over everything that I am.

Love him? No, his saying it first did not frighten me.

Love and passion are like a dammed river in full flood breaking loose, they cannot be denied once awakened. I want to feel his arms around me. I want to talk a hundred thousand million words. I want to share a shower, snuggle on the couch, take a drive down a moonlit road by the ocean, and lay in bed beside him as he touches all my secret parts. I want to whisper, and shout, and sing. I want us to be ourselves, and make mistakes, and be forgiven. I want to laugh, and cry, and giggle, and speak without any words at all.

I want the past forgotten, I want the present gone, and I want the future now. But if wishes were horses …

08-14-2005 — **Practical Matters – oh so practical matters**
Personal email to *Gabriel* from Anna

A long time ago (at least it seems a long time ago, because it feels like I've known you for such a long time) you suggested that it's never too early to discuss practical matters.

Considering the feelings that are growing between us, and the emotions you have already expressed, I wanted to bring up some practical matters to see if you had considered them – or if not, to let you consider considering them because once we are together we may not have the time or inclination to discuss such mundane things and I don't want <u>you</u> to be sorry later that we didn't.

About a year ago, I began putting together a "budget." What would it cost to live on my own – what would it cost to live with a roommate. I hadn't budgeted the idea of living with someone and not sharing fully in the household costs, as I'd always assumed I would be working.

Since I am not an heiress or a famous somebody with a personal fortune, it would mean a smaller contribution to our mutual expenses if I were not working full time. Not that your idea of my managing a home, entertaining, and keeping YOU happy is an unappealing idea – it is very appealing.

I think financial matters may be less of a big deal to you than they have been in my other relationships, but it's an important area and can cause so many problems if it's not discussed openly early on.

I've told you I am perfectly willing to sign any agreement so you, and your family, know your personal assets are protected. I ask only that if, once I'm there with you, we choose to end the relationship I am provided with enough to send me back to where I started.

Just so this doesn't get quite so mundane, please don't be sorry for expressing how you feel. It means a great deal to me that you are willing to be honest and romantic and passionate, and I'm so happy and so excited and so tongue-tied. Imagine – me – tongue-tied.

Thirty-seven days until we are in Baltimore … in the same place at the same time!

08-14-2005 — **Practical Matters**
Personal email to Anna from *Gabriel*

Dear Present Associate and Future Partner in Life:

The Business of living is always full of surprises, ups and downs, twists and turns. It can be exhausting and fulfilling, with an incredible amount of satisfaction. And that's only our sex life. Sorry I got sidetracked.

I understand your need for a businesslike approach to the possibility of a lifetime venture between the two of us. My opinion is that this venture may be a long and enduring one. As in all businesses, there should be certain safeguards in place.

I have read and have fully noted your suggestion that, should You or I feel it is time to disband this business of living life together, You should be provided with enough to sustain you through a period of readjustment. I agree to provide you with the funds needed to live comfortably for a period of two years. You should be aware, however, that should you leave there is the greatest of possibilities I would pack up and go with you (please initial here if you understand that possibility).

As far as contributing to the cost of the houses, they are paid for, but there is never a free ride in any situation. I feel it would be fair you pay something, as in paying a great deal of Attention to ME!

Unfortunately, because of the rise in the cost of utilities, and maintenance of the properties, I'll need additional payments in the form of many varied kisses, strokes, hugs, and at least one serious make out session per day.

For personal necessities, food and such (and I'll need this in writing), you must strive to achieve a certain level of happiness each day, to better your mind, achieve goals you have set for yourself, and never ever lose your sense of curiosity.

08-15-2005 — **Life With Mr. Lucky**

Poor Mr. Lucky is not terribly handy. When a light bulb burns out in the reading lamp above his head, he stares at it balefully, waiting for it to replace itself, and when it does not take the hint, moves to other end of the couch.

He will on occasion say, "I can do that for you." Some of you might even think that is exactly what he means.

What he actually is saying is "I'm only saying I'll help in hopes of getting brownie points for it. If you say yes, be aware that I will ask you what you want done, where the thing is that needs something done to it, and where the tool is located that is needed to do what you want done to the thing that needs something done. I will not be able to find the tool where you said I could find it, so you will have to come out to the garage and find it for me. You will have to tell me how to do what you need done, and how to use the tool that you found for me, and where the electrical socket is to plug in the tool should it need electricity. You will also have to help me move the object, hold open the door, and come and watch me perform my heroic task so I can later say with an absolutely straight face *"but I always help you."*

But I digress.

Today I did a whirlwind weekend pick up and laundry in preparation for an extremely busy week. **cue photos of raggedy dirty underwear left on the floor and an empty toilet paper tube on the holder** I am, without a doubt, due sainthood within hours of my expiration.

I feel like making a call to his mother to suggest a remedial course on "what if you were in an accident."

08-15-2005 — **Tricked**
Personal email to *Gabriel* from Anna

I'm driving along, talking to you on the cell, while trying to avoid an oncoming train and find an address in a completely unknown neighborhood, when right in the middle of a most regular call you tricked me!

I said, "Ask me something I can answer YES to!" and what was your immediate response? "Do you love me?"

You are a stinker, aren't you!

08-15-2005 — **Tricked?**
Personal email to Anna from *Gabriel*

I did no such thing … you said it of your own accord! Well I hope you did. So you don't love me? You were tricked and those words were hollow, meaning-less, they accidentally stumbled out of your mouth?

Oh, it is a sad day indeed.

I shall throw myself down my stairs … Okay I'm in my trailer and there are only three steps, and soft dirt at the bottom, but it's the thought that counts.

I shall thrust this knife through my heart, oops it's feeble plastic (they don't trust actors with anything sharp, especially made of metal).

I shall hang myself from the drapery, damn it's a tinted sliding glass window, bummer.

I shall hold my breath until I die … okay I feel a little dizzy, my head is spinning, my heart is pounding …

Anna, regardless of how you feel I still and will always love you NA NA ha ha ha sticking my tongue out. Good night Sweetheart

08-16-2005 — **Oh horror, Oh terror, Oh blood and guts begone!**
Personal email to *Gabriel* from Anna

Please do not toss your carcass down the stairs, off a cliff, in front of a train, or under a speeding truck. Please do not cut your wrists, stick a scissors in your eye while running, or put a peanut up your nose. Please do not strangle on a piece of hard candy while laughing, as I am too far away to perform a Heimlich and it is certain no one on the set will know how – as they only dress like doctors and nurses at Halloween. Please do not stub your toe, jump off a swing, fall in a hole, or hit yourself in the head with a surfboard.

We have talked on the phone for over 2800 minutes the last 30 days, not counting what seems like hundreds of emails, which have to count for something. So if a typical date is 4 hours, we've had just over 11 dates a month on phone calls alone. Can anything happen that quickly?

I ADMIT IT.

I fell for you on one of those dates who knows how many of those 2800 minutes ago. Remarkably, unbelievably, daffy about you. I think about you every day, and dream naughty dreams of you at night.

Thirty-five days until we meet in Baltimore. I know you can't understand, but I already know how I will feel when I have to walk away, have to watch you get back on a plane not knowing when I will see you again, touch you again, kiss you again.

Six months until February 12, until we won't have to say goodbye again. A lifetime of lifetimes stretching out to an eternity. Sogno di me.

08-16-2005 — **Six Months? Silly Girl**
Personal email to Anna from *Gabriel*

Darling I hate to point this out, but on my phone according to my minutes as of right now, I have spoken with you 2566 minutes. Then add yours, and darling we're at right around 3100 minutes and I must also point out that's not nearly enough.

On to the second error. After You and I have loved each other until we're bleeding, taken to the emergency room due to the most wondrous and lovely physical trauma a person could ask for, and I board my plane ... it begins.

As soon as I sit down, buckle my seat belt, and we lift off I shall begin planning our next Union. First, I know I couldn't go more than two weeks at the most without you ... but something tells me we might need the time apart to heal.

As I recall there's the little matter of us traveling to Dominica in October. Okay that's September and October, November, hmm, maybe the Thanksgiving parade in NYC, what do you think?

I know it will be hard for us to part but we'll do what we can. I think the last day will be the hardest. To stop kissing you will be the hardest thing I've ever done ... but Darling we'll have the next 40 years to kiss.

I'm pretty sure waiting through the next six months is going to be a tough time for both of us, but as in every true great Love story, the lovers survive some type of hardship and because of it, their love grows stronger. I know this will last, I can feel it in my bones.

08-16-2005 — **What is Love**

> *In a world where you can date without sex, screw without dating, and in the end keep most of your sex partners as friends long after the screwing is over, what really defines a relationship?*
> ~~Carrie Bradshaw, "Defining Moments"

In their rambling through what is becoming a relationship, Anna and Gabriel have begun to define what love is, and what trust is. Those are the easy questions. The hard one is "What is it not?"

Falling in love usually means accepting a person as they are, not as the person you believe you can change them into. We are all cursed with the personal irritations and foibles, egos and vanities we have acquired over the years, and part of getting to know someone is acceptance of all that they are. Is the reason love – and trust – dies because our partner/soul-mate can't/won't accept/work-around/talk about/compromise on the natural and inevitable changes that occur in each of us as the relationship begins to age?

My Dearest Gabriel,

If outrageous facts are a test of love and understanding – rather than just your seemingly inexhaustible supply of patience – then there is perhaps one last thing I should tell you. It is that, over the years, I have become selfish. And I want you to know about my top 10 selfish requests (in some particular order). You have never given me reason for concern, but promise me we will always find a way to work around/talk about/compromise?

1. I want to be your girlfriend/wife, not your mother.
2. Sex is a team sport, not an individual competition.
3. A girlfriend/wife is not a maid/cook that lives in.
4. Remember to talk to me, not at me. Conversation is more than jokes and headlines. If we can't talk about the things that live inside, I'll explode.
5. Don't make me be in charge of our life together. I want to fully participate, but I am a surprisingly old-fashioned girl.
6. Do something nice for me occasionally, no payment required. Take me on a date sometimes.
7. Don't ever lie to me unless it's to say "your ass would look great in anything!"
8. Sleep is a good thing, about seven hours a night. I do not wake with a smile at 5 a.m. Just because I sleep more hours than you does not make me lazy.
9. Holding a grudge is a bad thing. Anger, disappointment, jealousy, worry, and fear are normal human emotions. Talk about it, work it out, and let it go.
10. Silence is golden and being alone does not mean being lonely. Sometimes I just want to read, or sleep, or just sit and think – comfortable in knowing you are there for me and always will be.

I believe our finding one another in this place, and at this time, is more than simple Serendipity. I want to reach out and create a new past with someone willing to accept my imperfections. I want to stroll down the boulevard holding hands at 90. I want to look in your eyes and believe in always.

And the answer to your question will always be – Yes.

It's ok for love to be passion and obsession. For it is that ounce of excitement, that whisper of a thrill, that there's no sense living this life without.
~~Anthony Hopkins, *Meet Joe Black*

08-16-2005 — **Describing Me**
Personal email to *Gabriel* from Anna

You asked me to describe who I am, so here is the list! Sensual, Passionate, Empathetic, Loving, Compassionate, Giving, Understanding, Appreciative, Good humored, Occasionally witty, Truthful, Intelligent, Well-spoken, Confident, Steadfast, Faithful, Supportive

oh yeah, and Good in Bed

08-16-2005 — **Good in Bed?**
Personal email to Anna from *Gabriel*

Good in Bed? Are you saying that you never misbehave and are always on your best behavior, thus being good in bed?

Oh no, you must promise to be naughty in bed, much like myself. I want the part of you that has your claws dug into my back, who pulls away from a deep and very passionate kiss gasping for breath, and who half moans and growls for me to F*ck her. Oops did I say that out loud? See that Bad Boy does come out occasionally!

My list is much smaller. I am:

1. A Gentleman 24/7 compromised of many facets, complements, and components and I believe you will enjoy discovering and seeing them.
2. Someone who will Love and respect you for several centuries after you pass on to the next plane.
3. My life is an adventure I will share with you until it is finished.
4. As a man, I will love you as no other has before.
5. As a Bad Boy I will love you like you have never imagined, satisfying all urges, aches and desires you may have, and some you weren't aware of.
6. I am made up of basic parts used to their fullest extent. In doing so, I live life

completely. You will share these parts of me as I share yours, and life will be good.

There you have it ... Me.

08-17-2005 — **My Mother**
Personal email to Anna from *Gabriel*

So talking with my Mother last night, I mentioned that I had someone new in my life, to which Mom replied OH? Anna, first you have to understand, I haven't announced a new woman in my life for twenty years. So the fact that I mentioned there was someone in my life and no Holiday function in sight, caught my Mom by surprise. My brother, who likes to push over the anthill then sit back and watch, had hinted that I was seeing someone, and they took it for granted it was casual, like most of my relationships in the past 20 some years.

So today, I showed her the photo of you in your Capri pants. She said you were lovely. She asked if you were a model. I asked why she thought that. Well, she's beautiful and carries herself like one. Now wasn't that nice? My Momma Likes you!

08-17-2005 — **Blame it on the Pea**
Personal email to *Gabriel* from Anna

So darling, does this mean I should take down my internet dating profile?

I want your family to like me. So maybe they should think I'm a nice girl – absolutely no reading about me in *JournalLand*, ok? I should have one ex-husband (as I have to explain Morgan), no Mr. Lucky, and a reasonably normal past – unlike the real thing which has been far from normal but occasionally bloody fun.

When meeting them I shall try not to sit on your lap teasing you unmercifully in front of them by kissing, canoodling, and wiggling around on Rocky until he can't stand it (as he stands so easily!). I shall sit demurely by your side, keeping my tone soft and my hands to myself.

The only requirement is that you find out where they put me up overnight because I expect you to sneak in my room and keep me awake the entire night.

And when everyone asks why we look so tired, we use the excuse of the princess of old – and blame it on the pea!

08-17-2005 — **Nice girl, huh**
Personal email to Anna from *Gabriel*

Don't worry Honey my Mom loves you already, I think she went to Sunday night Mass to thank God you're (almost) the same age as me.

I told her today I haven't felt this way about anyone since Shane's mother. She was very happy for me. I'm sure she has already spread the word ... you know how that works, Telephone, Telegraph, Telle-my Mom!

Honeybunny the only thing that bothers me is where have you been? We should have met five years after my wife passed; I know we'd still be together and married. Then my son would be yours and your daughter mine. We have a lot of time to make up. But then again the next 30 to 40 years should keep us busy.

As far as your history, you must remember I'm my Mother's Son. There isn't anything you could tell them that would redden their cheeks ... Honey you're talking about my family here and everyone has a History.

08-18-2005 — **The Woman in the Moon**
Personal email to Anna from *Gabriel*

Darling Anna, the huge white Moon you told me about has risen here now. It is prettier than any other Moon has ever been for me before, because it came to me after you had gazed into it. And, as we all know, the Moon collects all things beautiful. The Moon captured your image and now it reflects your beauty all over the Heavens.

On this night of nights, everyone can see the Woman in the Moon and she is You. Tonight, Darling, you are close to me. You are shining through my windows, pouring through my skylight; I feel you watching me sleep and there is great comfort in that.

Please Anna, my Love, when the Moon rises Full tomorrow night, allow it to drink you in. Just one more night allow it to steal your image and wear your beautiful face for me. I will wait for you to travel across the starlit sky and rise in the East so that we may once again spend the night together.

Oh how I love the Woman in the Moon.

08-20-2005 — **And the Fabric of the Universe is Love**

I was blessed with a wonderful Auntie, my Mother's older sister. Given a choice, I would have chosen her to be my mom. Very late in her life I told her I had always wished she would have taken me away, but never had the courage to ask her. And she told me if I asked she would have tried because she knew how bad it was for me.

My Auntie was married in 1934. She and Uncle raised three children together, and were just beginning the task of raising three young grandchildren after the death of their oldest daughter, when he died suddenly in the 40th year of their almost perfect marriage. No one ever thought she would marry again.

Auntie and Uncle were the type to have a large circle of close friends. One of those well-loved friends lost his wife of many years shortly before my Uncle passed. Auntie and he were already wonderful friends of many years and began having lunch or sitting together at church, and before anyone realized what was happening, it blossomed into love. They were married three years later and he became my Uncle2. Auntie passed just short of their 27th wedding anniversary and Uncle2 soon thereafter.

In the later years of her life, Auntie regaled me with stories. One of them was how she and Uncle2 had reconciled the loyalty they felt to their original spouses with the love that was growing between them. She told me they both, in their own ways, asked permission of their respective departed spouses, and for their blessing. And she told me their budding relationship was infused with an overwhelming love and acceptance that flowed between, around, and through them all.

Past relationships influence future ones and Anna's relationship with Gabriel is no different. So one night, when she realized their teasing flirtatious friendship was beginning to turn into so much more, she went out to the patio. She turned her face towards the star-lit heavens, spoke her heart-felt desires, and asked permission. And, like Auntie before her, was surrounded with a warmth and acceptance that required no words.

We say atoms are bound by Weak Attractions.
Why not admit the Truth:
The Universe is held together by Love.
Michio Von Kerr, Wayist physicist, CY 9942
~~"The Banks of the Lethe"

08-22-2005 — **Random Ramblings – Sometimes Ya Just Wanna Talk**

Lost, yesterday, somewhere between sunrise and sunset, twelve golden hours, each set with sixty diamond minutes. No reward is offered for they are gone forever.
~~Horace Mann (290)

Did I mention that needles of any kind terrify me? When my migraine medication was first tested, it was only available in the form of injections. I had to give them to myself and I wouldn't do it until I was dying. No reason for that bit of information, just wanted to share.

Speaking of sharing, let me tell you about yesterday.

Mr. Lucky. "I need something business casual to wear next week. What is that?"
I describe it.

Mr. Lucky: "I think I need something new."
I suggest the local mall as it has Banana Republic, J. Crew, Abercrombie, Hecht's (Macy's) etc.

Mr. Lucky: "Go with me. I don't know what to pick out or whether it looks good."
Rats.

Why, would the more curious among us ask, does he need to go purchase new clothes for a one day event when he has hundreds of shirts, uncountable numbers of polos and tees, jackets and casual pants hanging in his half of the ginormous 13 x 21 foot double racked closet?

Because he simply must buy everything on sale or representative of a price point and style he remembers from the early 60's. Which means the poorest of quality, color, and fit. Then wear it to death and even though it has faded, shrunk, discolored, stretched, is no longer an appropriate size, or gotten holes in it, KEEP IT FOREVER ... just in case.

We went to the store and then, being as it was his birthday, we joined his family in the private room at their restaurant for dinner. Two restaurant regulars stopped by unexpectedly to say Happy Happy. These two know most of the family but have never met me. They arrived shortly before the cake was served.

Mr. Lucky jumps up from his seat beside me, very happy to see them, and after chatting for several minutes, wanders off with them to the bar. While 12 of us sit at the table waiting for his return so we can do the singing bit and cut the cake. I finally went to find him and he said his goodbyes as I stood there. Got some phone numbers as I stood there. Waved and walked off as I stood there. I returned to the room and served the cake.

By the way – this is not unusual. For the first ten or so years, we co-hosted a black tie birthday dinner and dance party every August and invited 350 of our closest friends – most of whom showed up. The other birthday host (a woman) and I put the whole thing together. It was a huge amount of work, and the clean-up took until the wee hours, even with staff.

Mr. Lucky and I would arrive at the party together, and I wouldn't see him again until it was time to leave. Along about the fifth year I was at the buffet when I heard two women behind me talking.

"I heard Mr. Lucky has been living with someone. Do you know who it is?"

"Nope. Wonder if she's here?"

> *See, the problem is that God gives men a brain and a penis, and only enough blood to run one at a time.*
> ~~Robin Williams (62)

08-23-2005 — **Safe and Sound**
Personal email to Anna from *Gabriel*

See – the burglar heard us talking and beat feet. As soon as he heard deadeye Anna loading her 9mm he pooped his pants and exited stage right!

What may have seemed an odd long-distance lesson proved to me you knew enough to properly load, unload, and aim at stuff. Believe me, should someone attempt to hurt you, and he had the misfortune of my catching him, I wouldn't kill him, but I might wear his skin for a year.

If you ever get scared again, day or night – call me. Because I love you.

08-23-2005 — I Hope You Dance – Winter 1968

For every door that closes, another opens.
Every trial that ends means one more chance.
If you get the choice, don't sit it out and cry,
Get up and dance.
Just dance!

I was a college bound high school senior with good grades in a very, very small Midwestern town.

I had been going "steady" for two years with a boy several years older than myself.

My mother was dying of cancer.
There was a war in Vietnam.
And that boy was drafted.

There was crying, and goodbyes, and promises. And an unexpected sense of freedom. He had been my first real boyfriend and we were always together.

Shortly after he left, I was introduced to a friend of a friend "just to take your mind off of things." He was cool, exciting, just out of the Navy after four years, and a gentleman. I wouldn't date him, but there were parties with mutual friends, he held my hand, and I began to feel an excitement that had been missing after three high school years with the same guy.

Four weeks later my steady called. He had been classified 4F and was coming home. I put the phone down, walked to my room, and sobbed hysterically. My father walked in, stood at the door a minute, and said quietly "Honey, are you crying because you're happy ... or because you're sad?"

I ended the relationship two weeks after he returned.
And two weeks after that the Navy man and I had been on several dates.
And two weeks after that I was pregnant.

We married in May, because that's what knocked up girls in small Midwestern towns did back then. I had known him for less than three months.

And so it began.

I learned about the lawsuits, then the DUI, then a pending assault charge. Then the debt collectors began calling. And he had trouble keeping a job. And there was the drinking. And the anger. And the yelling and door slamming and fists through walls. And I wondered why none of his friends, and none of his family, had told me any of this before I spoke those vows.

We moved twice, the baby was born, and my mother died within weeks of the birth. Daddy was heartbroken and lonely, but I knew I could never go home again … no matter what.

We moved again. He worked an evening shift and would come home at midnight (or one or two) drunk, wake up the baby, and begin to yell. Yelling became threats, threats became bruises, welts, sprains, abrasions, and finally cuts. And I learned where to hide and I learned how to duck.

Morgan was hospitalized with croup at 14 months. As I sat beside her, alone, watching her struggle for breath in an oxygen tent, I realized it was enough.

I had saved a few dollars and, as soon as she was released, went to the big city, found a job, an apartment close enough I didn't need a car, and as luck would have it, great childcare in the same apartment building.

I packed up one day while he was gone and didn't look back. I was 20 years old.

Someday I'll tell the story of when he found me. And how he broke down the door to my apartment, then the door to the bathroom, and how I climbed through a window and ran out in the street naked at two in the morning screaming for help. And how he kidnapped the baby. And how difficult it was those first couple of years with little money and no support system.

But anyone who has been reading here for a while knows that life changed and got a whole lot better, and I stuck it out (and pressed charges!!) and Morgan and I both became happy successful people because we wanted to, and because we deserved it. But the message today is something different.

Believe in yourself.
Believe you can have something different.
Believe in the dreams you have for yourself and for your children.
Believe you deserve to be happy, and satisfied, and triumphant in this life.
Believe there are people who are ready, willing, and able to help you achieve it, whether it's encouragement, friendship, a shoulder to cry on, a loan, a reference, or a room in their home for a while.

And believe you can do it.

You don't have to stay anywhere or with anyone. Not for your mutual friends, your parents, a vow you took years ago, and especially – most especially – not for the sake of the kids.

You are worth it and you can do anything you want to do. All that is required is that you take the first step. All the other steps will follow naturally. I am here to promise you, with absolute *I've been there myself* conviction, it may not be easy, and it might get harder for a while, but it WILL get better.

And, sooner than you think possible, you will look back, realize you aren't crying anymore, throw up your arms … and dance.

08-25-2005 — **Mathematics**
Personal email to Anna from *Gabriel*

I know you have heard me say this to you already but I'll never stop saying it. The distance between the Earth and the Moon is representative of how much I love you, but it is ever-changing so it must be Squared then taken to the 10th power every 5 minutes. When it comes to us, even math changes a bit. 1 plus 1 does equal 2 but the 2 of us equals 1.

I'm not sure if you read the Science section in today's paper. There was a great discovery made by a team of Anthropologists in Central America. While working in a Mayan ruin they discovered a very precise calendar and within that calendar two very important dates. The first gave the very date the world would end. December 21, 2012. The second, and most important, the date that Gabriel would stop Loving Anna. Carved in stone with its letters and numbers several feet tall it said "on the 12th of Never."

08-25-2005 — **Hello, Goodnight, and Ho Ho Ho**
Personal email to *Gabriel* from Anna

You make my insides flutter and sometimes my heart begins to pound so hard I think it's going to come out of my chest – like the old cartoon characters. Love, panic, fear, belief, hope, faith – everything so rolled up I don't know where one begins and the other one ends. I take each day at a time.

Remember when you were a kid, and the Christmas tree was in the stand, and mom was taking down the ornament boxes to decorate and had already laid the angel out on the table so she wouldn't get broken, and the stores were all playing carols, and the lights were already up in the windows of the house across the street (because they were always early with that sort of thing) and you KNEW it was coming soon but it was so DARN far away and just seemed to take forever, and you sometimes had to take a deep breath for no reason at all, and your tummy would do a little front flip each time you got to thinking about what was going to be in the little boxes under the tree? Yeah, it's like that.

Ho Ho Ho – may sugarplum fairies dance round your head.

08-25-2005 — **Love After Love Two**

> *and I ask myself for one more uncounted time, what to do … how to love again … who will ever understand that as perfectly wonderful as they are and as happy as I am with them, that they were still a second choice … who would ever put up with that fact and still love and stay with me? … nobody, I fear … but I do not want to be alone … so I dream …*
> ~~Candoor, August 26, 2005

It had been a long time since Anna had considered what it would be like to love another person. And what of him. She wouldn't be his first either. Would all their lost loves get in the way?

Anna finally told Bobbi everything. About how she and Gabriel had met, and would meet, and how she decided she would take the chance to love again.

Darling Anna,

I think it's wonderful that you talked with Bobbi. They help us see reality through the blurred vision caused by a swelling heart so don't be too hard on her if she says *What, are You crazy!?*

I know everything is moving so very fast but I think the best thing we have done is set that six-month limit. It gives us enough time to see, feel, and know if being together for the next 40 years is the right thing to do.

What better Valentine's gift could there be for both of us than knowing on that day we will start the rest of our lives together.

Maybe the past is like an anchor holding us back. Maybe, you have to let go of who you are to become who you will be.
~~Carrie Bradshaw, "Anchors Away"

08-26-2005 — Bye Bye Sweetheart
Personal email to Anna from *Gabriel*

I am all set and ready to tackle the trip to New Zealand to finish the last of the filming. I still have that creepy feeling in my stomach, but I guess it's because I'll be so far away from you and the time difference will make it hard to talk as often as usual. I just have to remember that the sooner this is done the sooner you'll be in my arms. You know I have to say I love you at least another 40 times to meet my quota of 100 times per day. I love You Darling and I shall miss you terribly.

08-27-2005 — Jinxed and Stuck in Hell
Personal email to Anna from *Gabriel*

Well, so far it's been a mess. Last night I couldn't sleep, we were delayed three hours, an hour and a half out of Honolulu we descended too early, circled Oahu for two hours, and without warning landed on the Military side of the Airport.

We were rushed off the plane into a holding area, held for an hour, then informed our plane had to be serviced and we had missed the next flight to New Zealand (the last one of the day). But they would put us up in a nice hotel (which they did) pay for everything (which they did) give us a ticket to anywhere for free (which they did) and told we will board a flight tomorrow at 9 a.m. (which I hope we will).

So Honeybunny I'm trapped in Paradise (oh poor Me) … I'm checked into the hotel, I am going to rent a surfboard and surf a spot known as Castles. After that, I'm going to dinner with some folks I met on the plane. I started teasing everyone about how pissed off I was being trapped in this God forsaken hellhole, tossed into a 20th floor fully furnished Suite overlooking the Ocean and that stupid hill called Diamond Head. I asked, I don't see any diamonds do you?

I, of course, shall spend dinner expounding on my darling Anna. I shall tell them of how my Heart feels and the New Man I have become because of you. I love you Honey and I already miss you somethin' Horrible.

08-27-2005 — **Poor Darling**
Personal email to *Gabriel* from Anna

Let's see, put up in a hotel suite in Hawaii (the perfect paradise), fed tidbits of 5-star cooking (the perfect meal), getting a chance to get in one more night of ocean (in the perfect surf) among a gaggle of new friends (the perfect date). Did you pick up any "diamonds" for me as a memento?

Oh please, let me feel sorry for you shall I? Although the plane may have had at least one serious problem, did any passengers suddenly "disappear" from sight? Threaten any of the stewardesses with rape and pillage comments? Display any manly items amongst their seat belts and blankies?

08-28-2005 — **Something Wicked This Way Comes**

prag·ma·tism: *noun.*
A practical, matter-of-fact way of approaching or assessing situations or of solving problems.

There are things I do best, things I do better, things I do good, and things I don't do good at all. Or is that well. One grammar rule I've never remembered. Yesterday, when I was attempting to be loving and sympathetic, I came across pragmatic, unable to verbalize what I am so often able to write.

Katrina is bearing down on New Orleans and Gabriel, having grown up there, is beside himself with fear as many of his friends, his childhood home, and most of his older family members are in the path. I can't begin to imagine what it must be like for him to sit helplessly, stuck in Hawaii for the next couple of days, while nature does what nature is going to do.

09-01-2005 — **Good Night**
Personal email to Anna from *Gabriel*

It was a very sad night for me, one of those kinda nights I needed to be alone. I don't feel quite up to discussing it yet so I'm going to skip the real sad parts for now. Please know that I love you more than anything and miss you something awful.

New Orleans is dying. The water is rising, the levees won't be repaired in time to stop the undermining of the older buildings, and there is talk that a large portion of the City will have to be razed. My family homes are damaged, but my aunties got out. The sewage, chemicals, mosquitoes, and bodies of Humans and Animals will set off a Plague like atmosphere throughout the city. Honey I'll talk with you when I'm able about the bad stuff, but for the moment, I can't.

No one is sure when they'll let folks back into the safer parts of the city so my plans are still up in the air. The Production company has released me from my obligation if I want. I haven't decided yet, but intend on making a decision in the next hour or so. Sorry about my state of mind today, it will improve soon.

09-01-2005 — **So Why Bother?**

> *I think a hero is an ordinary individual who finds strength to persevere ...*
> *in spite of overwhelming obstacles.*
> ~~Christopher Reeve (267)

The author Peter David in *The Woad to Wuin* (32-33) says that on one hand, we celebrate the belief that we are blessed with free will. On the other hand, whenever anything goes wrong we shake our heads and sigh, "It's the will of God."

We simply can't have it both ways. We can't choose to believe we are in charge of our own destiny while simultaneously believing that an all-powerful being retains the right to manipulate our path anytime He/She/They (and I'm leaving your choice of spirituality open here) choose.

In short, if you consider the relationships of gods to men, you are forced to one of two conclusions:

There is a God, in which case the desires of man don't matter. So why bother?

There is no God, in which case we are alone in the universe, there is neither heaven nor hell, and this lousy life is all we get, with no hope of eternal reward for the good or eternal damnation for the wicked. So why bother?

My head just spins when considering predestination. After all, if it is possible to predict some things in detail, shouldn't it be possible to predict all things?

My Sunday School teacher once said that God looks down upon us every day with great interest. Great amusement is more probable. One would have wished God might have preferred watching a funny movie or something, instead of indulging in merriment by inflicting hardship upon us.

But go argue with God.

09-02-2005 — Twelfth of Never

> *So how does it happen – Great Love. Nobody knows, but what I can tell you is that it happens in the blink of an eye.*
> ~~Will Smith, *Hitch*

Everyone's first reaction after hearing about Gabriel (well, after *WTF, ARE YOU CRAZY?*) is to ask various pithy questions about how the hell I am going to keep a long distance relationship going. (and isn't that what best friends are for? To ask the pithy questions?)

The total of his calls has been more time than some couples spend together dating – almost 3,000 minutes a month. Every single morning I wake up to an email, written the night before and sent while I am sleeping (darn time difference!) and one or more during the day. We are taking time – even though he's already set a date to merge our stuff in whatever style suits our fashion. February 12, 2006 (he figures six months is just right).

Am I still a little scared? Of course I am, I'm human. Maybe he will tire of the distance, and the inconvenience, (and the phone bills!) and move on to someone else in another few weeks when the glamour wears off. But until it happens, I'm going to ignore the other shoe up there, dangling like the proverbial sword above my head.

He says a person should not be afraid to ask the important questions. That honest and open communication is the only way to get the answers you need, and to build the trust upon which love is based. And he has always **always** understood the questions.

09-03-2005 — **God I Love You!!!!!!!!**
Personal email to Anna from *Gabriel*

You've ruined me. I have become an Anna Fiend, an Anna Zombie, and I like it! Sweetie, You are just exactly what I need right now.

Thank You Sweetheart, I Love You! I'll Call you as soon as I'm Home.

09-04-2005 — **Last Breath**

I've always had an entirely unreasonable fear that as I took that last breath, I would look around in sorrow knowing that true happiness had always been just a little out of reach. Not that there have not been happy – sometimes ecstatically happy – moments, but there was something else there just around the corner, just out of my grasp. I have so much love to give, so much heart and soul to share. I want to live forever just to know what I'll miss.

9-04-2005 — **I have thought of you every minute of this day**
Personal email to Anna from *Gabriel*

I have thought of you all day and into the evening. Although the news has been bad, and I still worry about family, there is a comfort inside of me. As my heart aches with worry, another shadow heart pumps Love and pushes kindness and comfort into mine. I know you have sent Your Heart to support mine in this time of need. As long as Your Heart beats, it will beat inside of me too.

For years I have walked through my life incomplete, a little off balance, lacking what is needed for life to flow freely. On the 12th of February, our personal

Twelfth of Never, you will come into my life for good. On that day I shall become whole again. I can't wait to start the next 40 years with you.

09-05-2005 — **Both Sides Now**

I wear a wedding ring. A triple wide gold band with channel cut diamonds across the top, topped by a 1.85 carat pear shaped white diamond. And it's not mine. And I'm not married. And the setting is not particularly pretty, but the diamond is sparkly and beautiful and something I never, ever, had before.

Mr. Lucky owns his own business, which I have helped to build and maintain since 1992. Our company is only one of a large number of vendors for a specific product and we've been Top Ten since the list began.

I tell you this because right before 9/11 Mr. Lucky and I were invited to spend the weekend at the home of another Top Ten vendor in the northeast. Their home was large, luxurious, and located in an upscale neighborhood. The vendor and his wife drove new, and expensive, "name-brand" automobiles. And his wife sported a very large diamond ring on her left hand.

We arrived home on Sunday night and Mr. Lucky immediately went to his dresser. "Here," he said, handing me a paper wrapped package "see if this fits."

Again I digress in order to say that when Mr. Lucky and his second wife were married, he purchased a diamond wholesale and (one of them) designed a custom made setting. She was very proud of it but, when she divorced him, she gave it back (or perhaps he asked for it, I've never inquired).

Now I was at their wedding, and I knew him and his wife when they were married, so I recognized the ring that lay in that package. I looked at the ring, then at him, and answered "No, it won't fit."

"Ok," he continues, "take it up to the jeweler tomorrow and have it sized. Then you can start wearing it."

Don't be mistaken, poppets. I am not confused by this conversation. I know exactly what he is doing and why.

"Fine."

And I did exactly that. And I'm not fooled about the reasons. I adore shiny sparkly things. And I don't mind wearing a lovely diamond belonging to someone else because it meant I wasn't asked the oh so many difficult questions by the oh so curious neighbors when we moved into his new, oh so luxurious, house in the upscale neighborhood a few months later.

In case you are wondering, I'm still driving my same car. And so is he.

> *We are not the masks we wear.*
> *But if we don them, can we not become them?"*
> Keops D'ao Tsumai, *Fortunes* CY 9683-301 AFC
> ~~"Pitiless as the Sun"

09-06-2005 — I Can Be So Spoiled Sometimes
Personal email to *Gabriel* from Anna

I've not put up some entries that I was going to because you read my journal and you are already very protective of me (yes you are – you virtually taught me to load a pistol one night). But mostly I don't want to add anything to your already overwhelming responsibilities.

On the other hand, it's my journal and I use it to vent, to get angry, and even to feel sorry for myself on occasion. It makes me feel better to write things down and hear advice from others who have had similar experiences. I'd like to know that it's ok with you if I continue to write about the things that happen to me.

09-06-2005 — This has been a long day
Personal email to Anna from *Gabriel*

This has been a long day and I'm not even working … not fair. I just feel sad and a little useless. We still have no solid news on those missing. I feel terrible for both the folks in Louisiana and what they have to look forward to. I sense their pain, but can't imagine what it's like being them – the future must look so dark.

As far as your journal, I expect nothing less from you, please express yourself freely and honestly – as you say, after all, it's your journal. As long you speak from a place of truth with no intention to inflict hurt on another, nothing you write will bother me in the least.

09-06-2005 — **Ask Anything**
Personal email to *Gabriel* from Anna

I want you to know I do understand the helpless feeling you have. I, too, am moved to tears and feelings of complete frustration over the hopelessness and loss felt by everyone involved. I want to do more, say more, contribute more in any way possible, starting with you who have lost family and have family who lost everything. Talk to me anytime you want, about anything. Ask anything of me. That's our agreement, right?

I understand your need to cancel some of our planned meetings. I am absolutely sure that when you can fly east for a day or two without feeling guilty, you will do so. We still agree on February and I will be patient (not my greatest trait, but probably a good thing to work on at this age, huh).

09-07-2005 — **Skinny Girls Are Nice Too**

I have been called a variety of names throughout my life. There are few I prefer.

When I was in grade school, I was the tallest, thinnest little girl you could ever imagine. Long stick arms and legs flying everywhere out of clothing that was always too loose and too short. Pictures of me back then show ankles that were never covered, and wrists that had never known a blouse, jacket, or winter coat that came down where it belonged. It was only recently that clothing designers agreed people who wore a size 2 were not always 5'2" tall.

Over the years I've been called angular, bony, emaciated, gangly, gaunt, lanky, lean, malnourished, scrawny, skeletal, skin-and-bones, skinny, slender, spare, stringbean, thin, twiggy, undernourished, and underweight (this last one from a recent doctor's notes). It was whispered I might have an eating disorder, when such things became known in polite society.

Apparently when you get my age you are supposed to settle into hips and thighs and bellies and droopy breasts and, well … you know … a "matronly" figure. But my weight has been the same for 40 years and it doesn't seem to be "matronly."

Despite the pre-supposition my size may place in your mind, PLEASE realize that my father was slender, my mother was slender, I am slender, and my daughter is slender (yes, my preferred descriptor). It runs in the family.

I watch my fat and cholesterol because I ate banana splits for lunch and Grand Slam breakfasts at midnight for too many years. Now I'm paying for it, and since Gabriel has told me I must outlive him (I think the exact phrase was OR ELSE, although I have no idea how he expects it would be any easier for me to lose him) the numbers gotta improve.

If there is a moral to this missive, or a message, it is this. Folks of all sizes fight their own demons. Probably best not to judge.

Who want dat girl wit' da' skinny legs?
~~A singer I can't remember (ok, I remembered, Joe Tex)

09-08-2005 — **Good morning angel**
Personal email to *Gabriel* from Anna

Yesterday was 330 phone minutes of bliss. A sinful pleasure for both of us. Afterwards, I looked up the quote I was trying to remember.

Go confidently into the direction of your dreams. Live the life you always imagined.
~~Henry David Thoreau, *Walden and Civil Disobedience* (para.)

(PS, two little pictures for YOU)

09-08-2005 — **I Love You!!!!!**
Personal email to Anna from *Gabriel*

JUST FOR ME!

Thank you, I love you ... but Honey it didn't last all that long I ate everything including my computer screen. YUMMY!

Honey, I shall love your body as my Heart Loves Your Heart, I will Love it like my Mind needs to connect to your Mind. I will love Your body with the same level of passion and desire that my Soul has to blend with your Soul.

09-09-2005 — **Bollocks!!**

Here is the price of freedom:
Your every drop of courage,
ounce of pain, pint of blood.
Paid in advance.

Sebastian Lee, "*The Rising Tide*" AFC 271
~~"Bunker Hill"

Morgan has known Mr. Lucky since I met him and, like most others, never liked him. Actually, I think she said she would not wish him upon anyone, including her worst enemy. (All right, maybe her worst enemy. And his cohorts. And underlings. And immediate family. But no one else. All right, perhaps cousins, but only if they were utter cretins in their own right.)

Her new husband, Jarred, after meeting him the first time last summer said, "But what's the problem? He seems like a nice enough guy!" They have visited several times since and I was unsure what his current thoughts were until I got this email just after their last visit:

My opinions about Toadface, otherwise known as Mr. Lucky.

I've realised what it is that bothers me about him – he's like one of those Harry Potter characters – the Detraqueurs (didn't read the books in English, sorry!) [*author note: Dementors*]. I always feel exhausted when I'm with him as though my energy is being sapped from me at great speed. He dominates conversations and forces one (mainly out of politeness rather than interest) to listen to him. This becomes tiring very quickly.

I've learned to just ignore him and not look up when he starts out with one of his "Of course, you know what I did when I danced/fought/boxed/fenced ... " (cue long inane speech bragging about some time past when he once did this or that, unconfirmed I might add, but making out that he did it on a regular basis.)

It's testament to your good nature and character and perhaps even a weakness on your part that you have managed to put up with this sort of bollocks for so long. I would have told him to f*ck off long ago.

09-10-2005 — **Such stuff as dreams are made of**

Don't marry the person you think you can live with; marry only the individual you think you can't live without.
~~Dr. James C. Dodson (211)

In 1968, I married because I had to. Because that's what good girls did when you found yourself in that condition in those days. Ten family members in a small chapel, then dinner at a local restaurant. I was filled with dreams.

In 1975, I married because I needed to. Because stability and a loving two-parent family were important for a young child. Fifteen family members in the back yard, then dinner and dancing at a local restaurant. I put my dreams on hold.

In 1989, I married because I ought to. Because everyone expected it, there was a house, and insurance, and taxes, I was getting older, it was lonely in a strange new city, and there didn't seem to be any reason not to. Just us, at lunchtime, at the courthouse. Facing reality was more important than dreams.

Next time I marry, it will be because I want to. Because you are never too old to dream again.

09-12-2005 — **Personals**

A while back, I started reading the personals. I could never contact anyone, although I was often amused and sometimes interested. I gave fleeting thought to writing my own, once things had changed, but what to say? Nothing in 25 words or less seemed to fit so I abandoned the whole idea.

Along the way, a dear friend suggested I start two lists, based upon the book *If Love Is a Game, These Are the Rules* (Carter-Scott). The first was a list of what I was looking for, broken down by must have, wouldn't it be nice, and deal breakers. The second, and hardest list, was what I could offer if he showed up.

In the last days and weeks and months, I have come to a profound realization. Maybe at my age the lists just aren't that important anymore. Maybe it's enough to have figured myself out. To like the person I've become. To understand what makes me happy and sad, passionate and committed. To appreciate honesty. To have the confidence to give, and take, and compromise, and forgive. To have learned how to fight.

To know what love is … and isn't.

> Ageless SWF seeks fearless handyman for new installation. Packaging includes all hardware and software required. Must be willing to read directions. Ongoing help desk available.

09-13-2005 — Virus Checker Loaded Here

Gabriel is sick. No, I mean legitimately sick, although he has pooh-poohed any attempts at commiseration.

It is tough, but I've been trying to do the virtual pillow fluffing, water/juice offering, chicken souping, and head/shoulder rubbing through the telephone wires for five days now while he wrestles the Southeast Asian flu to its knees. I may have discovered the **only** advantage to our relationship. Southeast Asian Flu is one virus you can NOT download via the internet.

> *Love and a cough cannot be hid.*
> ~~Francis Bacon, *Oxford Dictionary of Proverbs* (364)

09-15-2005 — Five Things I Miss About my Childhood

My Granddaddy was a big man. Tall, ruddy cheeked, big hands and body. He and my Grandmother lived on a farm about five hours south of us in central Kentucky.

The closest town was Penny, a one-room country store located at a fork in the gravel road surrounded by farmland. It had a wood stove in the middle, an unpainted screen door that smacked close with a rusty spring, an oak counter worn smooth over an untold number of years, and two faded red gas pumps out front with round glass globes perched on top.

Twice a year we would pile into the family car for the road trip to Kentucky, down miles and miles of two-lane roads.

"She's on my side" "No, she's on MY side" "Mother she's touching me" "Stop taking my colors" "Don't look at me" "How much longer?" "SHUT UP" "No, YOU shut up" "MOMMMMMYYYY"

When the tires hit the gravel road, you were almost there. We'd shut up, scoot forward, and start watching for the house that was set far back from the road. Like magic, they always seemed to be in the yard, under the trees near the well, watching for us. We'd pile out and run into their arms knowing the next three days would be as close to heaven as it was possible to get.

My grandmother could make country biscuits that would melt in your mouth. Her kids, her kid's kids, and some of her kid's kid's kids tried for years to make them but there was no duplicating the secret ingredient – homemade lard. When dinnertime came round, she'd go out into the yard, grab a chicken by the neck, spin it, and have its head off, feathers plucked, gutted, and fried before you could get washed up. Fresh green beans, tomato slices, corn on the cob from the garden, mashed potatoes and gravy, homemade jelly, and cold ice tea made from real tea leaves filled the table.

There was a hand pump at the kitchen sink for water. To take a bath you stood in a big tub filled with water heated in big pots on the wood stove and washed up with homemade soap. Drinking water came from the well, cranked up in an oak bucket and dipped out with a gourd dipper.

There were no sewers, so the toilet was a one-seat wooden structure behind the chicken house, barely held together with handmade nails and baling wire. A persimmon tree grew up around it. In the spring and late summer, it would be full of buzzing, stinging insects seeking the flowers or the fruit. At night, we had chamber pots so we wouldn't run into the foxes or wolves come to snuffle round the chickens.

On the farm, there was no stopping us from getting dirty. We rode the horses, chased the pigs, heckled the calves, drowned dozens of worms hung from bamboo poles trying to catch sunfish in the little pond, hunted for chicken eggs in the hayloft, found the blackberries, raspberries, walnuts and pecans, and climbed all the trees against every imprecation of our too-strict mother.

Many of our second and third cousins were older than my mother and were called "Aunt" this and "Uncle" that and when we'd go a'visitin' there were always new baby kittens, squirrels, hound dogs, and hugs and kisses and "my

147

how they've growed."

Granddaddy would sneak us off to Penny to "show off my grand-babies." We'd ride the tractor up the graveled road and he'd always let one of us sit on his lap and drive. Once there we'd get one of the little "coke-cola" six-ounce bottles from the red-lidded cooler. Remove the cap, tilt up the bottle without banging your front teeth, and let that fizzy drink bring tears to your eyes as it bubbled down the back of your throat.

On a few exquisite occasions, we would arrive at the same time as our slightly older cousins from Minnesota. One year we discovered a way to play that kept us occupied separately, and together, for almost eight years.

The wood behind the house was full of majestic spreading hardwood trees, which left the shaded floor nothing but a thick layer of dried leaves. We used rakes to clear trails through the leaves, defining living spaces and connecting everything together. Each time any of us visited, the newly fallen leaves would be cleaned off to extend the trails. The first thing we always did after lots of hugs and kisses was run out to see the new trails created by our opposites since the last time we were there.

Very early in this new game we found some good hard cattail reeds that were taller than we were. We cleaned off the leaves, and sharpened the points with a rock. Then, holding them above our heads, we would run barefoot down those hard packed dirt trails screaming at the top of our lungs …

"TTTTAAAARRRRZZZZAAAANNNN"

ok … some of us yelled "Sheena."

09-15-2005 — **Strongest Man Alive**
Personal email to Anna from *Gabriel*

So do you miss me? How much? Sweetie I want you to know nothing has changed about how I feel about you. I have just had the wind knocked out of my sails. Especially with my cousin, three uncles and an aunt missing in New Orleans. We are now hoping they will recover their bodies.

Three quarters of my family are, for the time being, homeless. I worry about their health, both mental and physical. I worry my Granny and older Aunties won't survive knowing their homes, and most of the city they love, have been destroyed. I can't remember ever seeing my Dad so sad. Or so many others openly cry. It is terribly sad and I am overwhelmed. Childhood memories and secret places have all been washed away.

Baby, please know I love you more than anything but it is difficult to be myself until I deal with all that is front of me. Once I'm actually working and rebuilding some of my family's homes and can see their lives coming back on line and order formed, things will increasingly get better, I promise.

I know you understand. I feel the glorious Love you have for me and I soothe myself in it. It is healing and a great comfort, and without it, I'd be in so much more pain. You are my elixir, my cure all. Your love pumps vitality into my heart and mind and, with you, I am the Strongest Man alive.

09-18-2005 — **Backyard Surf**
Personal email to Anna from *Gabriel*

The surf was gigantic yesterday. It's a little bigger today but tonight it's going to be huge.

Honey it was nice talking with you while looking at the Moon. While I was sand bagging the breach in our sand bag wall I thought of you and how wonderful life will be once you're here with me … then we can sand bag together … just kidding, we only do that twice maybe three times a year, except for last winter, then we had sand bags on our street for four months.

I still think I'll sell this place soon, maybe within a year or so. As much as I love this place, I think you and I should get something new. Once you're here, we can start thinking about our home. I want to build a new home in North Carolina, but if you don't like it, we can live elsewhere and lease it out. We'll be busy little Bees Honeybunny.

09-19-2005 — **National Talk Like A Pirate Day**

> **Wade "Cry-Baby" Walker:** [*after getting new motorcycle*] "You have made me the happiest juvenile delinquent in Baltimore."
> Johnny Depp, *Cry-Baby*

In th' summer o' 1989, me lass spent eight seven-days as an extra in John Waters first major production movie *Cry-Baby*. Th' only place ye can pick th' lass' ou' be as a non-credited feature extra called Polio Girl in one o' th' first scenes.

T' find a young lad fer th' role o' Wade "Cry-Baby" Walker, Waters boonswaggled $30 worth o' teen magazines, all o' which showed Johnny Depp o' *21 Jump Street* (1987) on th' cover. Depp be thinkin' th' script as funny an' strange, an' tookst th' offbeat role t' avoid bein' typecast as yur TV pretty boy.

Morgan, e'en then, be gorgeous. Her natural wiles attracted th' best lookin' bucko on the deck, Kenny Corcoran. On nights they weren't shootin', Kenny an' Morgan would meet up w' th' rest o' the hands at Club Charles. John Waters be generally thar as be Hep (th' hairstylist) many o' t'other Drapes an' Squares, an' a young Johnny Depp. Th' hands would get a table in th' aft o' th' pub, or e'ry lass in that rum-runners heaven would try fer t' o'erhaul Johnny boy.

Predictions be true, th' scallywag Hep would flirt wi' th' lass', John Waters would flirt wi' Kenny, an' ever' bar lass in th' place was tryin' t' shanghai purty Johnny boy. Morgan was eight seven-days tryin' t' talk me into joinin' them to splice the mainbrace wi' a wee clap of thunder. Sink me, I neredid.

When I asked th' lass' this mornin' 'bout th' now famous Johnny Depp, she spake o' some 'er fondest memories bein' o' them nights she be chattin' wi' th' lad about 'is musical days 'fore he took up th' actin' life.

> **Harbormaster:** Hold up there, you. It's a shilling to tie up your boat at the dock ... and I shall need to know your name.
> **Jack Sparrow:** What say ye t' three shillings and ye be forgettin' the name.
> **Harbormaster:** Welcome to Port Royal, Mr. Smith.
> *Pirates of the Caribbean: The Curse of the Black Pearl*

09-19-2005 — **If I Could Put Time in a Bottle**
Personal email to *Gabriel* from Anna

Three and one-half months ago, almost a quarter of a year, you said hello and thirty eight days ago you said I Love You.

We have shared three moons and six time zones.

We chose to respect each other for who we are, and for our differences – not in spite of them.

We have been blessed with understanding and acceptance by our friends and relatives.

We have found common ground as we overcome life's obstacles.

And each day, with a great and infinite wonder, I find myself loving you more.

9-21-2005 — **Mmm … Cake!**

> *Life takes a lot of courage, often more than we think we've got, and almost always more than we think we should have to find.*
> ~~Merle Shain (63)

In one of our early marathon telephone conversations I warned Gabriel that I had already experienced a long distance relationship whose chemistry, upon meeting, did not live up to expectations and I was apprehensive about embarking on another one. I remember saying that I feared one of us might feel the same way and we should not get in too deep too fast. Too late.

So I was surprised, a few days ago, when Gabriel asked me why I thought the chemistry hadn't been there.

The simplest answer was that after seeing Jason again, I began to realize that I had formed my renewed attachment to him based on the memories of what he looked like, felt like, how he sounded, how he smelled. When the real Jason didn't match any of those memories, I was able to look at everything else more realistically.

Genetically, I am a card-carrying female member of the human race and a product of its evolution. The evolution wherein the female of the species is naturally attracted to the male with the most colorful plumage, the loudest roar, the biggest horns, the fullest mane, the shiniest fur, or the tightest abs – face it, the cake with the best looking icing. Even if, intellectually, I know that once you lick off the icing, you are going to be left with the cake (so it had darn well better be a flavor you love).

I think Gabriel understood. We have exchanged many, many pictures – the good, the bad, and the ugly – and he often says that the old-fashioned way we are building our relationship feels like the best way. You see, in normal circumstances, the physical attracts you, then DIS-tracts you before you take the time to learn what's inside. In a balanced long distance relationship you still get to start with a picture, but then you take the time to know the other person's heart and soul before you add the sexual *Sturm und Drang*.

So I decided to trust him with my real self. To accept that if he will only love me with a false front, he doesn't love *me* at all, so I haven't much to lose.

09-24-2005 — **Ah yes – Spooky Action**
Personal email to *Gabriel* from Anna

Einstein was right you know – spooky action. We are nothing less than a perfect example of Quantum Entanglement. Even when we don't mean to, even when we don't want to. We're connected. Even when we try to be unaffected. Yeah. That's it exactly.

09-24-2005 **A Love Letter**
Personal email to Anna from *Gabriel*

Honey to say I'm impressed is a huge understatement. I had no idea you are interested in theoretical mathematics. I once wrote a paper on Quantum Entanglement using Love as the proof, and my professor joked I had changed the principles of basic math.

I wrote that when two individuals combine with the unseen element of love, the separate entities communicate as one. Thus 1 and 1 = 2 but when love is present, 2 = 1.

Honey you should see an enhanced Photo of entangled Photons. There are Two individual Photons connected as One. They are of the same Heart and Soul just like us.

09-25-2005 — **What a Day**
Personal email to *Gabriel* from Anna

I don't think I properly extended my condolences yesterday for the confirmed loss of your cousin and his father. I'm so sorry you've had to lose people you care about in all this mess and wish there was more I could do.

I've been thinking about you all day – and less apprehensive now that most of the levees in New Orleans made it through Hurricane Rita.

Your email love letter last night arrived – how much fun it was. Wish I knew what happened to the ones that go missing.

09-28-2005 — **Gratuitous something anyway**

gra·tu·ity: *noun.* First used 1540
something given voluntarily or beyond obligation usually for some service; especially: ***TIP***

I went to get my hair trimmed last Saturday. I don't normally go on a weekend, as it's an extremely popular salon (ok, *SPA*, and since they do fingers, toes, and facials I'll give them the pretentious moniker). It was a must do, however, since I invariably wait until the last minute, when I look in the mirror one morning, go "AAAAGGGGGHHHH" and hit the speed dial labeled "Romeo" (I am not making it up – that's his name).

Did I mention the salon is busy on Saturdays? Yes? It was so busy that the normally free park wherever you want parking lot was partially blocked off with ropes and politely printed signs announcing:

Complimentary Valet Parking
Tips Accepted

The youngsters handling the keys did not appear to be working their way through college, or supporting their families, or contributing their time for a worthy cause (which may have made the sign slightly more palatable).

Instead, these young teens displayed the looks and bored impatient demeanor of individuals forced into the trade only because they could not wheedle a new iPhone or portable Game Boy from their already overburdened parents. Is this a lesson in bad American manners or just consumerism at its worst?

I'm sorry.

Wasn't the concept of "tips" defined as a bonus for a job performed better than expected? Something you did not discuss in polite company. A dollar or two slipped almost imperceptibly during a handshake, or tucked into a pocket with a knowing smile, nod of the head, and a silently mouthed thank you.

When did gratuities get added automatically to the menu check, find their way into cab fare because the driver fails to carry change, or become so blatant as to have a sign asking you to pay for your "complimentary" parking spot that, on every other day, is FREE.

Before I get comments about poor harassed waitresses and bartenders who live on tips because they don't get a salary – yes I get it. Morgan lived on tips for years to put herself through college, pay for acting classes, and make the rent.

But she didn't carry a sign around her neck asking for them – she went above the call of duty in hopes of earning them.

I parked at a free space down the street.

The word TIP is also considered by many to be an acronym:
T.I.P. – "**T**o **I**nsure **P**romptness" or "**T**o **I**nsure **P**rompt" service

09-29-2005 — **Off to Borders**

> *It has yet to be proven that intelligence has any survival value.*
> ~~Arthur C. Clarke (109)

You've seen the movies. Handsome, intelligent, well-born Prince. Warm, affectionate, working class girl. They meet unexpectedly. She can't believe it's real, but he seeks her out, pursues her, and accepts her for who she is. Happy forever after the end. *sigh*

Well, in the movies at least. Usually a bad JLo movie (ummm, *Maid in Manhattan* anyone?) What about reality? Can a middle class high school graduate from working class high school graduate parents, and grade-school graduate farmer grandparents, be accepted into a family of doctors, lawyers, scientists, and politicians? What if, after the first get-to-know-you family dinner, the conversation over port in the library is 'Well, she seems nice enough, but ... ' which we all know is a polite upper class euphemism for 'What the f ... are you thinking?'

What can a plain Midwestern girl do? Take a museum course on French Impressionism? Refresh her memory on the works of Dickinson, Longfellow, Chaucer, and Thomas? Learn to ski? Spend some time with the Science and Discovery Channels? Buy some new books, like *Quantum Mechanics for Dummies*?

Or, perhaps, the best answer is to take her clue from the subjects they talk about during hours (and hours, and HOURS) of phone conversations each week. What does he dwell on, come back to, discuss, find amusing, and real, and diverting? What could she learn more about so that it might not matter being just an ordinary girl.

Let's see – yesterday they chatted intelligently for almost an hour on the comparative odors associated with farts, underarms, and poop.

Yeah, she'll fit in just fine. But she's still going to pick up the Dummies book (just in case).

09-30-2005 — **Fire**
Personal email to Anna from *Gabriel*

According to the last report, the fire attempting to accost my property has a 12-mile front and has burned 16,200 acres in LA County and 9,000 acres in Ventura County. The fire is only 5% contained and the 95% burning uncontrolled means none of us in Malibu feels safe.

Apparently being an ex-Ranger and a good Boy Scout serves me well. I thought about what you said this morning and decided it made good sense to empty out the rest of the house ... thanks sweetie. Even if it ends up like washing your car and it rains, should the worst happen, my stuff is safe.

I have a long day ahead of me, so I will get into the sleeping bag atop my air mattress. For the next 5 days or so I will revert back to my College days and live like the bachelor you once wondered about – sparsely furnished home, paper plates and all! But still no lawn furniture in the house!

09-30-2005 — **Good Night Honey**
Personal email to *Gabriel* from Anna

I'm glad you got everything else out. Although I don't know what "everything" means. Lord, it took me two weeks to pack the stuff that moved into this house and five people an entire day to unload it.

I'm pretty sure of one thing – now you can leave tomorrow to do what you need, and want, to do in New Orleans for the next few weeks without worrying about fires, hurricanes, earthquakes, burglars, etc. I guess 2005 will go down as "that was the year that." Call me when you can.

10-02-2005 — **Forget----my laptop and cell phone----ful**
Private message from *Gabriel*

I'm sorry I haven't called or emailed for a couple of days. I left my phone and laptop at Home. I guess I was a bit preoccupied. The idea of the Funeral, the fires, and seeing homeless family members under these circumstances made me a bit absent minded … or I'm just getting old.

The Funeral was beautiful but very sad. My aunt lost her husband and only son, her home, and her beloved neighborhood. For the first time I realized what people must have felt like consoling me after my wife passed. You want the pain to go away for them but it won't for some time.

Well, Sweetie I have missed talking with you and emailing, but I'll speak with you tomorrow. I am leaving in a few minutes but Dad is staying. I love you.

10-05-2005 — **Message from an Old Friend**
Personal email to Anna from Benjamin

Anna,

I stared at your picture for what seemed like an hour last night, because it reminded me so much of you. Last night I dreamt of you naked, crying out in the darkness, and my arms opening to hold you. Somehow in those moments you always trust me and I woke up believing you could trust me again.

I know I haven't been very communicative, but I needed time to think about us. Think about what it would mean to overcome my fears and imagine a life together. How I could make that happen in a way that would make us both happy with the outcome. Can you ever be willing to forgive me for hurting you, for abandoning us? We have so many years invested in one another.

I still can't be without you. Would you be willing to come visit, to talk, to consider our agreement again, to trust that I can be there for you someday?

Always, Ben

Dearest Ben,

Your email was sweet, and heartfelt, and unexpected. You will always be my dearest friend but I cannot keep the agreement we made.

It took too long to understand why we both kept trying to come together, when each time, each heartbreak, hurt more than the last. At the end, it was a little book called *He's Just Not That Into You*. I must have read it four times. In a row. Then I sat back and shook my head, finally knowing why, and why not. I am not broken, I do not need to be fixed, and there is nothing I can change that will make us work.

Ben, there have been so many times the last twenty-five years when I would have given up everything to be with you. What I understand now is that it is exactly what I would have given up – everything – and that's not the way it should work. You shouldn't have to give up ANYthing for love.

Your friend, Anna

10-06-2005 — **An Epiphany Day**
Personal email to *Gabriel* from Anna

I do so love the days you tell me stories, especially today. You said sometimes we forget them. Sometimes we bury them. Sometimes we refuse even to think of them. Those boogey men that exist, just out of sight, slipping in between the trees, hiding down deep in the closet. We don't go looking for them because we're just a little afraid of what we'll find.

You suggested that the only way to get rid of a boogey man is to get up, walk over to the closet, and open the door – no matter how scared you are of what is inside. That mostly you'll find out there's nothing there at all, or that it is more afraid of you than you are of it.

So I took a big breath, got up, walked over, and – just as you said I would – found the closet empty.

10-06-2005 — An Epiphany – Did you pop it?
Personal email to Anna from *Gabriel*

It's funny how we actually get disappointed if we can't find something wrong with what is going right. It offends our belief systems. People can't be trusted, everyone always gets hurt, nothing good ever happens to me, and something going right flies in the face of our truth. Instead of being happy and inspired we try to prove it is a cosmic mistake.

Nothing is 100% guaranteed, there are disappointments, and we are occasionally wronged. There is a constant stream of choices to be made and not every one is going to be the right one. What's important is to jump right back into life, knowing we have learned some great lesson.

Honey I don't know what's ahead of us, but I know I want to find out. The funerals stirred up some pain in me. If You died before me, I don't think I could live through it again. But I promised myself back then that if there's a road I wanted to travel I wouldn't be afraid to walk it, and together we will walk over, around, or through any obstacles.

10-07-2005 — Schedules, trips, and travel plans
Personal email to *Gabriel* from Anna

You sounded a little disappointed when I said I was going to visit friends in San Diego for Thanksgiving. Honey, a long time ago we made plans for getting together, but since Katrina/Rita/forest fires in Malibu, etc. you put all plans on hold until December or later when you were free to come here.

I understand your schedule is significantly more spur of the moment than mine. (yes, I know, just because I talk to you all the time you probably picture me at home eating bon-bons and watching SoapNet TV don't you?) So, since we don't know yours – the best option is to go ahead with mine.

I hope we will find the time, because if we aren't able to spend a few days together before February it will certainly be a very interesting first date! Just think of me as a mail-order bride who can speak English!

10-08-2005 — **Why Everything is Just Fine ... And You?**
(from the secret journal "*LuvACowboy*")

what's wrong, he says.
why nothing, I say.
but I sense there's something, he says.
oh no, say I, everything is wonderful.

Because what difference would it make if I said I don't understand. I would just be repeating, like a broken record, the same doubts and asking the same questions. And the perfectly plausible logical reassuring answers would still be the same while I nodded and said um hum, but of course I understand. Because really – I should.

There are only a handful of my close personal friends who know about my relationship with Gabriel and I don't know anyone, anywhere (including his "friends" on *JournalLand*) who has met the real person. Because Gabriel is a secret to everyone, even me.

He says he fell in love with me, and I suppose it can happen like that. We email and talk every day. Each time we say I love you, click off the phone, and I wonder at all that was left unsaid during those daily hours of talking. The days and weeks pass, and I am not just tired of asking, I'm afraid to ask. And being afraid of doing something is not a good foundation for a relationship.

Every meeting we had planned has been canceled – always for perfectly good reasons, mind you. So I've hinted that I would come to him. In the nicest possible ways, he refuses. There is always a reason, always an excuse. No, I'm not seeing anyone else he assures me. No, I love you he proclaims. I want to spend the rest of my life with you he vows.

I don't think I've talked to him at home more than twice in four months. He's always driving, out, at a meeting, in a restaurant, at work.

"I want you to talk to my family, my friends, anyone you want" has never taken place. "I'll have everything handled by my attorney" but when I suggest sending the documents needed before February, it's "not yet." "I have a package to send you." Weeks later, I don't have it. Two Priority Mail packages I sent to his home address never arrived and were never returned to me.

"Get a phone on my mobile network so we can talk for free. I'll send you a check, I'll pay for it." I got the phone in August. I'm still waiting for the check and too embarrassed to ask.

He says he works in the Hollywood film industry and I'm interested in seeing his successes. Not once have I ever gotten an answer as to why his name does not appear in the credits of the shows and movies in which he supposedly appeared (and I've never recognized him either).

"I value my privacy." So he is not listed in the phone book, his name does not appear in his industry directories such as IMDb, nor is he credited in any public papers, documents, or places where such credits would normally appear.

Effectively, the internet is completely silent on his existence.

Lies, or lies of omission? I said I would trust him, and I've tried to stay positive and loving when we speak or write. But increasingly I am left to wonder are they truly lies, his attempt to protect me, or his attempt to protect himself. Does he love, or is he enamored with the idea of loving again.

After all, these kinds of relationships are rarely anything but fun filled, flirtatious, adventurous, and sexy affairs of the mind. They have nothing to do with what's real, do they?

Maybe, as a friend suggested, he simply wants or needs the chase. The endorphins released during the chase are a greater high than the reality can ever be. And he fears the fall.

10-10-2005 — Are You Willing to Come Up

Anna and Mr. Lucky had been dating for about five months when, one night, he asked her to make it an exclusive relationship. An interesting request, since she was quite aware he had not been exclusively dating HER. She, in return, had not been exclusively dating him.

"What, exactly," she asked, leaning back against his upraised legs and facing him, "do you mean by exclusive?"

He looked at her quizzically. "You don't sleep with other men."

Anna raised her eyebrows. "And ... " she prompted.

Confused, he simply repeated the question. "And?"

She waved her hand, as if to draw out his response. "And YOU don't ... " However, she could tell he still didn't get it. "And you don't sleep with other women. Isn't that what you meant to add?"

"Oh ... ummm ... yeah, at least not without you." In addition, he laughed heartily.

Two weeks after this pronouncement, Anna and Mr. Lucky had just returned from a particularly steamy date. They were still in the hot monkey love part of their relationship – he was chasing her, romancing her, taking her on great dates, and spending endless time with their love-making. They entered the house tearing off clothing and in the midst of the passion, the phone rang. He popped her off like a used champagne cork and ran for the phone.

"I've got to go," he said, as he began to dress. "Betsy thinks her house may have been broken into and she wants me to come over." With a perfunctory peck on the check, he was out the door. Anna stood there, arms crossed over her nude body, wondering WTF?

Ummm, let's see. Betsy lived forty minutes away and was one of the girls he had been dating regularly. She was also a Washington lobbyist with a huge number of local family, friends, and acquaintances she could have called after the police.

He came back home the next morning with the most practical of reasons. Seems she didn't feel safe and wanted him to stay with her overnight. Right. But Anna didn't want to appear jealous, or uncharitable towards an acquaintance (yes, she knew Betsy) so she chose to believe him, and forgive her.

Not long after, Mr. Lucky asked Anna to move in, using the most practical of reasons "It just makes sense, you can rent your house for the income to help pay the debts Paul left you, and save the long drive down here." So she moved.

And using the most practical of reasons, he placed ads in the *Personals* section of the newspaper and passed the caller to Anna to give the "girlfriend blessing."

He eventually took a mistress. He was not careful, and the discovery included learning that he had been bringing the woman to social and family events, introducing her as the woman he "was in love with."

Given an ultimatum, he left the mistress and begged forgiveness, but she could never trust him again. Love died but, for the most practical of reasons, she stayed with him.

Anna isn't looking for practical. She wants someone who's coming up.

> *When a guy is into you, he lets you know it ... he's coming up!!*
> ~~Greg Behrendt *He's Just Not That Into You* (6)

10-10-2005 — **Good night or morning to You**
Personal email to Anna from *Gabriel*

Did you read *OnTheRadio's* last entry in *JournalLand?* She mentions having a couple of friends that are in an Internet long distance relationship that is starting to show telltale signs of not working out. If she were speaking of us, I'd prefer she keep her comments to herself or do it in private emails.

10-10-2005 — **Rock On**
Personal email to *Gabriel* from Anna

As you know, *OnTheRadio* has had a couple of bad experiences with long distance relationships so her observations are probably general ones.

I do not share our conversations with anyone else, although with your permission I have occasionally quoted from your emails to me. Despite being asked constantly by *JournalLand* writers, no one knows the identity of my online lover.

In other matters, I now believe I have heard you correctly about your plans for our meeting one another. It has been delayed in order to have a safe, unhurried, romantic meeting.

I'm happy to have you in charge, but if you can give me an outline from time to time I think it would help me ask better questions and stop being concerned about things for which you have already formulated a plan. Does that make sense?

10-12-2005 — **Love is**
Personal email to Anna from *Gabriel*

Elizabeth said, "how do I love thee"
William said, "shall I compare thee to a summer's day"
Byron said, "s/he walks in beauty"
and Solomon said, "I am the rose of Sharon."
Maybe Fyodor said it better – that Love at the closing
of our days is a blend of joy
and of hopeless surrender. (Tyutchev)
I say simply, love is all there is,
and I am so grateful you are mine.

10-13-2005 — **An Everyday Mundane Entry (go St. Louis)**

This is an entry about nothing. (go Cards).

White Sox vs. Angels
Astros vs. Cardinals (go Cards)

Tonight on Fox

During the Jim Hart era of Cardinals football, I was a very knowledgeable water cooler Monday morning quarterback. The rivalry between the Cards, Cowboys, and Redskins made every season worthwhile.

Then the owner absconded with the team to Phoenix. (go Cards)

Baseball was a favorite, but not in an "I know every player and their number and their statistics and all the history of the teams" kind of way. But I got season tickets for the last year the Orioles were in the old Baltimore stadium and have kept them for 10 years. God I love the sounds, smells, and fervor of summer baseball games! (go Cards)

So Gabriel, you know I love you with all my heart and will always support you in everything, even to cheering loudly for your hometown Los Angeles favorite hockey, soccer, football (as long as they aren't playing the Cowboys), and basketball teams but (sorry)
GO CARDS!!!

163

10-13-2005 — **Nighty Night**
Personal email to *Gabriel* from Anna

We are 10 minutes short of 50 hours on the phone since August 29. We have so much in common and yet so much not. But it's enough.

10-15-2005 — **Wheeeeeeeeeee!**

> *Runaway Mine Train was built for Six Flags Texas in 1966, and copied for Six Flags St. Louis in 1971 making history as the world's first tubular, steel track, full circuit, multiple car roller coaster. The ride consists of 2,484 feet of track broken between three lifts, the highest of which is 35 feet. The top speed of the ride is 26 mph.*

In 1979, when Morgan was 10, I chaperoned her Girl Scout troop to Six Flags St. Louis. One of the favorite rides was a roller coaster called **The Runaway Mine Train**, mostly because it had a water element and the lines weren't as long as the newly built **Screamin' Eagle**. We stood in line for it over, and over, and over again. Begging for the front seat, then the last seat, then the middle seat in order to experience it from all dimensions.

Now by "we" I mean everyone else. "We" does not mean "me." There was no possible way anyone was going to get me on a machine that went up, up, up — then down, down, down — really fast.

Morgan had a different idea. "Mom. Dad says you are too scared to go on this ride. I'm going and I'm only ten." Crap.

Wow, if mom is afraid of heights / roller coasters / the dark / clowns / the old guy down the street with the chainsaw, then I should be too, right?

You guessed it. I went on **The Runaway Mine Train** and it ran away with me. Paramedics from the aide station size panic attack. Morgan looked at me in disdain and never asked me to join her again on the million or so roller coasters she rode during the rest of her childhood.

The Monday after a big dance competition on Thanksgiving Weekend in 1986, I went to Disneyland with a large group of dance friends.

It was immediately apparent that many (ok, MOST) of the best rides in the park were roller coasters. In front of **Space Mountain**, and faced with the prospect of explaining why I was chicken to people who had just seen me compete fearlessly before 1000 strangers, I decided to conquer a 36 year old fear. I walked through the door.

OH MY GOD! For twelve straight hours we – and by "we" I mean "ME" – went on every ride in the park. Multiple times. Because of the holiday, sometimes there were so few people in line you could get off and get right back on again. I don't think I have ever had more fun out of bed.

Ok, maybe I did. In 1999, I spent the day at Busch Gardens, Williamsburg, VA. **Apollo's Chariot** had just opened. WHEEEEEEEEEEEEEEE!!

> *Apollo's Chariot is Busch Gardens Williamsburg's thrilling hypercoaster designed to reach great height and super speeds. The pulse-quickening journey plummets passengers a total of 825 feet, with 4.1 G turns. Continually voted "a top ten steel roller coaster," Apollo's Chariot is over 220 feet tall, has 4,882 feet of track, and boasts nine drops – the first of which plunges passengers down 210 feet of steel track. You will experience periods of up to 26 seconds of weightlessness, or "air time," as you race up and down the camelback humps at 73 mph.*

10-16-2005 — **Good Night Honey**
Personal email to Anna from *Gabriel*

I called a couple of times today but you weren't available, I missed hearing your sweet voice. I'm at my Dad's ranch again and by tomorrow evening we will have a plan regarding the homestead cleanup in New Orleans. I will dream of you.

10-16-2005 — **Another moon**
Personal email to *Gabriel* from Anna

> another moon races her way across the sky
> like a gaudy silver whore
> the fifth since you and i considered us
> and who knows the number before
> we shared the sight together
> you and i

I feel you everywhere, imagined reality,
there is a pain inside my bones
i can't grab hold of it, this longing
for so much more than the phone
even my skin hurts with the desire of
you and me.

10-18-2005 — Topsy Turvy, Inside Out and Upside Down
(from the secret journal "*LuvACowboy*")

He flirted and teased, made me laugh, turned my life upside down. My heart pounded waiting for the next call, the next email.

I began to trust him, to feel safe enough to tell him some of the not-so-great things — the testing things. Sometimes there were tears, but there were love letters, too, to ease the heart pounding of waiting.

Then there was an I love you and then everything went topsy-turvy. Two other women came into his life that just won't go away. They will each see him long before I will.

They took away the man I fell in love with and I want him back. My heart is waiting. Damn you Katrina, damn you Rita. I want him back.

10-18-2005 — Thanksgiving Schedule
Personal email to *Gabriel* from Anna

I have my flights booked for Phoenix. *sigh* Holiday Rip-off on fares. We'll make the drive from Phoenix in time for Thanksgiving dinner with *Randi's* family and be in San Diego all day Friday and Saturday, driving back to Phoenix on Sunday. What fun to meet my journaling counterparts in person!

And you want to meet me there! I'm so excited and keeping my fingers crossed you can make it! (of course, you know it means there will be a few *JournalLand* folks who will find out who "we" are)

I haven't stopped thinking of our conversation yesterday about your plans for the actual "move" in February wherein you show up with a moving truck and crew, pack me up, and off we go. I'm so excited about driving cross-country with you! Well, assuming we don't kill each other being stuck in a car for 40 hours over 2682.10 miles! (of course, the "breaks" will be the fun part won't they, the first one occurring approximately 2.10 miles away from my house when we stop and neck – then another 2.10 miles down the road when we stop at the closest motel!)

Then showing you St. Louis, and my little hometown, me seeing yours, introducing each other to relatives across the country. I am already looking forward to it!

I just realized calls from New Orleans might be hard without SAT phones – but I'm sure we will make do somehow.

10-19-2005 — **Now, Now, NOW**

> *Time and tide wait for no man. A pompous and self-satisfied proverb, and was true for a billion years; but in our day of electric wires and water-ballast we turn it around: Man waits not for time nor tide.*
> ~~Mark Twain (206)

We live in the NOW generation. Not "in a minute," not "as soon as I have time," not "just let me finish this" and certainly not "can I call you back?" It's RIGHT NOW.

I'm a baby boomer, one of the children born in the few years after World War II. It occurred to me today, as I was waiting for a call, that I have been infected with the same impatience as the Gen-X, Gen-Y, and whatever the heck the others are called.

When I was young, there were two ways to communicate. Type a letter on a non-electric typewriter (sometimes with a sheet of carbon paper between the letterhead and copy) or sit at a table and pull out your stationery. Then address the envelope, put on a stamp, walk it to the mailbox, and wait for a reply that might take a week, or even two.

The second was to pick up the telephone. However, if the call was to someone outside of your city it was expensive, and early in my life you had to go through an operator to make the call. There were no "800" numbers, heck, there weren't even area codes. My mother's phone book was filled with phone numbers that started with words – like "Metro3 6789"

When I began working, the typewriters were electric, there were zip codes for the addresses, and the telephone numbers had area codes. Personal letters were still sent, but not as often, and hardly ever by children unless forced to thank dear Aunt Martha for the birthday gift. Business letters still depended on paper duplicates because few businesses had things called Copiers, but we didn't have time to wait for return letters anyway. We picked up the telephone to conduct our business and if our party was out, we knew their secretary would write up a message slip to call us back the next day.

Fast forward a few years ... we duplicated the few letters we typed with the copier and put them in the new fax to send. Within seconds, they were on the other person's desk. Answering machines that could be accessed remotely took our messages. The expected response time to a letter or phone call dropped to same day.

Within milliseconds (as the Calendar of Time goes), there were computers, cell phones, and instant messaging. We expect responses within minutes, and immediate access via phone and text.

I have become a Baby Boomer member of the NOW generation. I don't save my allowance for six months to buy a new toy. I pull out plastic and pay for it six months later. I am impatient for a call, bewildered by the lack of response to an email, indignant when a message left on a cell phone is not returned within an hour. I despise being put on hold and apoplectic when I hear "press 1 for Parts, press 2 for Accounting," punching 0 repeatedly so a real person can give me the answer I want NOW.

Sometimes I feel the same way about life. Irrational as it sounds, I find myself expecting the same thing from my friends as I do my clients. I know the right thing to do is to take time, look around, relax, let things progress slowly and surely to the pre-destined end. Start at page one, savor the words, revel in the imagery, get caught up in the story as the characters reveal themselves little by little until, when you turn the last page of the last chapter, you cannot bear for the story to be over.

But there is this constant temptation to peek. To find out whodunit, is there a happy ending, does our hero win the girl, does she live happy forever after.

Don't you sometimes wish there was an IM service for happy endings.

Half our life is spent trying to find something to do with the time we have rushed through life trying to save.

~~Will Rogers (226)

10-20-2005 — **Now Wilma??**
Personal email to Anna from *Gabriel*

It was weird only talking to you once on a weekday. Maybe more tomorrow. I just talked with my Dad and everyone has their fingers crossed. Wilma could end up the biggest killer of all. I've also had some pretty nasty earthquake dreams ... maybe that's why I'm not feeling rested in the mornings. I had a couple of members of my writing group tell me today I'm looking rather pale and when I looked in the Mirror – I am.

I'm looking forward to seeing you soon. I'm dying to taste one of your kisses, feel your skin, gaze into to your big baby blues, and smell the sweetness of your hair. Can you tell I missed you today? I put one of your photos up in our writing group's makeshift office and everyone commented how pretty you look. I love you.

10-21-2005 — **Hello Mr. Bitchin'**
Personal email to *Gabriel* from Anna

Can you take some time off this weekend and have fun, get some rest, before the drive to New Orleans?

You didn't say – but I'm guessing you left your stuff in storage since you plan on being in New Orleans for several weeks.

Sounds like you are having another hellacious day with the writing group. You didn't say what time you got there, but looks like a long one. And what was that little hint you dropped about getting me to write? Harrumph. While I think the compliment was adorable, I doubt anything I write would interest more than you and a handful of *JournalLand*ers. Although it would be fun to write a story with you – it would keep us both laughing, that's for sure.

10-23-2005 — **I just wish**
Personal email to Anna from *Gabriel*

I just wish we'd finally open up and talk, this silence between us is killing me! My goodness – 2 phone calls: First, 2 hours 38 minutes. Second, 1 hour 18 minutes. Did you realize we actually discussed the California Alligator Lizard? In Detail no less! For tomorrow's topic, I am considering the effects of salt on the digestive tract of the common French/California Snail.

Did you know that said snail was imported from France to New York, and then sent to California as the yummy delicacy "Escargot" for the newly rich 49ers of the Gold Rush era? Unfortunately, the snails were set loose in the SF area and they multiplied, migrating throughout California. Then something odd occurred – instead of having a ready supply of Escargot, restaurateurs turned up their noses to the now common garden snail, continuing to import them from France even though they're the same exact snail!

Well, Honey got to get back to work so I can eventually go home lol. I love you Sweetheart. Sweet dreams.

10-23-2005 — **This Is My First Time**

It's been two years since Carol Channing's (85) December-December marriage to Harry Kullijian (86). Harry was her Junior High School sweetheart and Channing is still as giddy as a sophomore when she talks about the relationship. "I didn't realize at the time how rare it is to have such harmony," she says of her fourth husband. "I consider this my first marriage." On the *Martha Stewart Show* yesterday, she whispered, "Who could have imagined I could have found my soul mate after all this time."

We all look for that storybook happilyforeverafter romance. Women seek their perfect hero, knowing beforehand what our dream guy will be like when he appears. Mine has been the charming bad boy with a heart of gold – think Rhett Butler, or Errol Flynn, or Bruce Willis, with a side helping of Prince Charming.

For many years, I thought Ben was The One. And as we came back to one another time after time, it seemed proof indeed, even with that shoe constantly dangling above my head. Every time I made excuses about why it didn't work. It was me, it was him, we just needed time, space, understanding. He wanted to work through his issues; I wanted to give him the chance to do it. He could not let me go and I was unable to leave.

Sleeping Beauty woke up from her self-induced dreamland when reality slapped her in the face. Ben was not The One and I could sit around allowing Fate to write my life story, or I could start rewriting it myself. I deserved to be loved and loved properly. Just "settling" was not going to be the last chapter of my book.

What if I had never looked up whatever it was on Internet Explorer that led me to *JournalLand*? What if I had allowed Fate, or Ben, or Jason, or the years with Mr. Lucky to crush the little girl inside me so badly she could no longer stand up and shout "I BELIEVE"?

In our five months together, I know Gabriel better than I knew Ben after five years. But no matter how much Gabriel gives to me, I still think something is going to go wrong – because something always goes wrong.

We talked for a long time today – twice. Much longer than he should have with six people waiting for him to be in a meeting with them. In the midst of it all, he said, "I've tried not to ask for more than you were ready to give."

Maybe my questions are just the result of an overactive imagination.

10-24-2005 — Still unf*kd – are you listening God?

Yesterday morning, being Sunday and all, seemed to Mr. Lucky an appropriate time to attempt getting lucky. Rats.

Round One.
"Come over here so we can have some sex."
(I'm sorry, where did that "we" come from?")

Round Two.
"You wanna be on top or bottom?"
(Hey, at least he asked. But do I look stupid to you? Ya can't hide the distaste while on top.)

Round Three.

Sixty seconds later "OH GOD!"

(What's God got to do with it? If there was a God I would be anywhere else getting properly f*cked.)

Round Four.

"So, what's for breakfast?"

PS: I am so f*cking UNF*KD!!

10-24-2005 — **Interesting Facts**

Personal email to *Gabriel* from Anna

Did you know that 111, 111, 111 X 111, 111, 111 = 12,345,678,987,654,321

And did you know that nutmeg, injected intravenously, is a deadly poison? One of those factoids you pick up surfing the internet for … (shit, did I just say that out loud?)

10-26-2005 — **The one about groceries**

> *M'm! M'm! Good! M'm! M'm! Good!*
> ~~Campbell's Soup

Grocery shopping at my house is an interesting experience. In general, Mr. Lucky and I feed ourselves. No, really. He gets up at oh dark thirty every morning and does his thing. I get up with the rest of humanity, and do mine.

I work from home – so lunch is what I make. He eats oatmeal at the office. He once read it was good for you and anything that is good for you must be eaten daily. And if once daily is good, then two or three or four times must be better. Like dried breakfast cereal. Breakfast, mid-morning snack, after work snack and, usually, before bedtime snack. With dinner, I cook something yummy.

Me: I'm making dinner, do you want any.

Mr. Lucky: No

Me: *thinking* *goody, enough for dinner tomorrow night too.*

Me: *coming back to the kitchen to put away the leftovers* Um, where are the leftovers?

Mr. Lucky: I ate them. I didn't think you wanted any more.
Me:

Whether it is his monotonous, or my somewhat more varied, diet it requires groceries shopping to fulfill their destiny. And our shopping styles are as divergent as our diets.

Me: Drive to the closest market with a list of groceries needed to replenish the stock already consumed from the large pantry and refrigerator.

Mr. Lucky:
Step 1: circle all extra low price specials in grocery store flyers from Sunday paper.
Step 2: gather coupons and circulars, and then drive to every store in the tri-state area to buy items circled. List? I don't do no stinkin' list!
Step 3: it doesn't matter if either of us actually use the item, or need the item, buy it anyway because it's on SALE. Milk? Not on sale? Don't need it.
Step 4: the better the sale, the more you need of it. If two is good, ten is better, and if it comes in a case for five cents less ... WOOT!

When he married his second wife, she came with a dog. *(get your mind out of the gutter)*. Mr. Lucky bought a skid of bagged dog food because it was a great sale (and free delivery). They couldn't park the car in the garage for almost fourteen months. The dog food lasted almost as long as the marriage.

And the classic? In 1977, his nine year old son liked a dish using mushroom soup. Mr. Lucky bought mushroom soup. In 1993, when I moved in, I began to give away mushroom soup. To Boy Scout food drives. To Food Bank Canned Goods drives at Christmas. To the kids at Halloween (kidding ... sorta). In 2001, when we moved into the new house, I was able to sneak most of the rest into the recycling without him seeing me. This morning, I reverently placed the last three cans into the trash bin just before it was picked up. Whew.

11-01-2005 — **What I Heard**
(from the secret journal "*LuvACowboy*")

... he asked me what i did today.

oh, said i, i've been making lists. so i won't forget anything. like needing to get a

173

forwarding address, arranging to get doctor's records, making sure my prescriptions have enough refills, and that annual bills due early in the year are prepaid so they won't get lost in the move.

oh, said he, with an odd voice. it's a little early don't you think. after all, we haven't even met – things could change. *Huh???*

and i changed the subject so we could discuss general likes and dislikes, home decorating, company dinners, and matters that had no sense of romance or passion or moonlit nights and starry skies.

well, said he, perhaps we should have more of these conversations.

i think maybe i'm expecting too much storybook romance and should be satisfied with the everyday expressions of love on the phone, because the daily emails have become much less daily.

11-02-2005   **That Time of Year Again**

> *All it takes is faith and trust ... and a little bit of pixie dust!*
> ~~Peter Pan

It's that time of year again. Maybe it's the thoughts of the impending holidays. Maybe it's the smell of fall in the air, or the sounds of the rustling leaves as the wind whips them across the street, or the Christmas spirit that is already finding its way into the stores and radio stations.

It's the time of year when I would pick up the phone to hear Ben's voice ask the same question. Last night when he called, as I knew he would, I reminded him my heart is no longer his. It was easy, because it was the absolute truth.

Our relationship over the years was the stuff of bestsellers, and tragic poets. The sensitive, sensual quality of his mind and body made it simple to get lost in the physical desires of thirty years of mutual history. So when he called each year to ask again, it was the ultimate satisfaction for the woman he left years ago.

I would listen to the promises and leave full of hope. For a while, the loving, romantic, yearning emails would be there every single morning – sometimes two or three times a day. Sometimes when I was alone at night, he would call to whisper sweet nothings in my ear, making dreams and plans of our future, trying out our together forever.

But as the months passed the emails would get fewer; the subject matter more mundane, dwelling more on the whatif differences than things in common. As his fears grew, the letters would stop and the calls would go unanswered. Ben was always trying to make the perfect choice, rejecting what he had for what he hoped to find, betting the present on the future, and ending up missing both.

This year, Thanksgiving begins a new tradition. This year *OnTheRadio* and I are taking a road trip to *Poppygirl*'s house to see her piratey Peter Pan play. And Gabriel has confirmed he will definitely meet me there. Thank you, journal, for helping us to find one another, forever and always.

> *I believe in magic*
> *Just on faith alone*
> ~~Mary Moeller, "I Believe In Magic"

11-04-2005 — **Random natterings from a cluttered mind**

1. Where was your first real kiss? Late on beautiful summer day, I found myself on a porch swing with a somewhat older boy. He kissed me – a real kiss, and it was a lovely well-done French kiss.

2. Have you ever hit someone of the opposite sex? Does S&M count?

3. What is your biggest mistake? Oh my gosh, where to start. Life would have been so different if I hadn't married my first husband. Then again, I wouldn't be where I am now. And if I'd just toughed it out after breaking up with my first true love, instead of running away to another city, I'd never have met … well, everyone has those stories. Funny – my biggest mistakes have always had to do with relationships. Sometimes I wished there was a vaccination against falling in love. It has been my life's greatest tragedy.

4. Have you ever hurt yourself on purpose? Physically? No. Even getting my ears pierced was thrust upon me.

5. Did you have braces? Begged. Pleaded. Went to an orthodontist who swore I'd grow into my teeth. I hid my smile behind my hand most of my childhood and have noticed I'm doing it again.

6. What is the most romantic thing someone of the opposite sex has done for you? Remembered important dates. My birthday. Valentine's Day. The anniversary of our first date. Because it takes effort on their part to remember these things and do something about them.

7. When do you know it's love? When I don't feel like I have to run into the bathroom and put on makeup before he wakes up. When it's ok to disagree. When it's more important to stay, even when it's hard, than to leave. When he knows why I'm crying.

8. Can you dance? I can couple dance extremely well – Hustle, Swing, Lindy, West Coast (well, all the swing styles actually), Cha-Cha, Rhumba, Fox Trot, Waltz. Free style club dancing? Imagine Woody Allen dancing to "Smoke on the Water." yeah, it's that bad.

9. What's the latest you have ever stayed up? One time, 48 hours straight. I was hallucinating by the end. (oh, never mind, that was at the beginning … and the middle … and …)

10. Have you ever been rushed by an ambulance into the emergency room? Just once. By the time I got there, I was dead. No, really. And there was no going towards the light either. Sure hope heaven, as the Jewish religion suggests, is what we make of life here on earth.

11-06-2005 — **He Just Called to Say I Love You**
(from the secret journal "*LuvACowboy*")

"hi sweetheart. i had this overwhelming urge to call you and tell you i love you and how much i missed you today. i know you're probably sleeping by now, so this message is to let you to know how much you mean to me. Bye."

11-09-2005 — **Joe vs. the Volcano or Close Your Eyes and Jump**

I watched *Joe Versus the Volcano* last night. A sweet little movie with Tom Hanks as a man convinced he is dying of a terminal illness. He is paid by a wealthy man to throw himself into a volcano, and while enjoying his last few weeks of life, he meets Meg Ryan who falls in love with him.

As Joe walks to the edge of the volcano, determined to carry through his responsibility, Meg Ryan joins him. She twines her fingers in his, looks into his eyes, and says, "Nobody knows anything, Joe. We'll take this leap and we'll see. We'll jump and we'll see. That's life, right?" And they jump off the cliff together.

Life has been good to me. No, really. Things could have been much worse. Fortunately, I was born with a strong soul, a sharp mind, and a self-renewing heart that finds a way to mend itself each time it gets broken. Maybe my past lives mean it takes longer, but those lives, and tears, and bleeding, make me begin again, hope again, and give me every day courage.

I believe that when two people, separated by thousands of miles and a lifetime of U-turns, find each other in the same place, at the same time, it's no coincidence. I attach some great cosmic meaning to this, although I don't know what it is. It seemed we both pressed SEND at the same instant.

And I believe unconditional love is a rare gift and I don't ever remember seeing it before. I believe that faith, hope, and trust are inextricably intertwined and are what will allow me to take his hand and jump off that cliff on February 12 – the Twelfth of Never.

11-11-2005 — **101 Things You Know You Want To Know**

1. I was born in the evening.
2. I was the first living child of my parents who had lost several before me, including one that was born dead. Her name was Carolyn. I have no idea where she was buried.
3. I had chicken pox when I was 6 months old. My mother force-fed me water and I have never been able to tolerate the taste of tap water.
4. Two years ago, I found Fiji water and for the first time – I drink water! (is it the taste or the square bottles?)
5. I have one sister, 21 months younger, and we are complete and absolute opposites in looks, demeanor, and attitude. We haven't spoken for over fifteen years because, she says, I was mean to her as a child.
6. When I was twelve, I beat up the son of the local sheriff for picking on my sister. He wore a cape and thought he was Superman.
7. Every time I go in the woods I get poison ivy, but I still go in the woods.
8. My parents sent me to Red Cross swimming lessons at the local pool when I was five. I was afraid to put my head in the water.
9. As a teenager, I was on the summer swim team. Three years in a row I swam 100 miles during practices. That's 3200 lengths of the pool.
10. Getting dirty was forbidden when I was a child.
11. I have never broken a bone – but I had to wear bedroom slippers to my Confirmation because I cracked my little toe against a bookcase.
12. Four weeks after I began working on this entry, I broke my big toe. Karma?
13. I am an atheist, but believe all living things have a recycled life essence.
14. I do not like hotdogs, and never have.

15. I hated steak until I was twenty years old and was introduced to the concept of "rare," "broiled," and Filet Mignon.

16. When my daughter was thirteen, I dated a guy who didn't eat red meat. She has not eaten red meat since.

17. I love to play cards. Hearts, Spades, Pinochle, Canasta, Gin, Hand and Foot. And I usually win.

18. I like to win at everything, but I won't cheat.

19. I do not know how to play Poker.

20. In the winter, I drink a lot of tea, with cream and sugar, like the Europeans.

21. Indian Chai Latte, discovered during my trips there, is now my favorite and the easiest to prepare can be found on the *Serious Chai* website.

22. I'm afraid of heights, but do it anyway.

23. Another girl bullied me in grade school. She finally stopped when I fought back, threw her on the ground, got her in a leg lock, and pulled out her hair. She admitted later that she believed nobody liked her. Gee, ya wonder why!

24. My best friend in grade school was a boy. I caught cold easily and did not go outside for recess. We played chess instead, starting in 2nd Grade.

25. Thinking back on him – I think he was gay, but he has never come to a class reunion so I've never seen him since. (while writing this book I found his obituary. He died of cancer in 2008 – an unmarried well-loved singer, choral director, and supporter of the arts)

26. I have never felt funny around gay men or women.

27. I love ice cream, but rarely eat it in the winter.

28. I chill easily and carry a sweater or jacket with me at all times for restaurants, stores, and other overly air-conditioned environments.

29. My dream is to live on a beach and never have to spend a winter in the cold again.

30. I've always needed living space and even when I was dirt poor never lived in less than a two-bedroom apartment.

31. Buying a home on my own convinced me I was a grown-up.

32. I've always been extremely good at accounting – and lousy at math.

33. I could read before I was in kindergarten, but nobody taught me.

34. The first book I remember reading was a Reader's Digest.

35. I read most of Ian Fleming's "James Bond" books in their original release.

36. I adore Isaac Asimov and Robert Heinlein, Anne McCaffrey and Laura Joh-Rowland, Edgar Rice Burroughs, Jasper Fforde and Peter David.

37. I want to live long enough to witness the first contact with alien life forms. What a hoot it will be to prove we should have kept up the space program.

38. I love St. Louis style pizza – which uses a special cheese called "Provel," a

unique blend of Cheddar, Swiss, and Provolone cheeses. You can't get it anywhere else in the world.

39. Rigazzi's is the best Italian restaurant on "The Hill," no matter what anyone else says. Who doesn't like deep fried ravioli?

40. The 1975 St. Louis Cardinal football team, known as the "Cardiac Cards" was a thing of beauty. Jim Hart passed 2500 yards, Mel Gray and Terry Metcalf ran for almost 1000 yards and 11 touchdowns each, and eight members made the Pro-Bowl. Washington Redskins suck.

41. I lost my virginity at 15.

42. Everyone thought I was going to finish high school, go to college, and marry the boy I went steady with for three years in high school.

43. I knew my first husband for six weeks.

44. Marty Robbins was singing "A White Sport Coat" when my daughter was conceived in my soon-to-be-husband-but-we-didn't-know-it-then mother's bedroom and I missed my high school graduation.

45. I decided I wanted to go bowling when I was seven months pregnant, pulled a groin muscle, and was on crutches for two weeks. When I was 43, I was on crutches again for three months. I used the same crutches.

46. The first car I ever owned was a 1962 "titty pink" Ford Galaxy 500. My boyfriend bought it for me in 1972 because he was tired of driving into the city to pick me up for the weekends at his place.

47. We used to go to the A&W root beer stand when I was a kid, and you had to wait forever for a carhop to bring us large mugs of root beer and "push-ups" which were like Italian ice in a wrapper.

48. As a teenager, I worked as one of those carhops – and met my high school sweetheart.

49. I've worked as a ward clerk in a hospital, a secretary, a personal assistant, an office manager, a regional office manager, an insurance salesman, and a computer consultant. I also sold sex toys at home parties for four years.

50. I've only fainted once.

51. I've been knocked out twice – once by a man because I came between his fist and his intended target, and once by a woman who kicked me in the head with a well-placed savat kick when she thought I was trying to mess with her husband (I wasn't, he was – she should have kicked HIM).

52. Nudity didn't stop embarrassing me until I was in my 20's.

53. I've been married three times, but just once I'd like to be married for real. Not because I have to, or because it's responsible, or because it's convenient.

54. I've never had a real wedding.

55. I'd like to work because I want to. Not because I have to, or because the

boyfriend/husband lays a guilt trip on me for wanting to try something else, or because if I don't pay half the household expenses he'll kick me out.

56. I used to fall in love easily.

57. I don't fall out of love easily, but hold the feelings long after the relationship is gone.

58. When the feelings are finally gone … they're gone. I never look back.

59. Mutual respect is the #1 item on my list of gotta haves.

60. I love the taste of raw potatoes and salt, Hi-Ho crackers with peanut butter and grape jelly, and fresh strawberries with amaretto and cream.

61. The color blue is my favorite, but my home is buttercream, warm browns, apricot, aubergine, gold, and khaki.

62. If there's a fireplace, I want a fire.

63. If there's a candle, I want it lit.

64. I own Waterford crystal glasses and use them even when company isn't coming over.

65. I've been to the Caribbean, the Bahamas, Hawaii, most of the states, Ireland, Scotland, England, France, Belgium, Amsterdam, and India.

66. I want to go to Italy, Greece, the south of France, and see the Egyptian pyramids.

67. When I travel, I want to experience the history and culture first hand.

68. I could spend a week in the Louvre – every year.

69. Years ago, even when I couldn't afford it, I bought season tickets to the theater because it made sure I would go. Now I have tickets at The Kennedy.

70. The first play I remember seeing was *Cinderella* at The Muny, the outdoor theater in St. Louis. They brought a real carriage and four white horses onto the stage.

71. The first grown-up play I saw was *Marat/Sade* with Jason.

72. Chanel No. 5, Aliage, and Georgio were my preferred scents, but Mr. Lucky is allergic to scent so I put them away.

73. Give me tiger lilies, daisies, mums, or daffodils over roses.

74. Weeping willow trees make me nostalgic – there was a huge one in the back yard of the house I grew up in.

75. I lived eighteen years in the same house as a child, and then moved twenty-two times in the next twenty-five.

76. Having the courage to walk away from a relationship that had been over a long time made me realize I was ready to fall in love again.

77. When I was sixteen, a dog bit me in the face. I still have scars on my upper and lower lip. I sometimes wonder what people think it is.

78. I don't like hot, spicy food.

79. Cats are better than dogs, but both of them can sleep with me at night.

80. I'd rather sleep with the windows open than the air conditioner.

81. My mother believed her children should try everything at least once. Thus, I had tap and ballet lessons as a child. And trampoline, bowling, archery, piano, flute, guitar, swimming, tennis, roller skating, and a year at a "modeling" school that taught me how to get out of a car without showing my woo-hoo.

82. I sat first chair in the high school band playing my flute.

83. I've been without a piano for so long my hands have lost their coordination for difficult pieces, but I can still read music and play a little.

84. My guitar is in a corner and most of its strings are broken – but I keep thinking someday I will have time to pick it up again.

85. I've always wished I had the partner support to work full-time as a volunteer for worthy causes. I am legitimately good on committees.

86. When my mother died, I didn't cry.

87. When my father died, I couldn't stop crying.

88. Someday I'm going to write a novel.

89. I still want to go to college.

90. I haven't figured out if it's better to know a little about a lot of things, or a lot about a few things.

91. I started biting my fingernails when I was ten and saw my cousin do it. I stopped several years later when, on the first day of school, I noticed that a girl I disliked had stopped biting hers and she had beautiful hands.

92. I smoked cigarettes from the time I was 15 until I was 34. Morgan asked me to stop for her birthday gift and I went cold turkey.

93. I can't stand the smell of cigarette smoke.

94. I eat to live, not live to eat. But I absolutely love the taste and texture of food.

95. I am never warm enough in the winter, usually because I've never been able to afford to keep the thermostat at a comfortable setting.

96. Given a chance, I'd climb on a motorcycle and go riding.

97. I'd rather go sailing than do almost anything.

98. I've gotten more awards and compliments for my swing dancing than anything I've ever tried.

99. A kiss is one of life's greatest pleasures.

100. An unexpected compliment is a close second.

101. I know it's better to have loved and lost, than never to have loved at all.

11-13-2005 — **Good night my dear**
Personal email to *Gabriel* from Anna

thank goodness there is cellular coverage in New Orleans, even if no internet. i wonder if there will be anything left to talk about in February, or shall we spend the entire two weeks staying up all night making love and sleeping all day. and if we do, how will we ever get there?

just ten more days and your virtual arms will be around me for real. i love you.

11-16-2005 — **Junk Mail Isn't Always Junk**

Since I use a Safe List for my incoming Hotmail account, I have to check the Junk Mail folder daily for Junk Mail I actually want – Junk Mail I want, there's a non sequitur if ever I wrote one.

A few days ago, I got a Junk Mail and was compelled to answer, even if my answer never finds its way out of the Junk Mail jungle that is theirs. In the interests of, well, the interested, I present a part of it for your thoughts.

Hi Anna
This is something of a random note and, even were you to reply, I don't know if I would actually reply back to you.

The long and the short of it is that I have found "The One." But of course, I am married, she is married, and we both love our spouses and our kids, and from the get-go there were never any expectations to do anything but love the other.

The other day, she told me that she just wanted us to be friends. She says that her feelings for me haven't changed, but that she can't act on them, or speak of them, because it's too much for her to take. Pulled in too many directions by too many people, and so shutting it down.

I guess it's just a catharsis to tell someone random, someone who doesn't know me, doesn't know my One, doesn't know anything about our situation, and yet, I think, knows it remarkably well. I had toyed with emailing you, and then decided not to, but after reading your entry *Joe Versus the Volcano* tonight, decided to email you after all because you said:

"I believe there's no such thing as coincidence. That when two people separated by thousands of miles, and a lifetime of U-turns, find each other in the same place, at the same time, it's no coincidence. I attach some great cosmic meaning to this although I don't know what it is. It seemed we both pressed SEND at the same instant."

    X

Dear X,

For almost thirty years I believed I had found The One, my one True Love.

When we parted, the first time, I could not forget him. I locked him away inside a special box, imprinted with a message "In Case of Emergency, Break Glass" and we pretended life was normal.

But each time an emergency presented itself – his or mine – we would break the glass and try again. And fail again.

I was in love with a dream of coulda, shoulda, woulda. He may have been The One once, but in the end, he was a dream of Yesterday's Someday.

I believe when you find The One you will not let anything stop you from being with them. You will find a way around every obstacle. You will be willing to sacrifice everything but integrity. I believe True Love is as much Trust as Commitment, and as much Total Acceptance as Unconditional Grace.

Maybe she is The One, or maybe she only embodies what you dream of finding in The One. Whichever it is, she has given you a rare opportunity and a loving gift by releasing you to find The One who wants you as much as you want them.

You said you love your wife and, despite that, you found The One who, I assume, you also love. I believe it is possible to love two people at the same time for different reasons and in different ways. But I do not believe it is possible to love The One and any other. And I believe that when you find the one True One they will love you with a passion and commitment equal to your own, and I wish I had realized this years ago.

11-19-2005 — **I'd Be Better Off Naked**

Beauty is all very well at first sight; but whoever looks at it when it has been in the house three days?
~~George Bernard Shaw (116)

Hello darlings … it's a girl thingy time. Really.

I'm five days away from meeting the love of my life face to face for the first time after at least three re-schedules, and spending my time worried about the silliest things in the world.

What the heck should I wear? I want to appear pretty, and appealing, and … well … appetizing! So I don't think my standard 501's, t-shirt, and a sweater (hello, I'm ALWAYS cold) look like any of those things. Of course, now that I think about it – isn't it usually the MALE animal flaunting the brightest feathers?

But what if he doesn't like the fact that my knees are ugly and have a scar on them from falling down off my bicycle when I was twelve? And there's that dog bite on my face …

Or that my hands don't look like they are 35 anymore? Not that they ever did – they take after my father's hands with the crookedly little finger and all.

Or that I have to wear glasses to read a menu, map, or computer screen. I'm safe for everything unless it's close!

Or that I don't wear long pretty girly nails on the ends of my fingers. They use routers, and table saws, and hammers, and tend to break.

Or that every single time I eat ice cream, I sniffle? Ok, pretty much every time I eat anything cold. Or spicy. Or hot.

Or that I sometimes get scared about the silliest things, whereby I need a serious hug, and take on other people's worries too often, whereby I need another serious hug … and a kiss … and a little feel (oops, did I say that out loud?)

Or that I volunteer constantly, thereby keeping me exceedingly busy doing things having nothing to do with defeating the Republicans, finding a cure for cancer, supporting animal rights, fighting for a Pro-Choice court, creating World Peace or learning to paint.

sigh Of course he said he doesn't love me for my hair, or my clothes, or whether or not I need glasses to read. He can tolerate my toes, even if they are extremely odd. He knows my age, so that won't be any surprise – and he's seen pictures. He insists I wear something that is comfortable and "me" cause he's not a dress-up kinda guy and wants me in my native plumage (or was that Naked plumage?)

But the knees are a deal-breaker.

> *The lover knows much more about absolute good and universal beauty than any logician or theologian, unless the latter, too, be lovers in disguise.*
> ~~ George Santayana (151)

11-21-2005 — Theory of Everything

Having spoken about my odd toes from time to time in this space, I thought I would continue the scientific inquiry.

Stumbling into the kitchen one evening this summer I caught the edge of the grout line in the tile and pop – my big toe stayed behind while the rest of the foot went forward. It was forty-five days before I could walk without a slight limp and get back on the treadmill.

I bring this up because it is amazing what gravity can do to one's body after thirty plus days. Yes, yes, yes, I know I'm slender. It shouldn't make that much difference, but honey – it's GRAVITY. Lest we forget our basic physics, the four fundamental forces in the Universe affect matter:

1. gravitation
2. electromagnetic
3. strong nuclear
4. weak nuclear

Now, in a delightful scientific segue from the increase of my mass and the effect upon it of a fundamental force, I move on to something that Gabriel and I have been noticing with increasing regularity the last few weeks.

First, a little history:

At present, the deepest problem in theoretical physics is harmonizing Einstein's theory of "general relativity," which describes gravitation and applies to large-scale structures (stars, galaxies, super clusters), with "quantum theory" which describes the other three forces acting on the microscopic world of sub-atomic articles and based on tiny packets of energy called quanta.

The root of the problem, which has stubbornly resisted solution for 50 years, is that quantum theory and general relativity have two different physical pictures, and different mathematics to describe them. Einstein's dream was of a unified field theory, a series of numbers and symbols less than an inch long, which would constitute a pure, simple "Theory of Everything."

The "superstring theory" attempts to explain all of the particles and fundamental forces of nature in one theory. It is a revolutionary view of the universe in which all matter is composed of sub-atomic, vibrating strings existing in 10-dimensional hyperspace. ("Quantum Gravity: Simplified String Theory")

Like a violin string, these strings vibrate in an infinite number of possible frequencies corresponding to sub-atomic particles, or "quanta." According to this theory, the "notes" are the subatomic particles, the "harmonies" are the laws of physics, and the "universe" can be compared to a symphony of vibrating superstrings.

What's more, as the string vibrates it moves in time and space, causing the surrounding space-time continuum to warp around it and distorting the space-time continuum exactly as Einstein originally predicted. Thus, we now have a harmonious description that unifies gravity (as the bending of space caused by moving strings) with the other quantum forces (viewed as vibrations of the strings). *(*thank you Dr. Michio Kaku "The Theory of Everything" for assistance)*

ANNA's UNIFIED THEORY OF EVERYTHING:

Since Gabriel and I live in the same Universe, our bodies are connected through billions and billions (sorry, couldn't resist) of vibrating strings. I know, because he and I feel each other's emotional state across thousands of miles. We are aware of love and affection exchanged as packets of energy across the strings that connect us and marvel that our sleep has been disturbed of late by similar dreams, fears, and unrest.

And the gravitation of general relativity? Why, after the injury to my big toe occurred, I watched the distortion of the space-time continuum warp smoothly around the four extra pounds gained during the six weeks when this body of vibrating strings was a limping sloth.

HA – how about THAT for a unified theory of everything (didn't think I could do it, didja?)

11-23-2005 — **Prayers Needed**

Today I'll drive to the airport to catch a plane to the West Coast. I'll pick up *OnTheRadio* in Phoenix, and then drive to *Randi*'s family home for Thanksgiving dinner and on to San Diego for the premier of *Poppy*'s version of *Peter Pan*.

Gabriel, who was to meet me, at long last, during this magical trip will not be coming.

As I travel one direction, Gabriel is traveling the opposite way to be with his son who has just been diagnosed with terminal bone cancer. He has, maybe, six pain-filled months to spend with his wife, two children, and family.

Send a prayer out to your choice of angel, seraphim, Spaghetti Monster or Flat-Backed Turtle. For, to paraphrase Peter Pan – "You must believe in magic."

11-25-2005 — **Hello Sweetheart**
Personal email to *Gabriel* from Anna

When we *JournalLand*ers met this weekend – it was as if we were settling into the arms of best friends. We knew each other without ever meeting. We sat and talked as sisters. How could we not – we had been sharing each other's souls through our words for so long.

Honey – that's the way I feel with you. Meeting you only gives us a chance to share more of our senses. But we are already old, best friends. I don't care if we never meet until I land in LA in February. You are no stranger to me.

You asked me what I meant last night when I said, "Don't get lost." I mean, don't lose yourself. Don't go away from life, the people who love you or from your friends who can offer you help and compassion. Take all the strength you need from me and from the loving people around you to stay of this world. You still have great things to accomplish.

11-29-2005 — **And you wondered what we said**

Most of the trip to San Diego went as expected but there is a tale to tell.

On Friday night, after the play, *OnTheRadio, Randi, Queen of Rats, Poppy,* and I gathered at The Old Sod for a celebratory drink – or two – or so (ahem). It was 20-something loud, and louder still from the musical stylings of some unknown mid-aged fellow and his electric guitar. Conversation ebbed and flowed – mostly shouted into one ear or another and sometimes between people like playing telephone when you were a kid.

I suppose one might think I actually drink but, in fact, I probably have less than a six drinks a year – a Black & Tan on a hot summer night, or a glass of wine with a fine dinner. However, on my SECOND Black & Tan (courtesy of *Randi*), conversation came round to how daughters somehow turn from children to angry teens to best friends.

In keeping with what constitutes a best friend moment, I regaled the girls with a tale about the time Morgan called me for detailed instructions in one of my well-known, gold-star techniques. I later found out her boyfriend was right there with her, and she immediately practiced what I preached.

Yes, darlings, we talked about BJ techniques. In a bar. Loudly. Surrounded by a goodly number of young well-built men. Aside from the fact that women can't talk without using their hands (as most of you know), I can only imagine we raised more than one eyebrow as *Randi* used visual aids to describe (with appropriate embellishments) a particularly difficult movement.

The revelry ended around 3 a.m.

12-03-2005 — **And Baby Makes Three**

It's off to Manhattan for a visit with Morgan and her husband. Where I was greeted with the loveliest of news. ***And baby makes three.*** If all goes well, next July we will welcome a bouncing baby someone. We spent one dinner considering names. I teased that the best option is that they get the first and last names, and each family could choose one of the middle ones. The child would have six names (she/he will already have three last names) – but that's two less than Morgan's husband who has eight.

Jarred has begun calling it "Little Noodle." Gabriel, in the few moments we were able to converse, suggested in all seriousness "Cletus." My vote is for my all-time favorite "Michael."

12-05-2005 — **The Tangled Web**
(from the secret journal "*LuvACowboy*")

there is no time to talk. so the minutes grow less and less.
there is no strength to read, or respond, so the love letters are memories.
there is no courage to cry. so we force the laughter instead.
there is no hope for our February Twelfth of Never and i'm afraid.
Because all men leave

12-06-2005 — **My Time His Time**

> *I believe the moon is a piece of magic that comes out every night to remind us to look for the beauty in every day.*
> ~~*The Perfect Man* starring Heather Locklear

We crossed paths on a Monday, just over St. Louis. Maybe less than five miles away, as the crow flies. As we flew from opposite coasts. Physically closer than we ever were, and landing within moments of one another at our respective hometown airports. Back in our own time.

His time and my time have become intermixed. Next week, less than 48 hours apart, we'll trade coasts again. Him on mine, me on his. He will be hours from where I was and I will be less than an hour from where he would have been, in his place and in his time.

We have decided to move our timeline forward to "as long as necessary." So I accept forever never, unplanning all the plans, unchanging all the changes, erasing the files, closing the accounts and writing the checks.

12-08-2005 — **Believe in Magic**

Sometimes there is something we need to say. But the time is not right. Or when the time is right, there's not enough time. Or we don't know the right words.

Sometimes there is something we need to hear. But the time is not right. Or when the time is right, there's not enough time. Or we don't know the right words.

This time we both found the right time and the right words at the same time. He may never understand how much he said in a single sentence. "We are fine."

12-10-2005 — **In the Mind's Eye**
(from the secret journal "*LuvACowboy*")

"Sometimes," he said, "when you hesitate telling me something, I can see the fear in your mind. It's as if you see someone standing in front of you with a giant hammer hidden behind their back … waiting to pound you with it if you say something wrong."

And, of course, he was right. That is exactly what the fear feels like.

"By the way," he continued (off subject) "whatever made you think I would want to abandon you? Let's see, I'm facing one of the worst times in my life, so I'm going to punish myself even more, make everything even worse, by giving up the woman I love. Does that make any sense to you?"

Of course it didn't. It's just that I've not always gotten what I hoped for.

12-12-2005 — **East Coast Girl in L.A.**
(from the secret journal "*LuvACowboy*")

Well, with Gabriel on the East Coast as of this morning, I am NATURALLY headed to the West Coast in two hours. Just what do you suppose are the odds that two people, 3000 miles away, can miss one another AGAIN for the third time in as many months because they are crossing the country on different flights?

I thought it would be fun to invite one of the Brothers Grimm, who has acted as very interested parties to this whole relationship, to have dinner with me – or at least a cocktail – and ask them to pass along the Christmas gift I had purchased for Gabriel. After all, if one of your brothers said, "hey, the girl I'm in love with is coming to town and I can't be there, how about taking her to dinner for me?" wouldn't you take them up on it?

Did they? Nope. Not even a return email. I think that's called a double f*ck and a half.

12-12-2005 — **Strip Searches and Pretty Boys**

So there I was. Plenty early for my later flight (you weren't going to catch this ditz napping again) when, lo and behold, with all the ticket changes – and I'm guessing it was the one TWO HOURS before that did it – I become a prime suspect as a suspected terrorist.

So, no e-ticket check-in (please go wait in this line ma'am) and when I get to the head of that line I can't check my luggage (you have been selected, please go wait in that line ma'am) and when I finally get luggage checked and get to security it's "Spread em." I think that woman enjoyed patting down every square inch of my body. I suggested that perhaps the cute guy doing the luggage search could trade places with her. Ms. Butch was not amused.

I got a window seat on the three-seat side and at the last minute, the aisle seat filled with a tall lanky pretty boy in a rugged sort of way. He sat down and I swear went directly to sleep for the first two hours. Which left a dilemma. I had to pee. So I could either hold it, disturb him, or figure out a way to sneak over him. Sneaking seemed the most appropriate.

Getting out was a snap – I have long legs and over I went. Getting back in – I must have jostled something because he woke to find me facing him over top of his lap. He looked – and grinned. I looked – and grinned. I had to say it. "You know you are enjoying this."

I figure, ya gotta take life as it comes at ya – right? And it did my ego no amount of good to get a little flirt back from a pretty boy.

Hours later, as we de-planed, he looked straight in my eyes with a warm smile and said, "I'll be remembering this flight!"

12-13-2005 — I Don't Want to Talk About It
(from the secret journal "*LuvACowboy*")

i don't know why he will not read his email anymore. or maybe i do. he doesn't want to see the condolences from friends. they are too much reality. he wants each day to be as happy as it can be. but it means we have one less way to communicate.

he's almost himself most of the time on the phone – but with an intense layer of pain underneath always ready to break through. i know my role in all of this is to never ask, just listen.

it was funny a couple days ago. he was in a delightful mood. then, unexpectedly, began to talk about his son's condition a little. then stopped and said irritably, "this reminds me that every time i'm in a good mood people think it's a good time to ask me about it. don't they know that's not what i want?"

and i smiled a little inside – realizing he does want to talk some, just on his own schedule and only what he wants to say. so when he starts i keep my silence and just listen … hmming and uh-huhing and i understanding every once in a while until he says, "i don't want to talk about it right now" whereupon i immediately begin a funny story about something that has happened lately. anything that is completely off subject and as insanely ridiculous as possible.

12-18-2005 — Tripped upon a cloud somewhere

> *How did it get so late so soon?*
> *It's night before it's afternoon.*
> *December is here*
> *Before it's June.*
> *My Goodness how the time has flewn.*
> *How did it get so late so soon?*
> ~~Dr. Seuss

We both departed for home from our respective Florida airports yesterday.

It would be nice, just once, to land in the same city, at the same instant for even a moment. It is unfortunate we couldn't find a couple of hours to meet for lunch when we were just a driving hour apart these last few days. He says he would feel guilty, being happy when he should be sad.

I am so different. I would prefer my sorrow be punctuated by moments of happiness – no matter how brief those moments may be.

12-19-2005 — It Begins With Love
(from the secret journal "*LuvACowboy*")

the prognosis has been lowered from six months to three. sadness and desolation reign around a favorite holiday that is being made the perfect last wish.

i fear for him, but despite everything, he finds a moment from time to time. perhaps because he knows there will come a time when there will be silence between us as he finds his way to cope with the loss. perhaps because he knows i need to hear it. perhaps because he needs to hear it too.

we're fine.

12-21-2005 — And Suddenly It Rang

i was writing here about how it has been three days. and my silly girl heart could not help but feel the loss. he heard me, through the connection. he had to have heard me. because i did not even finish this short entry when the phone rang.

just three minutes to say so much. how everything was beginning to become too real. he had found photo albums. and gotten calls from family asking what presents to bring. he was back at home, alone, and it was too much.

as hard as it was to pick up the phone today, he did it because he knew i needed to know he was ok. even in this he is still thinking of me.

12-23-2005 — Bah Humbug
(from the secret journal "*LuvACowboy*")

He was offended by the Christmas greeting left for him in *JournalLand* so I removed it. I didn't think it would be the least bit disrespectful to his situation, as he frequently told me his friends and family knew about me, that we loved one another, and about his plans for me joining him in Malibu in the future. It seemed the best way to give him a gift without it being a gift.

"Lastly, to my darling Gabriel who has not been here for a little while, but who may return in time, I leave this for you to find. The world has asked much of you and somehow you have found the courage to go on and on and to keep me in your life, which is almost more than I had hoped. I cannot do less. You are my heart, my inspiration, and the greatest love of my life. You would accept no gift from me this holiday season, so I leave it here. It is a simple "I Love You.""

I'm also retiring the "Gabriel" character from any *JournalLand* entries, starting today, so I won't be tempted to speak of us again. Life, and Mr. Lucky, gives me plenty to talk about, after all!

12-23-2005 — Been There, Done That
(from the secret journal "*LuvACowboy*")

i wonder how many more times i can hear his 20-years long gone deceased wife's name. even though she was his son's mother, i feel more and more like i'm butting into a relationship that already exists. an appendage to something, an addendum to someone that will always be larger than anything i may wish for myself or hope for us.

12-25-2005 — Tis Better to Give, and Up Yours Santa

> *Humans say Hell is paved with good intentions.*
> *Why? Do they think there's a shortage of bad ones?*
> Karm'Luk P'an Ku, "*The Joy of Lucidity*" CY 8633
> ~~"Forced Perspective"

Betcha didn't know you could be quite f*kd being unf*kd.

Santa started in on me months ago. He's in collusion with the rain gods (Malibu mudslides), and the wind gods (Hurricane Katrina/Rita), and the fire gods (California brush fires), and every other god there is, to keep my love and I from ever meeting one another. They got together and decided Anna has obviously been a very bad girl the last year.

Some people would have said being bad is good. But these gods, puritanical farts that they are, started in on me in August. I remain unf*kd (or is that f*kd – sorry I keep getting mixed up) and will probably remain so for the foreseeable future.

And Christmas? Hey, I would have welcomed even a lump of coal in my virtual stocking, because it would at least have been something.

Oh yeah, the joy of the holiday is in giving isn't it. Must remember giving. (Hey, wait a minute. Mr. Lucky receives ... I give. or am I confusing taking with giving ... oh, never mind.)

Well, gotta go cook Mr. Lucky's holiday ham and wrap the presents. Mr. Lucky finally bought a few things but won't wrap anything. ("can't i just put a bow on the plastic bag they came in?")

I hope Santa's not gettin' any from Ms. Claus either so I can honestly say "Go F*CK yourself, Fat Boy." And that's just the mood I'm in.

12-26-2005 — **Mirror Mirror or Over The Years**

January – My father's death. Jason and Anna's first date.

February – Gabriel's birthday. The death of my mother and my wonderful grandfather. The anniversary of Ben and Anna's first meeting. And a lifetime later, a Valentine's realization that it will never be.

March – The birthday of my best friend Bobbi, and my stepmother, and my dear friend John, the musician bad-boy Alan and my son-in-law. The month my parents met, got engaged, got married, and when my father left to serve in WWII. And the month I was born. Not all in the same year, of course.

April – a boring month ... other than a harbinger of spring, nothing ever happens in April except taxes.

May – Two husband's birthdays, and two wedding anniversaries.

June – My mother's birthday, my daughter's wedding anniversary. And the anniversary of meeting Gabriel.

July – My dear father's birthday.

August – My second husband's birthday, and that of Mr. Lucky.

September – The death of my dear aunt at 93.

October – The death of my grandmother at 96.

November – Jason's birthday. The anniversary of Mr. Lucky and me that has never, ever been celebrated or remembered.

December – My daughter's birthday. Ben's birthday. The month Jason left. The month Ben left … twice. The beginning of the end of countless unremembered relationship possibilities. What is there about December and the demise of relationships? Such holiday expectations and such letdowns.

The only way to get through a year-end in my life has been to reach a non-aggression pact with the holidays.

How old do you feel my friends? I am not the age I feel, nor quite the age I see when I look into the mirror. I often wonder how long it will be before it is exactly the same. And how long will it be before love doesn't see how I feel, but what the mirror sees.

12-26-2005 — **I didn't say I love you tonight**
Personal email to *Gabriel* from Anna

There are so many things every day I want to share. And so very little time to do any of them.

The logical adult knows you absolutely should be spending your time with your family, and you give me an extraordinary amount of time and attention by phone. That's logic.

The child in me still hopes to find an unexpected email after two months, and optimistically wished for a Christmas anything. The child misses you.

Gabriel, I used to be so comfortable with you, and now we do an "I'm fine and how are you" dance. I feel like I'm intruding into a place, and a life, I don't belong. I don't understand what has happened to make members of your family think so badly of me as to force you outside in the cold to have our brief conversations so they won't know you are talking to me.

I want you to know that I am here for you, in any capacity you want me to be. I love you, but I don't want to add another item to your already prodigious to-do list at this time in your life. I want you to feel safe telling me what you need. Even though I don't want to step away – I can if it's what is best for you. You will not lose me – ever. I will be here now, or when you are ready to come back.

12-27-2005 — **Christmas Rubble**

Speaking of states of mind … Mr. Lucky was kind enough to pick up the son-in-law from the bus station Sunday. Son-in-law was an excellent accountant in his previous life, and apparently Mr. L wanted to brag about how he's creating a trust for his son and grandson, and putting everything he owns into it – including the business I helped build and the house I live in and pay half for. Perhaps he hoped son-in-law would break it to me gently?

The tree was beautiful, but the empty skirt had begun to remind me of the "Charlie Brown" holidays we shared when Morgan was little. We would go out and get a tree on Christmas Eve when the tree sellers were willing to practically give them away. Morgan would invariably pick the one everyone else had passed up as too small, or too crooked, or too spindly because "it looks sad and needs a nice home." We would haul it home and decorate it like crazy with a strand of lights, paper chains, popcorn, aluminum foil, and handmade ornaments. It always looked just like something magical.

No matter how poor I was, there were always gifts underneath, even if I had to wrap a set of something individually in Sunday's comic pages.
Santa (my Daddy) contributed something great every year – a rocking horse and cowboy hat, a red wagon, a tricycle, even a swing set.

This year, we took a hint from those years past, went out Saturday, and filled our shopping basket with lots of tiny little fun dollar things. Toys, games, stickers, pencils, Christmas mugs, and foiled chocolates. We wrapped every one of them, stuffing the stockings full to bursting, and it didn't look too bad.

Sometimes you just have to remember that the joy of Christmas is the love you share, not the stuff you get.

12-29-2005 — **Ta Ta – Been Fun**

A dear friend of mine told me recently I was afraid of being abandoned. I pooh-poohed the idea but perhaps he was more right than I would want to admit. Which makes me even more depressed in these post-Christmas days.

People do a myriad of things when they feel down. Some eat, some sleep, some cry, some write. I shop. I can judge my state of mind by my need to go shopping. I once cut up every single one of my credit cards because I knew I couldn't afford to buy anything. I am on the mailing list of every catalogue known to mankind. Computers haven't helped – I don't even have to get dressed to satisfy the urge. And when the mailman arrives with all the lovely boxes, every day is Christmas! It's ok though – I can usually control it.

Really I can … honestly … sorry, umm, gotta run – after Christmas sales and all. Ta Ta … been fun … BYE!

12-30-2005 — **A Revolution of Resolutions**

New Year's Eve is just around the corner, the time when many of us begin considering how we want to improve our lives in the New Year. I'm not sure why January 1 is the time we start, instead of December 23 or February 11 or April 4. Perhaps January 1 represents the proverbial clean slate, a significant milestone date less easy to ignore.

I have made dozens upon dozens of resolutions across the years. Most were forgotten by the end of January. Some would continue through another month or two, and then be buried under the pressure of everything piling on top of me. A very few would stick longer, getting lost from time to time amongst the rubble, then resurfacing to remind me of the promises I had made to myself and I almost always would try again. I suppose it was the thought that if they were strong enough to come back and haunt me, I should be wise enough to listen.

Design resolutions to improve your life and the lives of those around you. For making changes and moving forward in a positive way, for becoming the person you always wanted to be. Or for helping someone else to be the person they always wanted to be. Even if it's just one step, or one person, at a time.

I'm not sure how the above leads to this. Perhaps because I was reminded today that each person has within themselves an almost unlimited supply of strength and courage if we just take the time to look.

The following comment was posted on August 25 in response to my entry "I Hope You Dance"

> *jen – 08-25-2005*
> *the timing of the entry is eerie to me. sunday afternoon i mustered up the courage to tell him to leave. his response was to give me a swollen, bruised cheekbone, broken clavicle and a fractured scaphoid. my courage fled as i lied to the emergency room doctor, my children and friends. i wish i could borrow a cup or two of your courage. thank you for being real. your journal has been the best part of my day many many times. Especially today.*

I often wondered how she was doing and wished I could have helped more.

Today I got this in my email.

> *"jen – 12-30-2005*
> *A while ago, I came to this site and was moved by your experience with abuse. I left a brief message about my situation having been brutally attacked by my husband resulting in a broken wrist and collarbone. I just wanted to update you. I took a deep breath and faced the great unknown and started the divorce. I am safe. My children are safe and even though it is a struggle financially and emotionally, I have hope for my future. Thank you for sharing your story. It gave me a courage which I didn't know I had.*
> *Love, jen"*

Which goes to show that we all have it in us. We all have the ability to change and grow, to be greater than anyone expected of us. We all have the ability to be the person we want to see when we look in the mirror – the person that has been living quietly, sometimes hidden away, in our heart and in our mind.

So if you're going to make New Year's Resolutions this year, make one big important one. Make one life-changing or life-saving one. Make one that is big enough, and strong enough, to haunt you until you make it happen.

01-03-2006 — Sonic Boom
(from the secret journal **"*LuvACowboy*"**)

A call today and in the midst was a comment that his entire family, including his son, knows his papa is in love with a girl named me. i do wonder what everyone except the brothers Grimm (who DO know who i am and read my alter ego in *JournalLand*) thinks about why i've never, ever been around. why none of them have ever met the girl he "loves."

or is this just too f*cking weird to even think about.

ah well, i got "i love you sweetie" four times today, as if it is the most normal phrase in the world.

01-03-2006 — Loved talking today
Personal email to *Gabriel* from Anna

Seriously, I MISS YOU when you disappear for days at a time. Why, entire glaciers have moved across the face of the northern continent, species have gone extinct, Los Angeles suffered the big one (oh, sorry, wrong show).

That's it, enough for now. I will love you longer that the stars will burn in heaven, more than the drops of salt in the ocean waters, and with more dedication than George Bush for wire-tapping your phones.

01-04-2006 — Fantasia Redux

****CRASH, BANG, SPLAT, RATTLE … shit****

The sound of something large and glass hitting the kitchen's ceramic tile floor awakened me Saturday morning. With the accompanying **shit** that can mean only one thing … Mr. Lucky has been playing in the garbage again.

The first thing to understand is that Mr. Lucky only knows four things about the kitchen.

1. How to make coffee (don't get me started that his three year old coffee pot has never, in its entire life, been cleaned. Not even rinsed.
2. How to microwave a cup of the three day old coffee sitting in that pot.

3. Where the top of the stove is located so he can eat the leftovers of anything I make for myself ("were you gonna eat that?") and

drum roll please

4. Where the trash is located.

Yes, poppets, for all his miscreant ways, Mr. Lucky took it upon himself early in the relationship to be responsible for getting the trash and recycling out of the kitchen trashcans into the garage and from there to the curb twice a week. I can see the amazement in your eyes.

He was finally removing the overflowing recycling basket from last weekend when a large glass bottle flew out, covering the ceramic tile floor with 70 billion bits of shattered green glass.

I pause here to say, for those of you not familiar with Mr. Lucky, when he does any kind of "hands on" task   it is more a "fingertips on." As if it might bite, or scratch, or poke, or get him dirty. (I once asked him to help me move several pieces of 4 x 8 plywood and, I swear, the wood NEVER TOUCHED HIS HANDS!). Ah – to continue.

I sprang from the bed to see what was the matter, away to the window I flew like a flash, tore open the shutters, and threw up the sash. (oops, sorry, wrong story). I sprang from the bed all right, threw on a robe, and raced down the stairs to see what was the matter. There he stood helplessly, holding a tiny little dustpan and whiskbroom, staring at those 70 billion bits of glass.

"What's up?" I asked as he looked up and noticed my reassuring presence hovering in the door.

"I'll get the vacuum for you," he said, thrusting the whiskbroom at me and running from the room.

"Oh no," I said. "Glass will destroy the vacuum. Just use the big broom to sweep it up."

I saw it coming the very instant the words were out of my mouth. He turned dramatically, teeth gritted, jaw clenched, "I don't sweep."

And he's absolutely right. He swept once … using one finger, I think, and maybe a big toe. Like Mickey Mouse in Fantasia, it was an unmitigated disaster and a tale for another time. So I swept up all the little bits of glass and Swiffered it all shiny sparkly clean (which it needed anyhow).

01-05-2006 — **He said Just Trust Me**

I mentioned somewhere in the last few entries that Mr. Lucky had a long conversation with my son-in-law (an ex-accountant) bragging about how smart he was to consider utilizing a trust to protect his assets.

The idea of this trust, when it was first discussed, didn't worry me overly much as – knowing how he procrastinates – I thought I would be gone with some fair share of my contributions before it became an issue because although this state doesn't have laws for common-law relationships he doesn't know it.

Now, with a year-end reminder nudge from his brother, it appears he is going ahead with it. Which means, of course, that the business I helped build (but never got credit for except on the business card which read "Vice-President") and the house I've paid half the mortgage payments on (but whose name is not on the deed) will go into the trust for the benefit of his son and grandson.

I have come to a simple conclusion. When I entered this relationship fourteen years ago, I was working hard at a well-paid job I hated in an industry that had no future. I owned a house, furniture, lots of stuff, a working car, and (not counting the mortgage) was $40,000 in debt thanks to my ex-husband who decided one day while I was out of town to cash-advance all my credit cards for his benefit.

Thanks to this relationship I wrote a series of technical manuals which paid off the cards in less than a year, eventually sold the house and banked a very tidy profit, own even better furniture, a working car, have not a single penny of debt, and a great credit rating. I still work hard, but at a job I love in an up and coming industry. I've increased my retirement fund considerably, have a reasonable savings account for emergencies, and own more stuff than I will need for the rest of my life.

Yes, I put in thousands of hours redecorating the house we live in – but it was fun and I learned an awful lot that I can use the next time. And yes, I put in thousands and thousands of hours helping to build his business from a one-man part-time consultancy working out of the house to a $3 million dollar a year firm – but on average, my pay is better than minimum wage and I learned skills that are useful in other industries.

Once I settled down and stopped the poor pitiful me rant going on in my mind, I realized I'm coming out one heck of a lot better than I went in.

The only thing I've lost is the 122,640 hours that could have been spent with someone who actually loved me. If I was able to make it through 122,640, I can certainly make through another 8,760 and another 8,760 after that. Here's to counting the hours.

01-06-2006 — **Bawlmer and Other Foreign Places**

Finally, at long, long last – I am meeting the Princesses of Assholia, four ladies who write in *JournalLand* and live in Baltimore.

And I suppose you are wondering about the status of my co-star as it has been some time since Gabriel last appeared in an episode of my diary "Do You Believe in Always." Since there have been no crossover appearances in his show, it has led fans to wonder if contract negotiations have stalled and there will be a mid-season replacement announced by the network. All I can say is you may want to stay tuned to this station for the season-ending cliffhanger.

01-06-2006 — **I got your message last night**
Personal email to *Gabriel* from Anna

I am appalled at the news that you have been getting messages from some anonymous e-mailer warning you about how terrible a person I am. I appreciate that you have not wanted to worry me with this news until you had tracked down the perpetrator and handled it but …

My first reaction is F***&^%%$%K her/him. No one is going to scare me off with a lot of nasty gossip. But it affects you in an adverse way … so it's not just me to think about. I'm not used to it – and feel an innate distaste at being unable to defend my honor. I'm just stubborn like that.

01-09-2006 — **Ghost of Christmas Past**

> *I'm as corny as Kansas in August,*
> *High as a flag on the Fourth of July!*
> *If you'll excuse an expression I use,*
> *I'm in love, I'm in love,*
> *I'm in love with a wonderful guy!*
> ~~Hugh Fordin, *A Biography of Oscar Hammerstein II*

Christmas came down on Friday and is all put away. It is a melancholy moment, as I love Christmas. When it disappears for another year the house looks so empty (and this year the whole season seemed particularly hard, I'm not sure why). But leaving it up past the 12th day after Christmas is supposed to bring bad luck for the coming year … so away it went into the boxes and up onto the shelves that ring the garage about 10 feet up. I certainly don't need any more bad luck.

Sunday I made brunch for six members of Mr. Lucky's family. His mother (who is 82) has a new boyfriend (who is 87). Well, an old one I suppose. He was her boyfriend in high school. Yep, high school. I have no idea exactly what's going on, but he flew out here from Kentucky last week to see her after talking to her every day, twice a day, for a couple of months and they have nestled like lovebirds every day since.

But here's what I got to thinking – and it just goes to show where my mind is at lately. How long could they have together? If they forge a relationship, one of them will inevitably face the loss of the other. Wouldn't it be easier to keep their distance, just enjoy the butterflies in the tummy and the excitement of the possibilities? To keep it a someday, maybe, soon, we'll see? Wouldn't an arm's length relationship be safer, and hurt less, in the long run?

But that's not the way true love works, is it? Love is when you take all the chances. When you would rather face the world, and all its hardships and disappointments, together than be apart. When the desire for the other's presence is so strong, you cannot survive another moment without it. When all your dreams are of the other. When no matter what obstacles life throws at you, you find a way around them, over them, and through them. Because love is all there is.

*Love is the very essence and core of our being ... the energy that sustains who
and what we are. Everyone ... has a deep-rooted desire to love and be loved.*
~~Robert Abel (291)

01-10-2006 — i know it but i don't yet i do
Personal email to *Gabriel* from Anna

Does it make sense when I say that it feels odd not knowing "where" you have
been for so long. I think it's why I ask so often "where are you." I have an
innate need to place you on the map, visualize you in a city, on a street, in a
house, sitting in a blue room on a brown couch. I knew you were "in" LA, New
Orleans, New York, and in Connecticut for the holidays. Now you are "in"
Florida. Mostly you are always "in" a car, or truck, so I usually picture you
driving – one hand on the wheel, the other holding a phone to your ear while
talking to me.

What is my "where" to you?

I continue to encourage you to stay in touch – no matter what. You don't have
to protect me from your bad moods, your sad ones, or even your angry ones.
There is no such thing as bad company if it is someone you love with all your
heart.

01-13-2006 — **One of those MEME things**

1. **How tall are you barefoot?** 5'7" I've heard you shrink as you get older, but
I've had 5'7" on every driver's license I've ever had, including my first one at 16.
2. **Have you ever smoked heroin?** There is no point in smoking heroin. PCP,
coke, crack, opium, marijuana yes. There are more efficient ways to use Heroin.
3. **Rehab?** I rehabbed my house. I've rehabbed apartments. I've sent two
husbands to rehab. Does that count?
4. **Would you ever "do" someone in their parent's bed?** At my age that
would be weird, assuming their parents were even still alive. Although I conceived my daughter in the bed of my boyfriend's parents when I was a senior in
high school. Oh, give me a break ... like you've never done it.
5. **What do you think of hot dogs?** Is this about sex again? Oh well, no, I hate
hot dogs ... um wieners. Except at the ballpark and I get the kosher ones with
mustard and pickle relish that somehow makes them taste better.
6. **Do you do push-ups?** You mean exercises? Oh please. But I enjoy encour-

aging others to do push-ups. It's just been WAY WAY too long.

7. **Are you vegan?** I eat anything that doesn't eat me first. But if it does eat me first, I should only be polite enough to return the favor.

8. **What is your secret weapon to lure in the opposite sex?** The gold star on my forehead.

9. **Do you own a knife?** Kitchen – yes. Machete – yes. Do I CARRY a knife? Not since the airlines took it away from me and now with the whole 9/11 changes, why bother.

10. **Do you have A.D.D.?** No, despite what you think. And you. And you. And you too. Oh, that's paranoia isn't it. And I don't have that either. What were we talking about?

11. **Would you be a pirate?** Yes – but I'd rather be captured by one.

12. **What songs do you sing in the shower?** "Oh, sweet mystery of life at last I've found you"

13. **What did you fear was going to get you at night as a child?** Rodan, the monster from the horror movie, and atomic bombs

14. **Worst injury you've ever had?** A sailing injury that tore/strained the ICL and ACL on my right knee. In order to heal properly without major surgery they did orthoscopic, and then put me on crutches for four months and in a knee brace for six. Crap – football players are back on the field in 6 weeks, while I was still hobbling on crutches in a locked knee brace.

15. **What song do you want played at your funeral?** I'm not a religious person, but I love gospel music, especially the old revival ones. I suspect whoever arranges the service will find something they want, or need, to hear. I would want it to bring them comfort and joy. I won't need it anymore – I'll just be sitting beside them tapping my feet.

01-14-2006 — **You've Got Something to Talk About**
(From the secret journal "*LuvACowboy*")

this is one of those silent entries about things that are so deeply painful they are, of themselves, little more than anguished cries in the darkness.

someone claiming to know me well from before, perhaps before I came east, has been sending untraceable emails to Gabriel. Gabriel will give me no details (nor send me copies), although it is certain she reads my journal – and his – and has recognized (or been told) the connection between us. he only says they have been coming and contain unspeakable tales purported to be my past, disguised as truths and warnings that trusting me, or forming a relationship with me, would be ... misplaced.

i don't know anyone that has any reason to hate me. perhaps some, over the years, that have remained ambivalent, but hate? no – no one i have ever hurt so much and certainly no one that knows any of my deepest, darkest secrets.

this feeds into one of my oldest and strongest deep-seated fears – the inability to defend myself. what is being said? to whom? why won't he tell me? DOES HE BELIEVE HER/HIM?

we don't know anyone in common who can vouch for me. he would not have coffee with my daughter when he was in NYC, or talk to my best friend – people who could tell him i'm an ok kinda gal. he has never introduced me to any of his friends or family. and, of course, we all know i've never met him. the Brothers Grimm have already placed a scarlet letter on my chest, knowing about Mr. Lucky, and refused to meet me when given the opportunity.

that's all. i'm ok. it will all be better tomorrow. i just needed to talk about it here, in this safe place and wonder if i will be judged unworthy. after all, it is only my words against whoevers, isn't it.

01-15-2006 — **Believe It or Not**
(from the secret journal "*LuvACowboy*")

another night of troubled dreams, affected by his silence.

he doesn't believe any of it – in which case he is not telling me anything in order to protect me.

he's not sure whether he believes it – in which case he is checking the facts to see if it is true

he believes it – in which case he is not telling me anything just because.

and altho he calls me every few days, why is it i have never, ever been able to reach him on the weekends, no matter how hard i try.

01-16-2006 — **The Seven Dirty Words**

I remember distinctly the first time I heard the word f*ck. It was a hot, lazy, summer afternoon, I was about 9 or 10, and some of the neighborhood kids (mostly boys) were all sitting around on my front porch. A slightly older kid, son of the new assistant preacher, came round to chat and told a joke.

"What starts with F and ends with UCK?"

Everyone began to giggle when he shouted out "FIRE TRUCK!"

I didn't get it. What was so funny about a fire truck? So I asked my mom. She choked a little, got a very odd look on her face, then told me it was a dirty word and don't repeat it.

Fire truck is a dirty word? I'd been using in front of grown-ups for years without getting to enjoy the fact that I was breaking the rules!

Years later George Carlin did an entire routine on the seven words that you couldn't broadcast: Shit, Piss, F*ck, C*nt, C*cksucker, Motherf*cker, and Tits. (really? ... Tits?)

Crap, I've lost my train of thought with all that smut ... oh yes ... when I found out "fire truck" was a dirty word, I had only heard one of the seven.

I kid you not – my mother had a rule and even my father (a WWII army veteran) was not allowed to use dirty words. (He even went to "see a man about a horse" and my sister, who was equine nutty, kept asking him to bring her a pony).

I finally learned all about dirty words, and pretty much everything else one needed to know about sex, from babysitting my neighbor's kids.

Get your mind out of the gutter. I read the *Playboy* magazines in the closet!

01-17-2006 — **Who Is She**
(from the secret journal "***LuvACowboy***")

Gabriel has been frisky the last few days. his Son is feeling well despite the still terminal prognosis, the grandchildren are a joy, and the onslaught of email spam from whoever she was has stopped (he says the Brothers Grimm are relentlessly tracking her down).

whether she wanted him for herself, or wanted to hurt me, she did me a favor. i was distraught, as you know, torturing myself with thoughts that negative input, couched as "advice," and wrapped around lies, could make a difference. (silly me to think love flows from a faucet that can be turned off).

what she didn't count on is he will not allow anyone to hurt me. and he speculated that his protective silence about us could be interpreted in ways that may have been a contributing factor. or could be in the future.

so he says he is going to begin introducing this relationship into *his JournalLand* journal, and would i start talking about him again in mine. in hopes that our friends will play the game along with us in notes and comments – using the secret journal names we have given each other. then, at some point, i am to post a picture of Gabriel in my regular journal. letting those who know us in on the secret, and those who don't an opportunity to guess who he really is.

(i think he forgot i have the picture of him kissing a horse ... *giggle*)

01-19-2006 — **Happy Seven Month-a-versary**
Personal email to *Gabriel* from Anna

I often marvel at your ability to understand me so completely. Maybe we're a freight train. Or a tornado. Or the meeting of two pre-destined souls. Whatever it is – you can't stop magic.

Happy Seven Month-a-versary. May there be 10,000 more.

And on a return voicemail he said, "Beautiful Anna, you leave me shaking my head and laughing out loud. Your voice sometimes has such a fearful worried tone in it, as if not being able to reach me means something bad has happened. Do you suppose there is anything you could have done in the nine hours since we last spoke that could ever make me stop loving you?"

01-22-2006 — **Still Daddy's Girl**

King, Marion C
TEC4 U.S. Army, WW II
Date of Birth: 07/08/1923 Date of Death: 01/22/1993
Buried at: Section 1F Site 1297 Jefferson Barracks National Cemetery

Born in Booneville, Missouri of second-generation German immigrant parents, my father was the second of four children. He graduated from high school at 16 and left home to work in St. Louis. At 18, he met my mother while taking college night classes. They married in 1943, just before he entered the Army. He fought all over Europe, including the Battle of the Bulge, attached to the 308th unit of the 78th Lighting Division as a forward artillery spotter. Towards the end of the war, he was stationed in Paris and attended the Sorbonne – just because he could.

When the war ended, he went to work for the Pennsylvania Railroad as a yardmaster at Rose Lake Yards in E. St. Louis and never left – even though they went through multiple transitions and names. As the sole breadwinner for a growing family, he worked second or night shifts because it paid more money. My mother died in 1968 and five years later he married my stepmother whom he met in college, having gone back again to take more courses. I think he wanted to get the degree – even though he was the smartest person I've ever met. When they retired, they planned to travel – something he never got to do while raising a family.

In 1979, he suffered a catastrophic left hemisphere stroke that left him unable to speak or write words (including the use of a computer or typewriter) and partially crippled on his right side. Funny how it worked – he could build a doghouse, but couldn't make change at the grocery store. He could drive a car, but not sign his name. He could read the paper but not a book, only understand time and numbers if they were written, but understand mostly everything else that was spoken. He had difficulty confirming yes or no without thinking very hard. But, strangely enough, he could still curse.

Money was tight but they got to do a little traveling, just not as they had dreamed. He made the best of it, loving his wife, children, and grandchildren with a passion. When he was told he had six months to live, he didn't change a thing. He chose to remain home and forego the chemotherapy that may only have prolonged his life briefly. He died quietly of cancer January 22, 1993, exactly six months later. Like everything else – he made the best of it.

I love you Daddy and I still miss you all the time.

01-26-2006 — **Randi & Her Boyfriend**
Personal email to Anna from *Gabriel*

Randi and her boyfriend having problems? When folks continually fight and break up on a daily basis it's because of fear in one or the other, but in my opinion it's in both of them. I feel her boyfriend has never been in a relationship where he has felt secure enough to talk openly about his fears.

Communication is an absolute must and if they truly accept each other for who they are, not who they can make the other person become, they'll make it. Life is such a wonderful adventure, but you can take it to the tenth power if you share it with another.

I am entering into a terrible period in my life. I will soon lose the most valued thing in my life, my Son. What makes it so horrific is that I have been here before with the loss of my wife, I remember every minute of every day ... the fear, the agony, the never-ending pain of losing her.

There is an ocean of difference this time. There is someone who loves me. Someone whose love I can find comfort in. Someone I feel every day even though she is far away. When I am feeling my worst, I think of this person and there is instant relief. I replay her words in my head and my Heart warms. I feel as though I can breathe again. I think of her smile and my body relaxes. I see her big blue eyes and that smile and things don't hurt as much.

For most of us, our mind is a dark and scary closet where the boogey man lives. It's our fear of the dark, of what could be, not what is. Folks should remember you don't have to walk into the dark closet alone. Take hold of each other's hand and turn on the light. Talking about everything and anything has a tendency to chase the dark away.

I love you Anna.

01-27-2006 — **Things Change**
(from the secret journal "*LuvACowboy*")

Gabriel's son is home, looking noticeably more ill after just 2 weeks. he will go down to the islands soon – while he still can – with Gabriel and the children for dad/son surfer/fishing things during the day, and wife/kid things at night. i don't know if we will talk.

he said yesterday – things are going to change soon, things are going to be intensely different, you just have to hang in there.

i don't know what that means and i'm not sure he does either. i'm scared of things i don't know

maybe he will not feel like talking to me for days at a time. maybe he will simply take a hiatus that could last for weeks, or even months. he's told me that when he faces difficult issues such as these, he withdraws – and i've already experienced it firsthand. maybe he's preparing me to understand that our relationship will be on hold for an unknown long, long time. or maybe he will stay connected, but he may become short or appear angry at me – but he won't be and he wants me to know now before i have a chance to misinterpret.

or maybe it's all of the above. or none of the above. or maybe he just wants me to be prepared for anything, and to know that wherever his soul goes, he will come back to me when he can.

01-31-2006 — **The Illustrated Man**

My daughter, Morgan, has a tattoo. She got it from a Tattoo Parlor. Not a Body Art Emporium. Not a big deal today, but back in 1983 tattoos were primarily seen on people who made their homes in an 8x10 concrete room with bunk beds and a window slit.

It was the second day of a camping trip to The Lake of the Ozarks. Morgan broke the companionable silence around the campfire. "When we go into town tonight, I want to get a tattoo."

"NO."

"But ... "

"NO NO NO. You'll be sorry when you get older. You'll change your mind."

Whereupon she gave me The Look. The one that always came right before she uttered one of the classic, dramatic, extraordinary, statements of her childhood that I have repeated *ad nauseam* for over thirty some years.

"You've wanted a tattoo since you were my age and never did it. You haven't changed your mind in eighteen years. I am my mother's daughter. What makes you think I will feel any differently?"

The artist was a gentleman, carefully draping and conversing. Keeping her relaxed and laughing. She was fifteen that summer – and has never, in all these years, regretted it.

As I kept an eye on her, I began to look at the designs on the wall. Not surprisingly, when the artist was finished with Morgan, I took her place. Eighteen years after I first dreamed about it, I walked out with my own tattoo in exactly the place I'd always imagined it would appear.

02-02-2006 — **Three hundred and counting?**

My best friend called so I'm going to Tampa in mid-March to teach a class for her country club members. She tells me there's a fella who wants to meet me. He's about 46 or so, muscular, and quite attractive.

Apparently, a few days ago, having had a beer or two or three, he made a pass at my girlfriend. She turned him down flat, and then suggested he could take me out for dinner when I arrived.

After a few questions – he proudly suggested that he would be a good catch ... after all, he's made love to over 300 women in his life.

"300?" Bobbi questioned, "How do you know ... do you keep count?"

"Well" he sheepishly replied, "sorta."

Only 300? Sorry, Bobbi. I don't do amateurs.

02-03-2006 — **Valentine's Is Not For Lovers**
(from the secret journal "*LuvACowboy*")

on Monday, i got the courage up to ask again "can we get together for lunch on Valentine's Day? my girlfriend's house is only a couple hours from where you are. we can each drive halfway and spend a few hours with one another."

he got ... sharp? upset? angry? "you know i've said before it isn't possible to leave him. why do you ask me again? are you trying to make me feel guilty, having to say no again?"

and although Son's health has continued to hold up, and he isn't needed every day in the overly crowded household, i dropped the idea like a hot potato because his tone was almost nasty.

on Tuesday, when i took the time to apologize for upsetting him the day before, he said, "honey, you just make me laugh. i don't think i have ever been angry with you about anything you've ever said or done. and i'm not sure i ever could be."

then on Wednesday, he casually mentioned, "i have to renew my driver's license and two car registrations so i'm flying home February 12. my sister reminded me i'd agreed to do a presentation for the Mensa group i belong to, so i think i'll stay over for the week. i don't like to let people down."

how is it he has time to fly home to LA for 14 days, and does not have time to spend a single afternoon with me when i will be less than an hour from his supposed doorstep?

my dear friend, you are the only one to whom i can say ... i simply do not understand. i think I am learning, little by little, that should we ever actually meet or – by some miracle – get together as a couple, i may be meeting a complete stranger.

02-04-2006 — **Good Night, I Love You's**
(from the secret journal "*LuvACowboy*")

this last week I was away from home on a business trip. which meant Gabriel and i had the freedom to talk from three in the afternoon until I went to bed each night. sure enough, he somehow found the time to talk non-stop for four days. even after our goodnight i love you's he would call just one more time – rousing me for a last i love you.

i think he wanted to give me everything he could ... while he still could. these last few days were a reminder of what it used to be.

then, this morning, i wake to a new entry in the *Gabriel* journal wherein *Gabriel*, in his inimitable way, has announced to the world at large (and most especially to those in the know) the significant bond that exists between Gabriel and his sweetheart Anna. game ... set ... match?

02-05-2006 — **Smartest Man in the World**
Personal email to Anna from *Gabriel*

I have scored the pre-Mensa test you and "I'm the Smartest Man in the World" Mr. Lucky took. Your score is 13.5, Mr. Lucky's score is 3. The good news is you are 4.5 times better at solving problems and 4.5 times more intelligent than Mr. Smartest man alive. But the best news is you qualify to take the Mensa test.

That means you are who I have always known you were – smart both in knowledge and common sense. You have great comprehension and a wonderful ability to solve problems. Mr. Lucky, on the other hand, may end up in diapers and unable to care for himself sooner than expected. He does show some ability in math – maybe he's an idiot savant, brilliant in one thing only and an idiot in everything else?

Well, MS Smartypants let's measure my love for you in powers of ten. In the beginning it was

10 to the ninth power (a Billion) that's 2 groups of 3 zero's after the number 1,000 = 1,000,000,000. Then it took a massive leap to 10 to the 21st power that's 9 zero's or Sextillion, then to Quattuordecillion, 10 to the 45th power, and recently my love for you grew to the amount of Vigintillion, yes Darling that is 1 with 63 zeros behind it or 10 to 63rd power. By the time I pass onto the next plane I fully expect my love for you to grow to that of Centillion, 10 to the 303rd power yep 303 zeros behind it. Get the picture??

02-09-2006 — **With Quill in Hand**

In the old days … and I mean the days before Alexander and Bill hard-wired the world … people would often meet, court, and agree to marry based solely on letters sent and received. Miniatures – carefully rendered flattering portraits by a popular artiste, would sometimes accompany these.

I've always imagined the letter writers sitting at dainty desks with hand carved legs, carefully and considerately composing their words in order to make the best impression. Using quill and parchment, instead of dating rituals, to put their best feet forward. Speaking only of things that could be read aloud in polite company. Leaving out the worst of their traits and never, ever, sharing anything of consequence.

Considering the frequent, and sometimes required, lifetime-commitment outcome of that correspondence, it would seem to me that these letter writers should have done without the self-editing.

Our letters, such as they are, no longer adorn beautiful parchment, nor are they written at dainty desks. We write them in emails or texts, conversationally forgetting to clean and edit and then, with the click of a key, speed the random output of our cluttered minds to their intended recipients. Following this train of thought … circuitous as it is … .it follows that modern letter writers can be better than those writers of old.

Anna's letters to Gabriel, while not always acceptable for after-dinner enter-tainment, reflect her truest, deepest thoughts, beliefs, and passions. From the beginning, she pledged to write as her, and he did the same.

Each of you followed the story from the beginning, watching it happen. You have been our friends, our confidants, and our cheerleaders, anticipating the coming of the Twelfth of Never with a collective holding of breaths.

The Twelfth of Never would have been this Sunday that, by coincidence, is also his birthday. And Gabriel, in his usual extraordinary and loving way, gave a gift to Anna for his birthday.

He not only gave his permission, but actually requested that she post something very special, and long anticipated. This is one you will not want to miss.

02-12-2006 — Happy Birthday Gabriel!

> *Grow old along with me!*
> *The best is yet to be,*
> *the last of life, for which the first was made: ...*
> ~~Robert Browning (140)

Today, February 12, we celebrate the birthday of a remarkable man. A man that's been thrown out of cars, windows, buckboards, and bedrooms. Who has stood toe to toe with desperados, lawmen, and a few feisty ladies, winning some and losing some. Who's been bitch-slapped, punched, pummeled, knocked around, and beaten to a pulp. Who's been shot, stabbed, run over, burned, impaled on a pike, blown up, and buried alive. Even the Pacific Ocean tried to do him in.

He's fallen from the back of a horse, the seat of a runaway wagon, the edge of a cliff, and the side of a mountain. He dropped off a three-story building just last year. He's raced the oceans, dominated the surf, and sailed the high seas. He's stolen cars, expensive jewelry, bankrolls, and women's hearts. He rides a horse like a pro and can handle trucks, stagecoaches, sailboats, buckboards, and racecars with equal aplomb.

He's been a member of some of the most esteemed societies, clubs, associations, and organizations of the world, even walking the picket lines fighting for the worker's rights. But he's never felt the need to brag about any of them.

As a cousin, uncle, brother, nephew, in-law, grandson, son, husband, father, and grandfather he is devoted to his family – down to the last fourth cousin, thrice removed. When he calls you friend, it's for life.

He's visited the great cities of the world and made love to their beautiful women. He's traveled back in time. And seen the future.

He almost died in service to his country.

He's been a cowboy, a pirate, a painter, a poet, a chef, a thief, a soldier, a lyricist, a carpenter, a sailor, a writer, a fighter, a surfer, a black belt, a lover, a teacher, a singer, a stalker, a zombie, and a Neanderthal. And, no doubt, a butcher, a baker, and a candlestick maker at one time or another.

He's talked his way out of just about everything. And he's lived to tell about it.

When I met him, I had no idea how much my life was about to be changed … but then, how could I have known? He was The One that existed only in my imagination. He makes loving him the easiest thing I've ever done and I never want to go back.

So I ask you to join me, today, in wishing my darling Gabriel the most happiest of birthdays.

02-12-2006 — **Damn, You should write my resume**
Personal email to Anna from *Gabriel*

That's quite a salute you just gave me! Now remember you said it's okay to make my Valentine public? It's going to be mushy, real mushy!

02-14-2006 — **Names**

I wanted to start out today by reporting Morgan's healthy Baby Boy is now kicking up a storm. She says a Soccer Player has taken up residence in her tummy. The Expecting Moms modeling agency is already getting them both work (do they issue SAG cards to the unborn?)

Names are in order of course, and grandma is helping (ok, ok, hinting. A lot. Come on, just one of the middle ones. Pretty please?)

Anna, the name I use to tell my stories, is an English name meaning "Gracious"; probably from the Hebrew name Hannah meaning "Grace, Charm, and Mercy." My real name is Hebrew for "Bitter" and although a very famous blond actress used it, it never felt right to me. I much prefer the one I have now which is French for "Victorious People" and became mine at 21 – apropos, as that was about the time I took charge of my own future. So names are important and so, I think, are their meanings.

Today we celebrate Valentine's Day, a name that means "strength and honor." Valentine was a priest who served during the third century in Rome and may have sent the very first Valentine. When the Emperor decided single men made better soldiers, he outlawed marriage for young men. Valentine, realizing the injustice, performed marriages in secret. When discovered, he was sentenced to death. Valentine fell in love with a young girl who visited him in prison and before the sentence was carried out, wrote her a letter, signed "From your Valentine." Pope Gelasius declared February 14 St. Valentine's Day around 498 A.D.

An estimated one billion Valentine cards are sent each year, making Valentine's Day the second largest card-sending holiday of the year.

Happy Valentine's Day to my Love, and to all of you.

And for the *JournalLand* friends, supporters, and cheerleaders, who have been there for us since the beginning (occasionally – ok often – giggling under your breath when you figured it all out), we welcome you, at last, to share the romance of Gabriel's words to Anna by visiting his journal *Azrael999*.

02-16-2006 — **Questions Questions Answers**

How did *JournalLand* bring Gabriel and Anna together? The gorgeously exotic tantalizing Mistress *HissandTell* lent Gabriel to me. On June 12, 2005, she said (and I partially quote because the entry itself is a wee bit X-rated):

> ... *to distract me further from my tragically celibate state I managed to have a rather magnificent pornographic wet-dream featuring the breathtakingly-dexterous and abundantly-endowed "Gabriel" (well, he was a pretty damned dexterous and endowed cowboy-angel in my dream, anyway) ... Trust me; I spent the morning after ... searching the highway in vain for rugged Malibu men in cowboy hats and bandanas with two different-coloured eyes ... .*

Well, or something to that effect (as dear Hissy would say).

Which led me immediately (hello people – dexterous and well-endowed in the same sentence ... and from *Hissy*) to find out exactly who, or what, put her in such a tizzy. Lo and behold – that magnificent Malibu cowboy was right here in *JournalLand* telling outrageous tales of his Army experiences, his dreams, his friends and family, and his pea-brain.

Sometimes I'm asked – isn't it odd, or strange, or different. Starting a romance over the internet? No, just a little better. You see, he didn't meet me over cocktails or coffee, which would invariably have led to so much more before we even got to know one another. He didn't meet me in a chat room – where we could have gotten to know one another by carefully editing what we wrote for weeks or months. He met me by having read my journal and already knowing the rawest, most honest, and most personal details of my life. So I knew, when I picked up that phone for the very first time, he already knew me – and I was, well, worth getting to know better.

02-20-2006 — **Questions, Questions, Answers Two**

I've said before I am terrified of groups of strangers in social settings (I can stand in front of a hundred clients and teach a software program, or dance competitively in front of a thousand people – but a cocktail party with twenty strangers stops me in my tracks). So what scares me? Friends and Family. Not mine – they already know me and love me despite my quirks. It is all the ones I don't know.

I have an uneasy feeling some of his friends and family members may read my words – now that they have connected these writings to his "Anna." I thought long and hard about going back and editing like crazy. Changing the way I said things, passwording the X-Rated entries, hiding the emails dear Gabriel sent me and (with his permission) I quoted, and removing the entries full of my garden variety anxieties and fears about life in general. And most especially I suppose, the older entries about Ben, or the 101 Things or the ME ME ME entries which lay it on the line at times.

But you know … despite misgivings and second thoughts, I've decided to leave them. Because everyone knows that history is about what is told <u>and</u> what is left out. Eventually some of those friends or family may meet me, and I suppose it is better to know the real me than have to pretend to be a me that isn't me. Gabriel read all of me before he made that first overture, and everything that came afterwards. Besides, when I asked him long ago if he thought I should stop writing, he said, quite specifically "no way."

> … *when you love someone all your saved-up wishes start coming out.*
> ~~Elizabeth Bowen (146)

02-23-2006 — **Giving It All Up**

I've been thinking about giving up the stuff you love for the one you love –

whether it is the piece of furniture given to you by your favorite grandmother, a job that satisfies you, the cat that has stood by you, the first row center season tickets to the best theater in the country, the boat you spent windy summer afternoons sailing, or the place you hold in your local society. And what love has to do with it.

Do you remember the Christmas story where she sells her beautiful long hair to give him a chain for his watch, and he sells his watch to give her combs for her beautiful long hair?

When Ben (you remember Ben, don't you?) talked about us being together, I knew it meant walking away from almost everything. I finally knew deep in my heart I couldn't do it, even to be with him. Almost from the beginning, I've known deep in that same heart I was willing to give up almost everything to be with Gabriel. And he would never ask me to.

> *The important thing is this: to be able at any moment to sacrifice what we are for what we could become.*
> ~~Charles du Bos

02-23-2006 — I don't understand you at all
Personal email to Anna from *Gabriel*

In one sentence, you wiped out everything I did to reassure my family that you did understand our situation and what's going on with us … apparently I was wrong. Your quote about "giving up the stuff you love for the one you love" sent my son, my Mother, and a few others into a tail spin. Then your readers commented again about why we haven't met.

Let me spell it out MY SON IS DYING and LOVE DOES WIN OUT. I LOVE MY *SON* AND WILL BE WITH HIM UNTIL THE END. I LOVE MY *FAMILY*. I LOVE *YOU* BUT IF YOU CAN'T UNDERSTAND WHY I'M DOING WHAT I AM DOING THEN I SUGGEST YOU RETHINK OUR SITUATION.

Even my mother asked, don't these people know Shane is dying? Would these people leave a dying Son or Daughter for even a moment to spend time with someone they have known for less than a year? What kind of people are these? I thought I knew them, apparently I don't.

02-24-2006 — **the sound of the other shoe dropping**
Personal email to *Gabriel* from Anna

I cannot understand how my words could be interpreted to mean I wanted you to leave your son or your family for me, nor can I control what my readers may comment regarding our meeting one another.

The entry was about ME leaving stuff behind, and in the most loving and complete way I was saying that, unlike others, you have never asked or expected me to give up the things I own to be in a relationship with you. You wrote the same thing to me months ago – that no one should have to give up their "stuff" to be with the one they loved.

In my heart of hearts I believe you are exactly where you should be, doing exactly what you should be doing. I believe we are in full agreement that our meeting will come about in its own time and I fully support your continuing to dedicate the time and attention needed to matters in your personal life.

Your happiness and well-being are more important to me than anything else. And I have always tried to respect your wishes the very, very best I know how.

2-24-2006 — **I appreciate what you did**
Personal email to Anna from *Gabriel*
(written and sent before he got the previous message)

I know our friends want us to see each other as soon as possible, but to what end? I want to meet under better circumstances and when I'm not worried to death. My Son is dying and I want to spend every second I can with him. I doubt it would be much fun for you anyway, he would be on my mind every minute, and I would lose my mind if anything happened while I was away.

I apologize for reacting the way I did. It had been my son's first bad day since I got back and the anxiety and fear level has been very high among the family members. The pain has gotten much worse and his medication has been moved up to injecting Laudanum twice a day. It seems to help quite a bit, soon it will move to a Morphine pump.

Shane's turn for the worse caught me off guard. I will adjust to the fact that it has started and soon I'll be a bit more controlled. I'm just a little edgy now but my nerves will tighten and I'll continue to operate true to form in a day or so. Once again, I'm sorry. Tomorrow is going to be a long day and I have to be up soon, I already miss Pacific Standard Time. I love you Anna.

02-24-2006 — **Facing It**
(from the secret journal "*LuvACowboy*")

we finally faced it. we cried together on the phone, sobbing out our frustration, our anger, and even our fear. about different things, and the same things. then late that night, unknown to each other, we sat at the computer and wrote almost the same emails.

i finished and sent mine at 1:39 a.m. and when i rose the next morning i found the one he had sent at 1:40 a.m. each of us responding to the other's words and reassuring each other's fears without having read them.

now that we can talk about it, he also admitted he has always pictured our first meeting to be the beginning of a storybook romance instead of just a whirlwind coffee stop. i'm thinking – at the top of the Empire State Building.

02 25 2006   **Random Thoughts From a Common Mind**

Why are some people dump-ers (that's a technical term), and some people dump-ees? (that's another one) Ask anyone for a historical perspective. I'll bet most people in relationships are either (1) waiting for the other shoe to drop or (2) confidently in charge of its fate. And I'll betcha most of the ones waiting for the shoe to drop are female.

Maybe because he's typically in charge of moving the relationship along – he asks her out, says I Love You first, suggests moving in, and proposes marriage. For the dump-ee personality, talking with their husband or boyfriend about anything significant is like facing Wile E. Coyote with a giant mallet hidden behind his back. Afraid he will bang us over the head with a big "see ya" should we do, or say, the wrong thing. So instead of talking, instead of saying, "When you do that it makes me feel … " we bottle it up inside.

Where it festers, grows tentacles, knots us up, and causes headaches, upset tummies, and depression. We can't, or won't, speak up because that mallet could come swinging down.

In my opinion – if you find yourself with someone you can't talk to without fear of the consequences – be the Dump-ER for once. Then go find someone who honestly wants to listen.

03-01-2006 — **Call me "Annie"**

One evening Gabriel and I talked about voices. How the sound of a voice evokes memories, enhances emotions, creates trust, stirs us to action, sings us to sleep, or caresses our hearts. How we sometimes judge a stranger by the sound of their voice, painting a picture or envisioning a personality for someone we know little else about.

When Morgan was of dating age, so was I (dating, not Morgan, although I was certainly younger). As every woman can attest, there are times in a dating career that call for "the talk." You know the one … "You're a nice guy, I've enjoyed going out with you, but can we just be friends."

If I disliked and dreaded that talk, Morgan would rather have been dipped in milk, rolled in cornbread, and batter fried in boiling oil. Fortunately, our voices on the phone sounded exactly alike.

So I would give the talk to her *can we just be friends* , and she would give it to mine. It actually worked out quite well.

With Gabriel, we had already exchanged many long emails before we ever spoke in person and, while he had sent me his picture, it was some weeks before I sent him one of mine. I'm not sure the voice I expected, but it was not the voice I heard. I think I was expecting something smooth, rich, sultry, cultured, a little southern accent – a voice that would sing bass in the church choir. The voice I heard was completely unexpected and it took some time to reconcile it to the photos and writings.

The other day I asked Gabriel what he thought the first time he heard me.

"It scared me to death." "Why?" I questioned. *Could it have been that bad?*

"Because I heard a little girl and was terrified I had fallen for a precocious teen-ager who had been using a stranger's picture in her journal. And because I already wanted it to be you."

And I laughed so hard.

Then I told him my voice simply belongs to the girl inside. The girl that is exactly like Meg Ryan's Annie in *Sleepless in Seattle*. She is an adorably cute, blonde, curly-haired, button nosed, pert, tiny little bubbly person people will always refer to as a girl, instead of a tall, slim, dark-haired, poetic, romantic woman who carries elegant a whole lot more effectively than cute.

Of course, it would have been awfully nice if my voice had, in any way, grown up to match the woman outside, instead of the cute, blond, laughing, little girl within.

Perhaps when I called my character in this journal "Anna," it was simply a taller, romantic, and more elegant form of Annie ... the one who had just been waiting for her Sam.

03-02-2006 — **The Someday Boxes**
(from the secret journal "*LuvACowboy*")

Son has been hospitalized in very bad shape. Gabriel is not sleeping, eating, or even thinking straight. but he calls for a moment each day "just to tell you i love you." i'd like to think he just wants to hear my voice.

so things feel more normal, yet they don't. i wish i understood more.

long ago he gave me his West Coast address, but nothing i sent there ever arrived. he has never given me the address where he is living now – in fact, refusing to do so. something about respecting Son's privacy.

earlier this week he mentioned how his mail is being forwarded from his West Coast house to his Son's house, that he was expecting a FedEx package from the writing group and a UPS from a friend, all of which needed to be signed for. so i guess neither address is all that private after all.

i just put Christmas, birthday and the occasional card or picture or funny article i want to share into a someday box. that must be where the things he's always promising to send me are too. in a someday box. some days i am so angry.

03-08-2006 — **A Child's View of Life**

Brody, our secretary's seven-year-old son, recently participated in his Blue & Gold banquet for Scouts. Grace was said before dinner. As usual, the cub master said "Amen" at the end.

Brody looked at his mom and asked, "Why do they say Amen?" to which she replied, "It's a way to end a prayer, like grace ... "

Brody frowned and whispered, "Why can't they say all humans?"

03-09-2006 — **How Sweet It Is**

When I first met Gabriel, I could never quite figure out why a man as attractive, powerful, intelligent, well spoken, and diffident in the most seductive way, involved in an industry where the most beautiful and talented women in the world are readily available to him, was single.

And why, after the sheer accident of finding me and discovering I was 3,000 miles away, he still thought me interesting enough to get to know. Then how an attraction of almost epic proportions formed between us. How could that possibly happen? At last, I know.

It was Pi.

No, not pie ... *Pi.*

You see, Pi Theory explains the unexplainable – why things relate when they shouldn't. Pi is in the disks of the moon and the sun, the double helix of DNA, the rainbow, and in the pupil of the eye. Pi is in the spreading rings of raindrops falling into a pond. Pi can be found in colors and music, the tables of death, quantum mechanics, relativity theory, and number theory.

Why does Pi show up in all these seemingly unrelated places? No one can say. One of the great mysteries is that nature knows mathematics.

Pi connects, we just don't know how yet.

03-14-2006 — **A Love Doll For His Taste**
(from the secret journal "*LuvACowboy*")

today is my birthday. but no happy for me.

it's been a lifetime since my body was anything more than a real-as-life human sex doll, to be poked and prodded at will in the most emotionally degrading ways.

they say the opposite of love is not hate.

it is indifference.

03-15-2006 — **Full Moon Rising**
(from the secret journal "*LuvACowboy*")

200 miles. that's how close we'll be. again, for the second time.

we planned hours of late evening phone calls from today through next Friday, with me very careful not to suggest anything more. but something is wrong; there was no call yesterday or today. if Son had improved at all, he would have called.

and the full moon is back. damn Her, reminding me of so much that could have been. it is no wonder i believe Fate does not intend to allow this union.

03-16-2006 — **Floriday #1 – Redux**

I am in Tampa, Florida again, visiting my best friend Bobbi and my dreams last night were very, very troubled. But this is a subject for some other time.

My birthday was this week, and I find myself (despite best efforts) another year older. With a couple extra wrinkles, a few more saggy bits, and a lot more for L'Oreal Preference to handle. (by the by, thanks to so many of you for remembering and no, Mr. Lucky didn't – but you knew that)

Maybe because those good wishes were marking the passing of yet another life anniversary without resolution, they got me to thinking that, as diarists, we spend an inordinate amount of virtual ink on what we don't like about ourselves. Weekly, sometimes daily, entries dedicated to our "gee if only I coulda, woulda," "I wish it were different" changes and improvements we want to make.

Today, in honor of my birthday, I choose to dub the rest of this week "National Tell Me What You LIKE About Yourself" week. Go ahead, don't be shy. Brag a little. Tell the world what you like, no … what you LOVE about yourself. Then pat yourself on your deserving back and we will all raise a glass of something bubbly Saturday Night at 10:00 EST to toast our respective wonderfulnesses.

Here, in no particular order, are the top 10 things I LIKE about me:

1. It doesn't frighten me to fall in love, not even the hard work involved in maintaining the relationship.
2. I have dreams and I'm not afraid to go for them.
3. I have the courage to fight through everything life wants to throw at me, because in between the fights are all the good parts.
4. I am willing to take chances without knowing what the end result will be.
5. Being kind is extremely important to me. Not just to humans, but to all living things. I am so grateful when they are kind back.
6. I will stand up for what I believe in, without belittling the beliefs of others.
7. I have a good heart and will gladly give it where it is needed most.
8. I indulge my insatiable curiosity by making every day a learning experience.
9. I let myself have fun.
10. I want people to know the real me.

These are the things I hope people see. What's in me, instead of those saggy knees, weird toes, and the new lines that appear with every passing year.

03-17-2006 — **Falling Into the Abyss**
(from the secret journal "*LuvACowboy*")

i know the last words i said to him. "it's going to be all right. remember how much i love you." like a mother soothing a crying child.

i thought i could handle the silence. the not knowing. i've been preparing for it, mentally, emotionally. Gabriel has been preparing me, reminding me on each call that he loves me. promising he will come back.

it doesn't make it any easier. i am left alone to wonder. has he truly fallen into the abyss, or is it something i said or did. is he gone for a while or forever.

and today, after four days of silence, i realized there's no one i can even ask. no one at all.

03-24-2006 — **Best Friends Forever**

Bobbi, you are my best friend. You have broad shoulders for such a little thing, and I don't know what I would do without you sometimes. So I promise (*borrowed from one of those sappy chain emails*):

1. When you are sad – I will help you get drunk and plot revenge against the sorry bastard who made you that way.
2. When you are blue – I will try to dislodge whatever is choking you.
3. When you smile – I will know you've finally had sex.
4. When you are scared – I will tease the shit out of you about it every chance I get.
5. When you are worried – I will tell you horrible stories about how much worse it could be and demand you stop your bloody whining.
6. When you are confused – I will use little words.
7. When you are sick – Stay the hell away from me until you are well again. I don't want whatever you have.
8. When you fall – I will point and laugh at your clumsy ass.
9. When you're broke – I will remind you it was your choice to leave a great boss like Mr. Lucky, move to sunny Florida, and take a job that pays peanuts.
10. And if you ever track down Mr. Wonderful, that sorry son-of-a b*tch ex-husband of yours … I'll bring the shovel.

By the way, I tried to send this to 10 of my closest friends, then got depressed because I could only think of two, and one of them isn't speaking to me right now anyway. Sure glad the other one is you!

> *Remember: A good friend will help you move.*
> *A very good friend … will help you move a body.*
> ~~Edna Buchanan (125)

03-26-2006 — **Roller Coaster Rides and Courage**

The exciting thing about roller coaster rides is the adrenalin rush you get. Not quite knowing if you are going to walk away safely on the other end. But while roller coasters are fabulous fun every once in a while, you wouldn't want to ride one every day.

Relationships are the same way. I read somewhere that the entire first year of a relationship is spent learning to trust the other person. An entire year on a roller coaster of emotion that leaves you ecstatic one moment and terrified the next. I think the older you get, the longer it takes to trust, because we've got so much more history to overcome. So we protect ourselves against another loss by locking our hearts away in secret boxes of our own making. It's easier to close off the possibilities and run from anyone trying to find the key.

We are all scared. When we fall in love, we all have trouble unlocking a heart that has been badly damaged by past experiences. But consider that having found love, you have half of what you need. Raw courage is the other half.

The next time you feel like running, take a good look and decide what you're running away from. You … or your partner. Then decide when you're going to grow up and stop allowing your past decide your future.

> *I used to be a genuine romantic. Now love and reality are almost contradictory. It's easier to get together, have an exciting time, and watch him leave, than to deal with the day-to-day life of a relationship. I may miss him, but at least I'm not dying inside.*
>
> ~~Anna

03-29-2006 — **Midnight Hour**
(from the secret journal "*LuvACowboy*")

he calls again. every few days. as if he has to. with no explanation for the silences. each day, during the sunlit hours, i have a reassuring dialog with myself. each night with all the questions and none of the answers, i drift into sleep, gratefully embracing the Technicolor rainbow of happiness it brings.

03-30-2006 — **Dietary Challenge**

Those of you who have been reading for a while know about Mr. Lucky's diet. Or, lack of one. When I ask if he wants to eat the food I'm about to make, he always says no. Yet, he complains mightily about maintaining his ever-increasing weight, while his daily intake consists of rice, oatmeal, breakfast cereal and my leftovers.

He imbibes these gourmet goodies with an ever-increasing volume of gustatory sounds that would drive a sane person stark raving mad. They are the sounds of 10,000 soldiers marching with hob-nailed boots through the stone streets of Italy. They are the sounds that drown out the Washington Redskins game on Sunday afternoon. First time diners in my home look at one another in shock, while giggling nervously under their breath and trying to keep a straight face.

Sunday he woke up with a stomachache. "I don't feel good," he complained. "I can't go visit my mom and have lunch with her. I couldn't eat anything anyway." So around 4:00, I made myself some dinner. His olfactory senses, ever on the alert, brought him streaking downstairs to the kitchen, where he sat across from me and stared at my plate.

"How come your food always looks better than mine?" he queried.

"I dunno – because it's not brown in milk or white in tomato sauce?" I rejoined.

"Umm, is there any more?"

I looked at him balefully, and rose to fix him a cup of tomato soup. At least he didn't have to chew.

04-01-2006 — **The Greybody Factor**
(from the secret journal "*LuvACowboy*")

> *Strings interact by splitting and joining. When two closed strings become one, the worldsheet is theorized to be a smooth surface. Scientific study leads me to believe Feynman is more correct.*
> ~~Anna

It is the witching hour. The hour of midnight when the veil between the two worlds thin. Head upon pillow, poised on the event horizon of another black hole, I reach out tentatively to search among the uncountable number for the golden string linking us one to the other.

If I can find it, what will it look like? Is it shiny and bright like moonlight? Full-moon fat, gorged with love, laughter, bolstered by words spoken, lines written, promises made, thoughts passed through the very ether of existence?
Or is it but a single particle wide, so delicate that the sound of a falling tear could break it.

04-02-2006 — **The P Factor**

I HATE WATER

Ok, maybe hate is a relative word (ha, ha, get it ... Relative). Let's just say I'd rather be locked in a room with Mr. Lucky while he eats a 13-course dinner. Ok, that's getting carried away, but I would rather listen to fifteen war stories of his time in the Army (reserves) than to drink a glass of tap water.

I could count the number of glasses of tap water I've imbibed willingly in my entire life and can assure you it is less than the number of men I've dated (yes, I probably WOULD have said "had," but there are children reading this and we don't want to give them the wrong idea about me, do we)

Where was I? Oh, yes. Water.

I can taste every chemical, every additive (whether it's good for me or not), every toilet that has been flushed into my drinking water and supposedly cleaned. I can taste the fish poop and I know whereof I speak ... my second husband was an engineer with the EPA and worked with sewage treatment plants. People you do NOT want to drink that water. Trust me.
I've gotten myself sidetracked again. Ah, Water.

I get headaches. Lousy, rotten, stinking, down for the count migraines. Fortunately, the drug lords have invented several effective medications, including Imitrex. It takes an hour to "kick in" but it works wonders.

Yes, Yes, I'm getting to the water thing.

Gabriel has spent some time the past few months encouraging me (and I use this word very loosely ... for you can't imagine how emphatically he can ENCOURAGE one do something he wants you to do) to drink more water. While I'm fairly certain the causes of my headaches are either a)lack of sleep b)working too long on a computer under fluorescent lights or c)Mr. Lucky (in general, folks, just in general) I'm trying to be a good girlfriend and attempt to drink more water.

Years ago, we would have had a serious problem. Because not only does tap water suck, but most bottled waters are pretty much the same way. Aquafina, Dasani, and many store brands labeled "drinking water" or "purified water" is simply tap water subjected to additional purification before bottling at plants around the country. They all have a disagreeable "taste" and "texture."

However, four or five years ago I found Fiji water. This water is pure artesian water that comes from a source deep within the earth, protected by layers of clay and rock that, in turn, protect it from environmental pollutants and other contamination. It is bottled using a closed system and (according to the advertising anyway) untouched by anything until you open the bottle.

And it rocks! I LIKE it. Well, not as much as flavored liquids, but it is drinkable. So – taking Gabriel's advice to heart I've made a valiant attempt to DRINK MORE WATER.

Herein lays the interesting conundrum. Drinking the water is supposed to help with the headaches. But ingesting so much water wakes me up every couple of hours at night. Thus, I am tired. One of my headache triggers is being tired. See the vicious circle?

In deference to Gabriel who is only trying to help, I will continue to imbibe the water ... but I need to calculate when to STOP during the day if I'm ever going to get any sleep at night.

Yesterday I told you that the "Greybody Factor" is non-trivial frequency dependent corrections usually applied to black holes and string theory. In English, just think of it as important calculations needed to adjust the math so it works.

I think I'll call my water calculation adjustments the "P Factor."

I have never been compensated for recommending Fiji water. It's just that good!

04-03-2006 — **Sometimes**
(from the secret journal "*LuvACowboy*")

a little while ago today you said, "sometimes i don't call because I have nothing to say."

perhaps you don't know that "i know that." i understand how hard it is, sometimes, to even pick up the phone. hard to find the energy, the incentive, even the desire. i've been there too. but if i may venture a guess (and i don't mean to be presumptuous) don't you usually feel better after you talk to me than you did before?

i know i do.

so if you ever feel like dialing – then don't – what the heck, try it anyway. tell me you just want to listen for a few moments. you would be amazed at the healing qualities of "i love you."

04-04-2006 — **Grazing with Mr. Lucky**

I've regaled you with stories about Mr. Lucky and groceries. About skids of dog food, cases of mushroom soup, and giant economy size anythings – whether we use it or not.

If the words "on sale" are a potent aphrodisiac, "free" is an instantaneous orgasm (he could have saved the cost of the Viagra!). If it's free, Mr. Lucky wants one. Or two. Or Five. Even if he has to wait in line, or buy something to get it (you know, like Free Printer with Purchase of Computer).

When we go to a store giving away free samples of cheese, sausage, dessert slices, crackers (really, it doesn't matter) he will stop to graze at every station – then go back repeatedly. I have, literally, had to drag him to the checkout counter while he reaches out, whimpering, for "just one more" cheesy nacho with picante dip.

Don't get me started on the free imprinted mugs, calendars, water bottles, cloth bags, backpacks, pens, laser pointers, mouse pads, key chains, and assorted crap in his desk, strewn about on the floor of his office, and stashed in the kitchen cabinets behind the pots and pans.

Hotels? Each day he purloins the shampoo, conditioner, mouthwash, sewing kits, Kleenex – he will take the toilet paper if I'm not there to stop him. The closets are so infested with mini bottles and soap bars I have started donating them away to the local homeless shelter.

When the Sunday morning colored section arrives, those little veins in his forehead pop out, and he dances around the room circling On Sale ads whilst figuring out the most expedient route to the stores.

So, Mr. Lucky approaches me on Sunday and says "We never do anything together. There's some stuff I need on sale at the grocery. Want to go with me?"

We arrive at Wegman's, a fabulously wonderful store where I have actually learned to like grocery shopping. I grab a cart (please, you don't think Mr. Lucky would sully his hands with something as mundane as actually pushing a cart do you) and select some grapes.

"Don't buy those. They are cheaper at Shoppers." I arch my brow and refrain from mentioning that the closest Shoppers is several miles away and gas is approaching $2.60 a gallon. Let me do the math – oh never mind, I'll just come back later this week. I finish in the fruit section a few moments later and move to the bread. Mr. Lucky disappears to the left – heading into the coffee and tea area.

Where Wegman's always has a few pots brewing of various kinds, and tiny little paper cups set out so you can taste the flavors and, hopefully, buy some.

Forty minutes later. FORTY MINUTES. I've finished my shopping and Mr. Lucky is still nowhere to be found. So I call his cell phone. "I've been looking for you," he whines.

"Where are you?" I ask, restraining myself vigorously.

"I'm in the tea section" and a few moments later he joins me at the checkout, tiny little paper cup of tea in hand. I am, literally, embarrassed to ask, but just have to.

"So, you've been sampling teas while you were lost?"

"Yes," he replies, dancing up and down. "Hold this for me, would you? I've gotta hit the men's room."

Gosh – I wonder why.

04-06-2006 — **When Socks Come Home**

Some days are more remarkable than others.

I woke up yesterday before the alarm went off, which meant I wasn't jarred out of a deep sleep by a clanging bell.

A sock, long lost, came home to find its lonely partner. Which proves that sometimes things made to go together never, ever, stop looking.

All the green lights on the way to the office behaved, because when things are right in the world, even classically obstinate objects cooperate.

Gabriel called and expressed content that my hair was getting longer, pleasure at receiving new pictures, and a reminder that, while Mr. Lucky is an unpleasant part of my present, he will one day be nothing more a past memory easily forgotten by us both as we spend our years together.

And the song playing on the radio was "I Hope You Dance" which always refills my heart with new hope.

04-07-2006 — **Batter Up!**

Baseball season is upon us. Now, while I'm not a stand-around-the-water-cooler-and-talk-about-last-night's-games kinda' girl, I do enjoy watching a game. Particularly when I'm sitting in the stadium on a warm summer night.

Shortly after I moved to Baltimore my soon to be ex-husband and I quickly became the proud owners of six season tickets in the brand-spanking new/old edifice. We sold off what we didn't use and I continued the subscription for another ten years or so. It was hard to change allegiance from the Cards, but great players like Brady Anderson, Rafael Palmiero, Chris Hoiles, and Ironman Cal Ripken sure helped the transition.

Speaking of baseball, Gabriel and his son (to the extent his health allows) are helping coach his grandson's first Little League experience. For once, Gabriel has second billing as his son imparts some of his not inconsiderable skills and dedicated patience to the young admirers. I'm told the stands of the little stadium, which are typically empty during practice, have had a significant increase in parental attendance!

Speaking of parental attendance. Morgan played left field on a girls' Softball team (like Little League for girls) when she was slightly older than Gabriel's grandson, breaking four fingers in three years hustling after balls. Unfortunately for her dad, the games were in the late morning/mid-afternoon, so baseball moms were typically the only ones in attendance.

Hey, wait a minute. Baseball moms. Single baseball moms. Gabriel and single baseball moms. Gabriel and *pretty* single baseball moms. Gabriel and *pretty* single baseball moms with adorably cute kids. Umm, Houston, we have a problem.

Ok, just kidding. Mostly.

04-10-2006 — **A Ben and Anna Story**
(from the secret journal "*LuvACowboy*")

> *Because of you*
> *I never stray too far from the sidewalk*
> *I learned to play on the safe side so I don't get hurt*
> ~~Pennie Murray, *Giving Myself Permission*

You call me to ask how I am. I lie and tell you everything is wonderful. Because the truth hurts.

You call me because you truly care about me. I know that. So we laugh a little and talk about how things used to be. All those years when you and I knew everything about the us that was a we and you ask me about the new man in my life.

You call me and we still pretend to have no secrets, one from the other. We speak of how perilous it is to love and be loved.

You call me and your voice reminds me of how genuinely romantic I was then.

It's like I put all my romanticism into that one relationship, with its appearance of honesty and truth. When you left, so did hope, and I don't know how to trust anyone again.

04-14-2006 — **you, you, you BRUSSELS SPROUT you**

My parents taught me to look for the good in everything and everyone. I took their teachings to heart, although I do rather ~~hate~~ dislike Brussels Sprouts. Since I've heard the opposite of Love is not Hate, but Indifference, let's just say I hold Mr. Lucky in the same regard as I do Brussels Sprouts.

04-15-2006 — **The Name Game**
Personal email to *Gabriel* from Anna

Dearest one, you know I love you truly, but no matter HOW many times you refer to him as "Cletus," or "Rufus," or "Beauregard," those names are not going on the list of names for my Grandson! It's bad enough his father still calls him the "Little Noodle."

04-20-2006 — **BUT, Can He Boil Water**

The perfect recipe for Mr. Lucky's Famous Deviled Egg Sandwiches:

12 eggs
Water
Mayonnaise, mustard, salt, pickle juice, pepper, paprika
Pot, Bowl, Plate, Fork, Knife, Spoon
Anna

1. Decide you want deviled eggs.
2. Remove eggs from refrigerator
3. Go find Anna and ask how to cook eggs.
4. Put water in large soup pot and add eggs.
5. Go find Anna and ask if Step 4 looks right.
6. Go find smaller pot, remove half of water and add eggs.
7. Put pot of water on stove and turn on burner.
8. Come back 15 minutes later and move pot to the burner controlled by the knob you turned.
9. Come back to check on eggs when smoke alarm goes off.

10. Go to store and buy more eggs.
11. Repeat steps 1-7.
12. Check on eggs only because Anna asks, "Are the eggs done yet?"
13. Turn off burner and go watch TV show, leaving eggs in hot pot of water.
14. Return 45 minutes later.
15. Attempt to peel eggs.
16. Pry off chunks of eggshell with glued on egg white until egg yolk can be released into bowl.
17. Ask Anna how to get shell off white chunks, then, using the instructions provided, pry off shell with teaspoon and proudly display plate of shelled egg white chunks no more than 1" on any side.
18. Stare dolefully at yolks in bowl, unsure of what to do next and finally ask Anna to make the deviled part of the deviled eggs.
19. Slather completed devil on egg white chunks. Top with second egg white chunk. Repeat until you run out of egg white chunks.

Offer Anna some of your ~~funny-looking~~ famous "Deviled Egg Sandwiches."

04-22-2006 — **Two Minutes to Midnight**
(from the secret journal "*LuvACowboy*")

it's the two minute warning. Son's cancer ridden leg will come off within the week in an attempt to control the pain, even though he may not survive the surgery. if he does, it will be downhill quickly. it's simple right now. the horror of a waiting game where all sides lose.

Gabriel waits while Son loses the battle. and we all pray for as much time as possible, despite the inevitability of the conclusion. he will not admit – has even denied it (i tell you everything, he says) – but i believe one of the reasons he keeps me separated from that life is so i will not remind him of it in the future. i understand, so i don't push it.

04-25-2006 — **And Your Little Dog Too**

Sometimes I just want to be like Dorothy. All that power in a bucket of water.

Although if I used the house, I could at least keep the shoes.

04-27-2006 — **Send in the Clowns**
(from the secret journal "*LuvACowboy*")

i crossed our "not allowed to discuss" line this evening. Gabriel did not become too angry … just reminded me firmly that the timing was up to him.

you see, he wooed me last night with delectable tales of making love on a Sunfish in Mexico – where he wants to go for a get to know you month – and talked of returning to writing his show in the fall.

it was as if he was starting to think about his plans for the after and it got me to thinking too far ahead. i used the "we" word.

i've talked to myself quite firmly, taken a sedative, and rejoined the world i agreed to – where life is lived day by day, week by week, month by month. no plans, no – well – no more than the voice on the other end of that damn phone.

pragmatism – my new/old mantra.

05-06-2006 — **Brought to you by the letter "Ex"**

The following is brought to you by the letter "Ex" since I have good "Ex"cuses for not writing lately. Really.

I returned home from Manhattan last Thursday after four days. First hot weekend and I walked miles and miles. I called Gabriel from the Body Exhibit and expressed amazement at the size of the liver – largest organ in the body. My legs and feet started to swell which had never happened to me before – even when flying overseas. On Friday, I went straight to my internist after more swelling, pain and tingling in my left arm and hand, and general malaise.

I am, after all, no spring chicken – already older than my father's stroke at 55, and my mother's cancer at 45. I feared a stroke was brewing.

All normal, but got an RX for a stress ECHO because, as he said, "women are often under diagnosed." Gave me a diuretic and we laughed, figuring it was just the standing and the heat. Drink More Water he warned! (sound familiar?)

But I must admit to you, my dear friend, I thought hard about what to tell

Gabriel. I have never, ever lied to him – not even by omission. But I remember him telling me, early in our relationship – during those marathon get to know you calls – that good health was extremely high on his "gotta have" list, even extracting a solemn cross my heart vow to outlive him.

I think, no matter how much I look forward to our future together when the time is right, I would have had to find a way to let him walk away from someone he would most certainly survive, believing it was his decision. Because I will not hurt him and because I would not ever leave him.

05-08-2006 — **Do You Believe in Forever**
(from the secret journal "*LuvACowboy*")

he calls me the quiet, peaceful center of the storm that surrounds his every waking hour.

son's final surgery will be Friday – if he can make it through these last few days. then it will go quickly, four weeks, perhaps a little more.

05-11-2006 — **Shadow Dancing**

Ben: **text* are you there?*
Anna: *yes*
Ben: *where you been girl, can you talk?*
Anna: *yes *end text**
Ben: Is everything all right?
Anna: Yes … and no. Complicated, as always. And you?
Ben: I've missed you. I've missed the person I become when I'm inside of you.
Anna: You always missed me. But never enough to keep me.
Ben: Everyone changes. I still dream of you.
Anna: Only dreams because reality meant taking a chance. Moving forward. Putting one foot in front of the other on the tightrope that crosses the chasm.
Ben: I feared the fall. I feared I would fail. Let you down.
Anna: We all fear the fall. But to move forward, we have to trust someone enough to take the first step.
Ben: I still have time. Remember, you gave us until I'm 65. If we are both single then …
Anna: I remember … Ben?
Ben: Yes love?

Anna: I am so afraid that everything is going to go all wrong.

Ben: Trust is everything.

Anna: Only when it goes both ways.

Ben: Windows of opportunity open and close.

Anna:*laughing* You know what I always say. When one closes – Break the Glass.

Ben: Only if what's on the other side is worth the pain.

Anna: I think it is.

Ben: Even glass that appears clear can obscure reality.

Anna: Trust is everything.

Ben: Only when it goes both ways.

Anna: Goodnight dear friend. Peaceful dreams.

Ben: I will always be here for you. Goodnight.

> *Trust is, at its very essence, a duality; a path that runs in both directions simultaneously, back and forth. If trust is not shared without restriction, it is only the illusion of the word, a shadowy specter whispering across a moonlit night, melting in the light of day. It is clear that trust is not granted as freely as it is demanded. And that, sadly, is not the basis of a relationship. It is the foundation for a deception.*
>
> ~~beauty4ashes

05-13-2006 — **Vampirella, I Knew Ye Well**

Ten days ago, I came home from a visit to Morgan with legs that looked like giant sausages. My ankles had disappeared, and my toes looked like those Lil Smokies you stick with toothpicks and eat as appetizers. Only not as colorful. And not smelling as good.

I ran, without passing Go, without collecting $200, to the doctor. He performed the usual – well usual for him, unusual for ME – including an EKG (normal), stress test, ECHO, and a battery of blood tests.

This morning I got a call from doctor. The results of all those blood tests are in. He solemnly asked I come to the office to "discuss" them. Huh?

But it was good news/bad news. My cholesterol is fantastic. My white blood cell stuff is not so good and the AST and ALT liver enzymes seemed to cause him some heartburn. It could be several things, but the liver seems to be involved.

He sent me back to Vampirella who took FIVE tubes of blood using the old-fashioned method of large needle in small vein while suction popping tubes in and out (yucky, shiver me timbers cause I hate, hate, hate needles of any kind with a grandiose passion yucky). They took so much so fast I actually got lightheaded! I hate needles so much.

So no diagnosis yet, just more blood tests and an appointment on June 6 for an ultrasound CT scan of the liver/abdomen. Quite honestly, if the Doc's not worried enough to push the ultrasound sooner – then I'm not going to be either.

05-13-2006 — **Gabriel & Anna Update**
(Private email, by permission, to select mutual *JournalLand* friends)

Gabriel's son went into the hospital on Thursday. It was designed as a pre-op day, as his leg was to be removed on Friday. He had put it off as long as possible in order to go to one more of his son's Little League games.

During a dressing change, it was determined that gangrene had set in and the leg was immediately removed in a surgery that went as could be expected. He survived the surgery and on Friday, around noon, he was considered in guarded condition.

The trauma of the surgery will be substantial. It was not designed to heal, but to remove the cancerous limb that would have meant his immediate demise from the gangrene. The original estimate was 3-4 weeks after surgery. But he has been a fighter all along. For his family's sake, I hope it is a little longer – assuming it can be without significant pain.

05-15-2006 — **Toss One Over The Potomac**

We are told from birth that lying – even a lie by omission – is bad.

Honesty is the best policy.
Truth shall set you free.
I chopped down the cherry tree.

Whatever.

Women want to tell the truth. At least the truth as we perceive it to be. Lying eats away at us, making us uncomfortable, depressed, even weepy. It leads us into wanting to have the dreaded "talk."

On the other hand, every man is a liar until proven honest. They lie because it's easier for them.

The fact is, lying is a necessity for us all. We lie to our friends. We lie to our lovers. We lie to ourselves. We lie because the truth hurts.

Do you want to know why a sister is treated better than you are by a parent? Do you want to know if that dress makes you look fat? Do you want to know why your boyfriend came home at 3 am?

Do you want the whole truth, nothing but the truth? Do you really – really – want to know why?

05-17-2006 — **Puzzle Pieces**
(from the secret journal "*LuvACowboy*")

To paraphrase Jim Croce … I feel like a jigsaw puzzle with a couple of pieces gone.

I don't always know what to say.

If a laugh a little, smile a little, move the conversation toward a lighter subject I may sound inconsiderate and thoughtless.

If I express words of comfort, they may sound like insincere platitudes from someone whose life goes on.

If I feel overwhelming joy at the minutes our voices come together, so there is overwhelming guilt that the time may have been stolen from somewhere it is needed more.

No matter how sincere, at times like this any words of solace echo in a hollow cave.

I want to convey love, understanding, and acceptance as soundless whispers while he dreams. I want to join my voice to his and scream our anger out and up and over the landscape until it is spent in the far reaches of the universe.

05-19-2006 — **Vampirella Strikes Again**

So the doctor's office calls this morning and says – results are in from round #2 of tests, can you come in? Ok … *so again they want my $25 just to give me some test results.* Fine, I said … when. Today.

Gulp. *that's not exactly beating round the bush.* So off I went a couple hours later.

As I'm sitting in the examining room waiting for the doctor, Gabriel calls. "What are you doing?" Darn.

You may not believe it, but I tell pretty good ~~lies~~ fibs to strangers. With a perfectly straight face. Totally, absolutely, completely believable. To return merchandise, to wheedle a discount, to get a better seat on an airplane, to explain away a new pair of shoes.

But I seem to be psychologically incapable of lying to someone I care about when asked a straight question. The fib-o-meter over my head looks and sounds just like the last time you got caught doing 75 in a 30.

"I'm at the doctor's office waiting to see him about the blood work. Call you with the results?"

Then I got up, opened the door, and pulled my chart from the tray on the door 'cause I'm no dummy at reading test results. Except the results written there, in big red letters, were those least expected.

Hepatitis C virus antibody present.

You know, it's not dealing with a health issue. I intend to live forever and will do whatever needs to be done. But Gabriel has told me many times his chronic health condition makes him, literally, deathly susceptible to germs and viruses. It was one of the first questions he asked me – "*how's your health?*" I'm in the middle of it, tears flowing, when the cell phone went off.

"What did he say?" I couldn't tell him, so I handed the phone to the doctor who saw me with the report in my hands when he walked into the room.

"She's understandably not taking it too well," said the doctor. "The current tests only mean she's been exposed, not necessarily that it's active. We'll do more tests to see."

Gabriel asked to speak to me again and just said, don't worry. Everything will be just fine. He already suspected the truth, when we talked about the previous symptoms and test results. Besides, he quipped "Pamela Anderson was diagnosed positive and the treatment made her boobs get bigger!" Which made me laugh hysterically as I hung up to finish the appointment.

Back to Vampirella for yet ANOTHER three tubes of blood (we are now on a first name basis), a referral to a gastroenterologist, and a CT scan of the chest, abdomen, and pelvis to see if there are tumors. Oh well, I needed a mammogram anyway – I can do it all at once.

Gabriel called three more times with love you, won't leave you, we'll see this thing through together.

(oh, yeah, when I told Mr. Lucky? He said "Oh, guess that's why you haven't had the energy to do much work lately.") Asshole.

05-23-2006 — I Want to Live Forever

> *Is it less painful to leave in love, with all the memories intact, or to know*
> *that love left you and remains, out there, with another?*
> ~~Anna

Ben loved Anna. He will still tell anyone who asks that she may have been his greatest love. Maybe even The One.

Anna loved Ben. She made Holding Hands and Growing Old together Plans and they would live forever.

When It was done – whatever It was, whatever It is, whatever It might have been – Anna cried, and then she stopped.

She lived a Simple Daily Life, making the best of knowing there would be no Forever, just the grand finale of a last sunset, or a final moonrise.

There will be more needles today for more blood and a CT scan tomorrow.

Sometime this week there will be a phone call and maybe more I'm sorry's. And sometime next week a long talk about living forever.

05-26-2006 — **What Becomes of the Brokenhearted?**

> *What becomes of the broken-hearted*
> *Is that we do it ourselves.*
> *Hammers under pillows.*
> *We pull out the hammer.*
> *What becomes of the broken-hearted*
> *Is that we build the world out of our sorrow.*
> ~~Jan Heller Levi, "What Becomes of the Broken-Hearted"

A magical machine beeped and whirred over my head yesterday. Looking inside to see a part of the heart of me.

It saw what it was built to see. A muscle, moving the blood of life through hidden chambers. Each platelet moving through those chambers once per minute. It made measurements of continuity and performance, like miles per gallon city and highway, as I raced the engine going nowhere on a moving track.

I could have told them more if they had asked. I could have told them the heart story. The cracks and fissures, the patches and repairs made over the years. Machines cannot see it strain its bonds reaching out in love, or predict the new break that will surely come.

The young lady with the stress cardiogram machine and the little white coat did not request the story. She simply smiled and said, "You have a lovely heart."

> *In the stillness of the night*
> *I pour my heart out to you*
> *In endless gratitude*
> *You are the one*
> *The one to guide me through.*

05-28-2006 — **That Nagging Little Theory**

Last Monday I was forced from blissful sleep by a ringing phone.

"*umm … urp … coff …* Yeah?"

and this better be a damn life-threatening emergency because I am not the most pleasant individual when awakened from a sound sleep.

"Hi Anna. I'm at the airport and I left my keys in Minneapolis. Can you come bring me another key?"

WTF?

Mr. "I'm the smartest man in the world" Lucky proved, once again, that if his head were not screwed on tightly …

Did I mention that two years ago Mr. Lucky used up EVERY roadside service call available in our AAA Premium SuperGold Membership? In twelve months he locked his keys in the car three times (once while it was running) and lost them twice. He's too ~~cheap~~ ~~stingy~~ thrifty to have the gas gauge fixed ("there's an odometer") and ran out of gas four times. He had a flat tire (ok, that's legitimate – but not knowing how to change it?).

I began having duplicate keys made by the dozens, flinging them around in all the obvious places like confetti litter and STILL he calls me to save the $20 taxi ride.

Then there was yesterday. I preface this to say that he informed me at 10 a.m. (again) that we were having company at 5 p.m. For a meal.

"I'll help," he says jovially.

So I sent him to the store. I should have known better. In thirteen years of going to the store he has always managed to come home with half the list or substitute sale items (no dear, a head of lettuce doesn't make a Caesar salad). Of course, this assumes he doesn't leave the list on the counter when he leaves the house. This venture was no exception.

Ever try to frost an Angel Food cake with an aerosol can of Whipped Cream?

sigh

The news has been full of stories about preservationists trying to overturn well-established science. Darwin's Theory holds that, over time, natural selection weeds out the weakest of any species and advocates that when a creature is as moronic or pitiful as this, we must not help them. Rather, we must let them starve or die – victims of their own ineptitude – to ensure that their lowly, pathetic skill set can no longer infect the gene pool.

If any of you are still around when I leave here … you may see me wink.

05-31-2006 — **Welcome to My Journal**

A hearty welcome to any new readers who found their way here in recent days by clicking a banner ad. If you're an old (in the sense of time, not age darlings) reader who clicked through   Gotcha Again!

(What's that? You clicked through with honest expectations of a traditional daily journal describing dating rituals, diets, co-worker antics, whining kids, ex-husbands, and freaky in-laws? You just keep telling yourself that.)

You clicked that banner because there were subtle promises of quirks, eccentricities and, dare one say, perversions. (But we'll keep that just between us.)

Let me go on record by stating that while I may use sex to sell my journal, the accounts of my rapacious nymphomania are highly overrated and mostly confined to those X-rated entries that are certainly available in this space if you care to seek them out.

All right, as long as I'm being honest, there are those VERY few jpegs on the internet. Some of them are a bit graphic, but we're all grownups here. While they may picture a woman of no discernible inhibitions, the techniques are certainly innovative and a sight you won't soon forget. Go ahead, look. I'll wait.

Really, you hardly need me to provide hard-core entertainment value. The new JC Penny commercial uses "Everybody Wang Chung Tonight" as the background music while nubile nymphets parade across the screen (and the guys aren't bad either). Spammers bombard us with offers of SexxTonight, Rock-HardErections (his, I hope ... not mine), and Are You Looking For A Physical Relationship. Heck, the very hills are alive with the sound of bondage.

Dare we hope for an X-rated version of *Peter Pan*?

While I appreciate the opportunity to fulfill your fantasies (really, I do), I would much rather you take matters into your own hands. Because living this long has taught me one important thing. It is never too late to be what you might have been. Anyone can find within themselves the strength to persevere in spite of overwhelming obstacles.

Madeleine Albright, the first female secretary of state was once asked if she ever thought "Why me?" She shrugged and said "Why not?".

Face it – women who behave rarely make history.

06-02-2006 — **Sometimes, if it weren't for bad luck**

Well if this isn't the hottest patch in the heart of hell.

Remember all those tests? When my dear friend and (now) bosom buddy Vampirella withdrew so much blood from the Anna blood bank that I almost deflated? Seriously – sort of like a beach ball when you pull the plug.

Today was the day the doc would give me the final results. As I often do when faced with potential bad news, I sent a little prayer like thing up into the ether for whoever might be listening. Asking for a break. Cause it's time.

And well ... let's just say it's a good thing I don't invest heavily in day trading. Because God was not paying attention. (S)he is apparently off cooing over Brangelina's newest member, or sitting back eating bon-bons and watching *March of the Penguins* (no doubt trying to figure out what went wrong with the original design).

Actually – there's no real point in bothering God. I mean, God created luck as an efficiency measure. Otherwise, how would you explain horse races, slot machines, or lottery tickets? Without luck, picking a winner would be in God's hands. Which means (s)he would be spending all her time listening to whining people begging for a winner instead of coming up with cures for cancer, rockets to the moon, and a gorgeous, muscled, fabulous cowboy/pirate who adores me beyond all reason. (ok, two out of three isn't bad.)

The gastroenterologist (I'm turning into an old person – a specialist ending in "ologist" for every organ in my body) gave me the bad news that the original blood tests were completely correct – I have not just been exposed to Hep C – I have an active viral infection that, given enough time, will kill me.

He wants a biopsy performed wherein a long needle is stuck into the middle of my body to extract a piece of liver that is then checked for the extent of damage. After which (no matter the results) I spend the next nine months sticking needles full of poisonous drugs into my own body each week, while Vampirella (much too frequently for my taste) gets to do the same.

Adding to my pleasure are the potential side effects including chills, night sweats, fever, diarrhea, muscle aches, cramps, weight loss, headaches, hair loss, extreme to the point of suicide depression, and nausea.

Hmm, sounds a lot like menopause to me.

Or pregnancy without the reward at the end.

I tried so hard to wheedle out of some of the needles the doctor asked if I was a lawyer by profession. "No" I said, "by inclination."

Gabriel called during the exam, again, and they both pushed so hard to proceed with the biopsy I had to cave. Then more needles and eight tubes of blood this time. I'm running out.

Let's face it, sometimes luck runs hot, sometimes cold, and sometimes it's just right. You can't control luck. But you can play the breaks. Surround yourself with a supporting cast of characters. Stir the pot. See a full glass. Don't deny the power of positive thinking. Take charge and, if you watch your step, luck will go your way at least some of the time.

So go ahead. Jump in, pull the ripcord, ride the coaster, answer the email from a stranger, let yourself fall in love. Then say Damn! Am I lucky or what?

And when something doesn't go the way you expect, don't let it win.

I'm a great believer in luck and I find the harder I work, the more I have of it.
~~Thomas Jefferson

06-03-2006 — **Russian Roulette**
(from the secret journal "*LuvACowboy*")

Gabriel has been great. Calling every day. Telling me everything will be fine. But his doctor told him a relationship with me, considering his health conditions, would be like playing Russian Roulette. So he can't say it makes no difference to him and he doesn't say WE will be fine.

His son is in the hospital. His pain is managed. However, time is growing extremely short and the family is preparing for the end. Afterwards, Gabriel will go on walkabout. He will be back when he's back. Three months, four, six, a year. Whatever he needs without cell phones, email, or people asking him how he is.

I fear he will be gone before we can resolve this. I fully support him but I will miss him. I have grown to count on his presence, his support, his advice, and his love.

I've been going online, learning everything I can learn about this disease. I am afraid of everything, the tests, the biopsy, the treatment, the needles, and the coming sickness. I will undergo a chemotherapy consisting of self-injections and large numbers of pills for the 48 weeks. It reduces the virus in about half the people who do it – and some percentage stay in remission. Like any chemo, the side effects are brutal, but differ by individuals. There is hope that it was caught early, as the CT scans were clear of cancers and tumors in the liver.

Being without Gabriel during the worst of it will be extremely difficult for me. But I'll be fine because what he will be going through is so much worse.

06-09-2006 — **Side Effects**

My last husband can only be described as a case study in contradictions.

It was 1988 and Paul was one of those people you noticed. Confident, attractive, beautiful smile. I was enjoying the free appetizers after work (olives count as appetizers, right?) when he smiled at me from across the room.

An hour later I bade my co-workers goodnight and left the ~~bar~~ restaurant. He followed me out the door, excused himself, and handed me his business card.

"You fascinate me. Call my office and ask anyone anything. Then have dinner with me."

And walked back into the restaurant. I stood there, card in hand, and took a moment to shut my mouth.

I did. We did. And did again. Sometimes several times a night.

One evening there was a tiff. A disagreement. I was angry, he was hurt – or perhaps it was the other way around. "Perhaps I should just leave," he said, tight lipped.

"Fine," I spat. "I don't want you here. I don't need you here. All men leave, why should you be different?"

And, as I threw myself on the couch sobbing, he walked out the door.

And walked back in the door minutes later to gather me in his arms.

Paul wasn't The One I dreamed about. But Jason was gone these many years, Ben was lost to me, and he called me the love of his life. He moved in and we were married eight months later.

Why does commitment trigger the deadly disease that eventually kills relationships? I used to think it was the wedding ring. That when it slides on a man's finger it trips a hidden switch which re-inserts the real personality back into the shell you have been dating. But if that were the case, why does it happen even when there is no ring involved?

His glass of wine with dinner became two, then three, then a bottle. The occasional drink after work became a couple times a week, for several hours, coming home not the Paul I married, but an insensitive, belligerent lout. There were times when he insisted I go with him and, when he wouldn't give up the car keys at last call, I would walk home.

Just when I had given up, he and an old buddy started an extremely profitable business. He became focused – almost manic – stopped drinking, and the money seemed to roll in. Our finances were kept separate, so it was shocking when he told me six months later that he was almost broke.

One day I returned from a business trip to find he had "borrowed" most of my checking and savings, and cash-advanced my credit cards to pay off his creditors. And to buy cocaine.

It was only then I learned the truth. He could be completely sober and drug-free for years, and then go off the deep-end. Usually when faced with success. But no one told me. Not his family. Not his best friends. Not the girl he dated before me.

He didn't fight the divorce. Eventually he beat the cocaine, but not the alcohol. It took years, but I paid off every penny he borrowed from my personal accounts. Every month or so I get a small check from him. The online banking account name he gave me is "4life" which always makes me laugh.

I called him last Friday afternoon – first time in a couple of years – to give him the medical news and suggest he have himself tested too. He was already loaded. He called me, still drunk, three more times over the weekend. I told him not to call again unless he was sober.

Exposure to the "now I can just be myself" disease in your partner results in brutal, life-long side effects in yourself, including a lack of confidence in your ability ever to choose wisely again.

"I should have known … I should have seen … How could I have been so stupid?"

06-11-2006 — **Night Notes**
(from the secret journal "*LuvACowboy*")

"Ben?"

"Yes, love."

"I'm afraid."

"Why?"

"You have to ask me that? Because the time is almost here. I'm afraid he won't come back. That perhaps I just won't be … that I'm just not … worth it."

"Does he love you?"

"Yes. It is the one thing I am sure of."

"Then why can't you trust him?"

"Because so did you."

"Oh, Anna. Don't judge him by my actions."

"Faith, then?"

"Yes … faith. Always and Forever. Anna?"

"Yes, Ben?"

"My heart and soul will always love you, in their own way."

"I know. Goodnight dear friend."

"Goodnight."

06-13-2006 — **Biopsy Day**

Liver biopsy today. A neighbor drove me who happens to be a lawyer. I had redone my will, medical power of attorney, living will, etc. just in case. She signed and had it witnessed right in the waiting room. How grateful I am for friends like her.

In fact, it wasn't that bad, as the doctor honored my request to just "knock me out." I have no side effects from the drugs used in today's surgeries. In point of fact, it's a nice free high (unless you count what the insurance company has to pay).

At his insistence, I called Gabriel to tell him I came out alive. He was happy to hear, but his voice is distant and quiet. He feels the end will be any day now.

06-14-2006 — **Moon Magic**

> *My life closed twice before its close;*
> *It yet remains to see*
> *If Immortality unveil*
> *A third event to me,*
>
> *So huge, so hopeless to conceive*
> *As these that twice befell.*
> *Parting is all we know of heaven,*
> *And all we need of hell.*
>
> ~~Emily Dickinson (702)

The asphalt shimmered with the blinding heat of a hot yellow sun, requiring tippy toes to visit the mailbox. That evening, while the sun passed the moon, the heavens cried for the briefest of moments just before Gabriel and I took our walk together. As we do almost every evening.

On rare occasions, his voice will be in my ear. But more often not, it is just the silent phone tucked in one pocket, and me, secure in the knowledge his is tucked in a similar pocket somewhere on the other end.

Our full moon made its way into the sky during that walk, outlining each brick, each leaf, and each tree moving gently as if touched by nature's very breath. Throwing my shadow across the passing greenscapes.

Her light illuminated the pale, smoky mists rising from those hot asphalt streets. I watched in wonder as these ethereal phantoms, phantasmagorically swirled and rose upwards to accompany the moon in her journey across the sky.

She will be the steadfast companion for us both on this next journey.

06-16-2006 — **Mirror Mirror**

> Mirror Mirror in the hall
> Where's the girl that once stood tall
> Mirror Mirror on the wall
> Was she ever there at all?

I didn't like everything about the girl who looked back at me. Her mouth was too big. Her breasts were too small. Her legs were too thin. But she was full of laughter, lithe, active, with a slim waist, a flat stomach, and good health.

Then there was that day when the doctor sat her down and asked if she wanted more children – because it was now or never. She chose never, which meant the necessary little speech before a relationship got too far. Reality for her was a life choice for him.

Slowly, surely, the girl in the mirror disappeared. Small inevitable changes brought about by the March of Time. The life choice became less important. than the giving heart, quick mind, unflagging optimism, and good health.

And with all the pretty young girls in the mirror, it was never enough.

She settled instead for the security she had never known, the home, the healthcare, the friends, the joy of dancing. Watching her only child achieve everything she had hoped for her. Settled for making a life out of what she *could* have – instead of what she wished for.

Then there was that day when the doctor sat her down again. With good health off the list, all that's left to offer is her giving heart and quick mind. But with all the pretty, healthy girls in the mirror, she knows, instinctively, that it might not be enough.

06-19-2006 — **Time Passes**

It's time to decide when to start the drug therapy. I decided on August 1, or as soon as possible after my daughter's baby is born.

Gabriel called and asked about my doctor appointment. I just said everything was fine. There's time to talk about it later. For the first time in a year, he did not say "I love you" but I understand.

06-20-2006 — **Tears In Heaven**

Shane Michael
March 22, 1974 – June 19, 2006

Our dear friend Gabriel (*Azrael999*) has asked that I let you know his beloved son, Shane, was taken into the arms of the angels Monday morning at 1:30 a.m. with his family by his side.

He will be laid to rest later this week. His wife, two children, his father, grand-parents, and hundreds of loving aunts, uncles, in-laws, and cousins survive him.

Gabriel has also asked me to tell you how very much your thoughts, prayers, emails, and messages have meant to him over the last six months. While he could not answer them all personally, reading your messages, and knowing that you were each out there passing on strength and support during these trying days has brought him great comfort.

Thank you dear friends.

> *For there are no tears in Heaven!*
> *There, sorrow and sighing*
> *Have forever fled away …*
> *Oh no! there are no tears in heaven.*
> ~~William Frith, *Tears of the Pilgrims*

06-22-2006 — **Event Horizon**
(from the secret journal "*LuvACowboy*")

each day i wake up and know today will be better for me. but not for him. he suffers unbearable, unquenchable, unfathomable pain. he will not allow me anywhere near him. my mind accepts what he asked of me. but my heart, oh my heart.

how quickly we become accustomed to their presence in our lives. to ask a question, share our sadness, to make a decision, to reassure us, to fit exactly into the place in our soul that was empty for so long. when they are no longer there, the empty place where they once were expands until it is a great yawning black hole. the gates to hell where all souls are lost.

06-23-2006 — **Tell Me Everything**
(from the secret journal "*LuvACowboy*")

"I want to know everything and don't lie to me." He didn't say it harshly; he just wanted to make sure I wouldn't gloss over the results. So I got the printed biopsy results and read them to him. He seemed satisfied but it wasn't a subject he wanted to dwell on.

Tomorrow is the funeral and after that ... well, he will need to take care of himself for a while and we won't have time to talk. And I will never know.

He has called three times since Monday. But still no "I love you."

06-24-2006 — **On MY Baby's Daddy**

In all this sadness, I find myself going back. Reviewing the life-altering choices I have made. This is one.

In a recent blog, a fellow writer talked about how her young son had told a lie at school – that his father was dead – instead of admitting he simply was not in his life.

I could relate. I left my daughter's father (we actually got married, cause that's what you DID back in those days) when she was 14 months old.

We were not star-crossed lovers. We barely knew each other. We met in February while I was a senior in High School and fell in deep lust. I got pregnant within weeks and, to the obvious relief of my mother, we married in May. My beautiful baby girl was born in December.

He drank too much – perhaps not more than someone in their mid-20's just out of the Navy normally does, but more than I (who came from a tee-totaling family) thought the father of a new child should – and we argued about it. He drank more, stayed out later, got increasingly violent, and I left. I didn't bad-mouth him to my daughter ... I just didn't talk about him ... ever.

In her 20's my daughter admitted that as a very young child she always thought of him as some well-to-do Brady Bunch dad who would someday come rescue her. Like a knight on a white horse, he would show up at the door in sparkling silver armor and whisk her away to Perfect Land. Or at least send money to pay the rent or buy her the toy we couldn't afford.

She continued to believe in some version of this fairy tale, even through the angsty teen years, and even though she had a wonderful stepfather that adopted her and became her "real" Dad when she was five (and still is, years and years after our divorce).

When she became an actress, she took part of her father's last name as her "stage name." When I asked, she reasoned that perhaps, someday, she would be famous and when he recognized her, he would think – gee, look what I missed.

When she found him through the internet, he was astonished – crying – ecstatic to hear from her – could he come see her. Turns out, she was his only child. It was not until she met him that she realized he was not a knight on a white horse at all. He was a small, heavyset, balding older man with whom she had nothing in common except DNA, and who had made a conscious choice not to be in her life.

What meeting him did do was allow her, at last, to mend some broken fences with the Dad who was always her Dad and they are now closer than ever.

Had I to do it over again, I think it would have been a good thing to try harder to find him and let him know I would have given him a chance to be some part of her life if he wanted it. If nothing else (in our case at least) it would have answered an infinite number of nagging questions about why he didn't try and see her, and have made her appreciate her own "Dad" even more.

OK, ok, and maybe I would feel a little less guilty right now.

06-25-2006 — **Kisses Lost**

The doctor told Mr. Lucky we had to use protection until the chemo began working. It's to his favor actually. They give him another minute. Or two. Don't worry, we have TiVo so it's not like he'll miss anything.

Somewhere in the suspended seconds tonight between him removing my clothes and ramming it home, I realized this might be all the intimacy anyone will share with me for the rest of my life.

I wish I didn't know how wonderful it could be. Then I wouldn't miss it so very much.

06-26-2006 — **Curse of the Black Pearl**

Dear fellow diarist *HissandTell*,

As you know, we have thus far failed to settle our teensy little Krystle vs. Alexis squabble over a certain lithe, handsome, viral, pirate/cowboy with dual color eyes who, in a weakened moment, named his birthday surfboard "The Hissy" whilst parading around declaring undying devotion hither and yon to all who would listen. A board, I might add, whose main requirements are that he climb aboard and, while lying face down upon its smooth wet glistening surface, press down hard with his manly parts, adjusting appropriately each time he finds himself listing 90 degrees (for reasons not difficult to fathom).

We discussed the pugilistic rules with Gabriel (who, by the way, insists on being the referee) and make the following offers to your second:

> Adornments of lipstick red, or devilish black spikey heels, tiny bits of exquisite lingerie covering just the dangly bits in exotic animal prints (extra points for originality), shiny tiaras, twinkling diamante earrings, and lacey thigh high stockings held up by twirly ribbons. Weapons of choice, but strappy, whippy, crackly, or buzzy hand-held items strongly urged. Match to be held in a mutually agreed upon silk-lined boudoir with ceiling mirrors, champagne on tap, and bubbly bath waters ready and waiting.

I understand finding a mutually agreeable date for our ~~tumble~~ rumble has been overwhelmingly difficult (what with schedules full of stockmen, bikers, painters, singers, dancers, and general roustabouts taking up all of our time and attention). But let us persevere in the quest.

Love and mucho smoochy kisses, Anna Alexis

06-28-2006 — **Quantum Entanglement**

> *Whatever happened to one particle would thus immediately affect the other particle, wherever in the universe it may be. Einstein called this "Spooky action at a distance."*
> ~~Amir D. Aczel (122)

Quantum Entanglement theorizes that photons come in pairs, separated by space and time but always in instantaneous, inexplicable communication. Einstein called it "Spooky Action" and believed it was theoretically implausible. It may be that he hoped someone would find such proof – why else give it such an odd name!

Applied to lovers, this mathematical concept is actually quite romantic. We affect each other. Even when we try to be unaffected. Even when we don't mean to, even when we don't want to. We're connected.

In 1935 Schrödinger proved that if something disturbs the state of one photon, the other feels the effects as well, even when they are not physically connected. He wrote that the second photon could be affected in a predictable way, depending on the first photon's actions. (*Collected Papers on Wave Mechanics*)

It felt just *exactly* like that.

07-02-2006 — **Six Minutes to Midnight**
(from the secret journal "***LuvACowboy***")

Anna?

Yes Ben?

How are you?

You always ask me the same thing and I always answer with the same answer.

I know. But I'd rather hear the truth.

No Ben. You wouldn't. So my answer is the same as it was the last time.

Why are so afraid of saying it?

Because saying it out loud makes it real.

Ignoring it will not make it go away Anna.

I know. But I either live a life of dreams or a reality of quiet desperation.

Anna, it doesn't matter to me. I will not abandon you.

Everyone leaves. Sooner or later. For one good reason or another.

Not everyone Anna. Not everyone.

We will see, Ben. We will see.

Goodnight love.

Sweet dreams my friend.

07-04-2006 — **Game, Set, Match**
(from the secret journal "*LuvACowboy*")

no calls. no messages. i don't know where he is, although he had promised not to take off on his healing journey without telling me.

he stopped saying i love you on the 13th.

i guess i don't understand That.

07-05-2006 — **Until Later**
Personal email to *Gabriel* from Anna

i have turned the phone off for now. when, or if, you are ready to begin again, please email me or I will not know. it will be like old times when you were in Dominica and there was no phone service. those emails are still so special to me. i hope you will heal quickly darling Gabriel. and that the Spirits will help you in every way possible. you will have my heart Forever and Always.

07-06-2006 — **Is It Done Yet?**

The phone call from my daughter tonight says she feels my grandson's birth is imminent … starting to have some back pains. Even though gynecologist says nope, not quite yet!

Just before I left New York the last time, Jarred placed his head close to the baby and whispered, "Little one, aren't you cooked yet? It's time to come out and play!"

Ha, Ha, Ha – can't wait!

07-07-2006 — **Careful What You Wish For**

I've gotten my work projects ready to hand off to others while I'm cooing over the new baby – figuring by the time I get back two weeks later to start my Hep C treatments the first of August they will be mostly done and I just won't take on more until I can.

Mr. Lucky got pissed that he wasn't involved in the process of my handoffs. Finally shoved me in the chest with both hands, grabbed me by the arm, and slung me to the floor – hard – all the while screaming about how stupid I was.

Well. THAT hasn't happened before.

Then told me I was fired and there it was. My biggest fear. The ultimate boogeyman. The last nail in the coffin of my life.

No income. No insurance. No treatment for anything. Ever. Because I'm uninsurable now unless I move directly from one plan to another. The cost of the treatment without insurance is $10,000 per month. It makes you pretty sick for a while so going to another full-time job (assuming I could even find one) means I couldn't afford to be sick even a single day.

I guess I knew it all along. I think it's one of the reasons I am so very sad all the time right now. I'm really stuck here. There's just nothing to smile about anymore.

Oh, I realize I chose to be stuck all these years. I rationalized that while it isn't a relationship, the rest wasn't that horrible and maybe life would never offer me anything any better. Especially after Ben.

But between you and me? When things were especially bad, I would still creep to the window like a small child and wish upon a star that someday my fairy Godmother would stop by, wave her wand, and "Poof" everything would magically change.

You gotta be awful careful when you wish for something that hard. Sometimes you get <u>exactly</u> what you ask for.

07-08-2006 — Itchy, Itchy, Bang, Bang

I learned a new word when I finally got to a doctor to find out why my arms and hands were covered in itchy blistery areas that didn't look or act like poison ivy, oak, sumac, mosquito, flea, or chigger bites. Porphyria Cutanea Tarda.

Accumulations of excess porphyrins in the liver are transported by the blood plasma to the skin, causing damage. Precipitating factors include hemochromatosis, the use of estrogens, and Hepatitis C.

Great. I have all three, although the Doc is on the fence on the hemochromatosis until the next blood test in a week or two (just before I start treatments).

The first outbreak was in May. Just one area on one arm, and a little one on the other. This one – well, it was brutal. Definitive testing was NOT done because by the time I could get a doctor's appointment it was already responding to the super-strength steroid cream I got the first time. If it occurs again, I have orders to get to the dermatologist for a skin biopsy.

The recommended treatment for hemochromatosis? Oh, you are going to love this one. A procedure called phlebotomy, in which a pint of blood is removed every week until the person becomes slightly iron deficient, allowing porphyrin levels in the liver to normalize.

Again with the f*cking needles. I am living in my own circle of hell. With an illness that requires a flotilla of needles every time I turn around. All I need is Cerberus chomping on my feet.

07-09-2006 — **And the Devil Wore Shorts**

It is grim irony to think that the reason I chose to stay here the last six months was at Gabriel's behest. So he would know I was safe – roof over my head, food in my mouth, medical care when I needed it. While he was doing what he needed to do. Before. And After. It gave him peace of mind.

Today, I groveled to Mr. Lucky. Saying it was all my fault. I caused him to over react. To please not take away my insurance. Or the job that pays my bills. That I would do whatever he wanted.

He patted me on the shoulder, and agreed he would not change the locks while I was at my daughter's house for the birth and, knowing I needed it, he would keep my insurance in place for now. But the job? Well, he would decide later, because he did not intend to support me if I was not going to be well enough to work. Then he guided me to the floor, kicked off his shorts and, giving me no other choice, said "Eat me."

07-10-2006 — **As Scarlett Said**

I assume Gabriel needs some space and some peace. No contact means no "how are you" questions to answer so I don't have to lie and say "Fine" because I do not intend to burden him with this. It is one reason I locked this journal to even him. Those very few dear friends who can still read are enough to provide the support I crave in these crazy times.

It was hard enough telling him about the medical issue. Knowing it not only came at one of the worst moments in his life, but that it might make a difference in how he felt about me. But he knew I was seeing the doctor and insisted on the truth.

Besides, I am not a damsel in distress who needs a knight in white shining armor to rescue her. There is nothing he can do about Mr. Lucky and nothing he can do to help me except worry. I will not do that to him.

When he comes back to me, let it be because he loves me unconditionally, not because he thinks I need him to rescue me.

If the chemo is successful, it will be over in a year. In a grand about-face, Mr. Lucky has agreed to my staying here in the house and he will provide full support – food, housing, insurance, and transportation costs for the duration of the treatment. I don't need a salary with my disability insurance intact so I am financially secure for the entire period. I am starting with a roof over my head, food in my mouth, medical care, and an internet connection to search for work and stay in touch with the world at large.

It is the best of mostly bad choices. I believe in the life to come and I don't see any point in starting over twice. Now is the best time to do the chemo and get it over with and, well, I just need the time to make logical, well-thought out plans that will actually work. I've taken too many wrong steps, too many times, based on raw emotion.

It's not perfect. But it's a plan I can handle today. As for the rest, well, I'll think about it tomorrow.

07-11-2006 — **Promises Kept**
(from the secret journal "*LuvACowboy*")

what if i'm doing it wrong? what if he truly needs me? what if i should be breaking that promise to let him take the time to work things out for himself? perhaps he thinks it is i who has abandoned him.

so i got up. reread the messages from a year ago. when we were flirting. when we were falling in love. even then he emphasized honestly expressing your emotions when they needed to come out. Which one do i believe?

how do i keep my promise, and still keep my promise?

07-12-2006 — **Life is Worth $1000**

Something snapped late yesterday. It could have been inside. Or outside. Maybe it was something someone said. Or didn't say. Maybe it was just me. Tired of crying about things I can't change. Tired of wishing fate had dealt me a different hand. Tired of watching right now pass me by.

It's time to live each day like there is no tomorrow (what is that country song? "Live like you were dying?").

Even though missing him causes pain, it does not mean I don't support him completely in taking the time away he needs to heal. In reversed circumstances, I would expect no less from him.

Had we been together, physically, before … perhaps I would feel differently. Our commitment is sincere, but he does not owe me anything. He has broken no promises, betrayed no trust. Love comes in many forms and shows itself with many faces. He was absolutely honest with me, telling me for months the day would come when there would be silence and I agreed to respect his needs.

Meanwhile, as long as I have a good insurance company, a great doctor, a healthy grandson about to make his much-awaited appearance, dear friends who – even if they don't quite understand – support me anyway and well, even a Mr. Lucky who gave me a hug yesterday and agreed to keep the house straight and the flowers watered while I'm in NYC … isn't life just grand?

07-13-2006 — **Push!!**

The kids moved everything to the new place today and the nest is built. Her water broke and she's 4 minutes apart.

I'm leaving now for New York City (yes – it's 3 a.m. and I suck at night driving). Wish me luck! I'm not even sure where the hospital is – but I'll figure out something.

A new life is about to come into this world!

07-13-2006 — **Welcome Home Travis**

Travis Jarred King
July 13, 2006 1:24 p.m.
6 lb. 11.5 oz. 19" long

Mommy went to the hospital through the Holland tunnel in a Penske rental truck rented that day to move into the new condo (trucks not ALLOWED in the Holland tunnel – but what were the police supposed to do about it with a woman in labor sitting in the front seat!).

Grandma pulled away from home at about 3 a.m. EST and arrived (by way of the Lincoln Tunnel at rush hour in Manhattan!) in plenty of time to welcome her new grandson into the world.

Not everything went smoothly. At two points during labor, the baby's heart slowed and caesarean was considered as an emergency measure. But in the end, he arrived by natural means and is carrying a healthy dose of the family's "beautiful" genes.

07-16-2006 — **Lost Forever**
(from the secret journal "*LuvACowboy*")

oh beloved Gabriel, another milestone that will never come again. and it saddens me more than i can put into words. we have lost, in this gap (if gap it only is) a moment of pure beginning. an occasion to remember and celebrate in our life together. for if one life ended, now another has begun and we (if we is still what we are) could have shared in the joy.

my heart is already trying to protect itself. it is drifting, pulling back. building the wall back up. pushing the pain of you into the background. isn't it odd that for all you believe in your *ESPN*, it has been so silent – and so wrong.

07-20-2006 — **Seven Days and Seven Nights**

Travis is one week old today. He's gained weight, coming in at a nice round 7 lbs. 2 oz., up from 6 lbs. 5 oz. I am still here in New York, being a Grandma!

Life is one day at a time with everything else although Mr. Lucky told me my medicine had arrived at home. So when I get back … I suppose I'll get the final blood test and start.

07-25-2006 — **Something very strange is going on**
Personal email to Anna from *Gabriel*

Dear Anna:
A lot has happened since we last spoke. I would prefer to speak to you on the phone, but apparently you aren't answering it. Please call me. I have my cell phone now so call me.
Love Gabriel

07-26-2006 — **My Boyfriend's Back**
(from the secret journal "*LuvACowboy*")

Gabriel is back. he said that within days of Son's death he was hospitalized. so much was wrong. he had withheld the truth from me "yes, I'm eating. yes, I'm sleeping. yes, I'm drinking water." no, he wasn't so he paid the price.

he said family members confiscated his phone and laptop, and doctors made sure his needs were met over the next few weeks. but as I had often feared, no one bothered to let me know, because they either don't know i exist – or don't care.

the first day he had his phone back – he called seven times trying to reach me and when he finally did, everything tumbled out. he expressed an unwavering love. how he had missed me. how he had still felt that love and loss through the drugs that were supposed to make him feel nothing. which led to him making so many decisions about life, about us, about what he actually wanted.

"could you live with an artist?"

"of course dear one, i would live with a beach bum if that's what made you happy."

he still needs care and still needs to go through the grieving process that was denied him. but he has the help he needs, both family and professional. people who will surround him, who will make sure he does what is necessary.

and he says we still have each other.

I start my own journey on Friday – knowing he will be there to hold my virtual hand when needed.

07-27-2006 — **Quick As a Rabbit**

Everything is happening so quickly now. The insurance company approved the "good stuff" which is the 180 ml pre-filled syringes of Pegasys (peginterferon alfa-2a) with accompanying Ribavirin – the non-brand name of Copegus – (6 tabs a day for a total of 1200 mg)

The cost will be a little more than I thought though – $40 a month, plus $25 per week for the blood work, and another $25 a month for the doctor visit. Not so bad, considering the retail is in the thousands.

Now I just need the callback from the doctor to determine when to take the initial blood work and when he will do the first injection.

07-28-2006 — **Good News and Bad News**

Dear Journal (and anyone out there listening, you know who you are),

You used to be my space. Just mine. Even when others found you – you were still mine. I gave you all the things I could give no one else.

Giving it to you let it float away. I stuffed all my anxieties, fears, sadness, and loneliness inside *JournalLand* balloons – and turned them loose.

Then there was Gabriel and you weren't my space anymore. That was good news and bad news. The good news was that in sharing you with him he got to know me and love me. Even the me before him.

The bad news is that I could no longer tell you what I needed to write down. What I needed to get out in order to receive back from you the support, love, and occasional kick in the ass you have always been good for.

The worst news is that some of the very, very few people who still have the password access to read you have begun reaching out to him via notes and emails expressing chagrin, and chastising or belittling his supposed reactions and behavior towards me. Words that are causing him pain, bewilderment, confusion, and a belief that no one cares.

I thought I had made myself crystal clear. Leave him alone.

THIS JOURNAL IS NOW LOCKED TO EVERYONE.

7-28-2006 — **Good morning sweetie**
Personal email to *Gabriel* from Anna

It is so wonderful to have you back in my head. It was exceedingly lonely without you. So I just had to trust in what we have built between us.

And apparently, even in your psychotropic induced state … so did you. You are a very smart person, you know. Even on drugs. (hmm, I suspect that should worry me, but somehow it just doesn't seem important right now).

07-30-2006 — **Teenagers in Love**

We talk every second. It has long been our tradition that when he gets into a car he dials my number. He laughs and says it is as second nature as putting on sunglasses. Open door, insert key, put on glasses, dial phone.

Since he is not yet up to driving, one of the Brothers Grimm chauffeured him around from appointment to appointment the last two days. This meant we were on the phone a lot. Laughing, talking, catching up, saying all the things we have missed saying.

After about the third call Friday, poor Brother Grimm #1 removed the iPod earphones he had been using in self-defense, looked over, and with an amused grin said "What are you two – fifteen again?"

07-31-2006 — **Five Minutes to Midnight**

Anna?

Yes Ben?

How are you?

I am the same as last time. Nothing changes.

But it has changed, hasn't it?

Perhaps a little.

So, how are you?

I am …

What Anna? Say it.

I am ... fine.

After all these years, you still won't trust me.

You always expected me to be perfect ...

NO, I didn't.

You did.

NO, Anna, you wanted to be perfect for me. I loved the imperfect you.

Then I guess the joke's on me isn't it.

It won't matter.

You don't know that.

You don't either.

We never know anything do we? Life is a daily adventure, full of promises and denials. There is no point in the truth. No one listens.

Anna, listen to your heart.

No Ben. You listen to it. I can't be bothered with it right now.

08-02-2006 — **No Comment Required**

"You do realize you can be a real Drama Queen."

The accusation from Gabriel was pointed, and cut her deeply. It wasn't until later, with the label buzzing in her head like an angry housefly, that she gave it more thought. She was aware there are people whose lives are a lot worse off. It's just that the last two months had been a bit more difficult than usual.

Perhaps the empathy for his situation had worn thin. There was nothing she could do for him that doctors, relatives, and friends weren't already taking care of, so fewer howareyoufeelingtodays could be more useful.

Then there were those pesky doctors. Weeks of turmoil surrounding every test, every biopsy, x-ray, and needle, every appointment with crisp white pages of results. Wondering every day how, if she felt this damaged, would other people perceive her when they found out. On the other hand, it's not like it is a two months to live death sentence or anything.

And all those scary long drawn out tests at the beginning of her daughter's pregnancy. Even when everything looked great, there were reminders this child of hers was no longer a youngster, and having a baby is not always a safe or easy experience.

Of course, there was always Mr. Lucky. The threats. The possibilities. Difficult days indeed, coming on top of everything else.

Perhaps the label fit, after all. Drama Queen. Or maybe, just a Big Baby.

No comment required.

08-04-2006 — **Huh Me Top Ten**

Let's see now. I left at 3 a.m. on Thursday the 13th of July. I returned on Wednesday, the 26th of July, earlier than I had expected.

Ok – so let's see if I can get it straight. I was gone for 13 days. Let's run down the top 10 shall we? When I came home:

1. The work projects worksheet I spent hours preparing (and that he was so angry about not having sufficient input into) was lost. His response was "*Huh, what worksheet?*"
2. Cleaning? No.
3. Dishwashing? No.
4. Flower/plant watering? No.
5. Grocery buying? No. "*I figured you'd do it when you got home.*"
6. Bird care? "*well, I noticed the seed looked a little low yesterday and I added water a couple times. you always clean the cage.*"

7. Toilet paper? "*would you put TiVo on hold while I pee?*" "Um, Mr. Lucky, why are you going upstairs instead of using the powder room?" "*the paper roll is empty.*" Actually, it was empty upstairs too. He was using the guest bath.
8. Laundry? Piled in the floor of the laundry room. "*I brought it down.*"
9. Towels? "Um, Mr. Lucky, why is my clean towel so dirty?" "*It was mine. I traded with you.*"
10. The National Night Out event this weekend? He showed up an hour after it started. "*Oh, I forgot I said I'd help set up.*" An hour before it ended, he left. "*Oh, I have to take someone a computer.*"

I'm as prepared as I can be for my first Hep C treatment this afternoon.

And knowing there is no way in hell anyone else is going to help give me those injections, I've decided to do it all by myself. There's a certain independence in that, you know. See you on the flip side, poppets.

08-05-2006 — **Week #1**
(from the private journal "*cUnHell*")

Good news? The injections do not appear to be painful.

The bad news? Even the skillful doctor couldn't easily find enough "fat" on me to give me a sub-Q (subcutaneous, i.e. in the fat layer, not the muscle). He finally settled below my ribs after looking at, and rejecting, arms, tummy, legs, and even my butt.

"ummm doc, how exactly am I supposed to give this in my own butt?"

I also got an RX for anti-depressants. First time in my life. But better now than waiting until it's too late I'm told. Let's hope they have good results and don't turn me into a slightly stewed loon like Gabriel has become. One loon in my circle of loved ones is enough right now!

Ok – side effects. Let me see if I can describe it.

You go out and decide to run a 26-mile marathon, swim 15 miles, and do 200 pushups, 500 sit-ups, 750 squats. Wearing weights. When the most vigorous exercise you've done in, say, the last twenty years is lifting Godiva chocolates from box to mouth while lounging about on a cherry red sofa wearing your most tantalizing outfit and begging to be had. Your muscles, tendons, joints, and pretty much everything else having to do with the tissue that holds your insides in REBELS.

And your stomach gets upset.

And you are freezing to death, thereby needing a sheet, a blanket, and a quilt.

The only possible comfort you get is sitting up in bed, pillows behind your back, cradling your lower back and ribs that feel like they are ready to explode. Your arms, legs, shoulders, and neck are cramping and twisting so sleep is impossible.

This morning? Stiff neck, very light headache. But I'm hungry. That's a good sign … right?

08-07-2006 — 'night Angel
Personal email to *Gabriel* from Anna

Sure was nice having a few moments with the almost really real you tonight. Sounded like you are no longer loopy from the anti-depressants!

Watched the 3/4 moon up in the sky while we talked and was reminded of the old days.

Do what your lovely smart doctor says dearest – and always remember I'll be waiting for you on the other side. In the meantime, I'll be storing away plenty of ammunition as I giggle along with your looney toon antics over the next four weeks or so.

08-08-2006 — Tick Tick Tick

> *Somebody should tell us, right at the start of our lives, that we are dying.*
> *Then we might live life to the limit, every minute of every day. Do it! I say.*
> *Whatever you want to do, do it now! There are only so many tomorrows.*
> ~~Pope Paul VI

Life is swirling around me. Everything and everyone is changing, moving forward, taking the next step in life. I feel a bit … stuck. An SUV that sits, wheels spinning wildly, atop that last road-blocking tree trunk. A salmon swimming upstream. A rat, lost in a maze of my own creation.

We all know that Anna is occasionally sadistic. Being in exactly that mood this morning after yet another night of barely two hours sleep, I re-visited the oh-so-friendly web site *Deathclock.com*.

Using the Normal barometer (Optimistic is perhaps too much to ask for), I'll be around until

Saturday, May 26, 2029

719,331,422 seconds (and counting)

11988857 minutes

8325 days

22.8 years

At 6:01 p.m. tonight, I will have lived 20,602 days of my life. 56 years, 4 months, 26 days.

Ten years ago, everyone I knew had dreams. Ten years later, I am the only one who still settles for what I have, not what I want.

08-10-2006 — **Timothy Leary Incarnate**
(from the secret journal "*LuvACowboy*")

there are no words to describe this topsy turvy existence, and Gabriel too full of mind-altering drugs to notice anything. do you suppose there will ever come a time when i can say – my turn …

08-11-2006 — **Four Things Meme or Hey It's Friday and I Have No New News to Report so Why Not**

Four jobs I have had in my life:
1. Car Hop – A&W Root Beer Stand
2. Hospital Ward Clerk
3. VIP Party Salesperson (Very Important Playthings … yes, THOSE things)
4. Dance Instructor

Four movies I would watch over and over:
1. *Gone With the Wind*
2. *It Happened One Night* (ok, Clark Gable or Errol Flynn anything)
3. *Indiana Jones I* or *Star Wars IV-VI* (sorry can't decide)
4. *Pretty Woman*

Four places I have lived:
1. St. Louis, MO
2. Chicago, IL
3. Los Angeles, CA
4. Baltimore, MD

Four TV shows I love to watch:
1. *Doctor Who* & "Star" anything, especially *Stargate*, now with Ben Browder
2. *NCIS*
3. *Grey's Anatomy*
4. *House*

Four places I have been on vacation:
1. Disneyland – three times (but I was there for the U.S. Open Dance Comp anyway – so does that count?)
2. Amsterdam to Paris via Waterloo and Brussels (by car) – did you know that the little peeing boy is only about two feet high?
3. England, Ireland, Scotland (by car mostly – it was a LONG vacation)
4. India (twice – by car, train, plane, and camel) Yes, I said camel.

Four of my favorite foods:
1. Strawberries
2. Rib Eye Steak (rare)
3. Cherry Pie (tart)
4. Chocolate anything

Four songs that remind me of summer:
Songs don't remind me as much as singers, but I'll try
1. "Red Beans"
2. "Rocket 88"
3. "Shakin the Shack" (or pretty much anything that is danceable Beach Music)
4. Ok – I give up … Jimmy Buffett's entire catalogue and every disco tune that was every written (real disco, like Donna Summers, Evelyn "Champagne" King,

Edwin Starr, and Vicki Sue Robinson ...)

Four places I would rather be right now:
1. West Coast
2. Los Angeles
3. Malibu
4. Yes, there IS a theme here

PS: Yes, I know, I cheated. But FOUR? How absurd. Life is too rich, too full, and too HUGE to limit anything.

08-11-2006 — **Week #2**
(from the private journal "*cUnHell*")

For some reason I was unsuccessful at giving myself this week's injection with the Doc watching. Thing is, they don't hurt. The needles are short and small, smaller even than insulin syringes. It's just the whole IDEA of sticking needles into my skin. Quite honestly, thinking about having to do it contributes to my anxiety levels. Perhaps once I do it the first time or two it will be better.

He asked if I wanted a sleep aid, because it's been a serious problem. Since last Friday at this time, I've only had one night where I slept more than three hours – and that was with the help of a Tylenol PM.

Let's hope tonight's pain is better than last week – because my daughter and grandson are here and I don't want to live in zombie-land for the weekend recovering from the aftershock.

08-12-2006 — *JournalLand* **Post by** *Gabriel*
(In answer to emails directed to him from various "friends")

After the death of my son, I collapsed and was hospitalized. Once I was able to communicate, I waited a day or two before talking to anyone outside of my family. The first call I made was to Anna. Before the call I had checked my messages and Anna had left two very sweet messages telling me she loved me and that she was there for me ... I appreciated those kind of messages, especially now, and needed to hear them from someone who loves me.

Several days later, she finally shared how Mr. Lucky had treated her during my absence. I have always worried about him but Anna has always told me he was not cruel to her. After hearing her describe recent events, my mind began thinking of ways to hurt Mr. Lucky and someday he will get his. We have agreed that since I am not in a position to have her with me with her medical situation (because of the way her insurance coverage is structured) it is better to stay where she is – as long as he behaves.

Here are some basic facts … I LOVE ANNA … period. Why would I walk away from the best thing that has happened to me since my first wife and my Son? With all the bad stuff happening around me, why would I walk away from the one person who loves me with all her heart? Why would I want to make a bad situation worse? She is my bright light in all this darkness.

When the Doctors are done with me, I will take some time for myself to heal the best way I know how. This process is the best way and it works for me. We have talked about it, and I will tell Anna before I go. Then I will come back to Anna healed, the same man she loves, minus a lot of problems and heartache. I love Anna and will be with her until she tells me to leave, or that she's leaving, in which case I'll pack my bags and go with her.

Here are some other facts. Others will not manipulate me in my relationship with Anna. I am in a relationship with Anna, not the women and men from an on-line forum who call themselves friends. If you love us, let us live our lives. I'm sure we'll make a few mistakes along the way, but we're big kids – we'll figure it out.

I have not, and will not, abuse Anna in any way because I LOVE her. If, for some reason, our relationship should end, it won't be because we didn't try. If we have problems, we will work them out. God knows we talk about everything. I haven't found a single thing so far, nor do I expect to find anything, that will break us up.

08-15-2006 — **All F*cking Right Already – I Made The Call**

I called an attorney. In fact, I called two. They both had the same bottom line answer. It ain't gonna happen. There simply is no case law in Virginia – domestic, civil, or contractual – supporting my getting any part of anything when I leave Mr. Lucky.

They both suggested Mr. Lucky might be smarter than I give him credit for in protecting his assets and that the cost of arguing the case would outweigh any benefits I might receive.

Perhaps I put off talking with a professional to keep a little hope alive, because right this minute I am sure I knew in my heart I'd get screwed.

08-18-2006 — **Who Am I**

I am not a Mona Lisa, hands folded gently, head lowered, peacefully moving through life with a soft enigmatic smile. Do not picture an encircling halo, or a Madonna glow.

I will never be the focused Zen of a small burbling brook over smooth, well-worn rocks. Nor the glassy blue perfection of a perfect mountain lake.

My nature is not reflected in the dandelion seed, floating upon the wind this way and that without purpose or reason. The butterfly, happy to live the brief life laid out by nature is not of my design.

Do not look for me at the back of the room, the bottom of the list, the end of the line, or with the other cheek turned.

Spock would find me ... difficult.

I am Athene, Titania, Helen, and Hatshepsut. My hands play counterpoint to voice and conviction, my mind seeks the answer before you ask the question.

I am the Colorado River, full of sound and movement, urgency of spirit. Drop by steady drop I remove the hindering rock. My soul lives in the canyons I have hewn and demands attention.

I have the happilyforeverafter heart of a practical romantic – always preparing for the other shoe to drop.

I do not watch injustice, or inequity, I do not practice cruelty or deception. Everything you need to know is right here, right now and always has been.

Angels would find me ... interesting.

08-18-2006 — **Week #3**
(from the private journal "*cUnHell*")

Always start with some great news … I DID IT! Gabriel was such a help. He suggested a different way of holding the syringe so I could use my forefinger to give it a little tap without having to look at the needle going in.

The doctor said, "Wow, you did that just like a professional." Now I can do my injections at home each week.

The bad news … the blood work wasn't so great. On 1.25 pages of results, there were six alerts. Poop. The white blood cell, platelets, and neutrophils are plummeting. If they don't stabilize, I'll have to start another weekly injection to build them up. If they still don't stabilize, I have to stop the treatments for a little while which is something I simply refuse to do. I mean, what's the worst that could happen if I'm careful and am not exposed to something icky?

The maybe good, maybe bad news … side effects are still manageable. Depression light but very tired. Appetite down – lost two pounds but that could have been because SOME of my lower body parts seem to be working overtime here lately. BUT, the doctor said no side effects could mean it's not working, or that it won't get that bad.

"One of my patients never stopped playing tennis."

And MY friend that did the treatment years ago danced three or four times a week throughout. So who knows.

08-19-2006 — **Hello, Goodbye, Hello Again**
(from the secret journal "*LuvACowboy*")

in the middle of the night when there are more questions than answers, and i can't sleep despite the many sheep that pass through my head, i count instead all the additional ways the Twelfth of Never will be postponed.

already there was fire. then tides. then hurricanes, floods, and devastation. then work, illness and death. now more personal illness of the physical and mental kind.

and the prospects for the future?

he is at an age where parents and grandparents are at an age when any one of them can be laid low by an illness that would understandably, and deservedly, require time, attention, and focus, bringing about another inevitable delay in the course of our life.

when he, himself, having beaten the odds repeatedly, is suddenly attacked with a multitude of symptoms – some of which may have started 30 or more years ago.

and in those midnights, when even the moon does not show her face to comfort me, i count all the potential reasons for postponement during all the coming months, or years. is it no wonder sleep is an elusive dream.

08-20-2006 — **Golden Knights in Lexus Chargers**

"Hey, I'm going to be out in your neighborhood this afternoon. Join me for dinner?"

A welcome phone call from Golden Knight, my dear friend I hadn't seen in too long. He was one of the first people I told about my illness and the only one that didn't reply, "So, how'd you get it?" which always makes me feel ... a little soiled. He has followed up each week just to let me know HE knows it's rough.

Over the years, GK has given me many gifts. He took me sky diving to prove that heights are not scary, accompanied me (or I him) to innumerable black tie affairs because he knew how much I love dressing up, helped get me a job when I didn't know how I was going to pay the rent, argued with me without fighting, let me fly his plane, and never reminded me he was the one I never chose.

Friday, we celebrated friendship as two old friends do who only get together occasionally. It made my day when he said how proud he was that my needle phobic self had found the courage to give myself the injection after miserably failing the week before. Thank you GK for being my friend!

08-22-2006 — **Yesterday's Message**
Personal email to *Gabriel* from Anna

Between the dream you had and your last message yesterday I am a little disconcerted. I'm not sure what you meant to say, or were trying to say.

I told you many times I don't want to be one of the people poking you with sticks. There are too many people wanting too much from you already. So honey – just talk to me. Tell me what would make you happiest, and most content, at this moment and for the foreseeable future. And because I love you, and because I always will, I'll do whatever you need.

08-23-2006 — **Divine Intervention**

Human beings normally use a very small percentage of their brainpower. However, in emotionally charged situations like physical trauma, extreme joy, or fear, their neurons start firing like crazy, resulting in massively enhanced mental clarity.

Remarkable solutions to seemingly impossible problems often occur in these moments. Gurus call it higher consciousness. Biologists call it altered states. Psychologists call it super-sentience and Christians call it answered prayer.

Sometimes, divine revelation simply means adjusting your brain to hear what your heart already knows. Sometimes it means doing it the other way around.

"Each of us is a God," Buddha said. "Each of us knows all. We need only open our minds to hear our own wisdom."

08-24-2006 — **In the Land of Oz**

My sister came to see Travis for the first time last week. When she left, Morgan sent me an email to the tune of "ding dong the witch is gone."

Now my sister is not wicked, not by any means. She is, however, rigid. We are now, and have always been, complete opposites. She went to college; I got pregnant in high school. She had a house, husband, 2.5 children, and lived the life suburbia while I traipsed around the country having fun in urban settings. Her daughter has a wonderful personality and despite my (according to my sister) unsavory life-style – my daughter is Morgan.

During her visit, my sister admitted she had given up when she was six years old and some kid told her she wasn't likable. Or something like that.

Six years old – she gives up.

She became a bookish, easily offended, angry, arrogant, self-righteous individual with little humor. (But also a great parent who worked hard to help her daughter overcome a slight learning disability, supports her husband untiringly in every way, and is good in a career she likes). Of course, the entire mess of her childhood was my fault because I was older, bossed her around, and laughed at her because she was fat and had to wear glasses. (Ok, probably guilty as charged but who remembers when you were nine.)

It's not like I haven't apologized for my childish behavior.

And mostly she forgot the millions of hours we played together quite nicely.

At any rate – the rift grew wider and wider, especially during my mother's final battle with cancer when I was in high school. Then, of course, I got pregnant, moved out, and she was "left" behind. I was, perhaps, less than helpful in that I didn't care all that much for my mother anyway, had a difficult pregnancy, and an already challenging marriage. But I could have done more I'm sure. My sister never understood why I disliked my mother so much – but she didn't get hit like I did either. She was the "good seed" and I was not. Well, there has to be one in every family.

Her counselor told her years ago not to attempt a relationship with me, as I am not healthy for her – even though we are now in our 50's and the personality she tells him about is remembrances from almost 35 years ago. In my mind (and I'm not being judgmental here, really I'm not) another symptom of un-professionalism amongst non-professional shrinks, but who am I to say? I have long since believed that the hatchet should have been buried (and not in her back), but I'm not going to rock the safe boat she has created for herself.

With another generation born, however, it is difficult. Our family is extremely small and I don't believe we should exclude any of them. I often feel bad that things got where they are, or remained where they were – whichever is true – but despite several tries over the years, including Christmas 1999 when Morgan and her first husband invited us both to dinner (yes, at the same time), it doesn't seem to be fixable. I think both sides have to want to – and I've been the only side holding out a hand for decades.

Meanwhile, I suppose every family has to have one oddball you can talk about over Thanksgiving dinner. So when we are done talking about Mr. Lucky – there's always Sis.

08-25-2006 — **Week #4**
(from the private journal "***cUnHell***")

Another week. Absolutely the worst yet. But since there's no place to go but up, I'll just note the highlights.

Can't wake up, and then can't go to sleep. Everything hurts, muscle pain, migraine, insomnia, scary dreams, diarrhea, and bloody nose. Not enough energy to pick up a toothpick and the blood tests are starting to leave nasty bruises (although it might have been the new Vampirella).

Gave myself the injection yesterday without thinking about it. Just prepared it and did it. Yeah me.

Blood work for the week? Actually better. That's good news. White blood cell count up, liver enzyme down. But you can't count a single week; apparently my blood just changes on a whim pretty regularly and I'm not sure I trust this lab (this is the one that has LOST my blood on more than one occasion and when they found it, and tested it, got a radically different result than on the re-draw).

However, assuming the tests are even slightly accurate, the liver enzymes definitely appear to be down from the start. Let's hope that's good news.

Gabriel suggested yesterday I start taking the anti-depressants. Actually more than suggested. "I've been trying to say it in a subtle way."

"Just come out with it. I don't do *subtle* too well lately."

"Well, I've been hearing a change in your voice, and I think it would be a good idea if you filled the prescription. I don't want you to wait too long."

I did. Although I'm still not sure if I'll take them. They are contraindicated for my migraine medicine … fatal side effects in some cases … so I want to ask my doctor first (isn't it amazing they just write prescriptions and hope the pharmacy, or you, asks about everything else you take?)

I'm not sure how I *feel* relates to the treatment, the disease, or the side effects. Besides, you can't treat a sad heart with pills.

08-31-2006 — **Talk talk talk talk**
(from the secret journal "*LuvACowboy*")

There are talkers.
    And there are listeners.

Have you ever noticed that the phrase "We need to talk" is never, and I mean never, good news for the listener?

I could write about a thousand things. I don't know what he wants to hear. Or how much I can easily say.

I could tell him I feel like he's not always been honest with me. I don't think he has meant to be dishonest – I think he either didn't know the truth, or didn't think I needed to know it. I've tried to ignore it, figuring that someday the small dishonesties that have bothered me would cease to be important.

I could tell him that just because I show emotion does not mean I am crippled by fear, indecision, or worry. In the hundreds of emails and thousands of minutes of phone calls, has he failed to notice that we are both emotion-based individuals?

I could tell him that he takes umbrage at things that were never meant to be offensive. I won't call them trivial because they aren't to HIM. Like the time I mentioned I saw his house, (the one address he gave me) on Google Earth, and laughed that even Google didn't know he lived there. Is this the reason he has hidden all but the vaguest sense of his whereabouts from me since? If only he had said "sorry – but I don't want you to know where I am."

I could tell him that when I have to defend myself, explain, or apologize because he reacts in a negative way to actions that have no ulterior motives, it makes me feel like a child being harshly chastised for being a bad girl.

I could tell him that he has given me ultimatums many times and I don't think it's something I've ever done to him. Because ultimatums do not leave room for negotiation or understanding. Ultimatums feel like there is only one right resolution and one party has no input in how that resolution is crafted.

I could tell him that no one has looked forward to knowing, and being accepted by, the rest of his family more than me. Because they are so very important to him. But he recently said he would have to convince them to give me a chance.

Despite my recommendations, he introduced them to my journal in *JournalLand* before it was locked to the public and these very straight people (not the easy-going understanding folks he told me about) strongly disapprove of me.

I could tell him that despite everything, and against the advice of so many, I have steadfastly refused to give up on us and that I defend him, unconditionally, to anyone who asks … or questions his validity.

What I can't say is that I sometimes feel like I'm on a run-away stagecoach headed for the edge of a cliff and I don't need to be rescued by anyone. Because, should it become necessary, I am quite capable of making the decision to rescue myself.

09-01-2006 — **Week #5**
(from the private journal "*cUnHell*")

I'm getting very tired. It's been a long time and things are no better with Gabriel or Mr. Lucky or the world. Just worse. And worse. And worse. How many times will I be called upon to fight the same uphill battles?

Perhaps once I'm rested I can start living on 4-5 hours a night and finally get that book written I've been meaning to write for years!

09-02-2006 — **Reality is a Bitch**

> *For each of us there is a multitude of echoes and reflections, unto infinity.*
> Charma Besenchi, *Mirrors and Miracles*, CY 8545
> ~~Steven McDonald (46)

I ran from everything my childhood was, making all the wrong decisions that eventually led to making right ones.

But the bad decisions remained with me no matter how hard I tried to outrun myself. Reality is being left abandoned and alone to start over one more time with the same old fears.

It is Fear that keeps you alive. What kills people is the inability to make a choice. Real courage isn't about charging into the teeth of a problem with guns blazing. It's about being scared to death and getting the job done anyway.

I want to run away again, but I will just keep running into myself. There's here, there's now, there's this reality. Sometimes you have to accept the nightmare, and the fear, and keep going anyway.

> *Just as you get comfortable with the universe, the bitch*
> *hits you smack in the teeth … with a hammer.*
> Admiral Kadymae Keller, at the Delphic Conflagration, CY 8733
> ~~Steven McDonald (124)

09-04-2006 — **How Are You?**
(from the secret journal "*LuvACowboy*")

I wonder, dear Anna … dear friend … When he asks "How are you?" are there ever times you consider pulling the SIM card out of the phone and just banging it with a hammer?

09-05-2006 — **They call it LABOR day for a reason**

Sunday, 2 p.m. (48 hours after Anna's chemo injection)
Mr. Lucky: I just invited the neighbors over for dinner tonight at 6:30.
Me:
Mr. Lucky: Really, you won't have to do anything. If you're too tired, just stay upstairs. I can bar-b-que.

Sunday, 2:30 p.m.
Mr. Lucky: Wow, I just looked at my calendar. We're supposed to go to my birthday party with my family.
Me: The one re-scheduled from two weeks ago? Have you confirmed with them, because it's Labor Day weekend.
Mr. Lucky: No. I'll do that now.

Sunday 2:45 p.m.
Mr. Lucky: I can't reach anybody. I guess I had better tell the neighbors just in case.

Sunday 3:00 p.m.
Mr. Lucky: Ok, I invited them for tomorrow night instead. At 6:30.

Monday – Pouring Rain
Anna cleans. Does laundry. Cooks Moroccan chicken in oven. Makes noodle dish. Fixes a dessert. Makes fruit salad.

Monday: 6:00 p.m.
Anna sets table, lays out appetizers. Pulls out finished chicken. Puts dessert in oven to bake and prepares water for noodles.
Mr. Lucky: Oh, I just remembered, I was supposed to confirm with the neighbors. I'll call now.
Me:

Monday: 6:10 p.m.
Mr. Lucky: Nobody there. I left a message.

Monday 7:00 p.m.
Mr. Lucky: Well, I guess we can go ahead and eat.
Me:

Tuesday: 8:30 a.m.
Neighbor: Oh, I'm so sorry. Mr. Lucky and I agreed he would call early Monday to confirm. I didn't hear from him so we spent the day with friends.
Me: Oh, no problem. Don't think anything of it. We'll put it together another day.

09-06-2007 — **Full Moon Passing**
(from the secret journal "*LuvACowboy*")

another full moon. another month wasted. this week i realized he is exactly like the last one. just using new and more dramatic excuses as a reason not to commit.

demanding i defend my past choices, or else. as bad as Mr. Lucky can be, i never had to defend my past actions. nor did i ask him to defend his.

shouldn't you love someone for who they are, not what you can make them into?

09-07-2006 — **Must Love Dogs**

> *... fear is ... a subtle human flaw given to us by the gods so they can exploit us.*
> ~~Arminestra, "Between the Lines"

Lacking the energy to do much else on Saturday, I sat and watched a movie recommended to me a long time ago *Must Love Dogs*. In it, Diane Lane plays a 40-something divorcee, left by her husband for a younger woman. Everyone who loves her is trying to get her back into the idea of dating and eventually uses internet matchmaking sites to find her some suitors.

Sitting in the car one night after a family dinner, Diane's sister asks her about her ex, "If he hadn't left you, you never would have left him would you?"

"No, I don't think so."

"But you weren't happy with things as they were."

"Well," replied Diane, "I figured that was the life I picked, so I had to make the best of it. I'm not even sure I deserve a new life now. Sometimes I think that was my one chance ... and I blew it."

Christopher Plummer plays Diane's father, a widower who is also trying to get back into the dating scene. Diane sits down next to him one evening to talk about how one of his many lady friends is starting to fall for him. The conversation turns back to her in a sad dissertation on how difficult dating is for women today.

"All they want is a young, perfect, nubile, hard-body and to never, ever, have to say they are sorry."

Christopher smiles (as only Christopher Plummer can) and replies, "It's different for me. I've had the love of my life and no one else can ever touch that. No one can come close. So I'm just out there passing the time … tap dancing if you want the truth. Maybe if I dance fast enough I won't remember what I've lost, you see?"

> *My heart only ever had one thought.*
> *One want.*
> *One need.*
> *Despite all,*
> *In spite of all …*
> *All my heart has ever wanted is you.*
> ~~Stephanie Laurens, *The Edge of Desire*

09-08-2006 — **Must Love Dogs – Part II**

Mr. Lucky asked me to move in with him saying, "It would mean less traveling, and be less expensive." He had a pragmatic way of looking at things – and so did I.

I don't know that I had any illusions about the relationship. I enjoyed his company, I liked him, I may have even loved him. But he wasn't the One, and I wasn't his. So I suspect he had no illusions either. At 43, I was finally living a life I could actually call comfortable.

Three years after I moved in, he had his first affair (with a married woman).

When I found his love letters to her, I realized the words written in them were not the words of the man I had been living with. This was a complete stranger and, as it turned out, not one that I would ever meet.

> *It is very hard for both of us to be apart. But it would be even harder to try to call it off. Things will never be easy for either of us again until we are together forever. The thing that makes it bearable for me is that the prize is the chance to have you. You are my joy, my dream, my love, and I truly believe that you will be my wife.*

All of our friends, and his family, knew about Renee. It was humiliating in the extreme. When I confronted him with my knowledge, he wept like a child. I made it clear there was a choice to make – but it was his. Perhaps I believed that if he chose me, he was actually making a commitment, and that he might eventually feel about me as he felt about her.

I suspect she ended the affair – as I know she moved out of state with her doctor husband. But I don't know when.

I had a choice to make and, like Diane Lane in *Must Love Dogs*, figured that I was living the life I picked so it was simply time to make the best of it. Therefore, I settled for a man who did not drink or do drugs, who did not explode with jealousy or possessiveness, for a relationship with security, and without physical or mental pain. For one that did not have a shoe hanging above my head – because he had already abandoned me. There was nothing more he could do.

09-10-2006 — **Water, Water, Everywhere**

January 2006
Plumber: You know that dishwasher is on its last legs. The seal is ready to blow. I'd replace it pretty quick if I were you.
Mr. Lucky: mmm

April 2006
Me: Hey, dishwashers on sale.
Mr. Lucky: mmm

July 2006
Me: Hey, more dishwashers on sale.
Mr. Lucky: Zzzz

September 8, 2006
Me: Hey, the dishwasher is flooding the kitchen.
Mr. Lucky: Mmmrrrph, HUH?

September 9, 2006
Me: Great dishwasher. Shouldn't we have gotten the installation package?
Mr. Lucky: I can do it.

September 10, 2006
Mr. Lucky: Where's the circuit breaker?
Mr. Lucky: Where's the wrenches?
Mr. Lucky: Where's the plumbing tape?

Mr. Lucky: WTF – HOW DO YOU SHUT OFF THE WATER?!?!?!?!
Me:

09-15-2006 — **Week #7**
(from the private journal "*cUnHell*")

"How are you?" I've heard the phrase so many times the last couple of weeks it is beginning to grate. Because I still find myself answering the question. Ad nauseam. An unstoppable diarrhea of the mouth.

Only winding down to a stop when my brain catches up to my mouth and I realize the socially proper response should have been "Just great thanks, and how about you?"

09-22-2006 — **Cursed Happenstance**

I have the incredible bad luck to find myself constantly involved with relation-ship disasters – despite my best cross my heart hope to die efforts to stay out of their way.

Every person I've ever loved has left me, or tried to use me. Everything of value is lost and I wonder if these misfortunes are payment for past sins.

When romance once again presented itself, it was difficult. Would he stay, knowing the whole truth about the life I've led. Could trust and honesty make a couple out of two strangers?

My inner voice says it's over. But where is the feeling of … of completion. Life offers no requirement for closure or answers. In fact, the odds are that when you die, you'll die in ignorance at some level, no matter what.

09-23-2006 — **Afternoon or evening, depending on your time zone**
Personal email to *Gabriel* from Anna

hadn't heard from you for a couple of weeks – not a criticism, just an observa-tion. but you asked that I keep you apprised of the medical news.

two hours today to find out pretty much nothing. chest x-ray, lung capacity, blah blah blah. at least no needles. i'll try their three RX's of pills, inhalers, and potions for a while to help this constant strength-sapping cough.

meanwhile – it's do not WALK to the bathroom in the middle of the night without strapping a pillow to my ass.

09-25-2006 — **Your past**
Personal email to Anna from *Gabriel*

I haven't called or emailed you because I have lied about how my family feels about you.

They feel you and I are having an affair. They aren't happy with me and are angry that I would expose the younger members of the family to our bad behavior. They know about Mr. Lucky and it is not acceptable to any of them. Before he passed, my Son said, "If you work for a bank and its manager treats you bad, that doesn't give you the right to rob the bank."

I told my Son and family that we weren't cheating because we hadn't even met, much less consummated our relationship. Their reply was "No Gabriel, she's robbing the bank and you're driving the getaway car." They see you as not having followed the rules in the past, now I'm not, and that has been disappointing to my family.

Our relationship, and what they read of you and your past in *JournalLand* before you shut it down, has driven a huge wedge between me and my family. As long as I'm involved in this inappropriate behavior, I'm excluded from family functions.

I have been trying to work through this with the help of a shrink, but be warned my family will never tolerate your behavior. God I hope you're not a stalker? Because they are worried you are, and are going to bother them.

I love my family and I'm trying to save my place in it. If you ever loved me, let me work things out in my head. The last 3 weeks have been intense, my uncle Bob flew out for two of my sessions. I have had family and friends involved in my sessions. They all think I'm behaving badly, they never thought I'd do this kind of thing, but here I am.

I was asked not to speak with you until my sessions were over, but I guess I have to break yet another promise. Call me; I'll turn my phone back on. Why do you always have to make things so hard?

09-27-2006 — **Dearest Gabriel**
Personal email to *Gabriel* from Anna

Last November I was traveling a lot, and I thought of all those people who had lost a loved one without being able to say goodbye. So I wrote you a letter. In part, it said:

> *I want you to know one thing and I am writing it down so you can read it again and again until you believe in it. I have loved you. I would have followed you anywhere, any time. I would have waited for you. Given the chance, I would have held you, and cherished you, been there for you, and supported you in every part of your life until forever.*

I put this first, instead of last, because I didn't want to start with anger. I know what I wished for, but I must wonder – what did you get out of convincing me to love you?

I have never, ever lied to you. Not once. Not by untruth, not by omission, not by skirting the question or refusing to answer. Being called an internet stalker by someone who said four weeks ago they loved me more than they loved any woman alive was cruel.

I remind you that when we met, Mr. Lucky and I had already decided to split up but hadn't set a date. You and I talked a lot about when, and how, we would get together.

And we agreed, as partners, that my making an interim move was foolish, especially at the cost of losing health insurance and a share of everything I'd worked for (something you always seemed more anxious about than me). And that you needed the time to wrap up your own business commitments. So you set the six-month time limit to coincide with your birthday, saying it would be the right amount of time to make sure.

On December 2, when we agreed February couldn't happen, I said, "I'm going to leave anyway. I'm packed – I'm ready. It's just a choice of where."

You bluntly said to me, "Don't do this to me right now. I can't handle worrying about you too."

And I thought "you've stayed this long, it's not gonna kill you to stay until Gabriel is ready."

How could I have interpreted that statement as do it, just don't TALK to you about it?

The reality is I never needed your permission or your help to move, and I didn't want your money. I never, in all these months, guessed you were lying to me every time you said my staying here until you were ready was ok with you. On the other hand, considering how you feel now, perhaps your silence was the kindest cut because where would I be now.

I emailed you in September 2005 joking that since you were reading my journal (YOU, not your family members, or friends, or co-workers) would it be wise to start editing, or to lock it up to all but a few of my closest friends. You told me nothing I write would bother you in the least.

In December 2005, you made a choice to tell your family members about my journal and gave them my password, bragging about how cool and hip they were and how they would accept me just because you loved me. You knew it contained information we had already agreed did not need to be shared for years. If at all. Relationships, marriages, failures, sorrow, and most especially Mr. Lucky.

I'm old enough to know that if you want to be liked you must play by everyone else's rules. But apparently, it is too late. I am tried, convicted, and hung as "that" kind of woman.

I am devastated to learn how you have suffered because of me, because of my indecision, and I understand fully what it means to us. No matter how much you may want me, or what I could do over the years to prove I am a good person who loves you deeply, I would always be that trailer trash internet stalker and it would cost you too much.

Giving you up is unthinkable, incomprehensible to me. But I will give you whatever you need. I will delete, erase, or destroy everything in my possession and on my computer. You will have my heart Forever and Always.

09-28-2006 — **Week #9**
(from the private journal "*cUnHell*")

> *"I love you more than any woman alive," he whispered in her ear. She closed her eyes and smiled, listening to the sound of his voice. "There is nothing you can do that would make me leave you," he continued as he raised his hand gently and put two bullets in her head.*
> *As the darkness gathered around her, and all the boogey men came rushing in she saw his mouth move one last time, but could not hear the words.*

Today Mr. Lucky decided I can no longer work for "his" company. I'll still have my company paid health insurance and disability benefits because I have a written contract that forces him to keep them in place throughout my illness. But I will no longer be doing the work I love and enjoy.

He can't get over that I'm ill, jostling me awake or turning on lights. So I moved into the extra bedroom. He continues to eat the food the ladies of the Garden Club kindly bring over on Saturday evenings to help me get enough to eat during the week. When I do feel like eating, there's nothing left.

The coughing has been extra debilitating. I can stand for only a short period, and sit for a little longer. I don't remember when I've slept for more than an hour at a time. It's almost dangerous as there are times I cough so hard it causes stars in front of my eyes from the shortness of breath.

In the few hours I feel like doing something each morning, I've been discarding personal possessions. All those "things" I've been so worried about finding a place for. I'm going to have to sell my boat, my bicycle, my dragons, and Christmas. I will only have room for one or two rooms of possessions – it is easier to leave them now and forget about ever having them, than have to leave them later.

I feel like I'm living outside my body right now, as if I'm looking at something happening to someone else. I'm grateful for the wall the medication has put between it and me.

The ancient fear. A lonely old woman, dying poor and abandoned in an unheated third floor walkup. Coming true right before my eyes.

10-02-2006 — **In Memoriam**

Anna Maison
born: March 14, 1950 died: October 1, 2006

Anna Maison, popular character in a *JournalLand* series of novelettes died yesterday at her home in Virginia. It was reported she was alone at the time of her death.

JournalLand has learned through an unnamed source that a private memorial service will be held for friends and family during the Full Moon and her ashes will be scattered in the Pacific Ocean on the next Twelfth of Never.

Her final message was found just today:

> *If I could pass along a single thought, it is this. Extend to others — now — the forgiveness you may someday want for yourself. The greatest gift you can give is the offer of understanding acceptance and unconditional grace. Remember you can never know the path walked by a stranger, or the branches she needed to take along the way.*

10-06-2006 — **Week #10**
(from the private journal "***cUnHell***")

> *What is love? Lies and fairy tales.*

I've sold, given to charity, or discarded box after box of belongings. I've done well. There's a long way to go, but I've probably discarded 75% of the "stuff" that tends to lay around in dresser drawers, shoeboxes, and on shelves "just in case."

I keep working on it every day. Some stuff is harder than others, but I am resolute. There won't be room for it, and I cannot afford a storage locker – so out it must go. I have the winter to sell whatever else I can ... and what's left will go the same way as the rest.

Lungs are no better – I can handle 4 or 5 hours a day of light work, housework, paperwork, but not consecutively. So I do what I can, as I can, and the devil be hanged.

I'll get the results of the new tests this week. I'm interested in what they will have found – if just to stop taking so much extra medicine.

I keep thinking an apology will come. An explanation. Even an excuse. My friends and family tell me I will be happier in the long run with the silence. Then I can make my own explanations without the echo of words ringing in my head.

10-13-2006 — **Week #11**
(from the private journal "*cUnHell*")

These are the reasons I get up every morning and breathe. Because along with everything else, my best girlfriend Bobbi probably has bladder cancer and they found, during tests, a lump in her breast and something in her lungs. She refuses to do chemo or radiation of any kind or to quit smoking.

We were going to be the Golden Girls. Enjoying an inexpensive retirement in Florida, supporting one another. Being there until one of us kicked the bucket. She has always been my rock. I am angry at her for refusing treatment that could save her life – or at least give her a lot more years. I should be empathetic, understanding, supportive, be her best friend. Instead, I feel like one more person I love is abandoning me.

I watched *Pretty Woman* the other night and as he climbed that fire escape I shouted at the screen … Viviane, walk away now because in a year he'll be calling you names and telling you his family doesn't want your trailer trash self near them. Middle class girls should never Believe in Always.

10-20-2006 — **Week #12**
(from the private journal "*cUnHell*")

Once a week I check emails and phone messages to see if there has been an apology. An explanation. Something. There never is, of course. Soon I will discard the phone we used all these months together.

The lung tests came back. The good news is that my lungs are perfect; they are not being affected by any of the medications. The bad news is that all the pills and medicines they are giving me to solve the problem with the lungs, the coughing, the shortness of breath, the dizziness, and gasping for oxygen after any type of exertion are doing no good whatsoever.

So another test or two, discontinuing one pill a day to add 10 more. Yes, I said 10. Same medicine, but apparently they come in such small doses you have to take an abundance to get what is needed.

Just my fortune – three things I hate – inactivity, needles, and taking pills. Then I get an illness that requires a plethora of them all.

> *That which is impossible is only impossible until it is accomplished, at which point it becomes possible, if not necessarily probable.*
> Wayfinder First Order Hasturi, A.K.A. "The Mad Perseid," 217 AFC
> ~~Keith DeCandido (77)

10-21-2006 — **Good Afternoon Sweetie**
Personal email to Anna from *Gabriel*

You answered the phone! What a great talk we had, just catching up on everything that has happened the last few weeks and knowing that you understand what has been happening to me.

I'm so much better now, mentally and physically. I've worked hard to get well, and now I'm working hard to get back into shape and lose some of the weight I've put on!

Maybe this time away has been as hard for you as it has been for me. So Sweetie give me a call when you can, it's nice to hear your voice again.

10-22-2006 — **Eating More as you asked**
Personal email to *Gabriel* from Anna

Breakfast and dinner today, and let's not forget the 17 pills – surely they have SOME caloric content.

Still having problems sleeping. I'm wondering if it could be from the Prednisone they gave me for the coughing. That's the only thing different and the worst of the insomnia started about then. I'll have to look it up.

Hope you are feeling a little better. You said I should start leaving the phone on again during the day – so I will. I'm driving to New York to see Morgan and the baby on Wednesday and coming home the next Tuesday. We know what that means – lovely goodnight phone calls!

10-23-2006 — **I Tried**
Personal email to Anna from *Gabriel*

Sweetheart I'm sorry to report nothing has changed. The *JournalLand* women are now writing about me in their journals and that I'm a fucking lying creep and they are going to "do some digging" on me.

Sweetie, I need to ask you this, but first let me say if you told them any of these things I understand. Your chemo along with your worry about me, my emails, and that infamous phone call between us about my family's feelings could cause this reaction on your part.

Remember we promised not to lie to each other any longer … so if this is the case please tell me. Have you been talking about me to anyone? If so, I need to know the truth, I will stick by you regardless. This is completely unfair and it needs to stop.

You told me you asked them to leave us alone, to stop writing about us, or to you, in a public forum or via email. Please let me know immediately. We will get through this, hang in there, I love You.

10-23-2006 — **I Tried Too**

Please understand I can't stop what others write in *JournalLand* or in emails or messages to you. You must know that. I locked my *JournalLand* journal from public view in July – I write only for myself and talk to none of my friends from there, so no one is getting any information or ammunition from me.

As you may remember, you did not lock yours. In addition, each of us continued to read, and sometimes comment on, other member's diaries so we did not entirely disappear from the space, even if we no longer posted entries people could read.

Since messages by members, to members, are forwarded (and some writers have my personal email), I received a considerable number from my many followers asking why I stopped writing, and what happened between us. I answered a few from close friends by saying – thank you for your concern but please respect our privacy and leave us alone for now. The rest I ignored. I also got a number of calls that I did not return.

I did not tell anyone of the email or phone call I received from you accusing me of being an internet stalker and telling me your family did not approve of me or my past. I also did not say that because I loved you, I would not hurt your relationship with your family and, despite the difficulty involved in the decision, had decided to back away.

You told me you wanted to stop participating in *JournalLand* because it has become an uncomfortable online forum. Then let's do it. If people want to do some "digging" or "look us up" to find an ending to the stories we wrote, let them take their best shot. I am an open book – they can find me all over the internet.

We, and by we I mean You, should be above petty internet crap. It will blow over in a few days and who cares what readers in a little-known online journal site have to say about a writer they don't know, have never met, and whose alias they will not be able to crack?

If you tell me who is causing all the trouble for you I am happy to send a personalized email telling them, once again, to back off in no uncertain terms – that this is our life and I feel they are interfering ... and not as friends should.

10-27-2006 — **Week #13**
(from the private journal "*cUnHell*")

The last blood results came back. The one that measures the viral load (HCV Quantitation for medical minded folks). Let me put it in context.

YIPPEE YIPPEE YIPPEE YIPPEE YIPPEE

The viral load is undetectable and the liver enzymes are normal. It doesn't mean I'm cured – or that I will stay cured. However, it's a good start!

11-03-2006 — **Week #14**
(from the private journal "*cUnHell*")

My visit with baby Travis was spectacular. I LOVE being a granny!

It was a nice drive up. All the fall colors in the trees and a lovely warm sunny day. As usual, shiny stuff kept distracting me. A pretty leaf, a rock on the roadside, a cloud through the windshield.

Bah! That seems to happen a lot lately. No memory and no concentration.

Driving back, I was much more tired – even stopped at a rest stop and took a little nap. Unfortunately that put me in 5:00 Washington traffic.

Imagine being in the worst traffic jam you've ever been in. No, really. Even New York and Los Angeles vie with Washington. Our evening traffic jams start at 2:30 and end after 8:00. Really.

And remember that distraction problem?

I started from New York with half a tank of gas and figured I could get home. Now I'm on the Beltway with 65,000 of my closest friends and the Low Fuel light goes on. Yes – I know Low Fuel means there is still gas in the tank … but did you know how much depends on the age of the car and the amount of sediment in the tank? I made it, white-knuckled and all.

Fatigue, and three migraines, was the order of the day for the rest of the week – and itching. Yes – itching. Apparently, my body is reacting to one of the meds. I look like I have sunburn on my chest, tummy, back, neck – even my scalp. I scratch and scratch and scratch.

Ah – just another wonderful symptom to figure out.

11-10-2006 — Week #15
(from the private journal "*cUnHell*")

> *I hollowed me out*
> *Where my heart lies*
> *To make room for your dreams*
> *My intentions speak true*
> *Where my heart lies.*
>> "Love and Salvation," Ulatempa Poetess, CY 9824
>> ~~Ethlie Ann Vare (291)

I stopped taking all the medications prescribed for the lung problems two weeks ago. Lo and behold – the lung problems and the persistent coughing appears to have subsided. I'd said all along it might have been a low-grade infection that wouldn't show up in the blood tests.

Worst things going on right now (the fatigue doesn't stop, but I'm managing it) are infections and a horrific rash. Every little thing gets infected – from a bump on my leg to a hangnail. The rash itches like poison ivy – but no blisters or bumps. More like a horrible itching, burning, sunburn covering my scalp, neck, chest, back, and tummy. Since it's been going on for about 10 days, it's off to the dermatologist. At night, it burns and itches so much I can't even sleep.

11-17-2006 — Week #16
(from the private journal "*cUnHell*")

And I wonder …

What if Katrina had not intervened, would he have come to Baltimore on that planned visit?

What if he had not gotten the phone call, would he have spent Thanksgiving in San Diego?

Honestly – would the Twelfth of Never have happened? Ever. For any reason.

Was it me that suggested we "out" Gabriel and Anna in *JournalLand*?

Was I ever asked to stop writing? Or was it me that chose to lock the site.

Was it my idea to have his family read my past entries? And even if they did – did his friends and family love him so little to judge so much?

He repeats that something I must have written, or said, or thought led others to write, email, call, do background checks, etc. and come to a bad conclusion about his character. Then suggests I must have condoned it – as if I would have done so. He says his agent, manager, members of his writing group, the actors, and all the directors he works with will have nothing to do with him. That he is blackballed in the Hollywood industry in which he works as long as he continues to participate in our illicit "affair."

And still, how his family members just "don't understand" and assume I am some sort of … instead of trusting him to make good decisions at his age.

I've become fatigued at swallowing the anger I feel at being blamed for everything that has gone wrong in his life. I just eat it – and say "yes dear."

11-19-2006 — **Morning**

I have been very very happy the last few days since stopping the antidepressants. Happier, healthier, more energetic, laughing, and content than I have felt since May. It feels wonderful to have a few days "out of the fog" where your mind, body, and emotional state (both mental and physical) are cooperating with you. I needed the break.

However, I have been warned about stopping medications just because I think I feel better. I'm going to talk to the doctor on Monday and ask if there might be an alternate medication that won't return me to the same foggy place.

11-24-2006 — **Week #17**
(from the private journal "*cUnHell*")

My skin is on fire. It burns and itches, keeps me up at night. Already there are large patches of flaky alligator skin in my underarms and on my sides. I'm jumping out of my skin 24 hours a day.

The internet says most patients on HCV treatment develop some type of skin problem because interferon and ribavirin cause dry skin. The rash is not supposed to be dangerous but scratching can lead to infection due to the low white blood cell count that comes from interferon.

11-24-2006 — **Happy day after Thanksgiving honey**
Personal email to *Gabriel* from Anna

Tried to call you this morning and your phone message said the phone was not taking calls. Ha Ha – for once it is YOUR phone acting up instead of mine.

Your new job sounds like fun – running around all over the city finding just exactly the right location for movies and television shows. Your expertise at having been in front of the camera so long is coming in handy, isn't it?

11-25-2006 — **Some Thoughts**

He laid down his expectations after yet another accusatory conversation. We have agreed to keep our conversations of a general nature (weather, kids, work, football, etc.) that there will be no physical contact of any kind (or any discussions about it) and that anything about Mr. Lucky is a taboo subject.

The last injection date is still seven months away but I must start putting a plan together. I have some ambivalence about WHERE to move. I originally thought Florida would be best but, with Morgan and the baby in New York, the visits would be costly.

Apparently, he wants me to decide all these things without his input – and that makes sense considering his desire to keep himself separated from "this" life. I'm ok with it and understand completely. On the other hand, I would hate to be accused later of not including him in the decisions I make.

12-01-2006 — **Week #18**
(from the private journal "*cUnHell*")

So, today I had a skin biopsy (yes – poking hole, stitch, etc.) to see if the rash is something else. I can't stand it. Another RX as well.

We continue to dance the same dance. This time he broke his leg just below the knee. Never saw anyone that had more troubles associated with life. He still calls, but we talk about nothing at all. He's clarified that he wants nothing to do with the move, including input on the where. Send him the address change and call him when I get there.

Problem is – do I trust him to actually ever be there? Right now, the answer is no.

12-13-2006 — **Another phone call**

I woke up to another angry angry angry phone message. Monday he just hung up on me as I apologized once again for anything I may have done to make him so unhappy with his life. How can he assume I am trivializing what has happened. Just the opposite. I recognize that I am the object of his anger and resentment. I am trying hard to figure out how I will ever again be able to talk to him about anything important.

Will this be our life together – tip toeing around terrorized I will make him mad at me again and again and again. I cannot unwrite, nor force anyone to un-read. I am not in charge of emails from well-meaning friends or anonymous mailers that land in his inbox. Or the reported indifference and hostility of his friends, family, and colleagues because of my presence in his life (Jeez, doesn't he live in Hollywood?)

02-12-2007 — **An Interesting Breakthrough**

Yesterday was the anniversary of my Mother's death. She had her first surgery for cancer when I was 10 years old. My younger sister and I were alone in the house for almost six weeks – with the exception of the late night hours after my father got off second shift, and before he left for the hospital in the morning.

When she came home, the treatments started. Radiation mostly as I don't remember lots of pills and she did not lose her hair. When those didn't work, Mayo Clinic and trips to Mexico for the experimental drug Laetrile that was supposed to fight cancer. My sister and I didn't know she was dying, of course, although she figured it out before I did. Or perhaps Mother told her.

My Mother was not the greatest when I was young – although I suspect, in hindsight, that she was bipolar and did her best. The only example she had was HER mother, a country orphan that raised five of her own brothers and sisters from the time she was nine. After Mother became ill, she was much worse. Screaming, hitting, temper tantrums. Daddy, for all that he loved his children, adored his wife and became so absorbed with her condition he almost disappeared into himself. But I didn't get it.

Until now. Until yesterday.

She battled being sick almost every day for eight years while trying to be a wife and Mother to two children. Plus she went back to work in order to make sure we would have social security survivor benefits after she died. She still managed to attend all the band concerts, and choral concerts, and Christmas pageants, and make sure we got to Girl Scouts and gymnastics.

She cleaned the house, changed the beds, paid the bills, bought the groceries, and cooked the meals – including breakfast each morning until we were teens.

I've only done it for six months – with the knowledge that at the end, I'm going to get WELL – and it's harder than hell. Every day that I can't get off the couch, that starts decent and degenerates into an upset stomach, migraine headache, and skin that feels like it's on fire. Every day that starts with coughing and ends with coughing. Every day when more and more hair is on the pillow than on my head.

I can't imagine doing it day after day, week after week, month after month with the end knowledge that you are not going to survive no matter what you do.

It has taken many years, but I have finally been able to forgive the shortcomings I thought she had and apologize for not being more understanding, more helpful, and more supportive when I could have been. Despite our differences, I suspect she still loved me and did the best she could under the circumstances.

I say this because, well, because I miss talking with Gabriel. Especially about an important – if heartbreaking – breakthrough for me. The kind of thing we used to share and talk about in the relationship we used to have. I don't know where it's gone or whether it will ever be back. I keep believing he loves me, because he says so. I keep believing in August even though we have never discussed it since he first set out the rules of what I had to do if we were to have a future after my treatments were over.

Happy Birthday my darling. I think of you often and hope your day will be extra special.

03-13-2007 — **Hello**
Personal email to Anna from *Gabriel*

I am sure you have tried to reach me by phone, but Sweetheart that's impossible! I am at my Dad's new place that has no cell phone reception and didn't want to put a long-distance call on my Dad's landline.

I got his computer running today and decided to drop you a little note. This is the first time I've checked my email in a while and only read yours.

I hope you're feeling better than last week, keep the faith Sweetheart it's almost over. Well sweetie we'll be communicating via smoke signals (emails) for a while.

Email Me. Love Ya

03-14-2007 — **Hi Again**
Personal email to Anna from *Gabriel*

You're getting as bad as me about reading your emails. Oh well, I'm sure eventually you'll read these and drop me one. It's beautiful and very peaceful here. Well Honeybunny I'm going to get on the barn roof and watch the Sunset.

Goodnight Sweetheart.

03-15-2007 — **Hello Again**
Personal email to Anna from *Gabriel*

Still haven't checked your email, you ARE as bad as me. I thought I'd check in and see if you had dropped me a line … not yet. I'm going to hit the hay earlier tonight. I'm exhausted – this ranch life is killing me.

03-16-2007 — **re: Hello Again**
Personal email to *Gabriel* from Anna

Sorry – you sent emails to a Yahoo account I don't use very often. When you get back (or are able to get reception), you'll find a couple of phone messages from the last couple of weeks. I have missed talking with you; it was less than an hour last month.

I'm feeling – oh, who knows. Good enough to get to Garden Club where they got me a cake and sang happy birthday. Good enough to get more stuff sold on eBay. Good enough to enjoy the wonderful weather earlier this week, although it's back to mid-thirties and raining today. What a joy to see the daffodils and crocus coming up.

If your email continues to work, I'll check my Yahoo account a little more often. How long will you be there? Are you going to do the courier job? Have you quit the other job now? Is your brother back from Iraq? Did you get your car fixed/back? How is your mom feeling? etc. etc.

03-17-2007 — **Hello Again, and Again, and Again**
Personal email to Anna from *Gabriel*

FINALLY. See you are as bad as me! I tried to reach you today but every time I called it said *User Busy*. It's weird, I can use the Internet, but my cellphone won't work calling out of State. So check your email. Tomorrow we are going up the mountain so I'll try again. Sorry about your Birthday … Happy Birthday.

03-17-2007 — **No Luck**
Personal email to *Gabriel* from Anna

I'm not sure – but many people who have landlines have unlimited local and long distance. Since your father's family is mostly "long distance," he may have done exactly that. If so – you could call from his phone.

03-19-2007 — **It's Actually Cold at 11,000 ft. …**
Personal email to Anna from *Gabriel*

… but no reception. As for using my Dad's phone, I think its best that I don't. The less I speak of You and me around my family the better it is.

My Dad asked that I stay another week. He's 84, still active, and in the last week we have grown even closer. It feels like when I was a young kid and he'd teach me things like how to throw a curve ball. Things a good man should do in tricky situations.

When I head back to LA, I'll let you know the evening before and we can talk on the drive back.

03-19-2007 — **It's actually cold in Washington too!!**
Personal email to *Gabriel* from Anna

I thought your family had finally come to terms about us – which is why we put off everything again for another year. Guess I misunderstood.

We'll just have our own special times together and I've learned over the last seven months that "alone" time is actually somewhat enjoyable.

03-19-2007 — **Snow!**
Personal email to Anna from *Gabriel*

Yeah Sweetie I think you did misunderstand. I told you a little while ago, I had given up on the thought of my family and friends ever accepting the possibility of You and me as a couple. I guess we really should talk about this in detail eventually, but not now. Make no mistake, they don't approve and let's leave it at that. When I get home we'll talk about it, actually we have to discuss it if we are to continue on.

03-19-2007 — **If we are to continue**
(from the secret journal "***LuvACowboy***")

If? IF? Yes, I suppose we should talk about it someday. Here I've simply been trusting all along. Through all the accusations, the names, the anger, the frequent extended silences, and the fact that he has not said a word about a future together (despite my need to begin making my final plans) or that "we" still existed. I believed that all I had to do is get through the treatments, prove to him that the virus was gone, and he would accept me back into his life as a whole person.

But let me be clear. He says repeatedly he did nothing to cause his troubles – so his stay in the mental hospital, his extended absences, cancelling all his work contracts, and quitting his job(s) had nothing to do with it. Everything bad that happened to him was because I used to write a public blog.

Whatever happened, and for whatever real reasons, it doesn't matter. I completely and fully agreed to accept all the blame for everything, whether caused by me – or not. He agreed to "get up every morning and try to forgive me." I know I am a good person and nothing any stranger thinks will change who I am.

He has always asked me for complete honesty, even though he has rarely given me the same. He asked me to trust, but has never trusted me. He asked me not to give up, but has given up on me. He asked me repeatedly to just wait "until" ... and things would come together. I believed it and believed it and believed it. Now, almost two years later, we are an "if."

So, I keep thinking – even right this very second – that he is going to forgive me, make the decision that we (not our family or friends) have the right choose who we want to love, show up to wherever I move in August, and fall in love with me all over again, the world be damned.

03-20-2007 — **I need to calm down**
Personal email to Anna from *Gabriel*

I told you how my friends and Family felt recently and I am still a little touchy on this subject. Talking to you today hasn't helped my peace of mind.

Each and every day I forgive you for this friggin mess that I had absolutely nothing to do with. It has fucked my life up and yes, I am still very angry.

Now I think I need some time to calm down before we speak again.

Do not try to blame this on me. My friends and family care about me. I have never said a bad word about you to anyone; their conclusions have been drawn by the words you wrote – not by me.

Yes, we need to discuss this, but when I have calmed down because if we do it now we might as well walk away from each other – it won't end well.

03-24-2007 — **Interesting Reading**
Personal email to *Gabriel* from Anna

I have tried very hard during our talks and correspondence to stay away from any discussions on the subjects that upset you, as it doesn't do either of us any good. It makes you angry and explosive. And having already said I agree to take ALL OF THE BLAME, unconditionally, for everything bad that has happened to you in the two years you've known me – what more do you need for me to do?

03-27-2007 — **Speaking the Truth**
Personal email to Anna from *Gabriel*

When I tell you I need a couple of days, I mean it. I am telling you the truth. I suppose I should speak in very simple and plain English. I am still very angry about all the crap that took place last summer and all the wonderful things that happened because of it. I am still trying very hard to deal with what has happened and the changes in my life that have happened.

I feel you think of it as a small thing. Well, you had everything to do with this. People I know read your journal before you locked it up and found out what kind of person I was having a relationship with. I go to sleep at night hoping I'll awake in the morning and find out it's all been a bad dream.

I'll be honest. I hate my life the way it is now. I'm 59 and unemployed; everything I'd hoped for has vanished through no fault of my own. I was living my dream, it is gone, and it's not coming back. I know I have to deal with it and try to make the transition as painless as possible, but it is very hard.

I am going to be as honest as I possibly can. Part of me Loves you and a part of me wishes I had never met you. Sometimes all I can think about is you and how I can't wait to see you. At other times, I see my life as it is and get angry and ask myself why?

This thing is still eating at me like it happened yesterday. I have no one to talk to about this. My friends and family have made their stance clear and think I'm completely unreasonable and in a situation that will only hurt me worse. They think I'm on a self-destructive course and nothing good will come of this. I believe I should probably see the Shrink again. It all seems to be getting worse than better. I need to talk this out.

You are right; we are talking less and less. I sometimes feel so bad and angry I don't want to talk for fear I might explode. I said I'd never say mean, hateful things and I mean to keep my promise. Sometimes I feel the need to vent but there's no one here for me.

I told you we'd start over and I mean to see that through. But I'm serious, we are starting over. I want to meet you in person, get to know you, date you; we need to see if we are right for each other. I need to touch you and hear you say these things then I'll know if they are real or not. I fell in love with your words; they struck to the center of my heart.

But when you speak of us, you make it sound as though we are already an us. That is not true. When we meet, that's when the work starts. I hope that we will develop a trust in each other, and we will both know that this wasn't just based on a bunch of words. I will know when I can see and touch you in person. I'm not sure you truly believe in my ESPN but I do, it has never failed me. As they say, it's all in the touch.

I'm not going to lie to you and tell you I was not angry while writing this because it raised its ugly head a number of times. But the important thing was I got to speak the truth. I thought about erasing some stuff, but I believe I have made mistakes in the past by doing so. From this point on, I'm not going to be calm, placate, or make concessions for other's feelings. When the occasion calls for it, I'm going to lay it on the line.

This is going to be a rough time for me. I need some space so don't corner me unless you want the straight and plain truth. This doesn't mean I'm going to be mean or nasty on purpose, it means there will be times I need to be left alone until I get it right in my mind.

I want you to know I would never leave you during your illness. As a friend, I wouldn't do that to anybody. I will be here for you regardless. Even if we decide that we aren't going to be together, I will be here until you're better. In that same thought, we need to work hard if there is to be an US. I have decided it's best that I see my Shrink again. I need to talk to someone about this because it's killing me.

OK then I got a lot off my chest. I believe I needed to. I wish I could say that's all I needed but it's not. We have a very long and hard road ahead of us. Sweetie it's going to be painful and hopefully worth it. I'm willing to try, are you?

I hope you are feeling well. I'm sorry if this is upsetting to you but I had to say this, it was festering up inside of me. I haven't felt well in a very long time. It's not pleasant and it's painful but it needs to be done if anything is ever going to bring us together.

I'm leaving Dad's tomorrow evening and my phone will be operational on Monday morning. Please do not read anything into this other than what it is ... I am not kicking you to the curb, these are just things I needed to talk about.

Love, Gabriel

And I never heard from him again.

LAST DANCE PART SECOND

07-06-2007 — **Treatment Complete – Welcome Back**

An estimated 3.9 million (1.8%) Americans have been infected with Hep C, of whom 2.7 million are chronically infected. There are about 30,000 new infections each year.

Ten or fifteen years ago, I became one of the statistics.

How Do You Catch It

Hepatitis C is a virus that lives in the blood and can be spread in a number of ways.

*10-20% of people with Hepatitis C do not have identifiable risk factors.

I am one of the 10-20%.

80% of people have no symptoms of hepatitis C. By the time symptoms show up, it may be too late for adequate treatment.

How Do You Find Out If You're Infected

Don't wait. It has been suggested by the CDC and NIH taskforces that every person add a Hep C antigen test to their next annual physical. I have been infected for more than 10 years with no symptoms and perfectly normal blood tests. Only an antigen test would have showed that the antibody existed. I could have started treatment before my liver suffered damage.

I wouldn't have exposed friends, family, and the men I've loved.

Health Consequences Without Treatment

*75-85% of infected persons develop a chronic liver infection, which means that your body does not effectively fight off or get rid of the virus.
*Chronic liver disease causes death in about 3% of people.

*Chronic hepatitis C infection is the leading reason for a liver transplant.

*Chronic hepatitis can lead to cirrhosis of the liver (in about 15% of those infected with Hep C).

*Chronic hepatitis can lead to liver cancer and death.

There is no vaccine. There is no cure. There is only remission via chemo-therapy.

Conventional Treatment for Hepatitis C

*At the present time, optimal treatment regimen is considered to be a 48-week course of the combination of weekly injections of pegylated alpha interferon and daily oral ingestion of ribavirin. *******

*Patients with genotype 1 have a 40-45% rate of response to a 48-week course of combination drug therapy, meaning viral RNA is reduced to undetectable amounts for six or more months after treatment.

*The combination therapy is extremely expensive. Side effects include hemolytic anemia, nausea, diarrhea, headaches, muscle and joint pain, hair loss, constant fatigue, suicidal ideation, and severe depression.

***Author's Note: In 2013, new 12-week drug treatments were approved for genotype 1 Hepatitis C. Astonishingly, they have a 92% effective rate with minimum side effects. (*figures*)

I wrote the words above a year ago, just before the start of forty-eight self-injections, 1700 anti-viral pills, 35 blood tests, dozens of medical tests and procedures, two hospitalizations, and a plethora of drugs to treat the brutal and often debilitating side effects. The last injection was taken today. The last pills will be taken next week. The final blood test a week after that. It's over.

I love you more than any woman alive. I want to spend the rest of my life with you.

"I love you" means "until you do something I don't like."

"Rest of my life" means "until something better comes along."

09-23-2007 — **It's About Time You Updated**

Health: I am Hep C free. I appear to be one of the lucky 50% success stories. The treatment ended July and my hair is starting to grow back. There are those who call my short hair cute!

Job: Based on an agreement Mr. Lucky signed long ago, he had to keep my insurance benefits going. So I have health and disability through the end of this year and he is obligated to offer me federal COBRA starting in January if I am not yet covered at a new job. However, I've already sent out resumes and have six interviews set up with interested employers.

Home: I purchased a three-story two family home in Jersey City where my daughter, son-in-law, grandson, and I will live. We closed August 16. The moving truck arrives Sept 26.

My life the last fifteen years was almost complete – except for a loving relationship. After a year of illness, and looking at myself in the mirror thinking, "Who is that ugly, skinny, bald woman?" I realized I was getting no younger. And I missed having arms around me and whispers in my ear.

So life begins anew and, until the next time, a small piece of advice. If any one of you still believes life is a Disney fairytale with a happilyforeverafter ending, let me disabuse you of the notion. Think Grimm's. There are trolls under every bridge, giants in the woods, and the witch always – always – wins.

10-10-2007 — **All the Shtuff in Joisey**

I'm in New Jersey, just minutes away from Manhattan. Starting a brand new life. Still deciding if it will be any better than my old one.

My daughter, her family, and I moved into a 3-story house together, a relationship they initiated and I funded with most of my savings. Our contract is verbal, which may well have been a mistake, but it is what it is and it means I can see my grandson every day for as long as it lasts.

The house was built around 1915, with its inherent problems. Still living from a suitcase as everything remains in boxes or tubs – waiting for closet space, kitchen countertops, pantries, drywall finishing, etc. to be finished in my third floor apartment. I have a bed, a fridge, a stove, and a toilet that works. No shower yet, or kitchen sink. I'll just share until mine is working.

I have NO idea what to do with all the extra "stuff" there will never be room for. A shed in the back will house the tools, and a storage locker will keep the Christmas trees, keepsakes, antiques, etc. as long as I can afford to pay for it. But I fear the rest will go, little at a time, at flea markets, yard sales, giveaways, charity, or eBay. A new life beckons. After years of acquisition – I'm forced into a new, streamlined existence. Maybe it's a good thing.

The most interesting thing about that? It was one of the moving fears I had two years ago. How to give up my "stuff." Someone at that time said a move shouldn't mean having to give up anything. How wrong he was. Change means change. One cannot look back – always ahead.

First job interview was yesterday. They want me … which goes to show I'm employable at my age, and for the salary and benefits I'm asking … but is it what *I* want.

Who knows – maybe that job will look better when the boxes are empty!

10-17-2007 — **Cool Change**

> *Oh why is heaven built so far,*
> *Oh why is earth set so remote?*
> *I cannot reach the nearest star*
> *That hangs afloat.*
> *I would not care to reach the moon,*
> *One round monotonous of change;*
> *Yet even she repeats her tune*
> *Beyond my range*
>> ~~Christina Rossetti, "De Profundis"

It's not that I'm not grateful every single day to be where I am right now.

But late at night. When the moon is full, moving in glorious majesty across the dark sky. When that certain smell is in the air. In the moments just before drifting into sleep … I remember where I thought I would be.

Relationships end. They end with thunder and lightning. They end with pouring rain. They end in explanations, conversations, recriminations. They should never end with threats. Or anger. Or, most especially, in Silence.

12-16-2007 — **Sleepless in Jersey**

> *Blink and it's gone.*
> *A moment, a breath,*
> *A Dance of the Mayflies.*
> *Just enough ... For a Lifetime.*
> Ulatempa Poetess, *"Rhythms"* CY 9825
> ~~"Dance of the Mayflies"

Every day I pass the signs in Lincoln Park where a movie is being filmed.

It's where he was when we met. On a movie set. At least he said he was. I'll never know for sure. But I believed he was and imagined him there as I fell in love with him. Racing around the island of Dominica in a borrowed truck, constructing an antenna from spare parts to get better reception, talking to me during every break. As I said ... at least he said he was.

It's one thing to know the truth. It's another to suspect I never will.

12-25-2007 — **Having a Merry Elfing Christmas**

It's that time of year again. Just a few more days to spend lots of money on all those electronic "gotta haves," do up your lights better than the neighbors without falling off a ladder or killing the cat, extend Christmas dinner invitations to Aunt Tillie and Uncle Pete (who always arrives just a tad tipsy), and cook up a storm of high calorie, but great tasting, dishes (thereby paving the way for the perfect New Year's resolution).

So ... with home renovations taking up all the time I normally use to send out cards, here's my wish to each and every one of you! Merry Christmas!

12-31-2007 — **Happy New Year**

Another year, and another wish that the next is far better than the last. As the stroke of midnight sounds and that lovely shining ball drops, may I just say — And to all – A Good Night!

01-08-2008 — **The One With the Turtle**

I'm not lost. Just no one's found me yet!

I consider myself an agnostic, whereas you suggested that I am an atheist. I do not consider it an insult, but rather a compliment, for I do not pretend to know where many others are sure – that is all agnosticism means.**

Or perhaps we are ALL atheists. I just believe in one fewer god than you do. You dismiss all the other possible gods – I just dismiss yours. But with respect … because …

I believe in something, whatever that something is. Someday I may decide – but that day is not today and probably won't be tomorrow. Why, as I remember, there are a number of folks that believe the world is carried on the back of a large turtle (or is that tortoise).

**Thanks to Clarence Darrow (Scope's Trial) for that one*

02-12-2008 — **Twelfth of Never – Never**

today is the third Anniversary of the Twelfth of Never and his birthday.

i read somewhere that when you remember a relationship you must play the whole movie. not just the beginning and, most especially not just the perfect scenes of falling in love.

i wonder daily if what i yearn for is just an unattainable teen-age pipedream

because i have been reminded too many times that "i love you" does not mean "i want you"

because a relationship isn't give and take. it's give and give and give because men lie and then lie about lying

because even if i ever find anyone again – or they find me – will this same scene be played over and over again

because i'm not sure where to go or how to get there

because i've found "i love you" doesn't even mean "i love you"

because i'm selfish. you see i've always thought, these long years, that while i've made some bad judgments in relationships, i've also not stayed in them when they became unhealthy for either party. i've never just settled. now, at this point in my life, maybe i should find the courage again to just SETTLE

because i don't think i believe in always or that it is actually possible to find true commitment

you know, i've lived a life worse than some and better than others. even with the occasional bouts of mental self-flagellation i'm alive and the scars are well hidden. if i could pass along a single lesson, it is this

the greatest gift you can give is the offer of understanding acceptance and unconditional grace.

and remember you can never know the path a stranger has walked, or the branches they needed to take along the way.

sort of makes me think Luke had the right idea.

> *Judge not, and ye shall not be judged: condemn not, and ye shall not be condemned: forgive, and ye shall be forgiven:*
> ~~Luke 6:37. The Holy Bible, KJV

BASTARDO ROMANTICO™

02-14-2008 — Happy Valentine 2008

Happy Valentine's Day. May your life never be a prison – of your making, or of anyone else's.

02-15-2008 — Bastardo Romantico™

So I got tired of sitting on my ass hoping someone would come to me – and I joined Match.com. After all, it's been over a year since Gabriel and a LOT longer than that since anyone "real."

I've never done online dating before (unless you count "you know who," and I decided to do it my way. I didn't bother to look at a single profile before I did my own. Just jumped in and made it up as I went. It turns out mine is quite unique compared to the others on the site. Which could have been a good thing … or a bad one.

I've piqued the interest of several very attractive men and went out with one last night (Valentine's … me … a date … a FIRST date … with a real person that actually showed up). It was unexpectedly delightful.

We had dinner at a restaurant neither of us had been to before, but it was close to my office and we sat there a long long time just talking and laughing.

Since it was after 11:00 when we decided to bring the evening to a close, he loaned me his much-warmer hat and gave me some self-defense tips "just in case."

When I got home – I sent the following email:

The weather was cold.
The food was lukewarm.
The hat was toasty.
The kisses were hot, hot, hot.
And I didn't have to kill anyone on the way home!

And shortly after I arrived home, the phone rang and he sang "Besame Mucho" softly in my ear.

02-17-2009 — Just a Checkup

On-line dating takes an Excel spreadsheet to keep track.

I've decided it's all in the chemistry. Because attraction is not a choice. You can feel it, you can taste it. It runs through your body and makes you shiver just a bit. Even across the room. Eyes meet and it's there between you.

I've only met one person in my life that the spark came much later. It was Ben and I think I could have lived without the heartache that came after.

02-28-2008 — Johnny and the Subway

Here I am, coming home after work – subway train crowded as usual. And as usual, it makes a stop with no station in sight. Just stops – needing to rest or gather strength or maybe the engineer just needed to take a leak … who knows.

At any rate, the cute straphanger beside me says, very tongue in cheek (because trains stop *constantly* for no apparent reason), "Why are we stopping?"

And I pipe up, "Because they have to shovel more coal into the boiler!"

And it starts us both wondering. Just how DID those trains get around in the tunnels almost 100 years ago when the first part of the underground subway was built? Cause it's a TUNNEL. You can't use steam and if you used coal, you wouldn't be able to see!

This immediately led us to thinking of folks who work in coalmines and the recent spate of cave-ins, which left miners in the dark to die. (yes, an odd, dark, brooding segue, but we were on a *train* for heaven's sake with nothing much better to do).

"I think I'd rather die from lack of oxygen quickly than slow starvation," I pondered.

And he, little cutie NYC guy that he was, pipes up "yeah, you've only got so much time playing rock, paper, scissors in the dark before you get caught cheating. Then it's 'OH we're eating Johnny'."

Yep – ONLY in New York.

03-09-2008 — **Diatribe on A.M.**

I do not like morning. I have never liked morning yet, for some reason, morning invariably arrives to bother the shit out of me.

My grandson is still asleep (although I expect a call any moment) and I am the grand Pooh-Bah of caretakers this weekend while mommy and daddy are traipsing around the shiny streets of Las Vegas. Where was I? Oh, yes, I decided to get a few things done.

I ordered my new LCD HDTV which I have been putting off, I repaired a DVD player which absolutely refused to open up and spit out the DVD (my father would be so proud), I placed three containers of storage stuff resolutely at the top of the stairs, determined to finally get them into the locker.

I walked my daughter's damn dog who, despite his many attributes, simply refuses to learn how to walk himself.

Yesterday it rained lions and buffalos all day. When it cleared up, baby and I took an enjoyable walk, it being so warm and damp with all those lovely puddles to jump in. Within SECONDS of our coming home, the heavens opened up once again with renewed fury. Ah, Serendipity!

03-19-2008 — **Reality Bites**

I cancelled my *Classmates.com* membership eons ago. Mostly because I already traded Holiday Updates with the two high school friends with whom I wanted to stay in touch.

One of the two was my best friend. Really. My BEST friend, starting in seventh grade. We drifted a bit in senior year (hung with different crowds and all that) but still spent a great deal of time together.

Today I got an email from her younger sister generated through Classmates. It was addressed to a large group of people and noted, among other news of herself, that my best friend passed away sometime in the last few months.

And I find it immeasurably sad.

I guess I always thought we would sit down again. Relive some of the crazy times. Talk about our lives and the turns they took. She married the guy she went steady with in high school (I knew him too of course) and to all accounts was still married to him in the last Christmas letter two years ago. I guess that's why I didn't get one this year; I just thought it was cause I'd moved.

I bring this up primarily because it once again focuses the crosshairs on that damn reality button. It's still sitting out there taunting me, despite my singularly determined efforts to demolish it. I really hate that button.

03-28-2008 — **And The World Keeps Changing**

Another week, or is it 10 days, or perhaps 30. The days plow into one another sidewaysbackwardsupsidedown.

Speaking of boyfriends, or men friends, or bastards … whatever you want to call them … (we were speaking of them, weren't we?). Been out a few times with a half dozen or so, just couldn't quite find the attraction to move forward. But I have had two marriage proposals. Really. And kicked them both to the curb.

And the reason for that lack of attraction. Bastardo Romantico™. Who's still here. He seems to understand the me I've become and does not judge.

'Cause even though I always say I'm not, I am a little broken, I think. Between Ben, Gabriel, the illness, and years of Mr. Lucky, I seem to have gotten lost. Bastardo™ said I don't know that I'm pretty anymore and I think by pretty he meant desirable and perhaps he's right.

I've come to expect the dangling shoe is going to drop. So I speed up the inevitable by pushing all the buttons. Mostly unconsciously, but sometimes knowing I'm doing it yet absolutely unable to stop.

04-03-2008 — **F*ck Me and Love Me**

Bastardo™ has made it no secret he is also dating others … so I emailed his Blackberry with a hilariously funny, despicably dirty, outrageously sexy email when I knew he was on a date … daring him to read it. Which he did of course, and said he laughed so hard the soda came out of his nose. Endearing him no end to his date, I'm sure.

Boo-yah! A successful mission!

And when he says "F*ck me and love me" I understand it means don't lose the need, the overwhelming gotta have me some hot monkey sex now. Don't let familiarity breed 30-second Mr. Lucky smartest man in the world put the commercial on pause and get it on for the next minute and 45 so you don't miss the show sex. Don't lose the passion. Or the butterflies when you know who's calling. Or that perfect first nothing can be wrong with life when they are in it thought in the morning.

It's not time to share previous relationships, but if he knew the stories he would know that F*ck me and love me is just standard operating slut procedure. After all, what's the definition of a slut? Answer: Anyone who has slept with one more person than you have. For many of you, that's almost everyone.

For me, it's Paris Hilton.

And for him … ex-New York Governor Spitzer.

> *Out beyond ideas of wrongdoing and rightdoing,*
> *there is a field. I'll meet you there.*
> ~~Rumi (276)

05-04-2008 — **Sucker, or Lollipop**

The office manager quit, so what started as a nice easy get off at 5:00 without a care in the world job has ended up with me taking over as the office manager/accountant/marketing director with my very own secretary and a $20K a year raise plus full-paid benefits. (Hey, I hear you muttering "sucker" under your breath. It's ok. Really.)

05-20-2008 — **And the One After That**

> *Reality Concept: No One can take away My joy and positive outlook on the world, unless I give them the power to do so. My Reality is what I Create. Imagine the Reality I wish, and then Live It.*
> ~~Supervisor 189

My daughter and her husband do not like Bastardo™. Despite the fact that he is a well-respected psychiatrist, head of the psychiatric emergency room in one of the largest hospitals in Brooklyn. Now we are not talking about a "not fond of" we're talking about a "hate his guts and hope to die" dislike and let me know about it pretty constantly.

I'm not suggesting he's perfect, but it occurred to me yesterday that even if I stopped dating Bastardo™ (or he me) now, or in a month, or two, or six, what happens when they don't like the next one? Or the one after that?

What business is this of theirs and why is this feeling like reverse déjà vu.

05-30-2008 — **The Doc doc**

So it was off to the girly doctor today. All this use after months of disuse … well, it takes a while to get back in the saddle (as it were).

Since it was a new doctor, the standard formula applies. Come early. Fill out 17 pages of forms including every bit of intimate history it is possible to disclose. Sign the form that says they won't disclose what you've just disclosed (as if I believe that.)

Then it's into a freezing cold little room so the nurse can come in and ask you (sans knickers this time … you, not her) every question you have already answered on the forms she apparently does not have available in your chart.

Nurse: When was your last period?
Me: 1975.
Nurse: *(looking confused)* ummm
Nurse: *(having regained her place)* What medications are you taking?
Me: *(giving her the short list)*
Nurse: What surgeries have you had?

Me: *(giving her the longer list)*
Nurse: Any major illnesses?
Me: *(that one was fun ... just watching her face as I ended the list with)* Hep C
Nurse: Any drug or alcohol use?
Me: *(opting to answer the present tense tone of the question)* No, and occasionally. *(Let her figure out which is which)*
Nurse: Are you currently having sexual relations?
Me: *(why, are you jealous?)* Yes.
Nurse: Vaginal, anal, or both?
Me: *(only in New York, poppets, only in New York)*
Nurse: What protection are you using?
Me: *(good grief, why do you care ... so I skirted the truth. After all, I BOUGHT the condoms)*
Nurse: Are your relations with male, female, or both?
Me: *(opting, again, for the present tense tone of the question, but wanting to say "Both ... at the same time. Is that a problem?")* Male.
Nurse: Single or multiple partners?
Me: *(at once??)*

06-01-2008 — Closing Books

> *I got to thinking about relationships. There are those that open you up to something new and exotic, those that are old and familiar, those that bring up lots of questions, those that bring you somewhere unexpected, those that bring you far from where you started, and those that bring you back. But the most exciting, challenging and significant relationship of all is the one you have with yourself. And if you can find someone to love the you you love, well, that's just fabulous.*
>
> ~~Carrie Bradshaw, "An American Girl in Paris (Part Deux)"

In 2003, I closed the book on two men. The two loves of my life, Jason and Ben. I didn't just hide the key to my heart – I gave it back and it was over.

As for any others – well, those books were closed as they left. Or as I left. Snapped shut with the fanfare of a final tearful conversation or phone call.

Oh, there were the occasional "if only" lies and "could we try agains" but we gave each other the gift of closure and the resolve not to make those mistakes again.

I always hated those final conversations. But they were important to both of us. They absolved us both from blame, provided understanding and, ultimately, forgiveness.

And then there was Gabriel. The unexpected book that threw open its pages smack in the middle. No prologue, no setup, no cast of characters. Sort of like the first *Indiana Jones* movie. The adrenaline rush of the rock coming at you faster than you can run. It made me feel alive.

And we got to the final chapter. But like a book written for its sequel – there was no ending. It just stopped dead. Characters still in conflict, situations unresolved.

I want "The End." I want someone, somewhere, somehow, to write the final chapter about what was real. And what wasn't.

06-08-2008 — **Brought to You By the Letter P**

The letter "P" brings this entry to you.

Inspired, no doubt, with having a slightly less than 2-year old grandson who is beginning Potty training. This event requires that the adults in his life determine the correct terminology to use for the various and sundry Potty events.

Pee or Pee-Pee seems appropriate when discussing items emanating from his Penis, but just what to call the other side.

Barring the use of George Carlin euphemisms, we are left with Poo? Poo-Poo?, Poopy?, Just plain Poop? or – as my mother used to say – "Number Two."

Yes, in my family Poop was Number Two. I leave One to your imagination.

And unlike the Prolific bowels of dear Travis, I have been Plagued with Paltry Poop my entire life.

Well, perhaps THAT was my inspiration. The necessity of ingesting, once again, various and sundry Prune Products in an effort to increase the general Production of my Poop.

I long ago conceived the semi-famous Prune Principle. There is no such thing as a Perfect Prune Portion. However many you eat will be too many, or not enough. Period.

When I was Travis's age (and, quite honestly, continuing up until I refused to divulge my bodily functions to Anyone) the daily question was "Did you do a Number Two today?" and the answer was usually "No." The consequence of "No" was (wait for it) a large tablespoon of CASTORIA. A disgusting mixture of senna, sodium bicarbonate, wintergreen, taraxicum, sugar, and water invented in 1868 as a mild laxative for children with Poor Poo Production.

For some reason it never occurred to me to Prevaricate.

And, circuitous as this has been, I come to the moral of this tale. Once again, the dulcet sounds of a mother's voice are heard wafting through the air …

"Did you Poop?"

08-25-2008 — **The Lady or the Tiger**

I found out recently that Bastardo's™ occasional vague jokes about "all my other women" were not just cocky comments meant to keep me on my toes. I mean, if I've been with him every night he isn't working for the last six months (with its hot monkey sex for hours on end) and getting long drawn out phone calls every night he *is* working, when did he have time?

But when yet another joke was made I just asked point blank. Not using the feminine kidding style we all use to ask without asking in hopes of getting the truth we want to hear, and not the one we don't.

Is the joke the truth and, if so, how many. And what are they to him.

With an absolutely straight face, he told me. Three – and with at least one he uses the same I love you's he uses with me. Then adding "Didn't I tell you when we met I was dating others?"

(life lesson here ladies. sometimes a joke is NOT just a joke)

I had a choice.
A) Leave him.
B) Change the relationship to f*ck buddy and just enjoy myself while pursuing other avenues.
C) Leave the status quo and see what happens (but watch my back).

I think I would make a great columnist for on-line dating. No, really. I'm awfully good at giving other people advice, even if I don't use it myself. So, based on personal experience, this would be my first column.

"to women who decide to go on-line looking for a match"

If a man advertises on Match.com
(or any other online dating site)
the expectation is that he wants to date.
It's a dating site.
If he tells the woman this and she's interested, ok, she's interested.

If he tells her honestly, up front, he is also dating others,
she may even be ok with that too
Because she thinks to herself "Well, if he's happy in these 'relationships,' then why was he still on Match?"
So something must not be right.
I'll just play nice girl,
Or bad girl,
and I'll slide into position.

Not telling her the truth, that he is still dating others
after all those I love you's and all
Means she will assume she's acquired that position
Telling her friends and family,
Thinking of him as her boyfriend,
Even giving up anything she may have had going elsewhere
Or not starting any new possibilities
Because of that position.

And when something happens that finally requires him to tell her
all the details he's been holding back
about the who and how many and the intensity of

those other relationships
with a surprised, "Why, you knew when we met I was dating others, right?"
She can only assume he's been lying about everything.

You can't always trust the nice guys.
Sometimes you should trust the ones who say, right up front,
I like you, I want to fuck you, don't expect more than that.

"Fuck me and love me until the end of time"
Is nothing more than manipulative behavior

11-15-2008 — **The Dancing Sailor**

Although lousy at sports (no hand-eye coordination), I am lucky to have had
two hobbies I am pretty good at doing – sailing a Hobie 16 and Swing Dancing.
Mainly because there are no requirements for throwing, catching, or hitting a
ball.

I learned to dance on my father's toes, honing my repertoire in middle school
when the local youth center offered lessons in anticipation of the year-end
school dance. Many of us continued to Jitterbug and Cha-Cha in high school
and I've always belonged to a Swing Dance club wherever life took me.

Over the years, the movers and shakers of the dance community worked for
free running dance clubs, holding competitions across the country, and teaching
Swing to hundreds of thousands of eager students (and some are still at it): Jack
Nevel (Tulsa Swing Club); Terry Rippa (Dallas Push Club); California's Dean
Collins, Jack Bridges, Kenny Wetzel, and Jack Carey; and their East coast
equivalents Craig Hutchinson (Virginia), Tom Koerner & Debra Sternberg
(Washington, DC) and Margaret Batiuchok(New York Swing Dance Society).

Not to discount the contributions of the legendary Swing/Lindy dancers of the
40's (like Frankie Manning) but the swing competitors and teachers of the 70's
and 80's were the modern day equivalent of Vernon & Irene Castle. My mentors
included Harry & Linda Henderson, Bob Brooks & Stella (Star) Morris, Frank
& Val LaFemina, Gary Long & Judy Ford LaFemina, Mario Robau and Barry
Jones(with whomever they were partnering at the moment), and Dale Rouggly
& Sherry Lawson Martin.

Of course couple dancing wouldn't have been much fun without a partner. So to the ones who made me look good, thank you and I miss you all: Dick, Brad, Dale Rouggly (whose first competition partner was his 13-year old sister, Shirley), Tom Cameron (who can forget Popeye & Olive Oyl), John Hudson, Terry Rippa, and my dear Baltimore friend, Charlie Wyler.

Not for what they did last, but for what they did that will last.

As for that boat – blame David Miller. Before moving to Baltimore, Dave spent two years living in Atlanta, contracted a highly communicable disease for which there is no known cure, and had an 8-5 job.

It took 15 minutes of crewing on his Hobie 16 to be infected by the same bug. The most effective prescription was to stop whatever I was doing and IMMEDIATELY go sailing as soon as I felt the symptoms coming on. I worked from home, he didn't, and it was his boat. So I went shopping.

Buying the boat was easy. Learning a new language was not. I had to learn things like starboard means right and port means my other right, but only when my face was looking at the front (I mean aft or is that bow) part of the boat. A rope is not a rope, it's bedclothes, or deadclothes, unless it pulls up a sail, then it's something else.

OK. Got the boat, the trailer, all the basic parts, figured out how to rig it, got great wind, the water, the sun. NO CREW. Rather than stand on an Annapolis dock with a sign around my neck, I placed an ad in the local paper.

Wanted. Strong, young male for water sports. Must be good with sheets, knots, and canvas. Willing to take orders. Flexible schedule and own equipment helpful.

Ed, an experienced Hobie 16 sailor, answered that ad and we sailed together for several years. I had to sell my boat when I moved to New Jersey, but sometimes visit Ed and his family to take advantage of theirs.

Current circumstances have upended my participation in two things that mean a great deal – but I figure there will always be my retirement years to stage a comeback.

***author's note: On September 6, 2014 at 5:00 pm Paris time, over 3,000 dancers from 78 countries in 23 cities across the world, launched the first International West Coast flash mob. YouTube available. As are biographies of most of the dancers mentioned.

12-13-2008 — A Fall of Do-Overs

I think I left off last time still trying to decide what to do on the heart front. I had several choices. With all the time already invested, there was nothing to lose (except a little dignity) by taking option #3.

After all, while I thought his "I love you's" gave me the right to ask for exclusivity; perhaps it wasn't right to get mad when I didn't it.

So I took a deep cleansing breath, let him know how I felt, then gave him some time to work out what he wanted to do while I began accepting dates with other people as well (and honestly letting him know I was doing so).

We celebrate 10 months together tomorrow, the "others" have fallen by the proverbial wayside, and the "I love you's" seem genuine.

The entire family, and some friends, were together on Thanksgiving — yes, Bastardo™ too — and everyone got along just great. It seemed that a mutual do-over was decided which created a wonderful holiday.

In other news, I got laid off October 17, have already gotten, and accepted a job offer for yet more money starting January 5. I got severance and unemployment so won't suffer financially while enjoying the family and the tree and prezzies. If you are going to be laid off, do it at the Holidays!

Being off allowed Bastardo™ and I to spend endless time together. I may have mentioned he works nights, so it's been wonderful.

02-25-2009 — And the Bell Tolls for Thee

A few months ago (before he finally admitted it would be in his long-term best interest to consider monogamy if he was to keep me) Bastardo™ suggested it was only fair if I wished to go out with other men. In a fit of pique one night I said, "Well, at least I could have a champagne brunch on occasion." Cause, as we all know, his weekend night shifts preclude the Sunday brunch thingy.

So what does he do for our one-year anniversary? He rearranges his schedule and we go to a Sunday Champagne Brunch thingy.

With a gift, of course. The most beautiful gold heart on a delicate round gold chain. Engraved.

And what would you engrave on a heart? Why the exact thing I said when he whispered into my ear everything a girl could ever need or want to hear.

"Ditto"

03-19-2009 — Kayla Emmeline Comes Home

Kayla Emmeline
March 13, 2009 4:02 p.m.
6 lbs. 4 oz. 20 inches
Daddy, Mommy, Baby, Big Brother, and Grandma doing fine!

My second grandchild was welcomed to the World three weeks early. Quite a surprise … mommy called me at 1:15 p.m. on Friday from her doctor's office and said, "Come get Travis." I was on the train home with Travis by 4:00. When I got off the train 40 minutes later there was a picture on my phone … Kayla was born at 4:02. Apparently, mommy pushed three times and out she popped, happy as Larry. Mommy was eating a Turkey Burger and fries by 4:30!

Travis is very taken with the whole idea, coming over to pat her cheek and hold her hand frequently. Not too jealous yet – but when the family went out to eat on Tuesday he asked to ride in HIS stroller – something he hasn't done for quite a while. So perhaps a bit of "don't forget about me."

Of course – that's what Grandma is for!

01-05-2010 — As Time Goes By

A dear friend of mine sent a great picture of her and her husband over Christmas and just today reminded me he will turn 85 this month.

Unfortunately, it reminds me that I too will be reaching one of those count "down" side of life milestone birthdays in mid-March.

I remember the days when the 1/2 was incredibly important (I'll be 5 and ONE HALF).

Then it was the ALMOST. I'll be ALMOST 16 or ALMOST 21. Those lasted until we were STILL 39, then ONLY 45. Then I just started to lie as long as I could get away with it. In my late 40's. Early 50's. Then just 50's. Now what do I say.

Wait – I know – just say I have a 3 and ONE HALF year old grandson. Makes me sound so much younger!

04-22-2010 — **A Who's Who**

Fly like a who's who. Pay like a who's that.
Virgin America billboard 35th & Broadway, New York City

I worked in a job which put me in front of CEO's and COO's of Fortune 100 companies. I sat at the head of the table asking questions and they gave me the answers I needed to change forever some of the basic processes of their company.

I lived in a corner of the world where most of my neighbors knew me, or at least of me, because I volunteered for neighborhoody stuff. At the Annual Ice Cream Social, Pool Party, or Neighborhood Watch meeting most of them came up, smiled, and said hi.

I crewed or sailed Hobie 16's, winning races and regattas from time to time – as well as managing to finish the 150-mile *Down the Bay* race one year.

I danced and competed in a world where I was asked to judge other competitors and, with my partners, to teach seminars, workshops, and two summers at a dance camp. It was gratifying to be respected for a hobby I loved and to walk into a room full of 500 people and have a lot of them wave and smile and say hello.

And now?

I'm back to being someone else's assistant. I like my job, and I actually HAVE a job, but it's sometimes difficult because there was once a time when people not only asked for my input but also listened to what I had to say.

And I only know a couple of neighbors because it's not a real neighborhood. It's a house on a block, in a not-so-great neighborhood, in a city in New Jersey where there is no Annual anything.

I don't dance any longer even though I've told myself I need to start again in this city full of strangers and devil hang the consequences. But Bastardo™ is insanely jealous and does not want me in anyone else's arms, odd as that seems to me, and I'm tired of arguing about it.

The family I moved for – the ones that encouraged me, welcomed me, and were oh so happy for me to buy the house they picked out where we could all live and share the expenses of – moved out last spring for a high-rise waterfront condo in a cooler part of town, leaving me to pay the more than I can afford even with the raise mortgage, taxes, utilities, and upkeep on my own.

The daughter, who had been my best friend for 38 years decided six months ago that as a parent of two infant children, she knows more about raising children in the 2000's (with the help of me, the TV, the internet, and thousands of books and magazines) than I did as a single parent in the 70's and 80's (with the help of Dr. Spock). She and her husband have decided I was a terrible mother then and will be a lousy grandmother now. Really. Told me to my face.

I was told that until I apologize for not being the parent she thinks I should have been when raising her – and she "believes" my apology and its sincerity – I am not allowed anywhere near my grandchildren.

So, along with everything else, the whole reason I moved into this godforsaken part of the country is gone too.

My dear boyfriend tries hard. Despite his flaws, he is as kind, loving, and understanding a person as he is capable of being, and has stuck around for over two years now. At least one person in a sea of who's that still sees me as a who's who.

06-23-2010 — **The Punisher – Who Really Loses**

This morning I was walking to court … (Oh no big deal, just a neighbor hassle about a property line. After three court visits, 1.5 days of vacation time and a $750 attorney fee, the whole thing was dismissed. I think I will plant a dead body in the lot just to mess up THEIR lives). But back to the story.

... and who should be walking towards me but my son-in-law with my 15 mo. old granddaughter in a stroller.

The granddaughter (along with my grandson) I haven't been allowed to see since January because I am being punished for my 30 year old "sins" by withholding contact with the grandchildren I had been with since birth. No visitation. No telephone. No photos. No birthdays.

My son-in-law would not look at me as he passed. Literally averted his face.

Someday I will get a chance to show her and her brother the cards I've sent every week not knowing if they get them, and the web site I am keeping for them so they will know I think of them daily and love them more than ever.

I will have proof I've tried when they seek me out and ask "Grandma – didn't you love me anymore?"

08-20-2010 — The Whistling A*S

> I really admire the avocado because it's a vegetable that can make you fat.
> For a vegetable, that's gotta take some chutzpah.
> ~~Manning Krull via _Twitter_

So I'm lying all spooned up with Bastardo™ last night having one of those completely inane discussions that lovers sometimes have. In this case, determining what (if I was a man) would I look for in a girl.

Like most men, I have a type I admire. On the smallish side, slim to medium build, exotic features, full lips, and very nice natural breasts.

"Oh" said Bastardo™. "I once dated the perfect girl for you, and natural before the silicone inserts which got her the job as the Channel 11 weather girl. Had to break up with her though, cause I just couldn't stand her whistling ass."

Her WHAT?

It's not that little pooty sounds don't expel from various and sundry openings in the throes of vigorous moments. But a Whistling Ass?

And all I could think was …

Does she have a repertoire? Classical, pop? (like Flight of the Bumblebee … or YMCA – and imagining the Y part …)

Does it occur naturally or only during certain positions? Doggy style, mission-ary, cowboy?

"Oh, sorry, care to sing along?"

How does she explain the noise to hotel guests in the next suite, or while visiting family over holidays. Or perhaps she used a special cork?

And then I was hit with a wave of entrepreneurial spirit.

This is a million hit YouTube extravaganza. It's fame and fortune on *America's Got Talent.*

I'm seeing the New York double decker sightseeing bus … "on your left is the Empire State Building, on your right Top of the Rock, and straight ahead is Channel 11, with the famous Whistling Ass weather girl."

New York could close the budget deficit with the extra tourism. Just put a huge sign on the interstate at the state line: "Entering New York, home of the Whistling Ass"

And then, Bastardo™ speaks: "No silly, not a Whistling ASS … a Whistling "S"

Oh. Never mind.

04-19-2011 — **Lazarus Long**

> *A brute kills for pleasure. A fool kills from hate.*
> ~~Robert Heinlein (243)

two months ago, one day before our third anniversary, Bastardo™ walked out saying only that our relationship wasn't E-Z enough.

the issues between my daughter and I, the loss of my grandchildren, the house problems, the Bell's Palsy, the sprained ankle, and the job changes, had life in a constant uproar the last year.

mix in his continual (extreme) public and private jealous outbursts regarding any male figure around me – the tenant renting the kid's half of the house, the retired fix-it guy who does my home repairs, the salesman who sold me the new car, the waiter in any restaurant, the man sitting at the next table who glances over and nods hello, the friends, dance partners, cousins, and exes from around the world who occasionally call or email to stay in touch – and things had been close to breaking for a while.

and i questioned myself. because among the men i trusted who abandoned and betrayed me, there was only one common variable – me.

when all was said, separated, and returned, the computer he had set up for me happened to stop working. during the repairs, i found a backup he had made using his phone as the test, and in it all the lies he had fed me for three years about all the other women he had never stopped seeing.

i still haven't moved from disbelief or pain into anger and certainly not acceptance. can i rise, like Lazarus, or is this finally the end of me.

but even dead, i wonder – what was he that killed me?

maybe Bastardo™ was not a good man. maybe he was willing to lie about everything, even the most basic tenets of our relationship, just to get laid.

a good man displays honesty, integrity, emotional maturity, morality, respect for his partner, and maintains fidelity when he has promised it. he loves you AND likes you. he is non-judgmental, with a good heart and a kind soul and his partner should always feel absolutely safe with him.

5-10-2011 — **Information on Gabriel**
Private email to Anna

Anna, it was so nice to hear from you. It has been too long. You know, I've often wondered if you had the courage to research Gabriel as your friends did. I know how hard it was to face the end of that relationship, but I think you deserve the truth. For your use, I've attached the sources for the facts.

After he disappeared from your life, I decided to check facts. First, I called the "home" number he had given me shortly after the Thanksgiving weekend. The company that answered had never heard of him.

Then I reached out to my friends and acquaintances in the West Coast writer, director, and actor community. I received a call from a good friend who actually knew him. She said he was a well-known con artist. He had done some bit parts in TV movies and other shows, but he was not a movie star, a writer, or a producer. He would often pass himself off as such, leading people to believe he could help them make it in the business.

Not content with hearing a story second hand, I went to public records to fill in the rest of the gaps. Gabriel was not a career Special Services Ranger, he was discharged from the military after nine months (with no reason publicly listed). His first wife did not die young; records show they were divorced after only a few years of marriage. There is a birth certificate for a son (a few years older than he told you) who is still alive, married, and with several children and/or stepchildren according to Facebook. The names of family members mostly match those he gave, but the story of the dying ex-ballplayer son in Florida was a complete fantasy.

None of the things he told you ever happened. He did not live in Malibu. He was not independently wealthy. He did not have a disapproving family.

Things never added up, did they? Like mail never arriving, messages getting lost, never being able to reach him on weekends, and his always finding an excuse not to meet you. What kind of man who said he loved you would leave you dangling with Mr. Lucky? What kind of man with incredible wealth would not be able to support you, no matter what the medical costs?

In my estimation, what he did to you was a cruel hoax. He tossed out his stories and romantic comments all over *JournalLand*, and you were the one who got caught in the snare of lies. Many of us truly believed him, Anna, and we were rooting for you to find happiness.

It is time you stop thinking you did anything wrong. You were taken in by a master. People with pathological tendencies are very good at what they do and good people are often caught in their web.

So dear heart, this is what I know. Gabriel was a shit of the first degree. What he did to you was cruel and heartless and I suspect he finally disappeared when it was becoming clear you were going to find out the truth.

You deserve to be safe and happy, Anna. Holding guilt or doubt about why you fell in love with him, or what you could have done differently in the relationship, will stop any of that from happening.

I hope this information, late though it is, will give you closure, and you can finally heal from what must have hurt more than anything I can imagine.

05-25-2011 — **In Memoriam**

> *There's only one way to rid yourself of feelings. Shoot them in the head, drop them into a hole in the ground, cover them with lye, and shove dirt on top.*

I was angry when I discovered the real truth – that Gabriel was nothing he professed to be. That my emotional self had been played by a master.

But today I was forced to re-direct all the anger still left into ... well, I don't know into what. Because I was not only able to confirm all the information provided by my friend, but my in-depth searches for that confirmation revealed he is long dead. Exactly four years and three days after the first time we exchanged notes, the date we always considered our anniversary as it were, and about two years after whatever we were was no more.

In Memoriam
Gabriel Jonas Bresnell
aka *Azrael999*
February 12, 1948 – June 22, 2009

Lived hard, loved hard, tried hard, died hard

It is difficult to consider what finding this ending means to me. Our two-year relationship, if one can even call it that, consisted of hundreds and hundreds of hours of phone conversations and thousands of loving emails. It was extraordinarily passionate in its own way and extraordinarily unusual. An ocean of truth or a mountain of lies. Impossible to know one from the other.

Perhaps it is best to say that he had the ability to say just the lies you needed to hear, at just the time you needed to hear them. Which made him very special in his own inimitable way and someone I may never forgive, but will never forget.

He was the one who finally convinced me I didn't need to settle. That I could, or even should, give up the stuff I loved for a life of my own choosing. That the diagnosis of Hep C was not a death sentence when he made me laugh through my tears and gave me hope. That despite his own consistent personal issues – whatever they were – he still found the time to ask "and how are you?"

There were so many promises that were never kept, and he broke my heart at a time when it was almost the only thing I could count on. But that was the way his life operated. And it is difficult to fault someone for simply being themselves. After all – we all know the story of the scorpion, the river, and the frog.

Ribbitt … Ribbitt

09-23-2011 — **I'm OK, You're OK**

I have recently become acutely aware of the epic chasm between Good Enough and Truly Good.

Is it ok to just be "ok"? Or should life be more.

That's the big question, isn't it? IS there any more …

The problem is, I remember being more than OK. Being, perhaps, wonderful. Or fabulous. Or fantastic. Take your pick. At the very least being happy.

But I have a roof over my head, a good-paying job with a great group of people that finally looks to be permanent, a tenant in the house that covers the mortgage shortfall, and no debt – despite three layoffs in four years.

And I have my health. Which, considering the state of that a few years ago, is quite a positive thing when you think about it.

Maybe it is ok to be ok. At least it gives me a chance to consider what more I want, or maybe what I truly want, and the time to find it.

10-07-2011 — Compromise Hell

Don't believe what you've been told. The secret to a happy life is not compromise. The secret is to do what makes you happy – then find someone who finds their greatest joy in seeing you that way.

09-25-2012 — Another One Bites the Dust

It's been eighteen months since Bastardo™. A new guy I had been spending weekends with decided last night that he didn't see a future for us. I could have told him that a week after I met him – but it was summer, the company was not unpleasant, there were beaches and ice cream stands and he drove a Corvette convertible. Had he not brought it up, I would have in another week or so anyway, because summer is over.

Aside from the not wanting to do much of anything – the biggest problem was the usual one. Men my age are almost always quick-on-the-draw (or can't get it/keep it up), clumsy fingered, self-centric do me men who consider themselves great lovers – sprawling back with absolute satisfaction and a "was it good for you" look on their contented faces while the woman they are with spend a few minutes in the bathroom finishing what was started in the bedroom.

It baffles me that these men believe their own press. Why didn't at least one of the women in their lives speak up and make some attempt to teach them how to make love? Or perhaps somewhere, in the distant past, a woman did – and she was left in the dust when he just didn't see a future for them!

Perhaps Ben and Bastardo Romantico™ spoiled me completely and for the rest of my days. Years and years of outrageously perfect sex, their bodies fitting mine perfectly in every way, even if the relationships left a lot to be desired, and I just can't settle for less.

To paraphrase Hamlet in *Something Rotten*: Welcome to the world's leading enigma. Do you suppose I am truly mad, or mad pretending to be sane …

LAST DANCE PART LAST

When I think of you, it is a wordless sound. MMMmmmm. I don't know what it means, but I know it's what a woman says in the last instant just before her knees buckle from a kiss so intense it shatters her entire belief system.

You promised me honesty. You promised me integrity. You promised me fidelity. The most important promises I remember you making, and broken from almost the first day. Yet I continued to try and negotiate a relationship with you on your terms.

I just wanted your time, your attention, your affection. I pledged mine. I promised to listen to you without judgment. I promised to honor everything that you were. I promised not to try and change you or control you, and as you were NOT broken I could not fix you. My goal was to effectively communicate my understanding acceptance and unconditional grace.

The what if's of our time together stagger me. Even now, I want to sit in your lap, and I want to dance with you to a song you've picked out because it makes you think of us together. I want to feel your heart beat. I want your time, your affection, your friendship, your tenderness, your patience, and I cannot express in words how much I still want to find a way to be naked with you.

There is no doubt in my mind that the universe had some reason for putting us together in this place and in this time. In its quixotic nature, it looked around for a way to accomplish something truly spectacular. And we blew it.

If our beliefs make our reality, then my reality is that I have loved, and been loved, more than once – which is quite a remarkable thing.

Love is simple. Love is who you can't wait to tell about your every day, and who really wants to hear it. It's who you called first on 9/11. It's who you trust to be the real you with. It's who matters. Just because. I believe unconditional love is a rare gift and I don't know if it will ever come again.

Sharing love requires faith and courage. Courage to take a risk, accept setbacks, and overcome difficulties. Love is an activity that places us in a constant state of relating ourselves actively to the loved person. To love somebody is not just a strong feeling – it is a decision, it is a judgment, it is a promise, and it can bring pain and disappointment.

I believe that love, hope, and trust are inextricably intertwined, and I feel abandoned by them, like liquid slipping through my fingers.

Trust … trust your parents, trust your lover, trust your gut, trust your friend. Fool me once, shame on them; fool me twice, shame on me. Why, I once even did the third time around.

I used to start perfectly possible futures by laying a shocking fact about myself right on the table. Right there in front of him. Before the entree had even been served. Then looked him in the eye daring him to react. Poor guy had to come up with a passing grade emotional response to my startling revelation before he'd had a chance to cut his steak. Less a test of the heart, than a test of the stomach I think. Looking at my track record, maybe I should have started before the salad course.

How DO you learn to trust someone new? What does trust mean anymore (surely not the psychobabble we hear on daytime TV). How much do you need to know about another person, how many questions need to be answered, and is it genuinely about the questions?

Truth be told, at some point you have to decide which of the answers are REALLY the important ones, the big answers, the all-encompassing take it or leave it, double-down on the hold card, hail Mary pass answers like

Money doesn't grow on trees.
Beggars can't be choosers.
Your father has six months.
Breaking-up is hard to do.
You'll never have another child.
You make me feel like a natural woman.
All you need is love.
Imagine there's no heaven.
Santa doesn't really exist (does he?) or
that
People leave …

Meanwhile ... Remember this.

After all these pages, you should have learned the most important lesson there is to learn.

Men love you.
Until they don't.

WORKS CITED

Abel, Robert. *The Relationship Toolbox.* Denver, CO: Valentine Publishing House, 1998. Print.

Aczel, Amir D. *Entanglement: The Greatest Mystery in Physics.* West Sussex, England: John Wiley & Sons. 2003. Print.

"Angel Dark, Demon Bright." *Gene Roddenberry's Andromeda.* United Paramount Network. WDCA. Washington, D.C., 6 Nov. 2000. Television.

Anonymous. *AllGreatQuotes.com.* n.d. Web. 22 July 2005.

"Apollo's Chariot." *UltimateRollerCoaster.com.* 1996.Ultimate Rollercoaster, LLC. Web. 15 Jan. 2005.

Arminestra. "Between the Lines." *Xena.* Dir. Rick Jacobson. Writ. Steven L. Sears. Perf. Saras Govender. 2 Feb. 1999. Television.

Atsutada, Chunagon. *A Hundred Verses From Old Japan: a translation of the Hyaku-nin-Isshu.* Trans. William Porter. Singapore: Tuttle Publishing, 2008. Print.

Barabási, Albert-László. *Linked, How Everything Is Connected To Everything Else And What It Means For Business, Science, And Everyday Life.* New York: Plume Books, 2003. Print.

Beagle47. Blog Posting. *Diaryland.com.* Web. [c. December 2002]

beauty4ashes, Note to author. 11 May 2006

Behrendt, Greg, and Liz Tuccillo. *He's Just Not That Into You.* New York: Simon Spotlight Entertainment, 2004. Print.

Benét, Stephen Vincent. "A Child is Born: A Drama of the Nativity." *Cavalcade of America.* [Episode 310] Based on a story by: Stephen Vincent Benét. NBC Radio network, 21 Dec. 1942. Radio.

Bovee, Christian Nestell. *Intuitions and Summaries of Thought, Vol. II.* Boston, MA. Cambridge: Riverside Press, 1862. Print.

Bowen, Elizabeth. *The Death of the Heart.* New York: Anchor, 2000. Print.

Bradshaw, Carrie. "Anchors Away." *Sex and the City.* Darren Star, Creator. Prod: Darren Star Productions. Perf. Sarah Jessica Parker. Home Box Office (HBO). HBO East. Washington, DC. 21 July 2002. Television.

---. "An American Girl in Paris (Part Deux)." *Sex and the City*. Darren Star, Creator. Prod: Darren Star Productions. Perf. Sarah Jessica Parker. Home Box Office (HBO). HBO East. Washington, DC. 22 Feb. 2004. Television.

---. "Defining Moments." *Sex and the City*. Creator. Darren Star. Prod. Darren Star Productions. Perf. Sarah Jessica Parker. Home Box Office (HBO). HBO East. Washington, DC., 10 June 2001. Television.

---. "Ex and the City." *Sex and the City*. Creator. Darren Star. Prod. Darren Star Productions. Perf. Sarah Jessica Parker and Cynthia Nixon. Home Box Office (HBO). HBO East. Washington, DC., 3 Oct. 1999. Television.

---. "Hop, Skip and a Week." *Sex and the City*. Darren Star, Creator. Prod. Darren Star Productions. Perf. Sarah Jessica Parker. Home Box Office (HBO). HBO East. Washington, DC., 27 July 2003. Television.

---. "I Love A Charade." *Sex and the City*. Darren Star, Creator. Prod. Darren Star Productions. Perf. Sarah Jessica Parker. Home Box Office (HBO). HBO East. Washington, DC., 8 Sept. 2002. Television.

---. "Unoriginal Sin." *Sex and the City*. Darren Star, Creator. Prod. Darren Star Productions. Perf. Sarah Jessica Parker. Home Box Office (HBO). HBO East. Washington, DC., 28 July 2002. Television.

Browning, Robert. *Browning's Shorter Poems*. Newcastle, England: CSP Classic Texts, 2009. Print.

Buchanan, Edna. *A Dark and Lonely Place: A Novel*. New York: Simon & Schuster, 2011. Print.

"Bunker Hill." *Gene Roddenberry's Andromeda*. United Paramount Network. WDCA. Washington, D.C., 26 Jan. 2002. Television.

Burger King. "Marketing and Advertising History." *Burger King Corporation*. Archived from <http://en.wikipedia.org/wiki/Burger_King_Kids_Club#Childrens.27s_advertising>. n.d. Web. 12 Mar. 2005.

Burns, George. *QuotationsPage.com*. QuotationsPage.com and Michael Moncur. n.d. Web. 06 July 2005.

Campbell's Soup Ad Campaign, Ad. Firm: BBDO, New York.

Candoor. Blog Posting. *Diaryland*. (site access restricted). Web. 25 Aug. 2005.

---. "Candoor." Blog Posting. *Diaryland*. Web. Apr. 2003.

Carter-Scott, Cherie. *If Love Is a Game, These Are the Rules*. New York: Random House. 2000. Print.

catz-eyes. Blog Posting. *Diaryland.com*. Web. c. May 2003.

Chanel, Coco. "The Writer's Almanac." Prairie Home Productions, LLC. *Writersalmanac.publicradio.org*," 19 Aug. 1998. Web. 13 July 2005.

Chaucer, Geoffrey. *The Canterbury Tales*. New York: Penguin Classics. 2005. Print.

Clarke, Arthur C. *The Lost Worlds of 2001*. Boston: Gregg Press International, 1979. Print.

Crane, Dr. Frank. Quoted in *Business Education World*. Vol. 15. 1935.n.d. *wikiquote.org*. Web. 30 July 2005.

Croce, Jim. "Bad, Bad Leroy Brown." *Life and Times*. ABC Records, April 1973. Recording.

Cry-Baby. Writ. and Dir. John Waters. Perf. Johnny Depp. Universal Pictures, 6 Apr. 1990. DVD.

Cummings, Edward Estlin. "you said Is (XIII)." *E. E. Cummings: Complete Poems, 1904-1962*. Ed. George James Firmage. New York: Liveright Pub. Corp, 1994. Print.

"Dance of the Mayflies" *Gene Roddenberry's Andromeda*. United Paramount Network. WDCA. Washington, D.C. 23 Feb. 2002. Television.

"Decay of the Angel" *Gene Roddenberry's Andromeda*. United Paramount Network. WDCA. Washington, D.C., 15 October 2004. Television.

Darrow, Clarence. *Speech in Dayton, Tennessee* [defending John T. Scopes] 13 July 1925. Print.

David, Peter. *The Woad to Wuin*. New York: Pocket Books, 2002. Print.

De Blasi, Marlena. *A Thousand Days in Venice*. New York: Ballantine Books, 2003. Print.

DeCandido, Keith R. A. and Tribune Entertainment. *Gene Roddenberry's Andromeda: Destruction of Illusions*. New York: Tor Books, 2003. Print.

Dickinson, Emily. *The Complete Poems of Emily Dickinson*. Ed. Thomas H. Johnson. New York: Little, Brown and Company. 1976. Print.

Dodson, James C. *Love Must Be Tough: New Hope for Marriages in Crisis*. Chicago, IL: Tyndale House Publishers, Inc., 2007. Print.

Du Bos, Charles. *Approximations*. sn., 1922. Print.

"Forced Perspective" *Gene Roddenberry's Andromeda*. United Paramount Network. WDCA. Washington, D.C. 19 Feb. 2001. Television.

Fforde, Jasper. *Something Rotten*. London, England: Penguin Books, 2004. Print.

Fordin, Hugh. *A Biography of Oscar Hammerstein II*. New York: Da Capo Press, 1977. Print.

France, Anatole. *The Crime of Sylvestre Bonnard*. New York: Cornell University Library, 2009. Print.

Frith, William. *Tears of the Pilgrims; or, Words of Comfort to the tried, afflicted, and Bereaved*. London: S.W. Partridge & Co., 1883. Print.

Gari, Alan. "More Than Lovers." Unpublished. Writ. Alan Gari, Copyright 1971.

Gassman, Fabienne. *Hope, Joy, Peace, Love: Living Life Through Inspiration*. Indiana: Xlibris Corporation. 2011. Print.

Gibran, Kahlil. *The Prophet*. New York: Alfred A Knopf Inc, 1996. Print.

Heinlein, Robert Anson. *Time Enough For Love, The Lives Of Lazarus Long*. New York: Penguin, 1988. Print.

Hitch. Dir. Andy Tennant. Writ. Kevin Bisch. Perf. Will Smith. Sony Pictures and Columbia Pictures Corporation, 11 Feb. 2005. Film.

Hurston, Zora Neale. *Their Eyes Were Watching God*. New York: Harper, 2000. Print.

Jarman, Heather. *Star Trek Voyager: String Theory #3: Evolution*. New York: Pocket Books/Star Trek. 28 Feb. 2006. [paraphrased]. Print.

Jefferson, Thomas. *Quotationspage.com*. 2 June 2006. Web.

Joe Versus the Volcano. Writ. & Dir. John Patrick Shanley. Perf. Tom Hanks, Meg Ryan, Lloyd Bridges. Warner Bros. Pictures, 9 Mar. 1990. DVD.

Jones, M'Louise. "More Ways Than One." *State Normal Monthly*. Vol 10, No 1: 37. October 1897. Print.

Jones, Samantha."Easy Come, Easy Go." *Sex and the City*. Creator. Darren Star. Prod. Darren Star Productions. Perf. Kim Catrall. Home Box Office (HBO). HBO East. Washington, DC., 6 Aug. 2000. Television.

Kaku, Michio. "The Theory of Everything." *FirstScience.com*. 6 Jan 2001. Web. 21 Nov. 2005.

Kennedy, John. "Address Before the General Assembly of the United Nations." United Nations, New York, NY. 25 Sept. 1961. Keynote Address.

Krull, Manning. via Twitter as quoted on his *Facebook* page. Web. 4 Aug. 2010.

Laurens, Stephanie. *The Edge of Desire*. New York: Avon Books. 2008. Print

Leinster, Murray. "Sidewise in Time." *Astounding Stories*, 30 June 1934. Print.

Levi, Jan Heller. "What Becomes of the Broken-Hearted." *Skyspeak: Poems*. Baton Rouge, LA: Louisiana State University Press. 2005. Print.

Mann, Horace. *Why I Am A Temperance Man: A Series of Letters to a Friend*. (Google eBook). Pub. Thurlow Weed Brown, 1854. Print.

McDonald, Steven E. and Tribune Entertainment. *Gene Roddenberry's Andromeda: Waystation*. New York: Tor Books, 2004. Print.

Meet Joe Black. Dir. Martin Brest. Writ. Ron Osborn, Jeff Reno. Perf. Anthony Hopkins. City Light Films, Universal Pictures, 13 Nov. 1998. DVD.

Millay, Edna St. Vincent. *Letters of Edna St. Vincent Millay*. Ed. Allan Ross MacDougall. New York: Harper. 1952. Print.

Milne, Alan Alexander. *Winnie the Pooh*. New York: Dutton Children's Books. 1926. Print. [attributed to Winnie the Pooh in all resources]

Minority Report. Dir. Steven Spielberg. Based on short story by Philip K. Dick. Writ. Philip K. Dick and Scott Frank. Twentieth Century Fox Film Corporation, 2002. Film.

Moeller, Mary. "I Believe in Magic." *Inner Voices: A Collection of Poetry*. N. Amazon.com. 2012. Print.

Murray, Pennie. *Giving Myself Permission: Putting Fear and Doubt in Their Place*. Little Elm TX: GMP Publishing. 2012. Print.

Must Love Dogs. Dir. Gary David Goldberg. Writ. Claire Cook and Gary David Goldberg. Perf. Diana Lane, Christopher Plummer. Warner Brothers Pictures. 2005. Film.

Newman, Nanette. "Nanette Newman." *IMDB.com*. n.d. Web. 30 July 2005.

Numb3rs. Perf. Peter McNicol. Prod. Paramount Network television. CBS Television Network. WUSA9, Washington, D.C. Television.

Oliphant, Margaret. *Miss Marjoribanks*. New York: Chatto & Windus, 1969. Print.

Oxford Dictionary of Proverbs, The. 5th ed. Ed. Jennifer Speake. New York: Oxford University Press, USA, 2009. Print.

Peter Pan. Dir. Glyde Geronimi, Wilfred Jackson. Writ. J. M. Barrie based on an adaption of the play *Peter Pan*. Ted Sears. Perf. Bobby Driscoll. Walt Disney Productions, 1953. Film.

Philips, Emo. *Thinkexist.com*. [Paraphrased from actual quote: "Women: You can't live with them, and you can't get them to dress up in a skimpy little Nazi costume and beat you with a warm squash or something ... "] Web.

"Pitiless as the Sun." *Gene Roddenberry's Andromeda*. United Paramount Network. WDCA. Washington, D.C., 22 Oct. 2001. Television.

Pirates of the Caribbean: The Curse of the Black Pearl. Dir. Gore Verbinski. Writ. Ted Elliott, Terry Rossio. Perf. Johnny Depp and Guy Siner. Walt Disney Pictures, 9 Jul. 2003. Film.

Pope Paul VI. "Pope Paul VI Quotes." *Thinkexist.com*. n.d. Web. 1 Aug. 2006.

"Quantum Gravity: Simplified String Theory." Wikipedia.org. Wikipedia Foundation, Inc. n.d. Web. 21 Nov. 2005

Radner, Gilda. *It's Always Something*. New York: Harper Paperbacks, 2001. Print.

Reeve, Christopher. *Still Me*. Random House Digital, Inc., 2001. Print.

Rhade, Telemachus. *Gene Roddenberry's Andromeda*. Perf. Steve Bacic. United Paramount Network. WDCA. Washington, D.C., [c. 2005]. Television.

Rogers, Will. *The Autobiography of Will Rogers*. Ed. Donald Day. New York: Houghton Mifflin Co., 1949. Print.

Rossetti, Christina G. "De Profundis." *A Pageant and Other Poems*. London: MacMillan and Co. 1881. Print.

Rumi, Jelaluddin. *A Book Of Luminous Things: An International Anthology Of Poetry*. Ed Czeslaw Milosz. Trans. Coleman Barks and John Moyne. New York: Mariner Books, 1998. Print.

"Runaway Mine Train: Six Flags over Texas." *Wikipedia.com*. 1996. Web. 15 Oct. 2005

Saint-Exupery, Antoine de. *Wind, Sand and Stars*. Trans. Lewis Galantiere. New York: Mariner Books, 2002. Print.

Santayana, George. *The Life of Reason (Five Volumes in One)*. Middlesex: The Echo Library, 2006. Print.

Schrödinger, E. *Collected Papers on Wave Mechanics*. New York: Chelsea, 1978. Print.

Sciortino, Karley. "Breathless: I Was Dumped Two Months Ago, And I'm Still Heartbroken." *Vogue.com*. Conde Nast. 24 Sept 2014. Web.

Shain, Merle. *When Lovers Are Friends*. New York: Bantam Books, 1982. Print.

Shaw, George Bernard. *Man And Superman*. Stillwell, KS: Digireads.Com, 2009. Print.
"The Banks of the Lethe." *Gene Roddenberry's Andromeda*. United Paramount Network.
WDCA. Washington, D.C., 20 Nov. 2000. Television.

The Perfect Man. Dir. Mark Roseman. Writ. Michael McQuown, Heather Robinson.
Perf. Heather Locklear. Universal Pictures. USA-65 Washington, DC. 17 June
2005. Television.

"The Seven Year Witch." *Charmed*. [Actual Quote: "**Drake Robin**: The point is, Leo
and Piper's love, it's epic, it's massive. It's Romeo and Juliet, Anthony and Cleopatra, Brad and Jennifer. **Paige**: All tragedies, I might add."] Prod. Paramount
Pictures, Spelling Television. Perf. Billy Zane and Rose McGowan. The Warner Brothers (WB) Station WDCW-50. Washington, DC., 10 Apr. 2005. Television.

"The Sum of Its Parts." *Gene Roddenberry's Andromeda*. United Paramount Network.
WDCA. Washington, D.C., 26 Feb. 2001. Television.

Tex, Joe. "Skinny Legs and All." Writ. Joe Tex. Kent Records UK. 20 Nov. 1995.
Recording Single.

Their Eyes Were Watching God. Based on the 1937 novel by Zora Neale Hurston. Dir.
Darnell Martin. Prod. Harpo Films. Perf. Michael Ealy. American Broadcasting
Company. WABC-7. New York, 6 Mar. 2005. Television.

Thoreau, Henry David. *Walden and Civil Disobedience*. New York: Penguin Group,
1991. [Actual quote: … if one advances confidently in the direction of his
dreams, and endeavors to live the life which he has imagined, he will meet with
a success unexpected in common hours."] Print.

"Totaled Recall." *Gene Roddenberry's Andromeda*. United Paramount Network. WDCA.
Washington, D.C., 29 April 2005. Television.

Twain, Mark. *More Tramps Abroad*. 2nd Ed. London: Chatto & Windus, 1897. Print.

Tyutchev, Fyodor Ivanovich. "All Day She Quiet Lay." *Poemhunter.com*. 1 Jan. 2004.
Web. 15 Jan. 2005.

Tzu, Lao. *BrainyQuote.com*. Xplore Inc, 2013. n.d. Web. 16 December 2013

Unknown. "Love Messages." *Romanticlovemessages.com*. 2007-2011. Web. 29 July 2005

Vare, Ethlie Ann and Daniel Morris. *Gene Roddenberry's Andromeda: The Broken Places*.
New York: Tor Books, 2003. Print.

Virgil. *The Ecologues, Bucolics, or Pastorals of Virgil*. Trans. Thomas Fletcher Royds
(1922). New York: Cornell University Library. 2008. Print.

Virgin America. Advertisement. 22 Apr. 2010. [Subway billboard, 35th & Broadway, New York, NY]

Walcott, Derek. *Collected Poems, 1948-1984*. New York: Farrar, Straus and Giroux, 1987. Print.

Wang Chung. "Everybody Wang Chung Tonight." *Mosaic*. Geffen, 13 Sept. 1986. Recording.

Watts, Duncan. "Duncan Watts: An Experimental Study of Search in Global Social Networks." Dodds, et al. *Science*. 8 Aug. 2003: 827-829. DOI:10.1126/science.1081058.

Wilde, Oscar. *BrainyQuote.com*. Xplore Inc, 2011. n.d. Web. 17 July 2005.

Williams, Robin [quoted] Writ. Stuart Kantor and Mark King. *Beer, Boxers, Batteries, and Bodily Noises: {A Woman's Guide to Understanding Why Men Do What They Do}*. New York: iUniverse, Inc., 2004. Print.

Wyatt, Woodrow Lyle. "Quotes by Woodrow Lyle Wyatt." *Answers.com*. 2010. *Quotationsbook.com*. Web. 17 July 2005.

Yang, Julia, Alan P. Milliren, and Mark Blagen. *The Psychology Of Courage, An Adlerian Handbook For Healthy Social Living*. New York: CRC Press, 2009. Print.

BUT WHAT HAPPENED THEN

This book begins with birth and ends during September of 2012.

Visit www.nicidamon.com to see what more life has in store for our heroine and to read some of the earlier works that didn't make into this volume.

cat·fish: *noun*
gerund or present participle: **catfishing**
>   From the 2010 documentary film *Catfish*. A term for someone who creates false identities to pursue deceptive online romances. With one in five relationships starting online, it is important to check your facts early and often. Fully 30% of teenagers will try and meet in person the person they met online.

gas·light: *verb*
gerund or present participle: **gaslighting**
>   manipulate (someone) by psychological means into questioning their own sanity. From the 1944 movie *Gaslight* starring Charles Boyer

www.ingramcontent.com/pod-product-compliance
Lightning Source LLC
Chambersburg PA
CBHW071207250626
47159CB00001B/236